Adventures in Time

BOOK ONE

THE ACCIDENTAL TOURIST

OLIVIA ROX

Adventures In Time – The Accidental Tourist

OliviaRox.com

Illustrations drawn by Olivia Rox. Cover Art design by Tamara Van Cleef & Olivia Rox.

Printed in the United States of America.

Library of Congress Control Number: 2024922109

Hardcover ISBN: 979-8-9917724-7-1

First edition - Second printing

For my family, be they near or far, by blood or by choice.
Always.

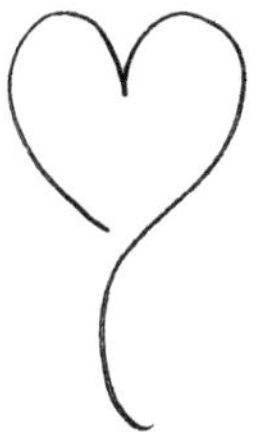

Acknowledgements

Thank you to my incredible parents Tamara and Warren for everything you do - you are both my rock keeping me grounded and the wind beneath my feet letting me fly. Thank you to my family & friends who were my first readers and biggest supporters; Joan, Ric, Bev, Dave, Gregg, Jay, Floretta, Ronnie, Jan, Marc, Ben, Mick, Ellen. To Tam and Miguel - thank you for helping me bring the audiobook to life, laughing in the studio and being such good friends the entire process. To my unwavering dear friends Vincent, Rose, Emma, Abby, Mary, Kristen, Emily, Santiago, Nicole, Dan, Ester. And to my multilingual friends who helped me authentically write in the 7 foreign languages inside; Marco, Miriam, Leo, Monica. To my friends around the world and close to home, who when we see each other it's like not a day has gone past. To my sweet animals who all sit by my side while I write and keep me company. I'm so grateful to have such an amazing support system, and I truly love you. Special thanks to Kitty for helping me get this book made.

To my Roxstars, fans and supporters around the world - thank you. Mostly, thank you to the person holding this book right now.

Love,

Olivia

"Time"

Time is beautiful.
It gives life, love, memories and joy.
We all think of time as something -
a saint or a devil, a giver or a taker -
but the truth is,
Time cannot be labeled.
It is everything.
Time allows flowers to grow,
which give us air to breathe.
Time lets a baby grow to one
day find love with another.
Time takes, and it gives.
And we accept Time for what it is,
how it works, and what it does.
We only wish we had more of that
wonderful, terrible thing we call Time.

Table Of Contents

Book One

PART 3

PREFACE

Time is a very tricky thing. We live it as though it is moving, with each second passing us by. But what if time wasn't linear and was happening all at once? Would that make it a constant? And if it wasn't fluid, would events in time be able to change? Or is everything already written, and we are simply experiencing history?

Each day of our life is governed by time. Without it, we are frozen and immobilized. But with it, we age and eventually die. It is beautiful, but cruel. Our hopes and dreams rely on time. The food we eat takes time to grow. Not a single thing in our reality can function without time.

But what is time?

If time was a place, would that place ever end?

If time was a dream, what if the dreamer woke up?

But what if, just what if - time was a person?

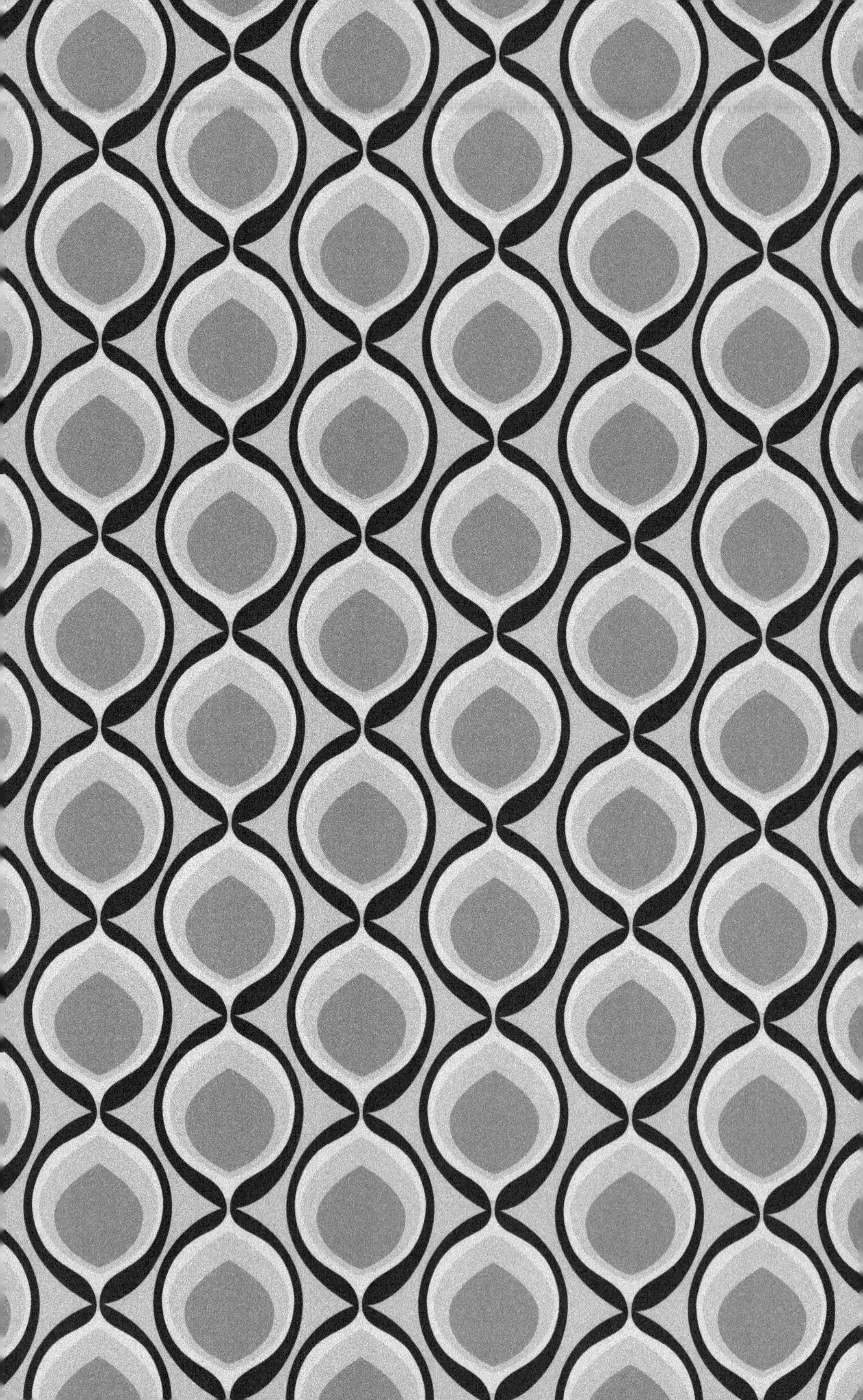

PART
ONE

CHAPTER 1

THE PARTY

Aurelia Quinn stood at the steps of the Los Angeles Public Library, staring at the massive building before her. Although she was a bookworm with a constant thirst for knowledge, she was shocked that this was the place her friends chose for her 19th birthday party. It was one of her favorite places in the world to be, and as often as she could, she came to this very library to wander the halls and find new adventures to read. Though she passionately loved it here, she had hoped her party would be something a bit more exciting than her quiet library midday on a Monday. It was meant to be a surprise, but she was quite an inquisitive person, and after hinting to her friends enough, someone had anonymously tipped her off that they were indeed planning something for her.

Starting a week ago, she had received texts from a blocked number, each day revealing more details of the upcoming event. Aurelia assumed the person planning the celebration must have been one of her closest friends, as the anonymous texts seemed to know so much about her. She was rather excited to see just what her friends had in store for her...

She knew the place to be, the exact time to be there, and she had already practiced her perfect "fake surprised face" in her car mirror at least a dozen times on the way there. Aurelia had worked out every single variable that might occur that night, and was completely prepared for anything - or so she thought.

She checked her watch to make sure she wasn't late for her own party, smiling gently at the reminder of her grandfather on her wrist.

'He would've loved this party,' Aurelia thought to herself.

In fact, he was the one who taught her how to read, and not just read the words written on the page - but to imagine, and see through the eyes of the characters and bring each and every one to life.

3:00 p.m. - right on time. Aurelia hopped up the stairs and headed inside the library.

She marveled at the beautiful concrete architecture surrounding her, and even though she had been there a thousand times, it still felt new to her. Her instructions were very specific - wait by the emergency stairwell until someone goes up the stairs, then follow them, and they would lead her to the party. Easy.

Casually, Aurelia picked up the first book on the shelf nearest her and made her way to the wall just next to the stairwell. She plopped down on the ground to wait for the mystery person, with the perfect vantage point to spy on anyone going up.

Just as soon as she sat down, her phone buzzed with a text from the blocked number: "Running late, be there soon - Meet you at the party. Have fun!"

Whoever it was that had planned this really wanted to stay anonymous! Aurelia couldn't help but smile as she imagined the exciting night to come.

She wondered if it was going to be a murder mystery party, with the cryptic nature of the texts adding to the theme. Or perhaps a game night, filled with trivia and board games. It probably wouldn't be anything too flashy or loud, judging by her friends' choice of location, but whatever they had put together would be perfect.

Within no more than a few minutes, three guys around her age walked past her and opened the door to the stairway. They were decked out in floral patterns, bright colors and bold fashion decisions - they honestly looked like they were straight out of Saturday Night Fever or an Austin Powers movie. Aurelia chuckled at their dated fashion sense, and stealthily followed behind them.

'Was it going to be a theme party,' Aurelia wondered? Even though they were dressed comically, Aurelia blushed at how well put together and good looking all three of them were.

She waited to enter the stairway for a few moments, hoping that would give the boys a chance to go upstairs first, but instead she bumped into them as she opened the door. They stood with widened eyes on the bottom landing of the cold concrete staircase, one of them beginning their ascension up the stairs.

"Are you goin' up?" one of the guys on the stairs asked her, motioning for her to go first.

"Uh, you go ahead," Aurelia said, unsure of herself.

"No, ladies first, I insist," he urged.

Was chivalry actually alive? Especially from what seemed to be college boys? They struck her as acting a bit strange, but perhaps it was just because of their ludicrous outfits that she felt that way. They shifted in their stance, glaring at Aurelia with skepticism.

Aurelia smiled with hesitation and started up the dirty concrete stairs. Would she know the floor when she saw it? She walked up slowly, and glanced down at the group below her, who all stood in absolute silence watching her as she walked up. She chuckled nervously as she made eye contact with them, and she hurried up a bit faster. Suddenly, her legs grew weak and her vision blurred. She grasped the metal railing for support and noticed her hands were shaking as well.

What was wrong? Had she been drugged? She had never felt anything like this before. Aurelia walked up the stairs even faster and realized that the guys had now started walking up behind her.

Was this some kind of cruel trick? Her chest grew tight and her heart rate quickened, her knees nearly buckling beneath her body. The staircase began to spin, and she started running up the stairs two at a time, nearly losing her footing. Her stomach turned and she looked behind her again to see the guys steadily gaining on her.

A random question flashed through her mind, 'Had there been wallpaper on the walls?'

"Are you OK?" one of the guys called out to her.

Aurelia didn't say a peep and instead continued to run up. Where was the exit? She looked underneath her and realized the stairs were carpeted - she could've sworn they were concrete. The guys were no more than a few steps from her, and Aurelia panicked as she started to question who had sent her the messages. Was there even a party, or had she been tricked into coming and drugged so that something bad could happen?

Then, just as suddenly as it came on, Aurelia began to feel normal again. The stairwell stopped spinning and her strength came back to her. She realized that she could hear music - and what seemed to be a party, coming from the door just a few steps away. This was it. She had made it. But what had just happened to her? Was it all in her head?

Before she went in, she took a deep breath and smoothed the top of her blonde hair, pulling herself together. She looked behind her and saw the guys slow down once they realized she was alright. Aurelia also took note of the strange stairway door, which unlike most, had a metal clock nailed just in the center of it. She burst into the room, and was delighted to find at least fifty people gathered in celebration. They were all dressed in amazing '70s costumes just like the boys, and a band played "Get Up" by James Brown. A disco ball hung just above the crowd, and Aurelia felt completely engulfed in bright, colorful lights. It was extremely authentic, and so impeccably put together. In fact - of all the times Aurelia had been to this library, she had never even seen this room! It was unforgettable to say the least. The only problem - she still hadn't seen a single familiar face. Given, she only had a handful of close friends and was a bit of an introvert, so she assumed the people surrounding her had to be friends of friends. Or perhaps they had taken her to an event that was already happening - either way, it was perfect.

The stairway door opened behind her and out came the three guys. Now that she knew they were harmless, she studied their faces a bit more and was speechless at how dashing they were. Did boys normally look that naturally handsome?

"Hey there. You feeling better now?" one of the boys asked her. He was the cutest.

"Mmhmm..." Aurelia stuttered, her mind still fuzzy from whatever had happened to her.

"I know they say it gets easier, but I still feel kinda strange every time, you know?"

Aurelia had no clue what he meant, but he sure smiled adorably, so she continued with her phrase, "Mmhmm."

"I'm Will, by the way," he said, looking into Aurelia's denim blue eyes.

"Aurelia," she said, shaking his hand and smiling back with an open attitude.

"Wow. That's quite a name."

"I know, it's a bit extravagant. You can call me Ari if you want."

"No - I think Aurelia is beautiful," Will smiled, unable to take his eyes off of her, obviously thinking more than just her name was beautiful.

"Thanks," Aurelia chuckled and looked at the ground flirtatiously.

"These are my friends, Benji and Mason."

"Hi. Nice to meet you. I'm Aurelia," Aurelia held out her hand to shake, which they stared at strangely before shaking.

"So, are you meeting anyone while you're here?" Will flicked his long, dark hair from his face.

"Yeah, I'm meeting some of my friends, although I have no idea when! They said they'd be here soon though," Aurelia laughed nervously, copying him by brushing her long blonde hair behind her ear.

"Oh, well, maybe we know them! What are their names?"

Aurelia chuckled, "Well - I'm not too sure exactly who I'm meeting, but I'm assuming it's either Jane or maybe Sarah who planned this?"

"Hmm... don't know 'em."

"To be honest though, the first thing I need to do is find a change of clothes!" Aurelia motioned to her little black flare-out dress and sleek crossbody purse, which were far from the '70s vibe happening around her.

"True. Not many people wear black here," laughed Will.

"Here, you can use this!" Benji said, holding out his bright multicolored sweater he held in his arm.

Flashing back briefly to a story her dad once told her, she realized she was the one in this group that was unprepared, a concept she despised.

"What? No - I can't take your sweater!"

"It's no problem! Really," Benji placed the sweater in her hand and smiled again.

She casually noticed the tag as she took the sweater from him, amazed that he had a vintage Halston. She had only seen his pieces in books and museums.

"Wow," whispered Aurelia under her breath, her knowledge and love of fashion showing through.

"Cool, right? He just designed it in his newest line!" Benji said, smiling with pride.

"Huh? But, isn't Halston dead...?" she said, confused.

"Not last time I was here!" he said, the group laughing along with him.

Aurelia joined in with a confused chuckle. What did he mean?

"Well, thanks!" Aurelia said.

"It's all about the camaraderie between fellow Members, don't you think?" Benji grinned.

Aurelia was surprised how enthusiastic he sounded about being a library member.

"Sure. I guess you're right," she smiled, putting the designer sweater on and directing her conversation back to Will. "Hey also, do you know when they added this room? I've never even seen this part before."

"Yeah, I think it's somewhat new. I remember reading about it being their newest addition coming soon in one of the flyers a few years back," Will answered.

"Huh. I never even knew about it!"

Aurelia couldn't believe the library had literally built an entire floor without her knowledge. She thought she knew everything there was to know about the building's happenings.

"Well, since it's your first time here, you need to really experience it! You wanna dance?" Will asked playfully.

"Sure!" Aurelia accepted, beaming.

Will reached for Aurelia's hand and held it cautiously, leading her closer to the band. Her hand tingled as his fingers wrapped around hers, and she couldn't help but smile as she realized just how much she instantly liked him. She wasn't normally one to fall for someone so quickly, and she hardly even focused on her love life at all, but there was something about Will...

Just as they began bopping to the music, the band finished the song and the lead singer relished in the moment of applause.

The singer screamed on the microphone, "OK Members, are you ready to party like it's 1977?"

"Yeah!" the audience replied, hooting and hollering.

"Hit it!" the singer ushered to the band and they began to play "Dancing Queen" by ABBA.

The crowd went wild, and everyone around Will and Aurelia danced like it was the best night of their lives. Will grabbed for Aurelia's other hand and danced playfully to the song.

Aurelia was blown away at how wonderful her night was going, besides the strange incident in the stairwell of course. Everything, from the room, the music, the costumes, to the company, was flawless. Will's face was lit up with a constant smile - he couldn't hide how he already felt about Aurelia if he tried.

Perhaps it was premature, but in that moment, Aurelia and Will felt like they were meant to be together.

Time flew by quicker than expected, and the pair danced for at least an hour, nonstop. Aurelia's friends still hadn't joined the party, which struck her as a bit strange, but she was distracted from dancing with Will, her head stuck in the clouds, her stomach filled with butterflies.

Every topic led into the next conversation, and their chemistry was undeniable.

"Aurelia?" Will asked.

"Yeah?"

"How have we never met?"

Aurelia laughed at his question, "I don't know!"

"No, but I mean it. When did you complete your orientation?" Will asked seriously, stopping dancing.

"What do you mean?" Aurelia asked back, puzzled.

"Well, see, I've known most of the Members since I was a toddler, and I've never even seen you before. Not at the parties, at Headquarters, or in any of the times I've been," Aurelia continued to stare at him, extremely confused. What did he mean, Headquarters? "I know, I can't remember everyone, but I'm pretty sure I wouldn't have forgotten you."

"I don't really get out that much, to be honest," Aurelia chuckled self-consciously.

"That's OK. So, when all have you been then?" Will asked with a sparkle in his eye.

Aurelia could've sworn Will just said, "when", not "where".

"Uh... I've been on some trips to Arizona and Northern California with my grandparents, but they don't like to travel too much."

"That's cool though. Mostly the 1900s then?"

"Sorry, what do you mean?"

Puzzled, Will looked at Aurelia, both of them confused about the conversation. They weren't entirely sure what the other was talking about, so they both fell into silence.

Aurelia's thoughts had wandered since the stairwell, hinting at the fact that something out of the ordinary was happening to her, but she continued to convince herself otherwise. Had she stumbled upon some sort of secret society? Why was there so much talk about "Members" and "Headquarters"? Additionally, Aurelia found it even stranger that everyone in the room was flawless and could very well be models. All night, she had disregarded each strange comment, but now though, she began to wonder if something was awry with these people.

Will hadn't filtered his conversation around her because Aurelia had come to the party on her own - so he wondered why she didn't have a clue what he was talking about. Doubts suddenly crossed his mind as he registered that she hadn't dressed in costume, and she did seem awfully confused about each topic he brought up regarding his travels. But it would be impossible to travel without a device, so it was out of the question that she was a permanent. He brushed aside his suspicions, for he concluded that she must be one of them - perhaps she was just new.

Aurelia broke the awkward silence, "I'll be right back, I'm just gonna step out and get some air," she said to Will, leaving him on the dance floor, both of them equally confused.

He nodded and she headed for the stairwell, stepping inside to the landing. She still hadn't come across anyone she knew, but she hadn't cared until now. Before she was only focused on Will. She took out her phone to see if there were any new messages, but it wouldn't even turn on. Suddenly, she realized that she didn't recognize the stairwell she was in at all. She must have gone through the wrong door. This staircase only had stairs going up - and she most certainly came from downstairs.

Stepping back into the party, she looked around for another door on that wall - but she quickly found that there was only one. She stepped inside again and inspected the landing. Everything was the same as when she came up - minus the stairs going down.

Something strange was happening here - yet she still didn't want to jump to any conclusions. In the back of her mind, every potential scenario she could think of wasn't a possibility, was it? There had to be a logical solution. But what had happened to her in the stairwell? Was it possible that she had blacked out? Had she been kidnapped? Plus, if this was meant to be her birthday party - where were her friends?

But she hadn't blacked out, as far as she knew. She had walked up this very stairwell to get to the party - hadn't she?

Completely puzzled, she stepped into the party, yet again.

She must have come in another way.

Frantically, she followed the wall of the room, wrapping all the way around to the side of the stage, when she finally spotted another door. She went through it, only to find herself outside on the street. A city street that she had never seen before. The air was crisp and the sky pitch black. She couldn't have been in there dancing long enough for it to be night already. She glanced at her watch, but it only read half past 4. How was it already pitch black at 4:30 p.m.? Perhaps her watch was wrong. But what if it was actually 4:30 in the morning? A bouncer looked at her with concern, wondering why she looked so flustered.

Where was she? It definitely didn't look like California.

"You OK, kid?" the bouncer asked her.

Nodding unhesitatingly to him and casting the doubt from her mind, she pulled out her cell phone yet again, hoping it would turn on by restarting it. How long had she been inside the party? Pressing the power button, the phone still wouldn't turn on. Had it died?

"PUT THAT AWAY!" the bouncer yelled at her, referring to her phone.

"What? Why?"

"Are you crazy? Someone could see it!"

Although confused, Aurelia listened to his harsh tone, shoving it back inside her crossbody bag - it was of no use to her at the moment anyway.

"Do you happen to know what time it is?" she asked.

The bouncer looked at his wristwatch, "Almost 8:30."

"*8:30?*"

She had been inside for five and a half hours? That wasn't possible, was it? What if she had actually blacked out in the stairwell? Plus, she was obviously in a different location than the Los Angeles Public Library. She must have lost time. What if it had been even longer than that? Was it even the same day?

Aurelia continued, "What day is it?"

"October 1st, 1977."

Aurelia broke into a laugh from his comical statement, "Ha ha. Very funny."

He was obviously still referring to the '70s disco party inside, taking his role-play a bit too far.

But the man just raised his eyebrows with a smile, "Look around ya, kid."

Aurelia looked around at the city street, trying to absorb every detail and see what he meant. Surprisingly, the few people that walked outside were all dressed similarly to those inside the '70s themed party, only perhaps less flamboyantly.

No. It wasn't possible. The bouncer was messing with her, wasn't he? Her mind was spinning - maybe she *hadn't* misheard Will's conversation when he spoke of when she had traveled to, and his friend's strange comments before that. What was going on?

"First trip, huh?" he said, studying her stunned gaze.

"...What? What do you mean?"

An old car drove by her and her heart fluttered as the realization sunk in. Could she have gone through some sort of portal to a different place? Even - a different time?

CHAPTER 2

WHAT IS AN OKLIOT?

White as a ghost, her very world spinning, Aurelia stepped back inside to the party. Will was headed in her direction, and she beelined to speak to him - after all, he was the only person that she somewhat knew at the party, so hopefully he could clear things up for her and dispel her insane theories.

"You OK?" he asked her as she approached.

He obviously knew when and where they were, but should she reveal that she didn't know? "Yeah, yeah, just a little turned around. Didn't we come in that way?" Aurelia pointed to the door with the staircase. She needed to get home, and he was her only way to get back.

"Yeah. Of course."

"Come see," she grabbed his hand and led him to the stairway, closing the door behind them as they entered. "Didn't we come from downstairs?"

Will's eyes widened. Where did the stairs down go?

"Uh.... maybe this isn't the same stairwell?" he guessed, flabbergasted.

"That's what I thought. It's the only one," she decided she needed to find out what he knew.

"But... I didn't know that was possible..." he muttered, utterly confused.

"Neither did I," she read his every expression, trying to decipher every twitch of his mouth as he processed the information.

He reached into his blue pants pocket and pulled out a small golden copper orb, about the size of a gum-ball. Aurelia was extremely intrigued, yet remained silent as he shook it near his ear. Aurelia could feel her heart flutter like when they had come up the stairs - she must be nervous.

Will looked at the copper ball to look for obvious signs of a malfunction, "It's still ticking. The portal should be operational."

Portal? Could it be possible? The bouncer was telling the truth?

Had they actually traveled in time?

Will looked around the landing of the room, inspecting it just as Aurelia had.

"Has this ever happened to you?" she asked him, playing along.

"No. Never," he muttered, looking at his orb again. "Did you check if yours is working?"

He motioned to the metal in his hand.

Aurelia panicked momentarily - she didn't have a golden ball like his.

"Oh, um, yeah. It is. Still, uh, ticking."

"I don't understand," he said, defeatedly.

"Well, should we try going up?" Aurelia suggested, hoping to triple confirm her theory.

"No, no. The portal might get stuck somewhere in time if the Okliots aren't functioning properly."

She was right. It was a portal. And the "Okliot" must be the name of the futuristic orb he held in his hand allowing them to travel in time! It was just as if she had entered one of her favorite stories - the perfect guy, time travel and adventure. Reality sinking in, she realized how real this story was, and that they were potentially stuck in the '70s.

"How are we gonna get back?" she asked him, fear washing over her.

Will took a shaky breath, "I don't know. We should try calling my contact at Headquarters."

Aurelia felt panic rush through her veins. Headquarters? She wasn't a time traveler. What if they found out who she was?

He reached into his other pocket and pulled out a small, clear device. It was extremely thin, and looked just like a piece of glass. It proceeded to light up like a phone screen the moment he placed his thumb to the center. It was sophisticated, yet it didn't seem too technologically advanced for her, compared to the smartphone technology that already existed in her time. He pressed a few buttons, and then set it on the ground in front of them.

Aurelia watched in anticipation as the device projected a holographic image of a man. Her eyes widened at the sight of this futuristic, full color projection, yet she tried her best to remain calm and act like she had seen it a million times before. She stepped aside to the wall to let Will talk somewhat privately, and so that the man he was speaking to hopefully couldn't see her.

"William," the man said, extremely business-like. He wore a perfectly-fitted black suit with a green patterned tie.

"Hi," Will said, standing up straighter than before. "I need some help with my Okliot. It doesn't seem to be working."

"What makes you say that?" the man replied, annoyed, keeping his eye contact on Will, completely ignoring Aurelia, perhaps not able to see her since she stood off to the side.

"Half of the, uh, portal seems to have vanished."

"Impossible."

"That's what I thought, too. But it has."

"Are you there alone?" the man asked.

"No... I have a few friends inside, and um, this is Aurelia," Will said, motioning for her to step towards him.

"Nice to meet you, Sir."

Aurelia nervously moved towards Will so the man on the projection could see her clearly. Suddenly, his face seemed to drain of all its blood and he grew white as a ghost.

"William. I have a team coming there now to assist you. Detain Miss Quinn until we arrive."

How did he know her last name? She hadn't told anyone at the party. Aurelia knew this was a bad idea. She took a small step back from Will.

"What? You mean Aurelia? Why would I do that?" Will said, finally breaking from his rigid stance.

"William. Do it now. Do you understand me?" said the man, in a harsh tone.

Aurelia's breath grew labored and fear washed over her. They must have known that she wasn't a time traveler. She looked at Will with a worried expression and tried to read his face. Would he actually detain her?

Will nodded at the man, and the projection ended. He was going to take her in, she was sure of it. His face was filled with worry and skepticism. Had he made his decision? They locked eyes, questioning what the other should, or would, do.

Will stepped towards her and Aurelia's eyes darted to see that he still held the Okliot in his hand. She knew that she had to make the decision for him. It was now or never. Making the fastest move she could, she grabbed the Okliot from his hand and ran up the stairs as quickly as humanly possible.

"Aurelia! No! Wait!" Will screamed, rushing up the stairs after her.

She couldn't stop. What would happen to her if they knew she wasn't a "Member"? Her feet flew underneath her, and she could feel the strange sensation building up in her body like before. Her muscles became weak, her chest tightened, her vision blurred.

She was traveling in time.

She looked behind her, and Will stopped in defeat, watching her ascend the stairs. Like a ghost, Will's body began to fade out of view.

She could faintly hear him screaming a warning for her, "Don't let them find you!"

He had completely disappeared from the staircase, and Aurelia stopped in her tracks to process what she had just done.

Did he have another Okliot? Had she just stranded him in the middle of the portal? Would he get struck? Would he be OK?

CHAPTER 3

THE ULTIMATE VACATION

Aurelia stood frozen in the stairwell, her thoughts catching fire.

Where was she? When was she? Was Will alright? How did all of this happen? Who sent her those messages to come to the party? Would she ever see her family again?

Tears welled up in her eyes, and she took a shaky, deep breath.

Why did they have her name? What did that even mean for her?

She looked at the golden ball in her hand. It looked as though it was pure gold, without any markings or holes on it except one small logo - a beautifully scribed letter "B". How did it work, Aurelia wondered?

She looked around her at the almost unrecognizable staircase. Before, it had been carpeted, with a flowered wallpaper engulfing her in color - but now, it had newly stained wooden steps and paisley patterned wallpaper. She glanced back down the steps she had just come up, almost hoping to see Will emerge from thin air, but instead, all she saw was an empty staircase. She couldn't go back down and look for him - not after he had warned her in such a dramatic way not to let them find her. Aurelia wondered how she would even know who "they" were?

Aurelia slowly stepped up the stairs, keeping her eyes affixed on the door that was just steps from her. As she approached the door and her hand grasped the cold, metal handle, a thought crossed her mind. If "they" were indeed time travelers, what was to stop them from being on the other side of the door - just waiting for her? She had to be cautious, she decided, and not go in the first, most obvious door. She hesitantly turned to face the stairs above her, and pondered what she might find if she kept going up.

Her mind was deafening, shouting warnings with every single step she took, but she continued walking up. This time, the strange sensations of her entire body going into shock as she walked up the stairs didn't seem as extreme, and she was able to keep stepping through it. However, regardless of the fact that it was now tolerable, the feeling was still sickening.

Aurelia squeezed the Okliot in her hand and realized that it was indeed ticking. Just like a clock, a constant rhythm came pulsing through the metal. What was making it tick? There didn't appear to be any way to look at the inner workings of it - since the smooth metal surrounded its innards perfectly. But even though it didn't look like it, it was indeed a mechanical object, created through some sort of advanced science.

As she increased her speed up the stairs, the changing surroundings blurred around her. They shifted though colors, patterns and materials, beginning to blend together in her mind. Finally, after running up nearly a dozen flights, her stomach and body couldn't handle any more time portals, and she stopped at the landing she was on. She shoved the Okliot in her purse, then just to triple check, tried to turn on her phone yet again, to no avail. She didn't realize that by going through the very first portal to the '70s, the harsh magnetic field in the stairwell had interfered with some of the circuitry inside, and the power had been drained by other means. It was unlike Will's clear glass device, which had been especially designed for frequent travel through the portals, even able to call home when somewhere in time with an official portal.

In front of her was a metal door with another clock on it. This time, before blindly stepping through, she looked closely at the metal clock nailed to the door.

It had multiple hands on it, not just two or three. Each hand was a bit thicker than a normal clock, and they were individually labeled with millisecond, second, minute, hour, day, year, and finally, century. Instead of just twelve numbers, the clock had multiple fields around it, corresponding to each hand of the clock. This particular clock was set to century 20, year 58, day 151, hour 8 and minute 12. Aurelia assumed this meant it was 1958, sometime in summer, at 8:12 a.m.

She opened the door and entered a diner. She must have been right about the year, because the place she walked into looked just like your stereotypical '50s diner. The vinyl black and white checkerboard floor was pristine, the red leather booths along the window appeared to have just been shined, and the bar looked like just the spot to have a chocolate malt whilst wearing a poodle skirt. Aurelia smiled at this picture perfect location, and a waitress wearing a fitted mint green dress walked out from behind the bar to greet Aurelia.

"Well hi there, love!" the woman exclaimed with a twang in her voice. "Would you like a seat at the bar or a booth?"

"Uh..."

"Or, are you just passing through?" she motioned to the door Aurelia had just come out of.

"Well, I'd love a coffee, but I don't think I have any money that'd work here."

"Not a problem, dear. We cater to 'your kind' all the time. Have a seat wherever you'd like and I'll get you that coffee," the woman said kindly, retreating to her station behind the counter.

Aurelia carefully stepped up to the bar and sat at the first stool. No one else seemed to be in the diner besides the waitress and herself. Her body sank into the barstool - she was tired.

"Do you take milk or sugar, love?" the woman asked, as she poured the coffee from a pot that was already brewed.

"Both, please," Aurelia said meekly, a small smile lingering on her face.

Aurelia ran through all that she was feeling in this moment, as she wasn't sure which emotion should take over. She was frightened for her life, found out that time travel existed, had met the guy of her dreams and then stranded him somewhere in time, and she had no idea what to do or how to get home. Yet even with all of the turmoil, the inner adventurer in her was saying that this was also the best day of her life. She smiled as the waitress placed the fresh cup of coffee with a small jar of sugar in front of her.

If this wasn't an experience of a lifetime, she didn't know what was.

"Thanks so much!" Aurelia poured a substantial amount of sugar in her cup, raising it to her nose to smell it.

She wasn't a regular coffee drinker, but today certainly felt like the time to have one. The scent of the hot liquid filled her nose comfortingly.

"So, what time did you come from?" the woman asked, grinning. She obviously knew everything about everything.

Aurelia hesitated. Should she tell her when she was from? Or would it be strange not to tell her?

"Uh, 2019."

"Ahh. That's a good year," smiled the waitress.

“Yup… How ‘bout you?” Aurelia asked, turning the tables.

“Well, they plucked me from 2203 - but honestly, I’ve been working as a guide all over the timeline.”

Aurelia had to hold back her enthusiasm as she wondered what life was like in the future - was time travel a regular thing?

“So, what made you settle on the ‘50s?” Aurelia was genuinely intrigued.

“Oh, just about everything. The opportunities are endless, and it’s basically the birth of new ideas and ways of thinking, you know?”

“Yeah… that’s true!” Aurelia said, dreamily.

“So, you’ve got plans while you’re here?” the waitress asked as she leaned against the back counter.

“No…” Aurelia brought herself back to reality. “Not really.”

“Well, I’ve got some great recommendations if you want!” she said happily.

“Uh… honestly, I don’t know how long I’ll be staying.”

“Well, let me show you some of my favorite things to do. I have a pamphlet in the back.”

The waitress rushed into the back kitchen, plowing through the swinging doors. Aurelia sighed. How long should she stay? Where would she go? Should she keep going up the stairs? Plus, this waitress was definitely one of “them”, like Will had warned her about. Aurelia wasn’t that good of an actress, how long would she be able to keep up this charade with her? The smiling brunette came jogging back to Aurelia, holding a small, sealed cardboard box with a stamped on label that read: “For Members use only”.

Aurelia’s eyes widened. Wasn’t that the term Will’s buddy used, “Members”? Members of what, Aurelia wondered?

“OK. I’ve got goodies for you!” the friendly waitress said. “Now, can I see your confirmation of membership to see how much you’re authorized for?”

Aurelia felt flustered. She didn’t have any papers showing confirmation of “membership”. She opened her purse and debated what to show the waitress. Should she take out her phone? Her eyes focused on the one thing she *knew* was part of “membership” - the Okliot.

She was filled with trepidation as she wrapped her hand around it, taking it out of her purse. Would this work, or would she instantly know that she wasn’t a Member?

The waitress looked at the Okliot, and suddenly, what looked like a laser came directly out of her eye, startling Aurelia. It quickly scanned the letter B on the Okliot and retreated into her eye.

"Perfect, love. That's all I need."

Aurelia sighed with relief, placing the coveted Okliot back in her purse. Was the waitress an android? Or was that the kind of technology they had invented for humans in the 2200s?

The waitress peeled back the tape on the box and opened it, giddy with excitement. Inside the box was something that's important in any time or place. Money.

"Thank you for being a premium Member," the waitress recited as if reading a script.

"Uh, thanks," Aurelia replied, examining the woman in front of her.

"Now, you said you needed money, right?"

Aurelia's jaw dropped as the waitress handed her three large, wrapped stacks of vintage money that were labeled $10,000 each. Aurelia was frozen in shock.

"Now, if you're coming from 2019... this is about the equivalent of say - a quarter million, OK?" the waitress said casually.

Aurelia was dumbfounded. This was more money than she had ever even seen in person - inflation or not. $30,000 was a lot of money - but the fact that it was worth almost $250,000, was - well, insane.

"...Thank you... I don't know what to say..." Aurelia was speechless.

"Not a problem, dear. This is just your standard starter pack I can give you with your B class membership for today. If you need more while you're here, don't hesitate to come back."

She rifled in the box and found a pamphlet, the reason she got the box in the first place, and handed it to Aurelia.

The pamphlet was just like any normal hotel paper of what to do in the area - perfectly laid out, with a map and everything. It had a picture of a stereotypical 1950s family on the front, smiling and posing like they were happier than any human could possibly be. The slogan read: "Things to do on your Adventure in 1958" and underneath was a logo that read: "Adventures In Time - The Ultimate Vacation". Could this be the organization that everyone was a part of? A vacation service?

Aurelia opened the pamphlet and was surprised to see the everyday things that the pamphlet suggested doing: "Go to the local market and taste REAL freshly grown food", "Join the latest craze - Hula Hooping" and even: "Meet a genuine '50s person". It was strange, because the pamphlet encouraged encounters with people from the time, and didn't even set guidelines as to what NOT to do or say around them. It was practically a free for all.

Almost magically - but perhaps mechanically, a golden bell set between the passthrough to the kitchen dinged. However, no one appeared to be there to ring it.

"Oh! Well that's rare," the intrigued waitress looked behind her at the bell, "I don't think I've gotten a new message in years."

If indeed it was a message from "them" - the "organization", perhaps it was about Aurelia. The waitress folded the flaps of the box together and pressed the already used tape against the edges.

"I'll be right back, love," the waitress acknowledged Aurelia with a bright smile.

"Well actually, I really should be going. Thanks for the coffee... and the money," Aurelia nervously folded the pamphlet and shoved the giant wads of cash in her tiny purse.

"Oh, not a problem dear. Y'all come back now, ya hear?"

"...Thanks," Aurelia stood from her chair and began her quick strides to the stairwell door. She had to get out of there - fast.

The waitress took the box to the kitchen and Aurelia watched her through the food passthrough as she giddily pulled out one of the glass devices that seemed to act as the organization's main way of contact.

Aurelia reached for the stairwell door, but hesitated. If they were indeed calling that waitress about Aurelia, wouldn't it make sense that they were on their way to detain her? She pressed her ear against the stairwell door, crossing her fingers for luck. Nothing but silence. She began to open the door, when she overheard the waitress speak in the kitchen.

"No, she's just left. And her Okliot checked out..."

They knew she was here.

Aurelia's breath quickened, should she run for it?

"Yes, she used the portal," she heard the waitress say.

They would be waiting for her at the next door in the stairwell, she was sure of it. Aurelia knew she would have to take her chances and hopefully find another way home. She silently closed the stairwell door and tiptoed to the front door of the diner. Opening the door, Aurelia stepped outside into the 1950s.

CHAPTER 4

THE SALESMAN

The warm air and bright sun flooded Aurelia's face, and she squinted to see the street in front of her. It seemed that she was in the middle of a small town, as only a few pedestrians walked down the entirety of the street. She made her way down the sidewalk, briskly, yet not obviously. If "they" were coming for her, she had to get out of town as fast as possible. They would quickly realize that she hadn't used the portal, perhaps in seconds, or a few minutes at the most. And it didn't help that Aurelia stuck out like a sore thumb with her little black dress and bright Halston sweater - she would be found in minutes. Taking off the sweater, partially for anonymity, but also because of the sizzling sun beating down on her, she sped down the street, pivoting to a stop when she realized she was upon a car lot. She could certainly get away faster with a car - and she did have $30,000 in cash, thanks to the waitress.

Aurelia glanced down the street behind her and it didn't seem like anyone had come out of the diner yet, so she hurried into the lot. A car salesman immediately approached her, with a smug, overbearing smile and far too much cologne, aiming to mask the smell of a long summer day spent in the hot, dry, Texas sun.

He tipped his ten gallon hat at her as a greeting, then speaking quickly in his thick Texas accent, and without hesitation, the salesman began his pitch, "Howdy Ma'am, I'm John, pleasure to meet you. I've got some beautiful cars on the lot today, what're you looking for?" Aurelia began to answer, but it seemed he hadn't finished his rehearsed speech. "I assume you're here for your husband, no? I've got the latest from Ford, Chevrolet, them fancy cars - you look like you deserve a luxury car-"

Cutting the man off, Aurelia got straight to it, "Well, thanks for all the options, but - I'm not picky. How about uh - this one, right here. How much?"

She pointed to a mint blue Chevrolet that screamed '50s all

American family with its rounded edges and low riding grill.

"Now Miss, you know just what you want, don't you. Original price is $2,350, but I might be able take its price down to $2,250 for such a pretty little lady like you," John buttered her up with a wink and side smile, revealing a cracked tooth amidst his straight smile.

"I'll take it, but I need to be on the road now."

"Perfect, you just follow me inside and we'll get that paperwork ready for your husband," his nonexistent sales beginning to bubble for the first time in months with the ease of this mystery woman.

Did she have time for this? Was she being stupid? She didn't *have* a husband, and paperwork could take ages! Plus, her driver's license certainly wouldn't work in the '50s. He would surely turn her away.

"Sir, I uh - *I'm* buying this car for my uh, husband, see? And I simply must get it to him now since he's coming home from a business trip. Umm... and I don't have time for the paperwork if I want to get it to him before he gets home...."

"Oh, pretty lady, see, we have to get you the pink slip for the car to be yours."

"Ahh... OK, OK. Quick as you can! I need to get on the road for my, uh, honey," the lie gritted through her teeth like sandpaper.

Aurelia followed the man inside a small office that reeked of cigarette smoke and mold. Kicking a few papers aside to clear the entrance, he ushered her to take a seat on the blue leather single seat sofa that had obviously already seen its day. Wiping the crumbs away from the worn leather, she sat hesitantly, eyeing the pine door as he shut it with a smile. Pulling out a fresh cigarette, he asked if she'd care for one with an eyebrow raise and hand tilt, Aurelia shaking her head no with a scowl. John, the salesman, collapsed into his chair across the desk with a plop, his belly jiggling over a large, silver belt buckle with longhorns engraved into it, that held up pants that seemed four sizes too small. He began rustling through his file cabinet with a lackadaisical

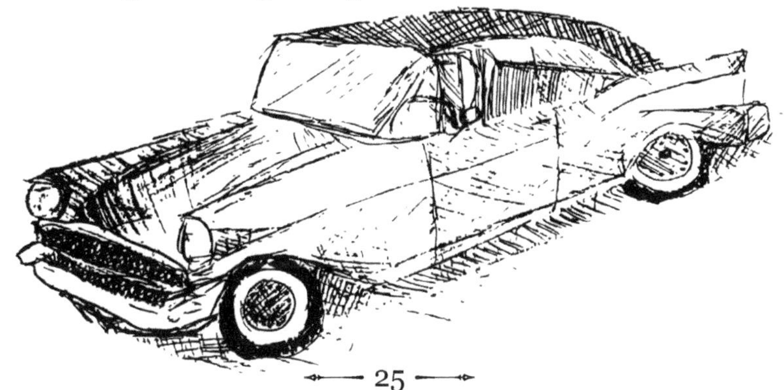

finger browsing for the right papers.

Aurelia glanced around at the claustrophobic closet of an office they were in, taking note of the stacks of books, papers and clutter, piled on the floor of the room, begging for a cabinet, and the mild bleach and urine smell that wafted from the open bathroom to the right of her. After her assessment, she kept her eyes glued to the window just to her left. Shaded mildly with white vertical blinds, yet revealing enough that one could people watch with ease. So far, only a woman with a baby carriage had walked by on the street that stood a good distance away, but her shallow breath grew stale with every second that passed, waiting in anticipation for someone to spot her.

The clock on the wall ticked louder in the silence, and the few minutes it took for John to collect the papers seemed like hours in the angst of the moment.

John broke the silence to explain where to sign and what to pay. $2,250, as he had mentioned before. She signed the papers, unthinkingly writing her own name, adding in a random home address of "1 Rose Lane, Austin, Texas" since they were somewhere in Texas, although she wasn't sure exactly where. Aurelia unzipped her bulging crossbody purse and turned slightly away from the man watching her, beginning to add up the money. She counted out nineteen hundreds before movement stirred in her peripheral vision, and she darted her head to see them; At least three dozen people walking from the diner's direction, all dressed in 1950s garb, methodically searching the street.

They had to be there for her. Some worked in pairs, such as some younger teenage girls appearing to giggle as they held each other's arms, casually glancing around corners, or the man and woman who walked side by side as if married whilst bending down to look under the cars in the lot. Then there were the few that walked alone. The man in the brown trench coat with Clark Kent esque glasses and a newspaper he held as if reading. Or perhaps the old man who walked with a cane who sat on a bench just across the way. The small town road had suddenly transformed into a bustling city in a matter of seconds. Aurelia's breath tightened upon the sight.

They knew she was here.

The money was damp with her hand's sudden clamminess, clinging to her tightened grip. With a sudden reaction, she counted out the remainder she owed, plus an extra $250, slamming the two and a half thousand on the table, startling John the salesman.

"Sir, I need a favor."

John's office door opened, and a man and woman, glued together like a couple, waltzed in together. They had already searched the car lot, and before they could move on, had found this closed door. The faded office sat empty, a fresh cigarette slowly burning out in an ashtray, and a crowded desk with flung papers and an open ledger laying stranded. The entirety of the office looked forgotten; an open bottle of liquor on the floor next to the door, the grey wallpaper peeling slightly at the edges, and a random photo of a sunflower askew on the wall. A coffee pot rested on the sink, cold coffee congealing on the sides, and a briefcase was shoved, not so conspicuously, underneath the blue sofa. Amongst the clutter and silly trinkets that rested precariously atop paperwork piles, they failed to see the wet signatures on the papers scattered across the desk that read, "Aurelia Quinn" - a blatant mistake on both sides that wouldn't be overlooked again.

Presuming erroneously that the target had not been there, chalking the scene up to bad taste and neglect from whomever worked there, the two left the room and continued their search elsewhere.

CHAPTER 5

TEXAS

Although the paved road in town seemed smooth upon first glance, in such a cramped, dark place and low-riding car, Aurelia felt every pebble and twist. The trunk of her new car smelled of leather and oil, and her head was wedged between the side of the car and the spare wheel which occupied most of her breathing room. Her long blonde hair sprawled across the metal, stray hairs catching easily on each edge it encountered. Squirming uncomfortably, she adjusted her purse and sweater to provide a slight cushioning to her back from the bumps, but it barely made a difference as the car jiggled along the road.

About twenty minutes had passed since she had bribed John the salesman to drive her to his home, hidden in this unprecedented way. Although the extra bills warmed his pockets, he still felt it a discommodious and nerve wracking task to have a young lady shoved in a trunk as he drove. But for a car salesman in a town with no more than a couple hundred people residing within the surrounding few miles, four mouths to feed at home, and a house payment that, unbeknownst to his wife, was months behind; any extra cash seemed like a blessing from God. The girl seemed nice enough, and although she apparently needed to beat feet, she didn't strike him as someone who'd be running away if it wasn't for a reason. So he had grabbed the keys and pulled the car away, nodding with a startled smile to the people that suddenly flooded his vacant car lot.

Now, as the paved road ahead of him began to crumble into dirt, he wondered what had become of the young girl in the back. Upon first sight, he thought her to be in her mid-twenties, but the moment he saw Aurelia in such a vulnerable state, he realized she wasn't much older than his oldest daughter, Margaret, who had just turned fourteen herself. He wondered how old the girl in the black dress actually was, and how someone quite clearly not from Texas had wound up in a small town outside of Granbury, all alone, with stacks of cash.

He ran over the scenarios in his head of what he imagined she'd be running from, and he settled on a rough theory that, as a God loving man, made him wince thinking about. It must be from some perverse nature, maybe even forced upon her, and she hoped to run away from that life of the Devil into the light. He shivered at the thought of what the poor girl had gotten herself into.

The car slowed as it turned into the cracking dirt driveway of John's home, a small farm once laden with cows. He had bought the home about a decade ago, when things were looking up for them. At first, the prospect of taking over a farmhouse seemed exhilarating, and to ease the workload they inherited an older gentleman that lived at the other end of the road, who tended to the cattle in exchange for the rent. But soon the rain stopped blessing his fields, and his hard-earned savings quickly dwindled. To compensate, he found a job selling cars that he hoped could save them, but it seemed the surrounding areas felt the same loss as he did, and only the upper class could afford the luxury cars they sold. Without sales at the lot, the cattle unsustainable and eventually dying from dehydration and disease, he came to loathe the sight of his home, barring the view of seeing his wife, daughters and son greet him everyday after work on that damned, creaky porch. Still, as the man of the family, he knew it was his duty to provide, and he hoped to one day restore the house to be even greater than before the drought, even if it meant an endless cycle of begging customers to buy cars in hundred degree heat.

Putting the car in park, John rushed to the trunk to let the poor girl out, praying she was unscathed from the drive. Besides sore muscles and an aching arm from laying on it for a while, she was unharmed. Aurelia stretched out with a grunt, crinkling her nose as she shook her arms out in satisfaction.

A voice from the porch said in a heavy Texas drawl, "John? What're you doing home so soon? It's barely 10 a.m.! And this better not be a new car! John?"

Despite the summer heat and without hesitation, he wrapped his tweed jacket around the girl as if she were an injured bird. He slammed the trunk and began walking towards his wife.

"Now before you go on and on about how I shouldn't've left early, this 'ere girl needed help gettin' outta a bad situation."

Jaw open, and arms melting from a tight cross, John's wife ran down the porch steps towards the stranger in black. Stopping just a step away from them, a stern and discerning look across her face, almost as if studying a piece of art at a museum, the woman stared silently. Then, without warning, the woman wrapped her arms around Aurelia in a motherly embrace.

"I dunno what you've been through, child, but I was just fixin' to make some iced tea. And iced tea makes everything better. How'd you like to help me in the kitchen?"

"I'd love that. Thank you."

Somehow, in a place and time far from home, Aurelia had stumbled upon a family as welcoming as her own. She felt a wave of relief wash over her, somehow knowing these strangers would protect her.

Louise, as Aurelia came to find out was John's wife's name, talked vigorously about the daily happenings of the town. She had spent the whole of the afternoon telling Aurelia about Patty down the road who was "brazen enough to get engaged to Earl - can you believe it? Earl! A whole six years younger than Patty", and "Lawrence!" the 40-year-old "over yonder" that had just won a scratcher worth three thousand dollars, "The chance!" Apparently Jacob down the road had just immigrated from south of the border. Louise explained that she tries to "speak louder for him to understand", but so far he doesn't give her much. Then there was Norma and Willie up near the Johnson's house. They've lived here longer than anyone else. Their family were original settlers of the town and apparently the house was built by their own two hands back in time.

It took knowing a full accounting of the small town's history before Louise realized she hadn't even asked Aurelia her name, nor anything about her. Flustered, and with an unsatiated thirst for new friends in a town unbothered with strangers, Louise poured more iced tea. John gave a pursed smile as he held out his cup for an extra helping, and zoned back into the conversation.

"Why don't ya tell me about you? How'd you meet John?" Louise asked her.

Aurelia cautiously answered, "Well. I bought a car from him. The one just outside."

"Where's that there accent from?" Louise pried with curiosity.

"California."

Two pairs of widened, startled eyes glared back at her.

"Well aren't you a long way from home!" said John, the first sentence since they were outside.

Aurelia nodded with a twinge of sadness. Somehow her

excitement for adventure had clouded her thoughts of how she would get home; the warm bungalow in El Segundo, California that her grandparents had raised her in.

Her grandmother, now probably alone at the kitchen table in present day, recently widowed and childless, yet a social butterfly with a 30-year-old's energy. She probably had her favorite soap opera on in the background to fill the silence, and was doing her afternoon reading with a piece of peanut butter and tomato toast.

She wondered where her grandparents were here in this time. They had met in high school in the early '50s, in the suburbs outside of New York City, and gotten married by the time her grandfather finished college. They would probably be settling down in the late-'50s or early-'60s, about to have their one and only child, a boy, Aurelia's father.

It all seemed so surreal to think that she could find her family before they even knew her, and she wondered if they would feel a familiarity towards her, or if she would always just be a stranger until she was born and grew up to be who she was now. She thought of the concept of meeting her parents, an echo of them lingering in her childhood memories. She was 6 when their car crashed driving to pick her up from school. It seemed like a century ago, and the memory of them faded a little more each day, only leaving the highlights left to dance in her mind amidst dreams. She could barely even picture the details in her parents' faces anymore - the few photographs of them pasted in her grandmother's photo book, blurry and faded.

Somehow, she remembered the day that they died more clearly than the six years before it. It was actually raining in LA, a rare occurrence that was always needed. She drew a smiley face in the fog on her back window as they drove to school, but it slowly faded from view. She had gotten to wear her new pink rain boots with a kitten charm on top, for the first time since picking them out that day at the strip mall with her mom - a prospect so thrilling that she had matched her sundress to them, and refused to wear a jacket, in fear that it wouldn't match her boots. In California, you don't need much more than one jacket, so the army green rain hoodie that lie on the seat next to her was sufficient.

They dropped her at school with their usual kiss on her forehead and "I love you" from her mom, adding in, "Lia, you'd better put your jacket on," and a mild tantrum followed, complaining that it wasn't pretty.

A short story from dad ensued, despite the cars behind them in the drop off lane honking in anticipation of getting to work on time, "I remember the day your mom and I met. It was freezing cold in the snow, but I was OK because I had my jacket. Wouldn't you know it, your mom comes running down the block with my friend to meet us, and guess who didn't think she needed her jacket?"

Aurelia giggled, "Mommy?"

Nodding with a wink, he continued, "She was the most beautiful girl I had ever seen - new in town, so she didn't understand how cold the snow could be - and I instantly won points by giving her my jacket. If I hadn't have worn mine, I wouldn't have one to give, and she wouldn't have looked twice at me."

Aurelia's mom scoffed and nudged him with an 'oh please' look.

"So maybe I shouldn't wear my jacket so someone can give me their's like you did for Mommy?" Aurelia said with a toddler's negotiation.

"No..." he said in a singsongy voice. "You're a giver, Aurelia. You should always be prepared to help someone, and you never know when you might need it to help yourself."

A deep message and an adage to live by, one that she would later turn over in her mind a thousand times, Aurelia smiled and took the jacket in her hand, running under the other students' umbrellas that walked in unison into the school.

"Bye Daddy! Bye Mommy! Love you!" she had yelled, waving back to them as she reached the dry awning.

Later that day, she sat outside in her pink sundress, her jacket next to her, waiting for her parents' car to pull up and take her home. As the rain grew stronger and began to blow under the awning where she sat, she stared at the jacket, and eventually, stubbornly, put it on. Hours passed, and the teachers brought her back in and called home. It was already dark when her grandparents arrived, grief stricken expressions and a hesitation to tell her the truth. They brought her to her parents' home that night - it was the last night she slept in her childhood room before moving in with Nana and Papa.

"So what brings you all the way to Texas?" Louise said, shattering the illusion of her daydream.

"Honestly, I'm not sure," Aurelia sipped her tall glass of iced tea that she clenched with both hands. "It's supposed to be impossible."

The husband and wife shared a glance of wonder.

"I think I used a time machine."

Aurelia had said it aloud for the first time. A time machine. As crazy as it sounded, that's what it was. Always wishing that magic actually existed, as it did in her favorite movies and books, somehow, she had finally stumbled upon something magical in real life. But then she remembered a quote by Arthur C. Clarke that she had once read in school, "Any sufficiently advanced technology is indistinguishable from magic". It was true - all technology is perceived as magic until it is understood. But turning over the Okliot, she was no closer to understanding its tricks than the moment she first held its warm metal in her hands. The B inscribed in the metal gave no clue as to its meaning, and mocked her as she stared. John and Louise had laughed upon the words "time machine", but had quickly realized she wasn't kidding. They sat silently with their foreheads crinkled, unsure of what to believe. To them, it sounded like a really well told story, but surely just that. Time travel wasn't possible. But then the idealistic dreams of the future began to pop into their minds...

"This is the device that brought me here," Aurelia said, placing it on the rounded oak table.

She needed someone to talk things out to - almost to help her prove to herself that she wasn't crazy, and everything was indeed happening the way she thought it was.

"What is it?" Louise said, nervous to move near it.

"They called it an 'Okliot'? And there was a waitress in the diner whose eye.... sort of - scanned it with like a laser as proof of membership. I don't know. I don't even know if it'll work again. Or how it works."

"You don't mean Sue?" John asked Aurelia. "In the diner?"

"Umm... maybe? I don't know her name."

"The diner near my car lot?" Aurelia nodded, and John broke into a laugh. "We've known Sue for years! She definitely doesn't have any lasers in her eyes!"

Jumping in, obviously a stronger believer, Louise asked with wonder in her eyes, "Do the cars fly?"

"Huh?"

"In the future - does everyone have flying cars?"

"Oh... no. Not in 2019 at least," Aurelia said, chuckling. She wondered if perhaps somewhere in time they would.

"2019? Well you're a long way away. Are there any farms left? Or is everything one big city?"

"Huh. Well yeah, there are definitely still farms, but most small towns have become pretty commercialized. You can't go a few miles without a Starbucks or McDonald's."

"What's a 'star buck'?" John asked, "Do ya mean from Moby Dick?"

Aurelia laughed, realizing that the company hadn't even been founded here yet, "No, no - it's a coffee shop. But they have a bunch of specialized drinks - hundreds even, and everyone likes something slightly different."

"Wow..." Louise whispered.

"How many types of coffee are there? Cream, sugar, or black. That's all you need," John mumbled under his breath, scrunching his forehead in doubt.

"But we also have cell phones... which are portable phones you can take anywhere with you," Aurelia opened her purse and dug for her phone, placing it on the table to show them. "It doesn't work here for some reason, but normally it lights up like a mini TV and you can call people, or text them, or play games, watch movies. It's pretty cool." Louise and John sat awestruck. "Oh! And we have robots that can vacuum for us, although not many people have them. And there are personal computers, you can order things online, and there's even an app that you can order food from. And almost everyone is a photographer now, since all of our phones have cameras built in. Then you post it on social media and share it with all your friends."

"Social, what? An 'app'? Are you sure you didn't hit your head in that trunk?" John asked.

"John!" Louise promptly hit his arm to stop. "How did you... get here?"

"Today is my birthday, er, I guess the day I left was my birthday, and I thought someone was throwing me a get together for it - like a surprise party. They sent me an invitation and where to be. But somehow I went through this staircase, um portal? And next thing I know I'm in the '70s. And I met this guy, Will, who had the Okliot. But someone, I don't know how, knew my name, and they said they needed to 'detain me', and then I just ran. I came out of the staircase into the diner, and I knew I had to get away - so I stumbled upon a car lot, and that's when I met John."

"Why did they wanna arrest you? You haven't done nuttin'

wrong!" Louise said with a motherly concern.

"I don't know. Honestly," Aurelia sighed.

"Bless your heart," Louise said worriedly, "and all this on your birthday."

"Where'd you say there was a staircase?" John asked.

"In the diner, through a door to the left when you walk in," Aurelia explained.

"Strange. I don't think I've ever seen that. Only a bathroom. Have you tried going back through it?" John said skeptically, as if he didn't believe a word of her nonsensical story.

"No. Not yet. I think they're waiting for me on the other side."

Louise shot her husband a worried look, "Well then you'll just have to stay here with us until it's safe. Won't she, John?"

"You're welcome here as long as you need."

It was quite a relief telling her story out loud. Aurelia wasn't sure if they fully believed her, but as Louise set up a few blankets on the couch for her to sleep, she realized it didn't matter. They were genuinely good people. Trusting, gentle, and even though they didn't have much, they gave her everything they could. Earlier, Louise had brought her upstairs to her closet and let her pick out whichever dress she fancied, to replace the short black dress that she had worn all day, and even found an old tan purse that she could use. She chose a blue, plaid, flare-out dress that fit comfortably, a little loose at the stomach and breasts, but a darling shape nonetheless.

Aurelia met the kids when they came home from school, simply telling them that she was a friend's daughter from California visiting them in town for a while. There was Margaret, a shy girl of 14, who had her mother's beautiful auburn hair and small lipped smile; Tim, a wild, boisterous 7-year-old with red hair and freckles splattered across his face like paint; and the youngest, Laura, a polite yet talkative 5-year-old with a brunette bob, porcelain skin with only a few tiny freckles, and a small, kind demeanor.

They had all crowded around Aurelia, this unusual girl from California that had appeared out of thin air, wanting to know everything about her. How it was living near the ocean, her friends, and how life was different for her at home in Hollywood. Choosing her words carefully, and timelessly, Aurelia answered their questions in delight. They asked her what her favorite toys were; growing up - Barbies, of course. Why she was alone and where her parents were; they wanted to go traveling so they left her with their friends for a while. Whose car was in the driveway; hers. How long she'd be staying; she wasn't sure yet. How old she was; 19, today, it was her birthday. This question provoked an excited reaction, and the kids all decided it was only right to bake her a cake. Running into the kitchen like they had won the lottery, they begged their mom for help and permission to make Aurelia something for her birthday. A reluctant "yes" garnered a frantic search for ingredients, piling them on the small kitchen table as Louise evaded the darting children running around her, while she herself cooked dinner.

Aurelia stood in the doorway, laughing under her breath at this dynamic little family. She of course asked to help, but the kids insisted that they could do it and would surprise her. Over an hour later, and a tornado of flour coating the kitchen floor, the oven beeped and out came a burnt topped chocolate cake. Aurelia melted the butter on the stove while the kids sifted the powdered sugar for the frosting, sneaking their hands in for a taste every time an adult would turn away. Soon, the cake was finished and at the same time, dinner was ready. Louise had made meatloaf, which as she said, was a specialty only for when they had guests. The younger kids squealed in excitement, pulling up their chairs and setting the small kitchen table with plates and silverware. Margaret helped her mother finish a salad, and John sat contently, waiting at the table. A big family, tiny kitchen, yet everyone had their place and their hearts were full just being together. Somehow Aurelia felt like an outsider watching a TV show as the perfect scene evolved in the kitchen, but the veil was popped when young Tim ran down the stairs with an extra chair from his room for Aurelia, and she was suddenly included in it all.

They ate as a family; talking about how school was, telling Aurelia about their plan to get a dog soon, and about Margaret's dream to become an actress. Margaret felt that since Aurelia was from California, all of her friends were bound to be movie stars in Hollywood, which Aurelia burst her bubble about - she didn't personally know any celebrities, much to Margaret's dismay.

Once their bellies were full, their minds talked out, and their bodies tired from the meat, they served the cake. A truly horrible tasting, dry chocolate disaster, that even the kids ate reluctantly. But it had turned into an unshakably perfect day regardless.

Now, as Aurelia changed into a borrowed pair of pajamas, she thought back about a story her grandfather had told her, of a friend's 20-year-old son who visited them from out of town. Her grandparents had apparently taken him in for a while to help him get back on his feet, sometime when Aurelia was a baby, and years later, they still spoke of him often. He stayed for a few months and was soon on his way, grateful and gracious. They instilled in Aurelia to always be kind to strangers, never expecting of anything in return, but you must give nonetheless. She wondered if the boy had felt the way Aurelia did now. Grateful, yet sorry to be in a place of need. It felt unpleasant to be accepting help from someone. Almost like she had a debt to be paid, although she knew they had truly opened their home to her out of pureheartedness.

She lay down on the scratchy fabric couch, pulling the knit blanket over her chilled limbs, and her head barely had to touch the pillow before she tumbled into a deep and epic sleep.

Morning sun crept through the white trimmed windows, a soft yet rude awakening as it tickled Aurelia's eyelids. In a brief misapprehended moment before her blurry vision cleared and adjusted to the light, the thought that crossed her mind was that she would be late for school. She was pursuing a fashion degree at a local, yet acclaimed school named Otis. A leading place to study art, fashion or other mediums. Her alarm should've nudged her awake, but before she could finish her thought, the day before flooded her memories. She was in Texas with John and Louise. In 1958. The time machine - the Okliot. The Members. The party in the '70s. Will.

Eyes bulged and breath quickening, Aurelia realized she had to get home. She had been biding her time the day before, waiting to be found.

A rush of fear overwhelmed her - what if she couldn't get home? What if she was stuck in the '50s? A mournful loss washed over her head like a sudden downpour, and she thought of her grandmother, her friends, her dreams.

"What's wrong?" Tim asked, leaning over the couch above her, a sweet, innocent soul untouched by the heaviness of the world.

"Just a bad dream. I'm OK, thanks," she smiled gingerly, wiping the wetness from her eyes.

"Mom says when I have bad dreams that I should drink more milk," the young boy imparted.

"Well that's very good advice, Tim. I'll be sure to try it."

Tim nodded firmly and ran off with a smile.

Sitting up from her cozy spot, she mindlessly felt around for her phone, before realizing that she still had brain fog from just waking up. Even if it wasn't in another room in her black bag stuffed in the closet, it wouldn't work in this time anyway. She moseyed into the kitchen disheveled and sleepy, her blonde hair in a rat's nest on her left side, with one borrowed sock missing and an obscure mind. With a proud look, Tim waltzed towards her, an overflowing glass of milk between his hands.

"Is that for me?" Aurelia gushed.

"For your bad dreams," said Tim, before monkey-climbing up the stairs with a sudden burst of energy.

Sipping the top, and setting the glass down, she grabbed a towel to wipe the spilled milk. Suddenly, a knock thumped at the front door just next to her. Unthinkingly, and out of habit, Aurelia opened it. A boy wearing a cowboy hat, white t-shirt and worn jeans stood with a flushed face. A wash of excitement and trepidation filled the air between them.

"Will!"

CHAPTER 6

WILL

"How did you get here? I was so freaked out that I stranded you in the portal! You're OK?"

Will nodded. Holding a finger up to his lips in silence, he motioned to be invited in to talk. She opened the door further, and he slipped past her with a quick movement. She closed the door, first scanning the empty surroundings outside, and turned towards him. Will's arms wrapped around her warmly, and he let out a sigh of relief that broke the initial tension. Realizing the familiar intimacy between them, and embarrassed by her undone appearance, Aurelia pulled away.

Mindlessly transitioning from the hug to sliding his hands to meet hers, Will looked her in the eyes with a fire, "A lot has happened. You explained it all to me, and I understand why you ran. In about an hour, after they realize you're still here, they're gonna search this time stream for you. You need to be gone before then."

Aurelia looked at him with a crinkled forehead, "What? I didn't explain anything to you. You're..."

"Like I said, a lot's happened since the day you went through the portal in 1977."

She slipped her hands away from his, closing off her body language.

"It was just yesterday. What's happened?"

"Right, right. Sorry. For you, yes. But for me, for their timeline, they've been at it for a lot longer. Listen. You need to create another portal and leave now. Do you understand?"

"I don't, I can't, create a portal. How? Do I use your Okliot again? I've been trying to activate it or something, but nothing happens."

"Wait, you... don't know how yet? How did you get to the '70s?"

"I don't know. Maybe because your machine was nearby?"

"No, no. You have to be holding it for it to work, and it has to be in a portal already active."

"Huh?"

"The Okliot's don't create the portals, they just allow us to move through them. Something else makes them, and you, future you, know the secrets of how it works. That's why I... never mind. I might know of a place we can find one, but it's far."

She suddenly realized she could go home.

Rushing up the stairs to John and Louise's room, she knocked gently and heard a muffled, "Come in."

Both of them were up dressing, John sat on the bed tying his shoes, and Louise powdered her nose in a handheld mirror.

"Will is here. He's gonna help me get home, but I have to hurry," Aurelia breathlessly explained after tearing up the stairs.

John knotted his shoes and hurried down the stairs to speak to the boy. Louise clapped her mirror shut and walked to the closet, shuffling through her dresses to find a light pink flowered dress with a dramatic neckline and large off-the-shoulder sleeves.

"Are you sure it's safe hun?" she asked, plucking it off the hanger. Aurelia shook her head no. "Can you trust 'im?" A hesitant nod yes, then her head slowly bobbed maybe. "Fine. I'm coming with you as far as I can."

Louise thrust the dress at Aurelia and marched down the stairs after John.

This time, the dress fit flawlessly. She slipped her black flats on and quickly combed out a few tangles in her hair with her fingers. She rolled her locks into a loose bun and fastened the dress's belt around her head like a headband to hide the flyaways. Grabbing the new purse Louise had given her in haste, she shoved the Okliot in the outside pocket. She had slept with the Okliot - her ticket home, tucked in a pocket of her pajamas. She ran out of the room, failing to remember that she had left her original black crossbody bag shoved in the shelves above her; her phone, wallet and 1950s stacks of money lying forgotten in Louise's closet.

Walking down the stairs, she realized John had been interrogating Will since she had left him. A fatherly response to protect a near stranger he'd only just met. Will's eyes darted to Aurelia, a stunning vision on the stairs, in a candy colored, princess dress that complemented her skin tone perfectly, and matched her natural lip color to a T.

"Are you ready?" Aurelia asked shakily.

Will nodded, reaching for the doorknob, "Oh... Sir, I don't suppose we could borrow your car out front?"

"No need to borrow it, it's hers," said John, fishing the keys from the dish on the living room table behind him.

Will shot Aurelia a surprised look, and she shrugged coyly. Tossing Will the keys, he opened the door in wait.

"Could I... could you give me just a minute?" Aurelia asked Will. "I'll meet you out there." Will nodded and closed the door behind him as he walked to the car. "I know you're gonna drive with us, Louise, but I just wanted to thank you both. You opened your home to me and made me feel so comfortable, even if it was only for a night. I don't know where I would've gone, and those people definitely would've gotten me if you hadn't agreed to help me, John. So thank you."

Aurelia reached her hand out to shake John's hand, but he instead hugged her with a tightly wound embrace.

"You're welcome here anytime," John said tenderly. "Just take care of yourself, ya hear?"

"Are you leaving already?" Margaret asked from the top of the stairs, her book bag slung across her shoulder ready for school.

"Yes. I am. I'm gonna go home," Aurelia smiled with a twinge of nervousness.

Running down the steps, Margaret hugged her, "Goodbye Ari. It was fine meetin' you."

"And you as well, Margaret. A true pleasure. Can you say goodbye to your brother and sister for me?" Margaret nodded sternly. "OK. I guess I'm off."

Will leaned against the gorgeous, mint blue, sleek classic car, his white shirt tucked into his jeans on one side, taught against his skin. He actually had a flawless body, Aurelia realized. Toned, his arms bulging the fabric at the sleeves slightly, yet not bulky like some overcompensating men she had seen who were consumed with their appearance. No, he seemed like someone who was naturally fit, blessed with height and a good constitution. His layered dark hair framed his face, with pieces curling slightly just above his cheeks, and others above his eyebrows. He held his black cowboy hat in his hands, turning it over in wait of Aurelia, as if counting the seconds with each turn. In the morning Texas sun, he looked as if he fit into this time flawlessly.

He would be the popular guy at school who maybe played sports and had all of the girls lined up for him to toy with. She wondered if that's how it was where he was from. He certainly carried himself with the degree of confidence you get when you're in the spotlight and everyone's inflating your ego with fallacies.

Noticing the stares from just behind him, he turned to see Aurelia standing on the porch. He lifted from his position and opened the passenger door for her, Aurelia nodding in thanks as she sat down. A perfect gentleman, Will let her adjust the fabric of her long dress inside the car before shutting the door gently.

John kissing his wife goodbye and good luck, Louise pulled the front seat up and slid into the back, a motion that triggered Will to look confused at Aurelia, "She's coming with us?" he asked her.

"Just to the portal," Aurelia said matter-of-factly. Will shrugged and got into the driver's seat. He trusted her judgement.

The black and teal leather seats smelled of new car, and the colored steering wheel hung low and large near Will's legs. Aurelia reached for a seatbelt, but realized the car didn't have any. The Bel Air roared to life, and they were soon on their way, John waving them goodbye from the neglected, peeling porch.

Even in the cabin, the car's shocks were almost nonexistent on a dirt road, Aurelia realized. Each gofer hole and cavity carved into the dry, cracking dirt shook their heads and blurred their vision as the car bounced over them, but it seemed the faster they drove, the smoother the ride. So far, they had driven in silence, an unspoken awkwardness between them. After a while, Louise had fallen asleep in the back, to the lull of the motor. Aurelia vacantly stared out the window at the brown, grassless dried mud that stretched for miles. Will, with one hand draped over the wheel, reached out for Aurelia's hand, and as his fingers touched hers, she retracted from her position, slightly startled.

"Sorry," she said, folding her arms on her lap, "I just, don't really know you yet. And you act like you know me a lot more."

"No... no, I'm sorry..." Will returned his spare hand to the wheel.

Aurelia glanced at him, his mildly square jaw now clenched and full lips pursed. From how Will acted, she assumed that future her was smitten with him, their relationship already blooming and progressing quickly. But so far, she only had butterflies when she looked at him - not a deep, lurching longing to be with him forever, as she imagined love would be. She could tell though that he was at least weeks, or perhaps months, into their relationship, and the boundaries that held them back now for Aurelia had all but vanished. It felt as though her choices had already been made for her, and the magic of the freedom of love taken away.

Perhaps she *had* to love Will, now that it had all, in a sense, already happened for him. Or maybe there were multiple scenarios that could still happen, and he was a fragment from one of them. She wasn't sure what "time" was. Was it ever changing? A butterfly effect of choices that shaped a new future? Or had the history of the world already happened and was set in stone?

Her eyes still fixated on Will, studying the complexities of his face, she wondered who he was. Now just a stranger in her eyes, but perhaps soon a trusted ally, a companion, a lover.

"Who are you, Will?" Aurelia asked, breaking the silence that hung over them like a dark cloud.

He chuckled. Looking at Aurelia, both of their blue eyes meeting for a fleeting moment, he said simply, "A friend."

Aurelia smiled, "I have a feeling you're more than that to me."

With a longing glance at Aurelia, Will focused his vision back on the road, "Maybe we will be. It's strange seeing you like this though."

"Like what?"

"Unsure."

Aurelia took a deep breath and returned her gaze out the window, "How... how long has it been for you since the party?"

Will smiled at the memory, "A few years I guess. It's hard to keep track."

"A few years? How... why... why did you come back for me now?"

"Because you would've done the same for me. Always."

"So what happens between us, Will? Do I ever get home? Do I ever see my family again?"

About to say his response, he stopped himself mid breath, "I don't know how much I can say. You're not supposed to be omniscient about your own personal future - it's one of your rules."

"*My* rules?" she questioned, to which Will nodded. "OK. Then, what about you? Where are you from? Who are you, really?"

"You really wanna know?" Aurelia nodded and Will opened the floodgates of his life, "I'm from a time when most people wanted an escape. We lived in filth, and wars, and famine, besides the royals and wealthy of course. My dad was a single father from when I was a baby, and he worked as a sort of... freelance blacksmith I guess you could call it. Then one day he gets a huge sum of money to work for one of the Lapites - they're one of the richest royal families, in the future. They sought him out and he became the inventor of the Okliots when I was little. I was sort of grandfathered into the company, suddenly the son of an upperclass family. I was five, I think? So I went from not knowing what it felt like to have a full belly to having birthday parties with businessmen's sons and princes."

"Wow," Aurelia exhaled, mesmerized, "tell me more."

"Well, with the Okliot's and the realization of the profit that could be made, the company was formed."

"So, is it a vacation company? 'Adventures In Time'... or something?" she interrupted, remembering the pamphlet she had seen.

"How did you...? Yeah! They cater to rich assholes wanting more to life than their bubbles and engineered air. But how do you already know-"

"The waitress. At the diner. She gave me a... pamphlet."

"Oh. Huh. Well she lied. She claimed she hadn't told you anything."

"You interrogated her?"

"Not me. My dad..." his voice trailed off.

"So... why are they after... me?" Aurelia asked.

"You didn't do anything wrong, if that's what you're wondering. You're just... an asset they need for the company."

"How? Why do they think that?"

Will looked at Aurelia with a conflicted mind. He couldn't say anymore. Not yet.

He remembered what she had told him in another time, "Don't you go taking the mystery out of it. Let me discover who I am on my own, OK?" her slow, flirtatious voice ringing in his ears and tugging at his memory. A stolen kiss ended any argument he may have had against it.

Pulled back into the present, he changed the subject, motioning to Louise sleeping softly in the back seat, "We're almost there if you want to wake her."

They pulled near an entrance to a mine. Their tires were thick with dirt and the sides of the car stained with splattered brown mud. They had driven at least four hours, if not more. With only a few small stops for gas, their bellies now rumbled and their hearts fluttered.

Turning to face Aurelia and Louise, Will explained, "Listen. This portal hasn't been used for customers yet, I think it's still sort of under construction, maybe one of their test portals as of now. So I don't want you to get your hopes up that it will work. But it's the only other one that I know of to get us out of here."

The two women nodded, hopes sinking with this piece of bad news that Will had conveniently avoided. The car parked, Aurelia reached into her bag for the Okliot, first opening the large compartment where she'd assumed her small black bag was shoved. It was empty, and immediately she remembered stuffing it in Louise's closet as she changed the day before, her money, phone and other items from the 21st century left behind. A hell of a lot of money to forget, but she had many other things occupying the space in her mind.

"How far in is the portal?" Aurelia asked.

"No more than a five minute walk inside," Will replied.

"OK. Can I have the keys?"

He handed them to her without hesitation.

"Louise?" she said, turning to face the lovely woman who cared so deeply for others. "I want you to take the car. If we don't come back out in twenty minutes, turn around and go home. That means the portal worked. My black purse is in your closet. I want you to take what's in it and have a wonderful life, OK? Just don't go inventing the iPhone before Apple does!"

Aurelia chuckled, small tears in her eyes.

"Oh, sweet girl. I'll keep your car for y'all and if you're ever in Texas again, y'all come back to see us, ya hear?" Louise said, reaching across the teal seat and hugging Aurelia with a tight embrace.

Aurelia placed the keys in her hands, holding her hand for a moment in thankfulness. She quickly explained a recollection of which roads they had taken to get to the mine, since Louise was sleeping for some of it, before thanking her again and saying goodbye. Will took off his cowboy hat and left it in his seat as he got out, leaving Texas behind with it. Then, just as quickly as they had met, Aurelia left the woman and walked into the mine with Will.

The curved walls of the mine dripped with liquid, and an eerie mildew smell filled the air. Stepping into the darkness, the light at the end of the tunnel faded slowly as they walked away from it. It seemed sudden, but it was indeed gradual, that her sight grew so dim that she called out for Will to stop. A blob of darkness shifted in front of her and his hand wrapped around hers tenderly.

"You OK?" he asked her, stepping towards her, his features becoming more discernible.

"Yeah. I just... don't like the dark," Aurelia said, thinking of her room she had equipped with a nightlight ever since she was little. A stupid childhood fear, she thought, but debilitating regardless.

"I remember. It's just a little further. Can you make it?" he placed his other hand over hers.

"Mmhmm. Yeah."

Holding his hand tightly, her eyes slowly adjusted to see the walls as they walked. Luckily, they only had to walk a short way in pitch black, and follow a few twists to reach their destination; an old wooden staircase, descending into darkness.

"You ready?" he asked.

"Yup," she replied, holding up the Okliot in her unoccupied hand. "Do you have one?"

"Yeah," he dug into his pocket for another, identical gold sphere.

"When are we going?"

"I have no idea."

Louise watched as the pair of young-ins walked into the mine, then waited in the heat for over two hours - aware that Aurelia had said to only wait twenty minutes, but unsure whether she should indeed leave the young girl alone. So before she headed back, she walked aimlessly through the dark mine, calling for them, and only met a rotting wooden staircase with a dirt wall at the bottom. Somehow, the mysterious duo had vanished from thin air. Perhaps she was telling the truth about the future, and she had indeed traveled in time to get there.

Louise drove home, questioning the very fabric of her reality, yet enthralled at the prospect of what Aurelia had sparked in her. A new belief. A magical existence. Something almost greater than her religion, which she didn't think possible. A girl from the future.

Hugging her husband and kids as she arrived home in the dark, she ran up the stairs to see what was in Aurelia's bag. Placing it apprehensively on the bed, she opened it with a gasp. $27,500, as she would come to count again and again in the coming days, lie bundled inside. Enough to pay off their house tenfold. Enough to live for years. Enough to send their three kids to college. The possibilities would be talked out for weeks, and yet it felt a distasteful task to spend the young girl's money, even though she had clearly told Louise it was a gift.

As Louise had promised, they kept the mint blue Chevrolet for Aurelia, on the off chance she returned. Covering it with a fabric absconded from John's car lot, and eventually building a garage that they could keep it perfect in. Then, as the time passed, and after the money had sat idle hidden back in the closet for a few years, they slowly began to put it to good use, each time eternally thankful to the mystery girl named Aurelia Quinn.

CHAPTER 7

ZHĒNZHŪ

The feeling of sickness hadn't gotten easier. Aurelia stood, breathless, at the bottom of a new staircase. The rotting wood and sediment walls replaced by a silver, sheet metal covering the entirety of the stairwell. They had come a long way down, meeting various doorways, each locked. After a few floors, they attempted to break the lock on one of the doors, and actually succeeded, using multiple hairpins shoved in the bottom of Louise's bag, and a rough knowledge from years of watching influencers try ridiculous things on the internet. Unfortunately, the door was just a facade, and the wall had continued behind it, trapping them in the stairwell. So they walked down countless flights before finally coming to the bottom. The last door. Will didn't seem to be as affected from traveling through so many portals, but Aurelia felt depleted, a mixture of tired muscles like after running a marathon, instant jet lag and bad food rotting in her stomach. They gathered themselves for a few minutes as the uncomfortableness dissipated, then ready to try their luck, Will opened the unlocked door.

What greeted them was unexpected. Will was back home. Unsure what time exactly, but definitely his sector, unmistakable from the hybrid smell of roses and plastic - the roses an artificial aphrodisiac that pumped through the oxygen tanks in higher class homes and commercial spaces nearby. Almost completely unnoticeable after years of living within the bubble of your class, but overwhelming to the senses when you're only a visitor.

The tunnel was empty, and a calming blue light emanated from small cavities carefully shaped into the palladium coated tungsten walls, indicating that it was nighttime. This tunnel probably led to homes nearby, and somewhere amongst them, the Core - every sector's main gathering place, equipped with a bullet train for traveling out of your sector, with nightlife, businesses - and in this particular one, the Headquarters of the company.

Will stumbled back a few steps upon the sight of being home, the cold, compressed air brisk on his face. Aurelia looked around at the smooth, rounded, metal tunnel, and then turned to see Will, the color all but drained out of his face.

"Are you OK?" she asked him softly, and he stared at her blankly, then without warning retreated to the stairwell. Following him, she closed the door behind them, "What happened? What's wrong? Have you been here before?" she asked as he sat on the metal stairs.

"I haven't been back here since... never mind..." Will said, looking away.

"Where are we, Will?"

"This was my home."

Will took a shaky deep breath, and Aurelia sat next to him, reaching her hand into his for comfort. He accepted the gesture, tracing his fingers along hers with a mindless movement. They sat in silence for a few moments, Aurelia unsure of how to soothe the near stranger that sat next to her, and Will with a troubled mind.

Then, like a switch flicked back on, Will stood up, and pulled two bendable metal bracelets from the back pocket of his jeans. He placed one over his own wrist and handed one to Aurelia, without looking. She grabbed it, and placed the slightly heavy metal upon her wrist, looking at him with curiosity.

"OK. Tap it once to calibrate, and again to confirm," Will said knowingly.

He demonstrated, and a lit projection from his bracelet appeared, reading "43-1".

"Huh."

"What?" she asked.

"This is the year my dad was hired by the Lapites. I've never been to this time. I mean I guess unless you count 5-year-old me."

He pressed the bracelet again, and this time, a razor thin mesh suit erupted from the metal, expanding and growing in a matter of seconds. It covered his clothes with ease, sucking in the bunches of fabric it encountered. Soon, it covered his entire skin, from his neck down. The projection on his wrist faded and an electronic bodysuit colored in dark blue and trimmed with large white edges on his neck, hands, ankles, and striped down his chest, now appeared where the mesh metal was.

"Ta da! Fashion of the 43's," Will said, turning around with a grin.

Aurelia, awestruck at the technology, chuckled in regards to the "fashion". It looked like a computer had a baby with a scuba suit. But Will was enjoying himself, back in his childhood garb.

Aurelia tapped hers, the same projection appearing reading "43-1", and tapped once again for the clothing to appear. As it grew, the metal tickled her skin as it clung to every pore on her body. Some would call it a second skin, but really it was designed to absorb radiation from the local surroundings, the specific metal like atomic structure acting as a barrier. If it detected unusually high amounts of radiation, it was also able to automatically cover the head and filter the air outside until breathable for the person inside of it. Some people didn't leave their home without the face covering, programming an emotion face into their metal that reacted to a face's subtle movements underneath, to make others aware of how they were that day.

"Great!" Will said, seeing Aurelia inspect her metal suit with discerning eyes. "I think you're gonna need to wear the headpiece here too - your immune system probably hasn't been exposed to any of our viruses here and who knows how you'd react," Will double tapped his bracelet and the blue and white mesh expanded over his head, where ominously long, white colored eyes and a large half circle smile populated. "See?"

"But, how am I safe around you then - what if you have some futuristic virus?" Aurelia asked, rightfully so.

Will double tapped again on his wrist, revealing his face, "All of us have to be decontaminated with nanobots before we travel. That way we can't accidentally kill the permanents."

Aurelia assumed he meant people like her, normally stuck in one permanent timeline.

Will had gotten his first suit when they moved here, eighteen years ago for him, but ironically the same year they now stood in. His father was 43 then, a long time to be without any type of shield, living in a sector much higher to the ground than this one, and with less barriers built in the walls. But the company had put him through rigorous tests to check his radiation levels, and even after finding poisoning on the lower end of the scale, sent him for a month long isolated therapy to flush the toxins away, as much as they could.

"I like the color on yours. It looks nice," Aurelia said, offering a small compliment referring to the vibrant, yet dark blue that covered his body.

"Thanks! Oh, right! I completely forgot, this is all new to you, isn't it?" he said. Aurelia nodded.

Will looked at Aurelia's suit, a blank, silver metal palette waiting to be programmed. Will identified as Blue, what most would call a boy in Aurelia's time, but now a gender in and of itself; the terms "boy", "girl", "man", and "woman" a dated concept that was the first hurdle to overcome when one wanted to travel to the past. Here, who you were viewed as was easily changeable. While you were still born with one part or the other, how you were treated was based on what you decided. Will, more stuck in the past than his friends, had always been the same, a boy who would soon be a man, or as they called it, a Blue.

Will explained, "Here, our identity is based on what color we wear. There are six standard main colors, Blue - like me, Green, Yellow, Orange, Pink and Red. Then there are the almost infinite mixes in between, different shades of colors like purple and teal, and you can also be a combination of colors."

"So is blue just your favorite color?" Aurelia asked, a likely answer to the explanation.

"No... we sort of categorize our gender based on the color you choose."

"So blue is a boy?"

"Kind of. Less 'boy' than leaning into what your view of a male would be."

"So wait... do you have a... um..." Aurelia struggled to find a politically correct way to ask him. "Uh... never mind," her face flushed.

"Penis?" he asked, chuckling. She nodded, laughing with him at the awkwardness of the question. "Yes. Always have, always will. For me, anyway," he said confidently, although patches of redness appeared on his cheeks.

"OK," Aurelia laughed, "good - I mean, good for us - I mean, not us, 'us', but I guess. I just like boys. That's all I mean... not that you can't be who you want to be... but... OK, I'm gonna stop talking now." Tongue tied, Aurelia put her hand to her face in embarrassment.

"It's fine! I like girls, too, so you're perfect for me," Will said, momentarily forgetting that this wasn't the Aurelia he knew yet.

"OK. Good. Good to know. So, what color is mostly for girls?" Aurelia asked, still flushed.

"Pink. Basically the two opposites are Pink and Blue - pop culture throughout history had already chosen those two. Then all of the in-betweens have completely different innuendos associated with them - Orange means you're permanently unavailable for any sort of relationship with another, sort of self-married."

Aurelia crinkled her nose.

'Who would want to be permanently alone,' she thought?

"And for instance Purple is used primarily for those who are open to possibilities. There's literally a whole class on this that everyone downloads."

He wondered what color Aurelia would choose to represent her. The only other times he had seen her in this time was without a suit. He knew her as elegant yet strong-willed, empathetic yet harsh, fashionable yet uncaring about her appearance.

"What does your white trim mean?" she asked.

"White means I'm..." Will stopped himself, realizing he would reveal too much.

"You're what?"

Hesitating, Will continued, "Um... with someone."

Aurelia's eyes widened, realizing he meant her, "Oh. I see..."

"We've just met, um, for you, so you don't have to feel pressure to put White in yours. Just choose your color and um... just forget I said that."

Caught between a rock and a hard place, Aurelia stared at the metal band on her arm controlling the suit. It stood just a centimeter taller than the rest of the outfit, smooth like the Okliot, yet bendable like fabric.

"How do I...? Um..."

"Oh here," Will reached for her wrist, "just hold both sides of the bracelet like... this," the projector popped up again, showing a round, grey button. "Now, just swipe through the main colors and tap to confirm. Then you can add other colors to your main to make a mix. And then you choose your, um... additional colors, if you want."

Aurelia swiped at the floating circle, and the grey button shifted green, then with another swipe yellow, then orange, and pink. She stopped there, tapping the pink sphere, and a range of smaller dots appeared showing hundreds, if not thousands of shades of pink. Mixes of purple to a slight reddish pink were scattered across the top and bottom, and shades of peaches, bubblegum, and blush all occupied the center. She chose a light pink, an almost pink lemonade color, and the projection shifted to the next view.

Will smiled at her choice - even without knowing the subtleties of the times, she had managed to pick a shade that complimented the basis of her personality; the lighter pinks mainly resonating with those who identified as feminine - refined, graceful, dainty, nurturing and kind. Although by itself, the color didn't necessarily cover the sharp, rebellious parts of her personality, the pink lemonade color was perfect for her kindhearted soul.

On to the next step, where you could add in additional colors to make a mix, all of the main six colors occupied the projection in little bubbles, this time adding white and black. Will, pretending not to pay attention, kept darting his eyes to see what Aurelia was doing. Hesitant for a moment, Aurelia pondered what she should do.

Will realized the awkwardness of the situation and spoke up, "Here, let me show you how to skip this part."

"No. No. It's OK, Will," Aurelia tapped the white and the other colors vanished. The dot pulsed in size, still waiting for confirmation.

"This is where you choose how much of the color you want," relieved, yet still nervous, he demonstrated. "You can expand it or retract it by moving your hand up and down," his hand moving upwards and expanding the sphere to a few feet in diameter and downwards to mere inches.

Aurelia tried it, the sphere moving between the sizes. She chose a size teetering on the edge of small and medium, about eight or nine inches. She tapped to confirm, and her metallic suit transformed pink, with one small edge of white appearing just where a necklace would be. Considerably less than the white on Will, Aurelia had, in a sense, drawn a line in the sand as to where their relationship stood as of now. Open to possibilities, yet unsure as to where they may lead. Will was relieved, yet saddened at thc sight, a kind gcsturc yct somcthing definitive about how she currently felt. He hated that he was home. He hated the decisiveness associated with it all. The white a wearable marker that had become synonymous with the popular kids growing up, and a reminder that Will felt love unrequited.

The sounds of their feet were dulled by the unique, soft metal now covering their shoes, Will and Aurelia crept down the hall of the sector that Will had explained was named B-udo. One level up from the ultra rich A's - the nicest of them all, the B's were filled with cities where most of the executives of the company lived and worked. B-udo was a "Members only" sector hidden beneath the ground of the earth, which was now completely uninhabited, as the atmosphere was all but disintegrated and the earth's surface now almost as cold as the vacuum of space. Most scientists agreed that the safest bet was to move underground when the air outside became unbreathable, the temperature rising to a tipping point, and the radiation levels unsurvivable outside of insulated habitats. Only a few spacecrafts were able to escape through the atmosphere, on missions to colonize elsewhere. While a few did, most of them were destroyed by debris and old inoperable satellites now a hazard circling at intense speeds that trapped most of the Earth from leaving, referred to as the Kessler Effect.

Many companies and countries saw opportunity in the chaos, and mega cities like this one popped up around the world. Some were interwoven and connected together, like the eight that the North America's had become, a huge booming economy. Each were planned to correlate underneath the largest tectonic plates at the time, hoping for the greatest amount of stability, and separating themselves from the other zones, except by a flexible, expandable bullet train. Despite precautions, two mega cities had already suffered complete collapse, one near where India was, from terrorist bombings, and another near Australia where a series of earthquakes destroyed the oxygen factories, and unbearable fatalities followed. Others had small incidents too, of course, but most of the issues that plagued the past were irrelevant in this new organized time. Recolonization was near impossible, and treason swiftly nullified.

Then there was the mega city Will had lived in, drilled somewhere underneath the Caribbean, this city called 珍珠, pronounced "ZhēnZhū", meaning "the pearl". Five original families buying up the wrecked, unusable ocean above to create their own new country of the future, themselves ungoverned by state, rather by CEO. Now, 431 years had passed since the last human left the Earth's surface, marking a milestone and new beginning.

Now, of the original five families, only one remained, a family called the Lapites. While the title of CEO began as a sort of democracy, voted into place by the company, the Lapites had begun to assert themselves into positions of power, until the title of CEO had become less a "job title" than a birthright. Now, CEO had taken on more of a monarchial meaning, passed down like royalty.

Most people felt lucky to even be alive, Will explained. The simplest of jobs treasured, and difficult to keep. He told Aurelia of his father, who was born on a P level, one of the lowest regarded levels. The levels, once simply a floor like a building, through the years had become a separated caste system of sorts that segregated the rich from the poor - a system unfortunately seen throughout time, repeated in poor taste. As the radiation on the planet's surface worsened, leaks began sweeping down through the levels, until it was decided to seal off travel between them. Most people were born and died on the same level. So in many ways, as an immigrant himself, Will still felt like an outsider here in B-udo. The fake faces ingrained in the suits that barely one person here would be seen without, a luxury of the highest regard in the other levels. Now, as they walked the barren halls, orienting themselves on where they were, both Aurelia and Will could feel the cold, negative energy of the past pulsing from their surroundings.

Stopping dead in his tracks, Will pivoted to a sleek, metal door they had just passed. Still maintaining the same uniformity of every other door they had seen, this one's projection just next to it read his father's name.

"This was my house," Will said, breathless. It had been so long since he had been home, that he had hardly recognized the twists and turns.

Speaking through her suit that covered her head claustrophobically, "Do you...want to...?" Aurelia motioned to the door.

Will smiled, a pleasant, distant memory of his father brightening his face. Before they had settled into this new upper class. When they were both still outcasts, he and his father clung to each other's souls for love. Holding onto that feeling, Will opened the door.

CHAPTER 8

ALEKSANDER

The room was dark, but the lights slowly dimmed on to the same blue hue that filled the hall outside. They stood in the massive ballroom, relics of the old world clung to podiums as art. Paintings that once graced the halls of vibrant castles now hung unseen in a room never used. To their right stood the respective rooms for gaming, music, art, and downloads. To their left was the dining hall, kitchen and drawing room, most probably still devoid of furniture. They hadn't bought many items until Will was in his teens, still feeling as if this dream could be ripped away from them in a flash, all of their belongings reallocated to someone who belonged here. Down a hall were the eight bedrooms, six of which remained eternally empty. Just in front of them, at the end of the looming ballroom, was a faux balcony overlooking a projection of Paris in the 1900s. A facade, but the basis for the home's design, and a hint of the past to serve as inspiration for the one man set to design a time machine.

A clatter from their left, and a weathered man appeared from the darkness, holding a frying pan as if to guard himself from the intruders. Weapons were strictly prohibited in the mega cities, except by the Guardians. His silk robe clung to his body, bare feet planting him.

"Who are you? How did you get in?" he exclaimed, holding his stance, his accent reflecting the melting pot of level P. Aurelia could see a slight resemblance to Will under his grey stubble beard, and his unkempt, ragged appearance. His eyes piercing like Will's, his nose almost the same shape, his body nearly the same height.

"*Tatko?*" Will said tenderly.

"What?" the man said, a glimmer of recognition.

"It's me, Dad. It's Will."

"Will? But you're... Does this mean...? No. This is a joke, surely? ...I figure it out?" Will nodded, a proud grin across his face. The man dropped the pan, a monstrous clang ringing in the air, and ran towards them. "My boy! How you've grown! Look at you!" he lovingly slapped

Will's cheeks and stared up at his face. He held him at arms length and looked him up and down, smiling at the white on his suit. "You've married!"

Completely caught off guard, Will and Aurelia looked to each other, Will only catching the darker pink shapes on the suit where her eyes would be. So they knew each other very well in the future. Will held the band on his wrist and the suit retracted into his bracelet, leaving him back in his white shirt and jeans.

Will's father's gaze drifted towards Aurelia, Will jumping in with a lie before a question was even asked, "This is a friend of mine... Miana. Miana, this is my dad, Aleksander."

"It's a pleasure," Aurelia said, holding out her hand as if to shake.

Aleksander stared at the gesture, then broke out into a laugh, "So you're from the past it would seem?"

He reached out with an unsure yet aggressive shake. Aurelia looked towards Will for approval, Will laughing at the interaction. His dad had clearly never shaken someone's hand.

"Here, we greet each other with a flurry," Aleksander explained.

"A flurry?" Aurelia asked.

"We all wear bands of some type, like the expensive one *your* suit is in, and when we say hello to someone, we send them a flurry," Aleksander still held her hand. "Was that long enough of a handshake, Miana?"

"Plenty. Yes," Aurelia chuckled as Aleksander pulled his hand away.

Will demonstrated, "Here, this is a flurry."

He pointed his hand wearing the bracelet towards Aurelia, his open palm upwards facing the ceiling, then quickly rotated his wrist towards the ground. A gentle chime arose from Aurelia's bracelet, followed by a tickle of sensation that quickly rose up her arm, through her chest to her toes, a darker hue of pink tracing where the sensation was.

"Wow! Well that's... sensual," the feeling giving her goosebumps.

"Why are you here?" Aleksander asked Will intently.

"Just passing through, Dad."

"But *how* are you here?"

"We came through an unfinished portal. They must have severed the link from the future and left part of it still open here."

"So I really do it then? The task of a lifetime?"

"You do. I don't know how, but you do," Will said proudly, letting the revelation sit on his tongue before continuing. "Listen, we need to get into Headquarters. I know of a portal out of here that, last time I checked, had an opening near this time."

"Really? It's been here all along? Why have we never seen it?"

"Because you can only travel if you have one of these," Will reached into his back pocket for the Okliot.

"What is it?" Aleksander marveled.

"Oh, I figured you had designed it ages ago. You call it an Okliot - It was your secret weapon," Will said, passing it to him to study his future invention. "So can you help us? We need to leave."

Aleksander looked at his son's face, a younger version of his best self, with his dimpled cheeks and pink, full lips a reminder of his mother.

"Headquarters opens in a few hours. Why don't you two get some rest and I'll bring you there in the morning. I assume you know your way around the house to a spare bedroom?" he said, chuckling.

"Thank you, *Tatko*," Will said, addressing his father with a warm smile.

Will gave Aurelia a room next to his spare room, creeping down the hallway past his childhood room where he assumed 5-year-old Will slept. Neither room Will or Aurelia occupied had been slept in yet, but luckily both had beds. Aurelia's was a Victorian era styled room, with a roaring fireplace, vintage tub and another balcony looking over a different view of Paris, the projection of the city dimly lit in the distance. Each room in the house was air locked separately in case of emergency, so Aurelia was able to take her suit off and sleep soundly that night. She felt drained - seeing new places and times was an exhausting endeavor.

Will chose a room with vaulted ceilings and a large fake skylight of the stars. He remembered coming into this room throughout his teen years, sometimes to be alone with his thoughts, other times to kiss schoolmates secretly under the night sky. His thoughts drifted to Aurelia in the room next door, and thought of what it would be like to kiss her here too. Probably passionate, long, dizzying. He drifted asleep.

A tender knock on the door mildly awoke Aurelia from her deep, satisfying sleep. The landscape on the projection had changed to a sunrise's orange glow sweeping over Paris.

"Lia, it's me," a voice from outside the door called softly.

Aurelia hadn't heard that nickname in years. Her mom used to call her that. The door crept open, and Will stepped inside, already dressed in his jeans and white shirt. He tiptoed over to her as her eyes half opened and he sat on the bed near her. Her eyes heavy with sleep, they opened fully as Will's hand gently brushed her tousled hair from her cheek. She looked at his face, a kind boy, who clearly loved her deeply, as hard as he had tried to hide it. His eyes, a sea foam blue, looked into hers with a longing.

Aurelia scooted up, bundling the covers up over her chest. She moved near him cautiously, his body apprehensive yet wanting. They could feel the distance between them as if it were filled with electricity, the near touch charged with possibility. Slowly, as their bodies moved closer to each other, the distance lessened and the feeling intensified. Will, tracing her chin with his fingers, could feel the newness between them. Aurelia could feel his breath quicken as she grew nearer, his heart filled as she stopped just inches away. She closed her eyes and leaned in to his lips, a confident kiss awaiting. His lips felt like they fit with hers, a missing piece finally returned. His fingers wandered through her hair, to her neck, begging for more. The kiss felt different than it normally felt for Will, Aurelia less steady and sure of herself, but as the seconds passed, she melted into the moment. Her soft lips pressed against his, moving with a slow cadence. Each space in between kisses intensified with a palpable energy and questioning of what the other would do next. Aurelia pulled back slightly, Will breathless, forgetting why he came into her room in the first place. She stared at his lips, wanting more but stopping before it moved so fast they couldn't stop themselves.

"Good morning," Aurelia whispered.

Will smiled larger than she'd seen before, the dimples in his cheeks amplified, his eyes squinted, "Good morning, beautiful."

They had gotten up about an hour earlier than Will was used to when he was growing up, hoping to avoid his younger self. Will brought Aurelia a small breakfast of genetically-made, nutritionally balanced food from the kitchen before they left, the harsh flavors overwhelming for Aurelia. Then, putting on their suits, Aurelia with it covering her face once again, the two waited outside the house for Aleksander. The tunnel was now filled with a yellowish glow, emulating sunlight. Within a few minutes, the front door opened, and there stood Aleksander, with a green and orange lined suit covering his body. Will had explained that orange meant you were romantically unavailable, but Aurelia wondered what the green on his suit meant. Aleksander began to step outside, when a small squeaking voice rang from inside. Quickly, the 26-year-old Will double tapped his wrist, and his head was almost instantly shielded with his suit. A young 5-year-old Will appeared in the doorway. Shoulder-length brown hair, bright blue eyes, and freckles which would soon fade, the boy was darling. His delicate hands held a clear glass tablet out to his dad.

"What's this, Tiger?" Aleksander asked, picking up the tablet to see a drawing of Will and his father.

"I made it for you! You said your office was boring..." a small, soft spoken Will said, just now noticing the two people in the doorway watching them. "Hi, I'm Will," the young Will said, sending the older Will and Aurelia a fast flurry.

Underneath their suits, they smiled at this pipsqueak's sweet demeanor.

"Hello there, Will. I'm... Miana," Aurelia said, remembering her Will's lie. Hesitantly, she pointed her hand at the boy and twisted her hand downwards, sending the boy a flurry.

He smiled, looking at the older Will, who stood silently, his suit covering any trace of his identity. He didn't remember this moment, but then again who would? A fleeting memory of two strangers outside his door.

"You go on inside now, Will, and let your Dad get to work, huh?" Aleksander said, patting young Will on the back.

"OK. Have fun at work, *Tatko*! Bye Miana!" the young boy said, running off.

Aleksander stepped fully outside, closed the door, and a collective sigh erupted from the group.

"You were so cute as a kid!" Aurelia whispered to Will, as they walked down the hall towards the Core.

"Pfft. Oh please. I was short and shy. And nobody liked me for a *lonnng* time," Will whispered back.

"What? Why wouldn't they like you?"

"Cause I was an outsider. I wasn't born in B-udo, which means

I could never be as cool as them."

"Well, apparently bullies exist in every time. But I bet they all became your best friends when your dad designed the first time machine, huh?" Will nodded, chuckling. "Everyone wants to be around greatness. I think they hope it'll rub off on them," Aurelia playfully bumped into his arm, looking up at him as they walked.

Soon, the hallway they had been in opened into a larger room, with several tunnels connecting themselves here like a hotel lobby. Will's smile dropped as he realized what came next. Various people stood in wait at the end of the room, waiting in preparation for the smooth metal doors to open. Will hadn't told Aurelia about this part of entering the Core. He knew she wouldn't have come so easily if he had. He was even a little nervous at how the scan would go for someone not from this time. But they had to get through. It was the only way out, as far as he knew.

"Listen to me. I need you to be brave right now, OK?"

"What do you mean? What's happening?" Aurelia whispered, wrapping her arms around his as they crammed into the space.

"Everyone has to be scanned before they can enter the Core. Just don't talk during it, K? Don't worry," Will squeezed her arm for comfort.

But of course she did worry, especially as everyone fell silent as the tunnels behind them sealed shut with doors that she hadn't noticed as they walked in.

"Don't move for this part, OK?" Will said, placing his hand on her hand that held him tightly.

Sometimes, Aurelia was braver than an infantry of soldiers - but Will knew that it was her worst nightmare to feel trapped.

With an ominous sound of metal scraping above them, hundreds of tentacle-like metallic arms protruded from holes in the ceiling. They slithered towards each person, attaching themselves to the bracelets that each person wore. Aurelia gasped as one snaked towards her, snapping to her wrist and pulling it above her head, towards the ceiling.

"Will...!" Aurelia choked, her body shaking with fear.

"Don't talk, Lia. It'll be over soon," said Will softly, himself dreading the experience.

Another part of the machine attached to Will's band, and soon it seemed everyone was attached. A prick stabbed Aurelia's wrist, and with a jolt, she looked up to see a small needle inside her skin where the metal held her.

Then, large red lights appearing below where each person stood, small glass tubes rose out of the ground towards their faces, stopping just in front of their mouths.

'The air,' Will thought to himself in a panic.

"Take a deep breath now and don't breathe in again until your suit is back on," Will whispered frantically, realizing she would be exposed to everyone's future viruses.

Aurelia quickly breathed in as much air as she could.

A pleasant woman's voice dinged from above, filling the space, "Please exhale."

The metal tentacle attached to Aurelia's arm now controlled the suit, and her face covering disappeared, allowing her breath to enter the glass tube in front of her. She exhaled a small amount, then held the rest of her breath in with anticipation. The tube lowered back into the ground.

Will looked at her worriedly, "Don't breathe in," he whispered.

She nodded, the seconds stretching. A pressure started to build in her throat, an urge to breathe in again. Her eyes locked with Will's as she held her mouth shut - her muscles involuntary gulping for oxygen.

Something was wrong. It was taking too long. She must not have passed. Will looked at his dad, standing a few feet in front of them, and he glanced back in worry.

"Please do not move while we collect your samples," the voice above chimed.

Will looked around, now realizing a young girl, who stood a few families away, squirming her arm as the robotic needle tried to steady itself. Tears welled in her eyes, she was clearly frightened - yet everyone else's eyes stayed glued on the floor in front of them. Will looked at Aurelia, her eyes shouting for help. He looked back at the girl. She seemed to be alone.

"Sweetie, close your eyes," Will said loudly, breaking the silence, "it will only hurt for a second, I promise."

A shriek of an alarm sounded, two bots coming from the sides of the room to detain who was speaking. Will lowered his head, praying they hadn't been able to figure out that the voice was his. Aurelia's chest heaved to his left, dizziness setting in, and on the other side, he could see the little girl tightly close her eyes - the needle finally puncturing her skin. A small squeal from the girl, but the bots above couldn't hear any intense disturbances and they returned to their docks.

Suddenly, a peaceful chime rang above them, "Thank you, enjoy your day."

The arm bands were released, and Aurelia's suit instantly returned over her face. Gasping for air, she collapsed into Will's arms as he rushed to hold her.

"I'm so sorry. I'm so sorry, Ari," he repeatedly cried, stroking and cradling her head to his chest.

Aurelia was physically fine, but traumatized from the experience.

"Why didn't you warn me?" she whimpered, instant regret washing over Will.

"I'm sorry. I'm sorry," he sobbed, feeling her trembling body in his arms as she panted for air.

The giant doors slid open in front of them, and people clamored past them to get through. Slowly, she calmed herself, her breath steadying and her head getting its equilibrium back. She looked up at Will, his face wet with tears.

"Is Miana OK?" asked Aleksander, weaving through the crowd back towards them.

She nodded, still hyperventilating slightly, but standing up fully, with Will still gripping the bottom of her arm as if for support. The lights of the Core in front of them glimmered with an intoxicating life.

"What was that?" she asked.

Aleksander explained, "Every person that enters the Core has to be tested for sicknesses. Colds, flus, genetic anomalies - you name it. If you're clear, you get to enter and interact socially, if you're not... or if you're a carrier... then..."

Will interrupted, "You get put aside and they flush it from your body with sort of like - temporary nanobots. It's not a very pleasant experience. But apparently before the precautions, we were almost wiped out by a plague that had an eighty-six percent death rate."

She was immensely relieved that she hadn't been singled out due to an immune system from 2019. While she was still feeling a little distrustful, Aurelia pretended to be braver than she was, and without a word, nodded at the boys and started marching towards the Core.

CHAPTER 9

THE CORE

For an underground city, there was certainly a lot of airiness. The Core reminded her of a huge shopping mall, balconies surrounding an impressively sized atrium. There was floor-to-ceiling glass at the balconies, separating them from the atrium. From the atrium's ceiling hung vines, and amidst them, wooden beams. Hung along the walls were hundreds of plant types - flowers, bushes and shrubs all in horizontal planters. Movement inside caught Aurelia's eye. She walked to the glass for a closer look, and realized the bottom was filled with large trees, plants and all sorts of animals. Just near where she stood, probably the movement she had seen, was a giant macaw perched on one of the planters. The vines stirred overhead, and when she looked hard enough, she could see it was filled with monkeys and birds playing up above. Down below, she could see a large pond-like glass tank pressed against a window, a slow bubbling fountain at one end. It was hard to tell what types of animals were surrounding the water from this height, but there were certainly a few dozen of them drinking.

"Pretty wild, huh?" Will said gently behind the marveled Aurelia.

She always loved seeing animals, but hated seeing them caged. Although, she imagined, this was the only way to keep their species alive now, since their natural homes above the ground were destroyed.

"How many species are in there?" asked Aurelia.

"Hundreds. A lot of the animals that can live together in a rainforest type climate are in there. And this is only one of many. We have over five thousand different species preserved throughout ZhēnZhū," Will answered, hoping to get back in Aurelia's good graces by talking about one of her favorite subjects. "Wanna see something cool?"

She looked at him curiously. He tapped the glass in front of them, pointing at the monkeys above, and a screen on the glass appeared instantly. It showed a closer view of the vines, a seemingly invisible camera tracking the animals as they swung gracefully. A picture list of all the other animals near the vines was just to the left, but according to the description below, currently they were tracking a breed of spider monkey. Aurelia tapped the glass, pointing towards the pond below, and the camera shifted to show a closer view at the animals drinking the water. Now she could tell that the animals were a mix of tapirs and capybaras, peacefully gathered in little groups. She could stay here for hours, just marveling at the animals, but she knew that every second counted. Who knew when the people chasing her would realize what time she and Will had traveled to? She spun around, taking in the sights around her, before stopping and looking at her two companions.

"OK. Which way to Headquarters?" she asked them, on a mission.

"Follow me," Aleksander said, smiling.

The three walked through the large, crowded halls as the bustling city around them stirred. In a lot of ways, it had similarities to the 21st century - with shops and things to do that occupied time. Here, it seemed life was only about appreciating the good things - art galleries, projection halls where performances could be viewed, sports courts and arcades all lined the spacious hall as they walked. Soon, they came to a grandiose unmarked door, and Will stepped ahead of them to open it for his dad and Aurelia. Entering a small room, each of them had to scan their bracelets for identification and security clearance to enter the next part. Luckily, Will's bracelet was given almost top security clearance in the near future, being the son of ZhēnZhū's most prized inventor. Will had Aurelia's band made last time he was home, reaching out to an old friend who had connections with the black market, to give it a false identity of a "Miana Reynolds". All Aleksander had to do was tap his bracelet to hers and a temporary security clearance was issued.

They all entered without suspicion, and in the next room they saw a bright white hall with faux stained glass windows, that looked like a train station's main terminal. It was the main hall of the Headquarters of the company, Adventures In Time. Still hidden from the people of ZhēnZhū, they had been working for years - centuries in fact, to create the most coveted invention of them all - the ability to travel in time. No breakthroughs had been made in decades, yet the Lapites had relentlessly continued the endeavor - throwing endless supplies and money at the project.

Already busy with people, they weaved through the stunning entrance to a room near the back, where a large laboratory led to Aleksander's private office. They scurried inside and shut the door.

"So, where's the portal?" Aleksander asked Will.

Will whispered slowly, "It's in Gira's office."

Aleksander's brows furrowed. Gira was his boss, this branch's department head - and a daughter of one of the Lapites. He couldn't get into her office. He had barely spoken to her since he was hired by one of her lackeys. Perhaps - just maybe - the office was empty. She was known to come in mid-afternoon sometimes, after lunch with her family. But it wasn't certain. Entering anyone's private homes or even offices without permission was a criminal offense - and if they were caught, they would surely be tried for breaking and entering - any crime on ZhēnZhū practically a death sentence. The prison level was nearest to the earth's surface - where the toxicity levels were supposedly almost unsurvivable. Even a small sentence there meant you could never return to B-udo, the radiation levels in your own body now a hazard to the other pristine citizens.

"Will. I can't. I'll be fired," the heaviness weighing on him.

"It's OK. I know where it is. Thank you for everything," Will held back tears, knowing how the kind, loving father he stood in front of now would disappear and soon change.

They hugged each other, Aleksander whispering into his ear, "I'm proud of you, Will. Of the person I knew you'd become."

Will couldn't hold his tears in, one rolling down his cheek to be quickly wiped away. They pulled away, his father holding Will by the shoulders to look at his face one more time.

"And you, Miana," Aleksander said, turning to her with his hand extended, "I'm so happy to have met you."

He shook her hand, his strong grasp squeezing confidently.

"You too, Aleksander," she smiled, softly.

As they left the office, Aurelia could tell that Will had wanted more time. His eyes shifted from her glance as they walked.

"You don't have to try and be strong for me, Will," she said sweetly, wrapping her hand around his for comfort. He nodded, his face still clenched.

They quickly crossed the main entrance, and slid into a large, clear door just to the right of it. The waiting room for Gira's office. Trying the door, and realizing it was locked, Will looked at the scanner to the left of the door. An extra lock. He scanned his bracelet, but nothing happened. He had been inside before with his friends - sneaking off to other times for parties. Then, a flash of memory appearing in his mind of his friend Benji - he recalled him typing a code to enter - something his mom had given him in case of an emergency. His last option - Will swiped in a Z pattern across the screen, then released and traced it backwards. The door clicked open and the two hurried inside to the dark room, a sigh of relief washing over them.

The lights weren't automatic here - extremely unique for any room in ZhēnZhū. They felt the walls for some type of switch, but no such thing existed. They could barely make out where they stood. Suddenly, a dull alarm began to pulse and they realized that they must have tripped some sort of security alarm by entering. Will blindly grabbed Aurelia's hand and started guiding them through the darkness to the other side of the room - where he remembered the portal had been, hidden as a bathroom. Swiftly, the ominous sound of metal scraping above them ensued, and another snakelike robot from the ceiling came down, searching for the intruder. Aurelia screamed as it attached to her bracelet like before - now even more terrifying in total darkness.

Will turned to see her behind him and grabbed the tentacle, ripping it off of her with sheer force. They both ran, but not quite fast enough.

The sharp end of the machine plummeted into Aurelia's back, attempting to grab her bracelet again. The claw-like metal tore through her strong suit and pierced her skin like putty. She screeched in pain - the feeling of knives being pushed between her ribs. The bot retreated from her back, blood oozing from the large wound, and realizing it had aimed improperly, it attempted to slither towards her wrist again.

Breathless and in shock - Aurelia attempted to keep moving towards the bathroom door - just a few feet away. Will, to the left of her, had found something strong on the desk and started swinging at the robot. He hit it a few times, and the arm simply retracted, then tried to reach for his wrist again. He knew it was only meant to capture and detain until the proper guards could arrive, but now he also knew of its strength, as Aurelia hobbled to the door. He couldn't tell how badly she was hurt, and in the moment, he only thought of getting them out.

Aurelia, gasping, opened the doorway to see a lit staircase - the residual light illuminating the office. Will could now see the blood covering the metallic arm above him and pooled where Aurelia had walked. He made one final swing at the conniving machine and darted for the door - slamming it behind them.

Aurelia, choking on blood, opened her suit's head to breathe. Collapsing on the ground, her vision blurred as she struggled to hear Will crying her name. Begging her to stay with him, sitting above her, his palm pressing her back's wound to try and slow the bleeding.

She wondered what her life would've been like with him. The stairway faded from view as she passed out.

CHAPTER 10

ELOISE

Will scooped up the bleeding Aurelia - struggling to keep his vision clear from his tears.

He ran down the staircase clutching her, continually sobbing, "You're OK. You're OK. Please be OK."

Coming to the first door, he swung it open with his hand under her legs. He ran through the same dark office, not paying attention to the clock on the door, and unsure when they had traveled to, although somewhere forward in time.

He opened the office door, and realized the company was now empty. It must be night. Frantically running through the main hall's large atrium to his father's laboratory - he placed Aurelia on the countertop and began searching for tools - anything that could help save her. Rattling through the hundreds of machines sitting on the counters, he didn't know what to look for, his red hands staining the metal of each object he picked up. He heard a door open and ducked beneath the counter as someone walked in.

Gasping at the sight of the girl sprawled on the counter, a man staggered backwards. Will glanced up to see his father standing above Aurelia.

"*Tatko?*" Will said - standing up and revealing himself.

"Will?" Aleksander exclaimed, stunned.

"You have to help me save her. Please. I don't know what to do," Will sobbed.

Aleksander looked at the unconscious girl, her blonde hair stained red.

"Put pressure on the wound," he barked at Will, and without hesitation, he ran to the cabinets on the other side of his lab.

Will rushed towards Aurelia, his bloodied hands pressing on her back. He couldn't stop the bleeding. It gushed between his fingers as he held her. Her breath shallow and gurgling from internal bleeding. Aleksander, running back with a plethora of tools, placed them out on the counter beside her. Holding what looked like a blowtorch, he pushed Will aside and began his work. He filled the wounds with a temporary bonding metal, meant for machines, but able to seal the wound quickly and stop the bleeding before he could get her proper help.

A bright light glared into Aurelia's sleepy eyes. She opened them, to see a bubble-like material around her - it seemed like a glass coffin, with a blurry additive which prevented her from seeing anything outside. Panicking, her claustrophobia setting in, she gasped for air - a sharp pain in her back stopping her in her tracks. She winced in pain, letting out a cry. A shadow appeared above the glass, and she froze in place, unsure who was watching her. The snowy material faded from view almost instantly, leaving only the clear glass in its place, and above her stood Aleksander.

"We were wondering when you'd wake up," he said softly, smiling.

Aurelia looked around at the bright white room she was in, with Will, passed out from exhaustion in a lounging chair next to her, and a young woman probably just younger than Aurelia standing on the other side of her.

"Miana, this is Eloise. The woman who patched you up," Aleksander motioned to the tall young woman with a blonde bob haircut standing next to him.

The girl smiled, and a familiarity crept into Aurelia's mind. She was reminded of her mother's smile.

"What happened? Where am I?" Aurelia asked, her voice crackling in her throat.

"You had a severe puncture wound in your back and lungs - it broke six ribs. You're lucky Alex called me when he did. I did the initial surgery to set your bones back in place, and now we wait for the computer to do the rest," Eloise said calmly.

"So, that's what this is?" Aurelia motioned to the glass tube she was in, "A computer?"

"There are microscopic bots floating in the air inside, healing you from the inside out with every breath you take," Aleksander explained.

"Speaking of, the best thing for you to do right now is sleep, and heal," Eloise said, tapping a glass tablet she held in her hand.

Suddenly Aurelia felt a sensation of relaxation overcome her, and she drifted to sleep.

Shortly after Aleksander and Will had moved Aurelia to the hospital, Aleksander returned to Headquarters, frantically sopping the trail of blood from the ground and counters. He hoped to have it cleaned up before his assistants came into the lab - or lest someone saw him still there after hours - a prohibited offense. Shoving the blood stained tools in a locked cabinet, he rushed back to the hospital, leaving just before the first employees began to arrive.

Will woke up after a few hours of rest - he had stayed awake all night as Eloise performed the surgery on Aurelia, then waited hours as the new day passed, hoping to be there when she awoke. She was going to be OK, but that same feeling of helplessness he had felt still bothered him.

He looked through the glass at his precious Aurelia - covered with a skin-hugging gown and placed on her side to help the nanobots work quicker as they moved through her body, repairing damaged cells and adding lipids, collagens and other proteins where needed. Somehow, she still looked as beautiful now as all of the other mornings, Will thought. Her lips slightly parted, her hair wrapped above her head.

He got up from his chair, about to stretch his legs outside, when Aurelia's eyes fluttered open at the movement.

"How do you feel, Lia?" Will asked, placing his hand over the glass.

"Like Snow White," she chuckled and Will looked at her with a confused expression. "You know - the princess in the glass coffin?" he still seemed to be puzzled. "The seven dwarves? Evil queen? Prince Charming? You have no idea what I'm talking about, huh?"

They both laughed, Aurelia scrunching her nose.

She wasn't sure how, but her body didn't hurt to laugh. She tested it and inhaled a large breath, pain free. Looking behind her shoulder, expecting to see a gaping wound, she saw nothing but a few red scratch marks.

"Does it hurt?" Will asked, noticing her attention to the area.

"No. Not at all, actually," Aurelia said, stunned.

"That's great! You had me worried there for a minute. Luckily we traveled to a time with ample healing tech and not the Middle Ages."

"Wait - did we actually use the portal?" she asked, her memory a blur after the pain.

Will nodded, "We're just a few years forward. You're in a hospital here. My dad had to pull some strings to get you an unmarked room."

"With... Eloise - was that her name?"

Realizing she had been awake before him, a small pang of guilt hit his gut, "She's apprenticing under my dad at the lab, but also luckily has an MD and hospital access."

"What? She's already a doctor? She looked 15," Aurelia chuckled.

"I think she's around 16," Will said, Aurelia's face asking how that was possible. "Oh! You guys still have schools in your time! We have downloads. You can get through med school in a few months."

"Well *that's* cool. So no studying?" an envious Aurelia asked.

"No, not really. It's all pretty much just there after the class is downloaded."

"So do you have like... a chip in your brain?" she pried.

"No! Definitely not! We just sit with a headpiece on and it forms the neural connections for us, creating the memories."

"So you have fake memories?"

"Not really 'fake'. They're curated, duplicated memories from other people working in the field you study. You just kind of live it vicariously through them, in a *much* shorter time. And when your class is over, the knowledge is now a memory of your own that you can access any time."

Mildly jealous, she wondered how much more creative and accomplished she would've been without wasting so much time engraining her studies into her mind, sitting through the endless boring classes that her school had required.

"So what did you study?" she asked.

"All of the base classes, of course, but later on my specialty was History and Languages."

"So you're bi-lingual?"

Will laughed, "You could say that," he realized that he'd lost count of the amount he'd learned. "I speak most of the Germanic languages like Icelandic, Swedish, Danish, Norwegian, Dutch and of course German. Russian, Polish, Czech, Ukrainian, Croatian, Macedonian, Bulgarian. Arabic and Hebrew, Turkish And Greek."

Immensely impressed with Will's vibrance, Aurelia scoffed, "Wow. I just studied Spanish in High School, and I can barely remember it."

"Oh yeah Spanish, I almost forgot. I actually love *all* of the Romance languages; French, Italian, Portuguese, Romanian, Latin, Catalan."

It seemed he spoke everything, Aurelia thought, "What about Chinese?" she asked, playfully hoping to catch one language he didn't speak.

"Yeah, I speak most of the dialects across Asia, obviously Mandarin, and Cantonese, Hindi, Japanese, Mongolian, Vietnamese, Korean, Malay, Persian, Turkish, Thai. And most of the Bantu languages; Swahili, Zulu, Xhosa, Kinyarwanda. Oh - and my favorite are the early world languages like Coptic, Sumerian, Sanskrit, Old Norse, Etruscan, and Akkadian - for so long lost in time."

"So, basically just the essentials. And English apparently too, right?" Aurelia laughed, in awe.

"Yes. English too," Will said, realizing he had been babbling.

"I wish I lived here with you," Aurelia dreamt, just realizing what she had insinuated. Will smiled at the thought, his cheeks flushed with red, dented with dimples. "Speaking of - when do you think I can go home?" Aurelia asked, thinking of her grandmother.

"Home?" Will asked, confused.

"Yeah, my home. 2019?" Will's smile faded as he realized she hadn't yet understood their predicament. "What is it?" she asked.

"I thought you knew... Aurelia - you can't go home. It's not safe anymore."

"What do you mean? Ever?" she asked, almost sitting up underneath the glass capsule.

Will's furrowed brows said what he couldn't.

Aurelia continued, "I don't... why not? Why isn't it safe? I lived there my whole life before I went through that damn portal!"

"Listen. In the future, you and I blocked all the portals in the early 2000s so that you could grow up without being found. But in order for you to be here - now - and all that's to come for you - we stopped at 2019. There are portals scattered everywhere there. You'd be safer staying here in 43-4."

"I don't understand. Why...? How...?"

"They'd find you, Ari. They'd find your entire family. You can't go home."

"No... no! What about my nana? She's alone. She doesn't even know where I am. I'm all she has left, Will! ...What if I just went back to get her?"

"You *have* to trust me - she's safer this way. There's too much you don't know about yet. You'd be putting her whole life in danger if you went home - her past and present," Will said, sorrowfully.

"So you're expecting me to live on the run, my entire life, for something I don't even know I did?" her heart was breaking thinking about the life she was building at home, everything she had to give up.

Her friends, her dreams of being a designer, her nana's home she had lived in since she was 6 years old - thirteen years of her life. She thought of their little street, tightly packed single-story houses filled with love and joy. Her kind neighbors that had paid her a few dollars to walk their dogs starting when she was 7, the parties they had celebrated on the front yard filled with memories of foldable plastic tables and cold pizza - uncreative, but still unable to be etched from her mind. Halloweens and Christmases their neighborhood's specialty - each house decorated to the nines, as cars from nearby towns would drive through, hoping to find a parking spot, just to look at the "effortless decorations", that in reality they had planned all year.

She remembered going to craft stores with her nana, Aurelia in heaven perusing an ocean of fabric; her nana always improving the house with little homemade knickknacks. The road trips they took on occasion - camping under the stars with her grandfather, her nana safely tucked in the tent avoiding the bugs, Aurelia laying by the dying fire as her grandfather told endless ghost stories, which he claimed to all be true. Trips around the city to libraries and museums. Rich with culture and a zest for learning, Aurelia's nana took her somewhere every Sunday. She remembered the first time she had been to the Los Angeles Library. It was the biggest one she'd seen yet. They wandered the halls in wonder, Aurelia filling her arms with books until they shook.

It all felt a world away now. Days ago, she had woken up in her own bed, with a frilly bedspread she had sewed sprawled over her, cocooning her in bliss. If she had known it would be her last day home - maybe she wouldn't have gone to the party. Maybe she would've given up this new life. Maybe.

But giving up this new life would also have meant never meeting Will.

"Are you OK?" he asked, breaking her heavy silence.

"I don't know."

A few hours passed and Eloise returned, smiling, holding clothes in her arms.

"Seems as though you're all healed up, Miana," she said, tapping her tablet sitting on the table to open the bubble around Aurelia.

Realizing she didn't have her suit to block the air filled with potentially lethal viruses - she shrieked at the sight of the glass retreating to the sides of the bed, gasping for breath before it vanished completely.

Will chuckled at her reaction, eliciting a glaring look from Aurelia as she held her breath.

"Don't worry, it's safe now!" he said. "Eloise added some permanent bots to keep you virus-free on our travels."

Aurelia let out her breath, breathing in the chilled air for the first time.

"So is it true what Aleksander was saying?" Eloise whispered to them. "You're from the past?" Aurelia nodded, their enticing hidden secret expanding. "Wow. What's it like?"

"Which part?" Aurelia asked.

"The sun?" Eloise marveled.

Aurelia realized that Eloise had never been outside before. Never experienced a hike or a bike ride, playing on a swing, sitting by the ocean. Never felt a warm island breeze surprise you on a chilled autumn day. Never walked barefoot down the street, the hot pavement burning your toes. Never felt the sun on her face, revealing a smile you didn't know was there.

"It's... incredible, indescribable, irreplaceable," Aurelia replied slowly, thinking of her beautiful earth that she had taken for granted. "Maybe you can visit, one day."

Eloise grinned, joy bursting from her soul. She wondered what she would do first in that new world.

"When does Aleksander invent the machine?" she asked, directing her question to Will.

"Soon, actually. I think the first prototype was sometime this year," Will said, remembering the day his dad came home and lifted him up over his head - an 8-year-old Will not an easy lift.

At the time he hadn't told Will just *what* he had achieved - only that he had done something no one else in history had been able to do. One day, he said, Will would get to enjoy the fruits of his labors.

Eloise gasped with excitement, her thoughts filled with images she had seen of the earth's surface.

"One day then," Eloise exhaled in wonder, thinking of her near future. "Well, Miana, how do you feel?"

"Really good actually. No pain."

In fact, she felt more energetic than she had since she was little. Her muscles danced with angst and her feet longed to move.

"Well then, I guess it's time to leave," Eloise simpered, slightly saddened, extending her hand, holding out a folded outfit for Aurelia. "This was the only thing that seemed like the 1990s to me. I do hope it fits."

Aurelia sat up, looking at the grey culottes and button-down white shirt, a smile creeping onto her face, "So we're going to the '90s?"

They waited until all of the staff and visitors had left the hospital, returning to their homes for the night, leaving the corridors empty in the Core. As with all of the levels in ZhēnZhū, people were expected to clear the Core by nightfall for cleanings and airlock tests. Aleksander had been testing his limits as of late, trying every possible combination of materials to make the time machine - sometimes secretly working three days in a row without returning home. It had been three and a half years since he had seen Will and Aurelia - and the thought that he had the invention locked somewhere in his mind almost drove him to madness. So he had studied the nights the airlock tests were performed; he knew when the last employee left and the first one arrived; he knew which rooms were decontaminated nightly, and which ran on a schedule; and he watched his boss Gira closely - soon picking up on the codes she used to enter her hidden hallways that led from Headquarters to almost every important place in the Core - including the hospital.

So, it was Aleksander that led them from room to room - navigating them all back to his lab. Eloise's heart palpitated from excitement, Aurelia clung to Will, in fear they would be caught. But they made it to the lab unscathed, Aleksander's confidence warranted.

As the group said goodbye in his office yet again, Aleksander pulled his son aside before they departed, "I need to know - how do I do it?" he asked Will.

“How do you do what?” Will asked, confused.

“How do I invent the Okliot?” asked Aleksander, remembering the sphere Will had shown him years ago.

“Umm... I don’t...” Will stumbled.

“Maybe you were the one who sparked it for me, Son. You told me a secret today that allowed me to invent it? But I need something. I’ve tried everything.”

“*Tatko* - you never told me how they work. You never told anyone the whole truth. That’s why you’re irreplaceable to them.”

Defeated, Aleksander sighed. He was no closer now than he had been the first day on the job. The only thing he had managed to build were the prototype shells of the Okliots.

Saying farewell - Will and Aurelia used the staircase in Gira’s office once again, this time running to the stairway to avoid the security bot above them.

Weeks had passed since Will and Aurelia left for the second time. Aleksander, after a long two days of work, had fallen asleep on his desk from exhaustion. A soft ticking sound filled his dreams and he woke thinking someone must be there with him. But no one was. The ticking transcended his dream and very faintly ticked steadily. Like an alarm clock shoved in a cabinet. Like a heartbeat barely pumping in your ears. His mind zeroed in on the sound, seemingly raising its volume as he concentrated. Standing up, he began to rustle through his things to find the mystery sound. Tearing his shelves apart, ripping the paintings from the wall - his office looked like a madman’s. He frantically shuffled through his tools in his desk’s drawer, finding the tools he had forgotten to clean after Will’s last visit, shoved away. He tossed them aside one by one, the sound of the ticking seeming closer - somewhere. He pulled his drawer out, dumping its contents onto the floor. The sound moved with it. He collapsed to his knees, rustling through remnants of his old inventions he had stuffed inside the drawer ages ago. A gravity manipulator, molecular entropy transformer, and a compact fusion reactor, among others. All had successfully done their original task, but none of the theorized modifications had panned out in regards to manipulating time. But now - years after being made - the fusion reactor ticked. He held it in his shaking hands, confirming the sound was there by moving it from ear to ear.

Sliding the rest of the contents from his cluttered desk, he sat to study the machine. Why? Why did it tick? What had happened? And what did it mean?

CHAPTER 11

TESS

Will led Aurelia through the portal in Gira's office, going forward in time to 44-4, multiple years after the company had launched its public persona, Adventures In Time. Offering incredible locations, the vacation company had instantly become the only thing that everyone wanted to do.

Will remembered his first trip many years before - he was one of the lucky few in the company who got to be amongst one of the first test groups that traveled, before Aleksander's invention was even officially announced. They had gone to Vegas in 1973 to see Elvis Presley perform. It seemed a ruse at the time. Surely just a projection of him on stage, like every other concert he'd seen. But the crowd's enthusiasm bubbled with a raw energy that you couldn't deny.

Leaving early, his dad walked the 10-year-old Will outside the Hilton theater, leaving the ostentatious Elvis still onstage in an iconic black and gold embroidered, bedazzled suit. The air was filled with cigarettes and desert heat. The sidewalk covered in tar, the car fumes sickening - but it was real. Will remembered looking up at the sky for the first time that night - the smog and lights around them covering most of the stars - but he could see the moon. He had never seen the moon before. A bright sliver in the sky that shone through the noise. When they returned home - all Will could think about was going back.

Now, Will and Aurelia walked through Gira's office, coming into a completely different looking Headquarters. Aurelia thought the main hall was large before - but now all of the other main offices and labs had been relocated - and the ginormous open room now held check-in points for each place you wanted to travel. Enormous lines like a ride at an amusement park stretched outside of the atrium. Each person already in costume, having spent their month's or even year's earnings on the experience for them and their families.

Hundreds of doors with ushers scattered the walls - all with a stairway inside, leading to another time.

Will wore long, black, pleated pants, an olive patterned shirt and a long, wool coat. Aurelia donned high-waisted culotte pants, a large, white shirt tucked in, and a black and white Versace-esque herringbone jacket with gold buttons, with her same black flats on her feet. The two walked side by side, shoulders glued together, Aurelia with her hands effortlessly slung in her pants pockets.

Avoiding the long lines of hundreds of people altogether, Will walked confidently past the front of them to near where his dad's lab had once been. As they walked nearer, Aurelia could see there was floor-to-ceiling glass separating the masses of people from the stairway doors and ushers. Will walked up to it, staring at one of the ushers behind it, his arms opening wide, and a smile erupting from his face.

"Plinar!" called Will, the glass automatically parting for him as he stepped close enough.

"Will! How are ya, buddy?" Plinar responded, embracing Will in a brotherly hug.

Plinar wore a suit the shade of teal, with hot pink accents. Aurelia wondered what gender that made him - or her.

"This is Miana - I don't think you've ever met - have you?" pretending Aurelia was a local.

"I can't say that we have. Nice to meet you!" Plinar said, attempting a flurry towards her but realizing their bracelets were already away in preparation for traveling. "Lemme guess - you're using the new '93 portal, huh?" Plinar said, motioning to their outfits. "I swear we've already had a dozen people today for it. Want me to walk you there?"

"Absolutely! And one of these days I'm gonna get you to come on a trip with me."

"Well some of us actually have to pay for it, Will," he said facetiously, laughing.

They walked down the glass corridor, passing dozens of doors. A few of the other ushers knew Will as well, and each remarked something different to him.

One boy in a deep blue suit greeted him with a chest bump and a loud booming sports call of "go team" - another person in yellow simply bumping fists with him as they walked by.

Aurelia thought about what Will had said about not fitting in as a child - circumstances had definitely changed. He was now in his element, oozing charisma and the epitome of the popular guy in school. She smiled at the sight, wondering if he had missed being home.

They approached a doorway with a projection to the left of it showing a video of fun things to do in 1993. Will scanned his Okliot in front of the screen, and it dinged with permission to enter, Aurelia, using the same one she'd had since taking it from Will at the party.

"Hey - bring me back a souvenir this time, would ya? Maybe one of those hot '90s models?" Plinar said jokingly, fist bumping Will with a wink.

He hardly paid attention to Aurelia, probably because Will was known to always have a different girl on his arm. She smiled to Plinar, despite no response, and they walked into the stairway.

Will and Aurelia stepped out of the stairwell into an Egyptian hall of the British Museum in London. Crawling with tourists flooded around the Rosetta Stone, this hall's most impressive breakthrough discovery for linguists and historians alike. Stone statues and artifacts loomed over the crowds, each a story unto itself.

This portal entrance was perfectly disguised for anyone from the future, as each person around them was eclectic in their own right - dotted with both foreigners and locals. They remained silent as they walked, to keep themselves from drawing any attention, plus Aurelia was speechless from the impressive art surrounding them, and her eyes bounced from piece to piece as they quickly passed the eight foot statues of deities and kings. She wondered if she would ever visit Egypt or really any of Africa or Asia one day. It seemed such a world apart from her life at home. But then again, she never thought she'd go to London, either. She didn't even have a passport, she was embarrassed to say.

Sliding through the interconnected hallways, Will led Aurelia to a gift shop, where a swift scan of his Okliot led to the man behind the counter handing them each a welcome gift bag from inside a locked cabinet, disguised as if they had just bought a museum souvenir. Before Aurelia even had a chance to look inside at what they had just received, they scurried to an exit, into a center courtyard with a library housed in the center connecting the museum. In a few years, the courtyard would become the Great Court. The cool crisp air filled their lungs as Will and Aurelia walked outside. They had just come through a maze of culture, their minds still spinning from the sheer magnitude of it all. The early-spring afternoon sun glaring in their eyes, they walked to the street nearby. Will proceeded to hail a cab, and the two got in the ever so spacious black taxi.

"Heathrow Airport, please," Will said to the driver, as he began driving.

"Where're we going?" Aurelia whispered.

"To meet a friend who can get us across the border."

"Which terminal should I drop you at?" the cab driver said in his cockney British accent, interrupting himself from a long drawn-out story about how he once drove Bono and the Edge from the band U2 in his taxi - an experience he surely told every customer about.

"We're flying private," Will answered abruptly.

Aurelia shot him a stunned look. He nodded, a smile creeping across his face. That quickly stopped the cab driver from telling his story about U2, as he realized he was driving a couple that were perhaps American celebrities themselves.

"So what do you two do? You also musicians?" the cab driver pried.

"I wish. No, she just comes from a *really* rich family," Will said, jokingly. Aurelia smirked - if only.

They rode in silence until pulling into the terminal - the cab driver studying the mysterious duo in his rear view mirror. He wondered who they were, and how two so young could be so well-off. He dropped them off, and Will reached into his bag from the museum, grabbing a few fifty pound banknotes from a wrapped stack of money inside, thanking the man.

They hurried inside, and briskly walked to the counter, where an older gentleman greeted them with a jaded smile.

"Hello. Is Tess available?" Will asked immediately.

"I'm sorry, who?" the man asked.

"Uh... I mean, Deja?"

"I'll see if I can reach her. And who should I say is asking?" he asked, picking up a phone on the desk.

"Tell her it's William Kovachev," Will said confidently, the man behind the counter beginning to dial.

"So is that your last name? Kovachev?" Aurelia muttered to Will.

"It's one of them. Most people take their mother's name where I'm from, but I use my father's when I need something from someone," he smiled, raising his eyebrows in mischief.

"So what's your mom's name?" she mischievously asked back, subconsciously copying his expression.

"Phoebe Branson," he smiled nostalgically.

"So your name's William Branson?"

Will nodded, thoughtlessly wrapping his fingers around hers, a habit he longed for whenever he felt uneasy. A beautiful young black girl walked up behind them, tapping Will on the shoulder.

"Tess!" Will said, turning around to see the stunning girl, her naturally springy, curly hair effortlessly wrapped in a bun, with ringlets framing her face. She wore a blue dress with small heels, the color complementing her radiantly glowing skin.

"Now where have you been these past few years, stranger?" she said in a peppy voice, hugging Will. "You had me worried - I hadn't seen you in so long, I thought you had stopped traveling altogether," she laughed in relief, her eyes moving to Aurelia. "Ari?" she hugged Aurelia like an old best friend, Aurelia's arms unsure of whether to reciprocate. "I've missed you! What are you doing here? And with this rascal?" she said jokingly about Will. "I wasn't expecting you for another month! Wait - is everything OK?

"I... um..." Aurelia stumbled to find the words to say to the stranger, as Tess's arms still clutched Aurelia's.

Tess watched patiently as Aurelia's eyes studied her unfamiliarly, "Oh my God. We haven't met yet for you, have we?" Tess whispered.

Aurelia laughed, the awkwardness shattering, "No. We haven't!"

She laughed, holding out her hand to shake, "Well I'm Tess, your best friend."

They had moved into a private room now, so they could talk freely. Tess had called a connection of hers who would help make Aurelia and Will fake passports within a few hours. So now, with their photos already taken by Tess's friend, who had just left, they only needed to wait. Will stepped out to go buy some snacks and carry-on luggage to avoid suspicion by flying without any belongings.

"So, I'm confused. *My* Will is *him*?" Tess whispered to Aurelia, sitting on her chair's arm to gossip.

"Him who?" Aurelia chuckled.

"*The* guy? The one you're always running after?" she teased.

"I guess so," Aurelia said, her future once again dictated by others. "I think we're... married - for him."

"Wait - so how long has it been for you, then? You certainly don't seem very in love, yet."

"A few days," Aurelia said, uncomfortably, Tess's eyes widening. "I mean, he seems perfect. But it's been weird - getting to know someone who already knows everything about you."

"Oh, I doubt that."

"What?"

"That he knows everything about you? You're the most secretive person I've ever met."

"I am?" she said questioningly - she had always been so open about her life before.

"Pfft - I once had to get you sloshed in the 1800s just to get you to tell me what year you were actually from. Up until now I didn't even know that *your* guy was *my* cousin. I can't even believe you kept that from me!"

"Wait - Will's your cousin?" Aurelia asked, the entanglements getting deeper.

"Yup. First thing Uncle Alex - that's Will's dad, by the way - did after he... basically became royalty, was buy a place nearby for me and my parents."

"In B-udo?" Aurelia asked, piecing it all together.

"How do you already know that name?" Tess asked, realizing Aurelia was a quick learner.

"I've been there, actually."

"So, now you see why I live here, huh?" Tess joked.

"It seemed nice. I mean, a little psycho, but nice," Aurelia laughed.

"*Right?* It totally is. It's literally like living in an ant farm."

"So, why choose the '90s?"

Tess sighed, "I've lived in a lot of times. We've lived in a lot of times together, actually. I guess you could say I just... um... enjoy traveling... so I switch somewhere new pretty often. I'm going on my second month here," Aurelia's face grew stale. "What's wrong?"

"It's just so strange."

"What is?"

"Being the only one who doesn't know anything about my life."

"All in good time, Ari."

"Can you just tell me one thing?" she asked, not necessarily wanting an answer. "Do I seem happy in the future?"

Tess bit her lip as she smiled, "Very."

Their new Dutch passports were stuffed in the large carry-on handbag that Will had bought, with fake identities Hannah Van De Berg and Lars Janssen, a somewhat newly engaged couple. Tess guided Aurelia and Will out of the terminal to the awaiting plane. Hugging Will first, then Aurelia with the same enthusiasm, they parted ways, until the next time.

A new Bombardier Challenger stood at the ready on the pavement, the cabin crew at the bottom of the stairs. Aurelia, giddy with excitement, ran to the front of the plane just to marvel at it. She had only ever been on one plane before - a high school trip to Washington D.C., which she had begged her grandparents to allow. She remembered the crammed middle seat she had near the back of the plane, a crying toddler just one row behind her, and the smell of someone's homemade fish sandwich filling the stale air. It wasn't a very pleasant trip - although her time in D.C. more than made up for it.

Now, standing at the nose of the private jet, Aurelia couldn't wait to fly again. Will stood at the bottom of the stairs, handing their new, empty luggage to the flight attendant with a nod, trying to conceal how happy he was to see Aurelia with such wonder. She had somehow always managed to keep that sense of awe, but he could see it burn even brighter than before now. He held out his spare hand to Aurelia, and she walked over to him with a pep in her step. Grabbing his hand, the two ascended the stairs, following the flight attendant.

"Remember - we're supposed to be Dutch going home from a two day getaway," he whispered to Aurelia as they walked up.

Reaching the top, the pilots stood just outside the cockpit to greet them, as the flight attendant placed their bag in the closet.

"*Goedendag!*" Will greeted them in Dutch, shaking their hands and nodding with a smile.

Luckily, Dutch was one of the countless languages Will was fluent in, so passing for a local came naturally. Aurelia on the other hand, had only just had a crash course of the greetings about an hour ago. She mumbled the greeting after Will, copying his hand shakes and smiling.

"How was your stay in London?" the pilot asked them in English.

"Wonderful, thank you!" Aurelia said, politely.

The flight attendant, a redhead wearing bright pink lipstick, introduced herself in an Irish accent, "I'm Shannon, I'll be taking care of you this afternoon. Can I get you any refreshments before take off?"

"No, thank you. We're ready to get home," Will said, hoping not to dilly-dally any longer than they had to, in fear that Aurelia may still be spotted in London.

"Well then, we're ready to go when you are, so take your seats and we'll be off," the pilot responded, holding out his hand, directing them towards the cabin.

Aurelia looked at it expecting to see other guests, but the twelve seats were completely empty.

"Aren't we waiting on the other passengers?" Aurelia asked, pivoting back to look at the cabin crew.

"No, Miss Van De Burg, you have a charter today," the pilot smiled.

Aurelia looked at Will, his usual smirking, dimple-filled smile surprising her with this exciting experience. They settled into the light brown leather seats, choosing two facing each other in the middle of the cabin. The flight attendant closed the cabin door and walked to the end of the aisle, doing her cabin check, then sat down in her seat. Quicker than Aurelia had ever expected, the plane began taxiing and headed for the runway. It literally was less than ten minutes before they were in the air and the captain came on the speaker to tell them the time to Amsterdam - just over an hour flight.

Shannon the flight attendant stood up at the end of the announcement, walking over to Will and Aurelia, "Is there anything I can get you two? Champagne perhaps?"

Aurelia hesitated for a brief moment as she thought of the fear they'd been in the past few days - running from her future - but then a thought raced in her mind - this was going to be her life from now on. She could either be scared, always looking over her shoulder, or enjoy the crazy ride.

"We would love some champagne to celebrate, wouldn't we, dear?" Aurelia said, solidifying their fake story of being newly engaged.

Will glanced at her with confusion, not knowing what had changed so suddenly.

The flight attendant walked off and Aurelia explained, "Look... I know we don't really know each other yet - err - *I* don't know you - but I want to. Obviously future me loves you enough to marry you. And from what I can tell, this 'running', is always a part of our lives together. So let's enjoy it. Let's have fun. Let's be rebels. Let's go to museums, and meet new friends. Try new things, listen to good music, see the world. Let's eat all the best food, and drink the best champagne together. What do you say?"

Will looked at Aurelia. *His* Aurelia.

"I say… I've missed you."

The hour in the sky flew by - with Will and Aurelia talking about nonsensical things, sometimes the most freeing conversations to be had. Tipsy on bubbles, the two landed in Amsterdam. Aurelia's first time drinking champagne, she found it had instantly gone to her head, so Will thanked the crew for them and they disembarked. The sunset already upon them here, the March air was still and fresh. Immediately thrust into a private customs terminal, Aurelia remained quiet besides a reciprocal informal greeting, "*Goedenavond*" while Will conversed in Dutch with the agent reviewing their papers. Luckily, they were quickly passed through, no red flags raised and greeted with a smile from the agent, welcoming them "home".

A car service was waiting for them, complimentary of the private jet's company, and they navigated through the city to a townhome just east of the historic De Wallen city center. As they drove through the flattened landscape, dusk barely lighting their surroundings, the tan colored buildings created a perfectly contrasting base palette for the new pastel greens, pinks and yellows that emerged on the foliage. The streets, dotted with elms and plane trees, among other species, began to light up as they drove - magical street lights illuminating the canals and giving way to brilliant reflections in the water. Castle-like historic buildings lined the stone streets, and hundreds of people walked the city at dusk. Aurelia had never quite seen anything like it. She was used to traffic by car, not pedestrians and bikes. In fact, she couldn't remember the last time she actually walked from her home in El Segundo to go somewhere in town. The energy in the air was palpable, the laughter contagious. They drove over a canal and stopped just in front of a corner home, squished together and sharing walls with the home next to it, as did every house on the block.

"This is it. Are you ready to see?" Will whispered to Aurelia, as the driver got out to open their doors.

"See what?"

"Home," he smiled.

Aurelia had just assumed that this was yet another pass-through time, and perhaps they would stay in a hotel for a few days before moving on. Her brows furrowed, she wondered what Will's definition of home was. About to ask him, the driver opened her door. Muttering "*Dank je*", a simple phrase of thank you Will had taught her hours before, she got out.

Bikes were locked against metal rails that surrounded the street, and a faint smell of skunk and dampness filled her nose. Will, grabbing their bag and tipping the driver, held out his hand for Aurelia to take. Still giddy from champagne, she took his awaiting hand and swung it slightly to show her nervous enthusiasm, her fingers tingling from his delicate hold.

Leading her to the raised door, he quickly looked around to check that no one was watching, and pried a loose stone free on the steps, revealing a hidden key. He opened the darkly painted wooden door, and they stepped inside the dark room. Flipping a switch, the long room awakened. The entryway held built-in cabinets, where coats and shoes were stacked messily. In the middle of the room, a squared off, white washed, wooden, winding staircase filled the space, and to the back of it, a door with a closet for bikes and other large items. Taking Aurelia's hand again, this time not inviting hers to take his, he walked her up the stairs.

"Will, what is this place? Where are we?"

"This is one of my places. I actually bought it years ago in the early '80s for me and my friends to come visit, but we all sort of forgot about it after so many new locations and times opened up to visit. So for now, I figured, this can be our little secret home, hidden in time."

They entered the living room, adorned with a small fireplace, wood floors and leather couches. Windows lined the front of the building, letting in the lamplight from outside, and a stunning view of the canal. Behind the stairs, a small kitchen sat unused. Continuing up the stairs, they entered a loft-like bedroom with a king-size bed and a sitting area in the window.

"And, this is the bedroom," Will said, turning the lights on to reveal it in its entirety. "There's a bathroom just here," he opened one of two doors next to the stairs, "and tomorrow I thought we could go shopping for you to get some new clothes," motioning to the closet filled with mostly menswear, and a few dresses left over from his friends.

"So, how long are we staying, then?" she asked, realizing he had planned everything out.

"Well - I'll need to make some regular trips back to 44-4, so I can bring my Okliot back and forth since we had to use a company portal. The times move at the same rate for all of their portals, whether you're in the past or the future, and if anyone stays longer than a week somewhere they send a team to find you - so we'd better not take any chances. But otherwise, I figured we can stay as long as you want..." he paused, realizing his error.

He hadn't asked Aurelia about any of this. He had simply assumed she would follow him wherever he had planned, but this wasn't his Aurelia yet. She hadn't built the same amount of trust in him that he had in her.

"Does that sound OK?"

Aurelia tried to choose her words carefully, "Yeah. No, yeah. It's fine - this house is... beautiful... it's just..." swallowing her words, she realized she was much less inhibited and still slightly tipsy.

"What?" Will asked, clutching his emotions.

Shyly, Aurelia stumbled, "Well... you're basically asking me to move in with you. And... one bed?"

"No! I know you don't know me yet. Oh God, no. I'm sorry. There's another bedroom above us that I was gonna take - and we don't have to... I mean - we could just get a hotel instead? I just figured this was somewhere we could have a little stability at, but no, you're right, um-"

"No, no, no - this is perfect. We don't have to go anywhere. I just, this is normally a big step. And we're kinda just skipping all of the other firsts, like dating, and... you asking me to be your girlfriend."

Will looked at Aurelia's familiar face. Her freckled button nose and kind blue eyes with a flame that burned bright with confidence. It was almost like they were getting to know each other again, and he instantly knew what to do.

"Aurelia Quinn... Would you go on a date with me?"

CHAPTER 12

AMSTERDAM

The morning April sun filtered through the blooming elm tree outside of Aurelia's window, the bustle of the city already booming in the street below. The smell of bacon filled the air and she could hear the distinctive sounds of someone in the kitchen coming from the open staircase, mixed with a faint sound of music. Throwing a robe over herself, she walked down to see what was happening. Will, with a fire engine red apron on over his brown t-shirt and faded jeans, scooped the bacon onto a large plate. A stereo softly played an album by The Police, and Will hummed along to "Every Little Thing She Does Is Magic", his body moving to the music as he cooked. A small breakfast table in the room, already set for two, held a coffee cup of pink tulips, two cups of freshly squeezed orange juice and a plate of fresh bread, cheeses and berries.

Leaning into the doorway to watch Will as he worked, his back to her, Aurelia interrupted softly, "What's all this?"

"*Goedemorgen!*" Will greeted her good morning in Dutch, turning to see her with a wide grinning smile. "Did I wake you?"

"You woke my nose, but I'm not complaining!" Aurelia chuckled.

"Well I figured we'd want some breakfast before we left, so I ran down to the market and got some of your favorites. Also..." he reached for a bag on the counter, "I saw this in a window on my way and thought you'd like it."

Aurelia, completely stunned by all of his sweet gestures, opened the bag to see a dark, muted red dress. She held it up to her body, the flowing dress hanging just above her knees.

"Wow! Thank you! I love it!" she said, putting it back in its bag and watching as Will placed the plate of bacon in the center of the table.

"Of course! You ready to eat?" he asked, scooting a chair out for her.

How had she stumbled upon someone so great? He seemed too

good to be true. She sat, and they quickly filled their bellies as they talked for the next hour.

Aurelia changed into the red dress that Will had given her, pairing it with brown leather grunge boots and a men's long brown coat she had found shoved in the closet. Inspired by their location, she Dutch braided her blonde hair into two long pieces, her love of fashion shining.

Walking downstairs to the living room, Will sat reading as he waited. His eyes doing a double take at her, he stood up abruptly.

"Wow... you look amazing...! Are you ready?" he asked, grabbing his black leather jacket he had slung on the chair next to him, overly excited for their date, hoping to impress Aurelia.

She nodded bubbly, "So... Where are we going?"

Will smirked, his face hiding something, "I have a few ideas."

Taking two bikes out of the downstairs closet, they hit the street. The sunlight finding its way through the lush landscape, patches of light flooded their vision occasionally, the clear April day picturesque and bright. As they rode, smells of smokers, murky water and paint interrupted the steady flow of blooming flowers and freshly made food. Coming to a large grey building surrounded with green grass, Will pulled in, lifting his leg over the bike as it still moved, and hopping off when he was close enough to the building. They quickly found somewhere to park their bikes, and walked towards the entrance.

"I know how much you love art and fashion, so I figured why not take you to see *my* favorite artist's work?" Will simpered.

"And who would that be?"

"Van Gogh," Will said dreamily, spinning to face her while walking backwards. "It's amazing because you look at some of his lesser known work, and you can see such varied styles, with absolute symmetry and... precision - and then most of his well known pieces are of course the ones with curves and an impasto paint style. It's almost like in those main pieces like *Starry Night* or his *Sunflowers* series, the imperfection was what drew people in."

"So is that why he's your favorite artist?"

"He's my favorite artist because each piece is emotional. When you look at the *Olive Trees With Yellow Sky And Sun* painting, it's almost like the trees themselves have thoughts. They wither away from the bright light, but the colors intertwine and somehow show that...

need for sunlight. Almost like there's a struggle happening... with the wind and sky, and light and trees."

Will opened the door to the museum, a rectangular grandiose building with a square, clear stone glass ceiling. They walked around, Will explaining each work to Aurelia, who stood in awe over the body of work. She hadn't realized Van Gogh's depth before this. However, it seemed none of the popular works were on display, and Will soon found an usher to ask where they could be found. It turned out, Will said like someone had died, that the paintings weren't on display because of an incident, only a few years before, where twenty paintings were stolen in an art heist. Luckily, they were all quickly retrieved - but many of them had to be restored, with great pieces like *Wheatfield With Crows* being damaged. Then, to make matters worse, many of the other popular paintings were on loan to other museums.

Will felt horrible for the ruined date, "I'm sorry, I thought this was the perfect place to take you but I didn't even realize-"

"Will, stop. You don't need to apologize - this is amazing!"

"But you didn't get to see any of the main pieces - why I brought you!"

"I'm enjoying the sketches a lot! I loved working with charcoal in my college classes," she said, remembering sketching out extravagantly dressed models for a fashion class.

"How are you so easy to please?" Will said, tenderly grabbing her hands in his. His fingers wandering along hers.

"Am I normally difficult?" she joked, to ease the intensity she felt of his hands drawing her closer to him.

He sneered, "Oh, you're normally horrible. Just despicable to be around," stepping towards her, slowly.

She smiled sarcastically, "And what do I think of you?"

"Me? You think I'm... conceited... and a really bad joker... and a horrible kisser."

Almost magnetically, they moved closer to each other by the second.

"Really...? Hmmm. I wonder why I'd say that," she said, the space between them closing.

Her lips embraced his and chills raced down Aurelia's spine. He slowly, yet eagerly demanded more, and she gasped at the intimacy building up between them. His breath meeting hers, his eyes fluttered open just to look at her as they paused for a brief moment, before his warm hand found its way to her neck, pulling them together again.

Her free hand slithered to his mid-back, feeling his muscles relax as her fingers gently roamed. She could feel the tension amidst his movement, the way he subtlety stopped himself from showing her just how deeply he felt.

Pulling away, her breath shaky, the feeling of him lingering on her mouth.

"So?" he asked, delicately.

"Yeah... you're right. Horrible," she giggled.

They rode their bikes down the interconnected roads, crossing over the Amstel canal and eventually coming to an outdoor farmers market. Walking their bikes through, they stopped to get a few things from the stands. Sampling the homemade cheese, they got a small wheel for later, and coming upon a bakery stand, they grabbed a few pastries for desert, but instead ate the irresistible delicacies as they walked. Vibrant fresh fruits and vegetables lined the tables, and the market's overwhelming good vibe was unmatched.

They continued riding, some new goodies stuffed in their wicker bike baskets. Coming to a coffee shop, Aurelia stopped and realized she would love a little caffeine.

"Let's stop here!" she said, getting off her bike spontaneously.

"Oh - that's not a coffee shop, Lia," Will chuckled.

"What do you mean, what is it?" she asked, as she walked her bike to a pole to lock it.

"It's a... um... cannabis shop," he jeered, knowing she would be vehemently opposed.

"Cannabis as in - pot?" he nodded. "So that's what I've been smelling all over town!" she laughed.

"Yeah!" Will laughed with her, about to get back on his bike to leave.

"Well, should we go in anyway?" Aurelia said, a hint of curiosity behind her voice.

She had never smoked before in her life - but it seemed her life was completely changed anyway, so why not try something new - and seemingly legal? At home, she never would've even tried it - her gut always leading her down the straight and narrow path.

"I mean, when in Rome, right?" Aurelia rationalized.

She locked her bike and started walking in, her nerves overpowered by her desire for adventure.

Will, dumbfounded that Aurelia would even try it, quickly followed after her into the cafe. He had actually been there before with his mates way back when. Their experimental phase where they tried lots of things as immature boys, mostly from dares. Marijuana wasn't as taboo in the future, just one of many vices that almost everyone had indulged in at some point. Plus, with the technology of the future, any negative effects of such things could easily be reversed. He chuckled at the memory, realizing this Aurelia was still only 19, just a few years older than he had been. She stared at the wall of choices, organized like a tea shop, in awe. She wondered how there could be so many choices for something so simple.

The man behind the counter helped another woman, and Will smiled with pursed lips.

"What's wrong? Do you wanna go?" she asked him, reading his worried expression.

"No! I just... can't believe you want to!"

"Remember what I said on the plane? Let's be rebels and try new things. This seems like the perfect example of that," she smiled, the woman in front of them finished.

They stepped up to the counter and Will explained to the man in Dutch that Aurelia was very new to this, and to give them something small, smooth and subtle. He understood, and within a few minutes, they had a blunt rolled for them. Stepping outside to a cafe table, they sat down in anticipation. Will lit it up, taking a deep inhale, and passed it to Aurelia. She stared at the lit crinkling paper and paused. Should she do this? Her grandmother would have a heart attack if she knew what she was doing.

"You don't have to have any, if you changed your mind," Will said, studying her face.

She shook her head and tried a tiny puff. The smoke burning her throat, she coughed uncontrollably, while Will laughed.

"That's disgusting!" she choked.

"You want some water?" he asked, still hollering from laughter at her reaction.

She nodded, setting it down on an ashtray. Will stepped inside and a moment later came back with a tall glass of water, which Aurelia sipped quickly.

"I don't feel anything. Should I feel something?" she asked, paranoid at what was to come. She liked to be in control of her body.

"I think you coughed it all out," he chuckled, picking up the still burning blunt and taking another hit.

"OK, lemme try again," she said, nervously. He passed it to her and this time she took a deep inhale, trying to hold it in as long as possible but quickly coughing it all out again. "How can you do that?" she laughed, trying again with another deep breath.

"Go slow, Lia," he cautioned, as she let out another cough.

"Am I supposed to feel something, yet?" she asked, catching her breath.

"Um... just a little relaxed, I guess."

"I don't feel that," her voice cracked with another large inhale.

Realizing she had almost smoked the entire thing, he reached for it and took a final small puff, then snubbed it out on the ashtray.

Within a few minutes, she definitely felt it. Her lips loose and

her mind unfocused, she rambled. For no obvious reason, telling Will all about her grandparents' house's floor plan, she grabbed his hand and pulled him from the table to walk him through "her house". Imagining the cobblestone street held her bungalow's walls, she guided him through the front entrance, explaining the deep purple walls and scratched, yellow oak floors. Immediately to the right was their kitchen, which had a door that opened to the living room. Then in the center of the house was her grandparents' room. Just to the left, connected by the hallway near the front entrance, was Aurelia's room and her grandfather's study, which shared a Jack and Jill bathroom. Forgetting what she was doing, she changed the subject to tell Will about her grandfather, who was an author. He had mostly written mystery thrillers, which for him never really saw their day - but still paid the bills, a success for most writers. She then realized she could write a book - about her adventures in time thus far - but quickly remembered her grades in high school. She was certain no one would read it, which made her overly sad.

Will, with the effects of the weed already wearing off for him, the small amount he had tried barely affecting his tall body, couldn't help but smile and laugh seeing Aurelia so uninhibited. He loved it - every random story she shared. He was falling in love with her all over again.

With Aurelia realizing how hungry she was, they walked their bikes down the canal in search of food. Coming upon a small pub, they parked their bikes again and went in for grub. The brick walls added to the allure of the dimly lit atmosphere, the place already crowded in the early evening. Ordering an array of hearty food, soon a large platter with a slab of meat and largely cut chips arrived. It had to be the most delicious meat Aurelia had ever tasted. The meat juicy and perfectly charred, the chips crisp and soft like butter inside. The waiter convinced the two that beer was almost a requirement with this type of food, so the pair ordered a local Heineken, served with bitterballen, a popular Dutch meatball with a round, crispy, fried exterior and a gooey, mouthwatering center. It was almost like a hot, fried pâté that you could dip in mustard.

Aurelia realized she'd never had such fun. Always the example of her friend group, never letting her hair down like this. But with Will, he made her feel free. Like he was going to be there for her no matter what she may do or say.

Rather quickly, Aurelia came back to reality, and her talking slowed. The small amount of beer very mildly replacing the effects of the pot. She laughed, realizing what a fool she'd made of herself the past hour.

"So that was strong, huh?" she chuckled, eating a bitterballen.

"What was?" he asked, facetiously.

Aurelia whispered loudly, miming it with her hands for him, "The weed?"

Will laughed, almost falling out of his chair, "You don't have to whisper, you know? It's legal here. Practically everyone does it."

"Oh! Right!" Aurelia said, laughing with him, yet feeling slightly embarrassed. "Just forget everything I did tonight, K?"

"Why? You were so cute! You wouldn't shut up!" Will razzed.

"Hey!" she tossed her napkin at him, playfully. "Well, that's probably a first and last for me."

"You didn't like it?"

"I guess... I just wasn't myself, you know?"

"Hey, to each his own. Now you know what you're missing," he smiled. "So where to next?" he asked, snatching up the last bitterballen.

An awfully long first date, but she still didn't want it to end.

"Well what's there to do at night in Amsterdam?" she inquired flirtatiously.

"I have a few more ideas," Will grinned.

Riding to a live music venue that Will knew of nearby, the duo parked their bikes and looked inside, the place packed. The already sold-out show anticipated the music that would start soon, the audience imbibing while they waited. Bribing the usher with a stack of banknotes to let them in, they stood near the entrance hoping for a seat to open up. None did, but as soon as the jazz show started, standing created the perfect atmosphere to dance to.

Blue tones mixed with vibrant reds and purples, the loud music surrounding them in colors, the sound tingling their skin. Samba overtones mixed with jazz fusion, the drummer brushing with finesse, the pianist filling the gaps and the saxophonist creating a wide space for himself musically. The song ending and moving effortlessly to the next, the crowd cheered. Now an orange sun emerged, with the song taking them to a bright day in the city. Frantic, yet thoughtfully placed, the melodies entwined like traffic. This song was less danceable, but was still executed flawlessly and stunning to hear.

Modulating, improvising, quickly flowing from one chord to the next. The song came to a close and the sax player finally introduced himself. A Canadian in town for three nights. The audience applauded as he began to play the next song. A slow dance he had written for his fiancée. Many of the couples in the audience stood, one of them inviting the other to dance.

Will looked at Aurelia, her eyes full of happiness watching people of all ages in love.

"May I have this dance?" Will asked her sweetly, holding his hand for her to take.

"You may," she gently placed her hand in his.

Their bodies swayed to the music. The slow tempo engulfing them in reds, pinks and tenderness, their bodies touching as Aurelia rested her head on Will's chest. She could hear his heart beating quickly, his breath deep and strong. Her body fit perfectly in his, her tall, lean figure still small enough to be surrounded by his arms. She thought of the last week. It all started with a dance. The 1970s, the 1950s, the future, and now here in this moment. She could see why she loved him in her future - what was there not to love? He was, in all ways, her dream guy. Her possible future flashed before her eyes - living here in Amsterdam with Will, every day filled with the same energy as today. She could get a job, one day have kids, and grow old with him, the familiarity of almost the next three decades already laid out for her.

The music culminating like an eargasm, the crowd cheered and called out for the sax player. Her illusion faded back into the current moment, and she looked up from Will's arms to memorize his features. His brown hair, his blue eyes. His dimpled cheeks, and his tiny worry lines.

"I have a question for you..." Aurelia asked him, still in his arms.

"What?" he brushed her hair from her eyelashes.

"Will you be my boyfriend?" she asked, already knowing the answer.

"Hmmm... Well, I guess I could be convinced," he smiled, reaching his head to her lips. A soft, thankful, yes.

CHAPTER 13

JOHANNA

Six days passed like a sunset, long awaited yet quickly gone. Will stood with a small satchel packed with some money, food and the Okliots, ready to go home to 44-4, only for a few hours. The plan was simple; once a week, Will would travel back to rescan his Okliot, thus not triggering any alarms by staying too long. This first time, he would take Aurelia's Okliot, and leave it in the future with a friend - that way, if for whatever reason he couldn't get back to her, she wouldn't be found.

He would take a jet back and forth each week, with Tess's connection at the airport arranging the details. Each time he arrived back to 1993, he would be able to take another gift bag, thus enabling them a steady flow of popular things of the time like watches and jewelry, pamphlets with upcoming events, and of course, large sums of money. Each gift bag varied with the time, but the constant between all of them was local currency. After all, you couldn't be a proper tourist without buying things, could you?

Standing at the door of the townhome, Will and Aurelia gently kissed goodbye, still strangers in many ways, but slowly becoming closer by the day.

Will paused Aurelia's lips, "Listen. If I don't..."

"Shh..." she shushed him, continuing their goodbye.

"No, Lia - listen," he said, his seriousness kicking in, "if I don't come back, meet me where we had our first kiss."

"In the future?" she asked, remembering that stolen kiss before the madness ensued in what was it... 43-1?

Will chuckled, realizing that had actually been her first kiss with him, "OK, *my* first kiss with you."

"But I don't... That hasn't happened yet," Aurelia said, confused.

"Exactly," he said, snatching one more kiss. "I'll see you tomorrow."

Bewildered, Aurelia stood in the doorway watching him go. What if she didn't see him again? She didn't have her Okliot anymore, so she couldn't follow him into the future. How would she meet him again? Where would she meet him - *when*? Could the timeline change and instead of her meeting a younger Will, she would instead be stuck here alone forever? Knowing that this was the only way she could stay hidden, she swallowed her fears and instead smiled at Will as his taxi drove away.

He would be back any minute, Aurelia thought. At this point, she had timed out almost exactly how long it took Will to go to the future and back, right from the time his taxi drove off, to the minute he opened the locked door of their *rijtjeshuis* - or townhouse as it was known in English. She was seated on their rooftop terrace to indulge in her daily tea with Johanna, her older neighbor next door. Johanna sitting on her side of the three foot wall, Aurelia on hers.

To everyone who knew her here, Aurelia went by her fake passport's identity, Hannah Van De Berg, born in the countryside of the Netherlands, yet raised in America, which helped to explain why she was just learning Dutch. Now, after meeting her boyfriend Lars when he was traveling in the States, she had moved in with him here, supposedly after a few months of trying long distance.

Their life, as foreign as it was to her, had slowly begun to settle over the course of the last three months. A subtle routine taking hold of her life here. Each day she woke up alone, waited for Will to come down from his room above them as she got dressed, then the two of them would walk to the market for breakfast and groceries. After returning home for a brief time, she would ride to the flower shop where she worked a part-time job. Then a few hours later, she would meet Will at his new part-time job working at a cafe, and grab a bite to eat, after which, she would ride to class - where slowly, she learned to speak Dutch. Then after class, riding home to meet Johanna to indulge in tea and cookies together, a tradition Johanna called, *gezelligheid.*

Aurelia would wait with Johanna for Will to come home, the lonely widow next door who simply enjoyed the attention. Then, the night still young, Aurelia and Will would explore the city a little more each day. Finding their favorite haunts, new and old, invisible and overlooked by most tourists. Each time they were out, learning more and more ways to be unnoticed by society. Turning away from tourists taking photos, keeping to themselves as much as possible, and hardly making friends.

There were three days of the week that deviated from their steady schedule; Saturday, when Will's cafe required him the full day, due to a local market set up in the street outside, consequently sending dozens of tourists inside their tiny restaurant for food.

Sunday, her favorite day of the week - when both Will and Aurelia had no set plans. Sometimes Will would drive them out to the countryside to see a new town; some filled with endless, floriferous tulip fields, or farms of sheep and cattle, others with castles and gorgeous architecture. Each place, somewhere new that Aurelia could try to sketch, with Will slowly teaching her his favorite hobby. Drawing had never come easily to her, but each new landscape improved her hand and hobby, each page realizing more and more life around her.

Then there was Tuesday - today. A dreaded day when instead of happily meeting Will for lunch, she instead said goodbye after breakfast, never knowing if it would be the last time she'd see him. She would go to class with an absent mind, then meet Johanna and count the minutes. It generally took him seven and a half hours to drive to Amsterdam's local airport, then fly into Manchester Airport, drive to The British Museum, go to the future to continually reassert himself in society there, then finally reverse the entire process and come home.

Glancing at her small golden wristwatch, Aurelia noted the time, 4:21. Will should be back by now. He was at least fifteen minutes late.

"*Hij staat waarschijnlijk vast in het verkeer, lieve,*" he was probably just stuck in traffic, Johanna noted in Dutch, her sweet voice cracking from smoking throughout the years. As far as she knew, every Tuesday Will drove out to see his parents in the country for the afternoon.

"*Ik ken.* Sorry," Aurelia responded she knew, in broken Dutch, each late afternoon *gezelligheid* with Johanna improving her conversation skills.

She didn't need to apologize, "*Je hoeft je niet te verontschuldigen* - you love him," Johanna smiled, switching to English so she would definitely understand her sentiment.

"*Love* him? I... no, I don't... I can't... he's just..." Aurelia sighed, searching for the right words. "I don't want to lose him."

"That's what most of us call love, Hannah," she smirked, "when you can't see yourself with anyone else. That's what I felt with my René. You know I moved to Valencia to be with him?"

"Spain?" Aurelia asked, Johanna nodding yes.

"He was an athlete on tour here who came into my parents' shop downtown. We met, and it was instant. I remember him courting me that whole week he was in town. Then he left, and I thought I'd never see him again. I was sure he had girls in every city he was visiting on that tour. Months pass and I get a call - he was home and couldn't stop thinking about me. He asked me to move there to be his wife that day. I knew I loved him right then, because I could've given up everything in my life just to be with him. So I did."

"Jo, that's so romantic!"

"So, would you?"

"Would I what?"

"Give up everything to be with him?" Johanna asked.

Aurelia had already given up everything the moment she walked up those library stairs. She had chosen to follow Will to the future, and then here to 1993. But that hadn't been out of love. That was survival. If she had known the consequences of that day - would she have still given up everything?

Aurelia's knee bounced as she sat in the living room alone, a coffee steaming in her hand. Will still hadn't returned. Looking at her delicate watch again, the time read 11:30 p.m. He had been gone for fourteen hours. Almost twice as long as it normally took him. Something had happened. She was sure of it.

She thought about what he had told her to do if he couldn't return - meet him where they had their first kiss. The only way she could find out where that was, is if she met him again after the party in the '70s. After she had trapped him in the portal. But she didn't want that version of Will. She wanted the one who already knew her quirks, who had the confidence in their relationship.

Sipping her coffee, then making frequent trips to the kitchen for more, Aurelia stayed up waiting.

Somehow, through the caffeine, she had still managed to dose off for an hour or so. Now, the summer birdsong and pedestrian bustling had begun outside, slowly waking her in the chair by the window. She got up, changing from the day before's outfit. Her long hair a curly tangled mess, she began brushing through it gently, her hands shaking.

She was alone. Will was gone.

She had no idea how to travel out of this time, with her Okliot still in the future. Barely able to continue, she glanced at herself in the mirror - her makeup smeared from the day before, her face puffy holding back tears. In that moment, she couldn't hold it together anymore. Holding her hand to her mouth, she silently sobbed in the mirror.

Was Will OK? What had happened that had caused him to not come back? What if he was... no. She couldn't even think it.

A knock on the front door startled her, and wiping her tears as she ran down the stairs she prayed it was Will. Who else would it be? He had come home.

Flinging the door open, her smile melted when she saw sweet Johanna standing with a basket of breads and tarts.

"You seemed so worried when you went inside last night, and then I didn't hear you and Lars talk at all," the walls between their homes paper thin, "so I figured I'd bring you breakfast and we could wait for him together," Johanna said, holding the basket out to Aurelia.

Her sobs returning, she embraced the kind woman with a deep hug, thanking her for her kindness, "*Dank je*, Jo."

Even with Johanna there to help pass the time, the breakfast table didn't seem the same without Will. Each morning usually playing a new CD, the two of them having just returned from the market, deep in conversation.

Now the silence surrounded them. The laughter nonexistent.

Johanna placed an apple tart on a plate and put it in front of Aurelia, who vacantly stared at the stairwell.

"Have you eaten?" Johanna asked the young girl.

Aurelia shook her head no, "I don't think I can."

Her stomach was twisting with unknowns.

"Well it sure would be a shame to tell the baker you didn't want it."

"Who's the baker?" Aurelia asked.

Johanna nodded her chin to show it was her. A small fleeting smile from Aurelia, and she took a bite of the pastry, the slightly salty, crisp outer layer flaking in her mouth, the warm gooey innards of cinnamon, sugar and apple exploding on her taste buds.

"*Heerlijk!*" Aurelia complemented, telling her it was delicious.

A small sound emerged from downstairs, the door handle jingling. Dropping the pastry, she ran down the steps, her breath quivering. Just as she reached the bottom, the door opened, and there stood Will.

"Will! Oh my God! What happened? Why didn't you come home last night?" she said, running into his arms.

"I'm so sorry Lia. I... they asked me to do something and I couldn't say no or it would've been too suspicious. I'm sorry," he said, stroking her head, his breath shaky.

"Who did? What did they need you to do?" she asked, pulling away enough to see his face.

"No. Nothing that matters," the lie burned his throat, "I'm still the son of the inventor, that's all."

Johanna walked downstairs, carrying the empty basket.

"Well I should be going," Johanna said, "Hannah, dear, see? I told you he'd be back," then, she turned to Will, "But Lars. Have some decency to call next time and tell your girlfriend you were safe. The poor girl thought you were dead." Scoffing with spunk, she passed the two and walked out the door.

"I'm sorry," Will muttered, turning to face Aurelia, his eyes welling up with tears.

"I don't know what I would've done if you never came back. You're my life now," Aurelia whispered, holding back from sobbing.

"And you're mine," he kissed her forehead, a tear rolling down his cheek.

"But, I don't want to live this way anymore. Never knowing if the man I love is going to just one day disappear into the future forever."

"The man you... love?" Will said, his voice crackling.

It had slipped out subconsciously. But, her heart had ached for him. She couldn't fathom living without him. If this wasn't love, she didn't know what was. "Yeah. I do. Love you," Aurelia said, tears now streaming down her face.

Will's forehead crinkling as his emotions took hold, he kissed her fervently. He had waited far too long to hear those words again.

Pausing to look at her, he whispered, "I love you Aurelia. I love you so much. Always."

He began to kiss her again, but she placed a finger in between his insistent lips. Aurelia silent as a dove, walked to the stairwell leaving him standing breathless near the door. Halfway up, she turned to look at him, his hand scooping his layered hair back from his forehead as he panted. Motioning for him to follow with a tilt of her head and a smile, he rushed after her. He would always follow her.

Only at the kitchen, he passionately grabbed her hand from behind, not able to wait another second to continue their kiss. But instead, Aurelia yet again pulled away from his begging lips, and slowly continued up the stairs, this time holding his hand to make sure he was right there behind her. Reaching the top, now in Aurelia's room, Will scooped her up into his arms. Her arms dangling over his shoulders, their kiss impatient and longing. Gently setting her head on the pillows, her body on the tan bedspread, their lips inseparable.

Aurelia tugged at his linen jacket, pulling it from his shoulders as he aided her in getting it off. His T-shirt now the only thing between her hand and his chest, she could feel his heart racing as her palm moved over his muscles. Their kiss still thrilling, his brown hair just barely long enough, falling to tickle the sides of her face. Her hands that held space between them, growing curious. She twisted the fabric of his shirt in her hands, the soft, light blue cotton bunching between her fingers. The sensation of his skin tingling her hands as she moved them cautiously.

Sitting up, Aurelia's breath tremulous, she guided his hands to her mauve button-down shirt that was tucked neatly into a grey pencil skirt. His fingers found their way to each button of her shirt, the warm air between them brushing her skin. His fingers gently wrapped around the sides of her stomach, creeping to her back. Each touch electric and noticed. His lips wandered from her face, gently moving down her neck, then collarbone, then shoulder, Aurelia gasping at the affectionate touch. With his shirt draped over her hands, she pulled it over his head passionately, seeing his bare skin for the first time. His muscles retracting with each breath, his warm, smooth olive skin, flawless and soft. Her hands running from his chest, to his stomach, then hitting the top of the fabric of his tan pants. She wanted him. All of him. After all, for him, they were already married. She began to unbutton his linen pants, and his kiss pulled back from her shoulder.

"Are you sure?" he panted breathlessly, a flame of mischief in his eyes.

Aurelia nodded slowly. She was sure.

CHAPTER 14

RED RAIN

It had been over seven months since Aurelia and Will had first arrived in Amsterdam. Now, the chilly November air mixed with a frequent rain here, the sound of water landing on the canals, a favorite of Will's. The smell of rain hung in the air even when the streets were dry. A few months before, they had found out that the roof leaked, dripping into the upstairs bedroom in multiple places. Luckily, the pots and buckets contained the water, and it wasn't like anyone was sleeping up there anymore.

Christmastime was already upon them here, the festivities of Sinterklaas starting in mid-November. Each year, Sinterklaas would make his appearances in the capital. Then secretly, The Good Holy Man, or *De Goedheiligman*, as he was known in Dutch, would deliver presents to the deserving children of the nation. On December 5th, children around the Netherlands would place their shoes by the fire in hopes that in the morning they would be filled with presents - a tradition that the children longed for each year.

The streets were quaintly decorated with twinkling lights, and a few large trees placed around town brought feelings of Christmas spirit. Although it most likely wouldn't snow, or if it did, it would melt almost instantly upon hitting the ground, the feelings of a cozy winter were already upon Will and Aurelia.

Will was out and about in town on this particular Saturday, since he had time off from the cafe, so he went out searching for a Christmas gift to give Aurelia next week. Aurelia had been working on his for weeks; a charcoal sketch of the two of them in the middle of a bridge, overlooking the canal they viewed from their window. Summer foliage and tulips overflowing in bike baskets, the atmosphere had been easy to capture. Drawing the lines of two dynamic people, however, seemingly impossible. Each attempted sketch having limbs that warped and bent like tree branches, the side profiles of their faces seeming emotionless. So each day, another try. She had one that she had just started yesterday that sparked her imagination. Somehow filled with life and color even with the monochromatic charcoal. She took her time with this particular one, and today hoped to finish it.

First, she was meeting Johanna around the corner to help her with her grocery shopping. The old woman quickly declining in loneliness, despite Aurelia's efforts. She spoke often of her four children, three boys and one girl, who were scattered across Europe, preoccupied with their own new families. One of her boys had come to visit for a few days in the summer, bringing his wife and two daughters. She had stories for weeks from that visit. But now, the short winter nights turning dark and sallow, each day seemed a struggle. So Aurelia helped as much as she could, filling her time by practically being a second daughter to the kind woman.

The rain began to fall on her cheeks like teardrops, but she didn't bother to pull up her puffy coat to cover her, as she was already less than a block away from the market. Briskly making her way inside, she instantly spotted Johanna - smiling and greeting her with three kisses on the cheeks. They did their shopping, Aurelia helping to bend and reach the things that the old woman needed, and soon they were at the register. Aurelia couldn't help but notice how unusually crowded the quaint store became as they shopped, with almost ten unfamiliar faces in a time of year when tourists rarely visited. Casting the thought aside, Aurelia didn't mention a thing to Jo.

Their canvas bags now full of food, Aurelia draped most of them on her shoulder, with Jo insisting to at least carry one. Stepping outside, Johanna's umbrella covering them both, she realized the unfamiliar faces left the store just behind them, not buying anything. They walked in the rain, the heavy sound of water hitting the pavement muting the sounds of footsteps behind them.

"Aurelia Quinn," a man's deep booming voice said from behind them.

They had found her. She didn't know how, but they were here for her.

"Jo. I need you to keep walking, go home and lock your door. Do you understand?" Aurelia whispered to the woman.

"What? Why, Hannah?" she said, startled.

"Can you do that for me?" Aurelia asked again, as they began to turn the corner onto the canal they lived on. They were just two blocks from home. The woman nodded worriedly. "Don't look back. Just keep walking like you don't know me."

Aurelia stopped, Johanna continuing home, the safety of the umbrella gone with her. Slowly turning around, she could now see the sheer number of people following them. At least three dozen people, all stopped about a block away, with a man, obviously in charge, in the middle. His face was familiar, and she briefly remembered him as one of the men in the '50s - then wearing an ominous trench coat and glasses. Now he wore all black with a leather jacket wicking away the rain.

"Hello again, Miss Quinn," he said in English, the owner of the low voice.

"What do you want with me?" she said coldly.

"We need you to come with us."

"Why?" Aurelia shouted over the rain.

The man blinked in annoyance. Then without saying a word, he raised his hand as if to say, 'she's all yours' to the others. Having nowhere else to run but towards home, she took off, dropping her bags of groceries where she had stood. Her feet slick on the worn stones, she ran as fast as she could, quickly coming up to where Johanna walked, now only a few yards from her home.

"Jo, run!" Aurelia shouted as she approached the old woman.

Johanna quickly turned around to see Aurelia being chased, and she gasped in horror at the sight, stopping in her tracks.

Aurelia skid past her, realizing she meant to try and stop the onslaught of people.

"What are you doing?" Aurelia shouted, stepping back for the woman and grabbing her arm to keep her moving - but Johanna had planted herself there stubbornly.

"*Ik sta niet toe dat je haar aanraken!*" she wouldn't let them touch her, Johanna shouted in Dutch.

The man in the middle swiftly reached in his jacket and pulled out a hand gun. Aurelia could hardly comprehend what had happened, it happened so fast. The sound of the bullet still ringing in her ears, she looked at her friend, the kind Johanna, who slowly collapsed to the ground, her chest bleeding. Aurelia reached for her as she fell, blood soaking her arms as she held her.

"NOOO!" Aurelia screamed, the reality not even setting in, incomprehensible. "WHY? SHE WAS MY FRIEND! SHE HAD A FAMILY!" Aurelia sobbed, collapsing on her knees, holding the old woman, already gone.

The others in the group stopped in shock, staring at the woman laying lifeless, her blood diluted with the rain, staining the cobblestones red.

"And that's what I'll do to every friend of yours, or acquaintance, or lover," the man said without remorse.

Aurelia thought of home, her grandmother. This was what would've happened to her if she had gone back. Then her mind shifting to Will, her lover, her soulmate. Luckily, he wasn't home this afternoon, otherwise he'd be in imminent danger too. What if this had been him? But it was horrible regardless. Her closest friend, a trusted soul in a scary new world, now gone in an instant.

Johanna was gone.

"I warned you before Aurelia. This is what would happen if you ran."

"NO! You didn't. I've never even met you!" Aurelia cried on the ground, her tears mixing with the rain.

The man, still holding the gun, tilted it to the others as if to say, 'What are you waiting for?'

The people around him hesitantly started towards Aurelia, who quickly got up, shaking from shock. She turned and ran as fast as she could. Johanna's unlocked house was only a few steps away. Flinging the door open, and quickly slamming it shut - locking it, she looked around for a weapon. There was nothing. A similar floor plan to her house next door, the kitchen was one flight up. She could grab a knife there. A bang erupted at the door, the lock blown off by a bullet. She darted for the stairwell, her heart racing, her wet feet slipping.

She had never felt such fear before in her life.

The man shot at her multiple times as she ran up the stairs, a bullet hitting her arm. She screeched in pain, still running up the stairs. The people behind her raced up, shouting at her to stop. Another round of bullets erupted, this time hitting her thigh, the pain searing through the adrenaline.

Suddenly, the staircase began to change. The carpeted stairs quickly turning to metal, then concrete, then brick. She wasn't sure how, but once again she was traveling in time. The dozens of voices fading like a dream.

She couldn't believe Jo was gone. She kept running, as the brick below her feet turned to stone, before her vision darkened at the edges, and she passed out.

Will had found something perfect to give Aurelia. A sewing machine. He knew she would love to get back to her passion in this strange new world, devoid of her hopes and dreams. Lugging the huge package across town in a taxi, he arrived home in the rain, thanking the man and carrying the heavy box to the doorstep. His heart dropped when he saw his neighbor's door wide open. Johanna would never do that. Quickly opening their house to put the sewing machine inside, he stepped back into the rain to check on Jo.

Johanna was on the ground. Her body had been dragged inside, soaked with rain. He rushed to her side, hoping to wake her, but within seconds he realized the blood. She was shot. He looked around at the hall. Bullet holes lined the walls of the stairs, a trail of blood going up.

Aurelia.

Panic rushed through his mind as he screamed Aurelia's name in bloody murder. Running back to their house, he called for her, receiving no answer. His body in shock, his hands shaking.

Open in her chair was Aurelia's sketchbook they had been enjoying together as he taught her how to sketch, and his eyes fell onto the unfinished charcoal drawing of the two of them that she was going to surprise him with, his eyes filling with tears.

She was gone. They had her. And he knew he would never see Aurelia again.

PART
TWO

CHAPTER 15

THE AZTEC PEOPLE

Aurelia woke up abruptly. Her left arm writhing in pain, her right thigh throbbing. She was in a small, torch lit, stone room, laid upon a short, woven, reed mat. Moving her arm to look at her wound, she could tell her injury was still wet and open. Looking on the ground next to her, she saw two flattened, metal bullets soaked in blood. Apparently someone had removed them. Thankful, she sat up to look around the room more, dizzy from the small motion.

Coming from behind a corner, a petite Aztec woman began scolding her in a language unknown to Aurelia, Classical Nahuatl. Aurelia shook her head no, she didn't understand, but she had to leave.

"Where did you find me?" Aurelia asked the woman slowly, hoping she spoke English. The woman continued in her mother tongue. "The stairs?" Aurelia mimed with her hands.

She had to get back to the portal. It was a fluke that she had been able to travel again, she figured. Probably from being so close to dozens of people with Okliots, that the energy in the air allowed her to go through a portal. It had to be something like that. But if that was indeed the case, she was certain the portal wouldn't last long.

She stood up from the ground, a wash of wooziness overcoming her as she stumbled to the exit, the woman obviously telling her she shouldn't be up, as she was badly injured.

"Please. Help me. I need the stairs?" Aurelia begged, the woman still speaking in a language she didn't know. "I don't understand. I'm sorry," Aurelia said, shaking her head at the woman, who wore a long handmade tan dress, with loose pants.

Aurelia looked at her own clothing - black leather boots, a fashionable blue cashmere sweater with jeans - once underneath a long puffy coat that now sat beside her - all of which was now stained with her blood. She definitely looked out of place here, compared to the woman.

Where was she? When was she?

Looking to her wrist to check the time, a flash of sadness swept through her body, realizing she no longer had the only memento from her home in 2019 - she had left it on her bedside table that morning in Amsterdam.

Amsterdam. Aurelia's thoughts flashed to 1993. Will. Johanna. She was gone. Jo was gone.

Clutching her mouth to hold back from sobbing, Aurelia collapsed back down on the reed mat. The woman attended to her arm wound quickly, still babbling on, trying to speak to Aurelia, who couldn't understand a word. She looked around the room - everything seemed smaller here, but perhaps that was just because she was tall for a girl. She wondered who this woman was, and why she had helped her.

Coming in from a short doorway, two stocky young men entered the room, their faces full of curiosity. The men were dressed in loose fitting loin cloths that covered their bodies, tied at the sides, with small threaded embroidery at the edges. Speaking to the woman, who now stood, they couldn't help but glance at Aurelia. Who was she, they wondered? Her blonde hair, blue eyes, and tall, lean figure, a complete anomaly to the women they were used to. They had watched her seemingly appear out of thin air - racing up the stairs of a local temple they had been praying at, when she collapsed onto the steps. Rushing to the girl, they realized she was severely injured, with two metal pieces lodged in her arm and leg. Completely unsure of where this large mystery girl had come from, they carried her home in the hopes that they could help heal her wounds. Perhaps the Gods had sent her, they thought.

Aurelia sobbed gently, exploring the severity of her situation in her mind. It seemed obvious that she was back in time, although unclear when exactly. Where? It seemed somewhere in Mexico, if she had to guess. But the people around her didn't speak any Spanish she had heard before. She thought of her Spanish classes in high school, and the difference was undeniable, this language unrecognizable, so she wouldn't be able to communicate with them. She was seriously injured, and doubted that the medicine here would be of much use to her.

She couldn't blend in if she was truly back in time in the ancient world - cultures didn't take strongly to foreigners back then. She doubted that they had ever seen someone that looked as she did. She had absolutely no clue where the portal was that had allowed her to enter this new time, or even, how she was able to travel without an Okliot. She was stuck here.

How would she get back to Will? She thought of him coming home to their *rijtjeshuis* in 1993, realizing Aurelia was gone, yet never knowing what had happened. He would try to meet her where they had their first kiss. But that still hadn't happened for her. There was no way to get back. How would she ever see Will again? It seemed impossible.

The two men stepped over to her and silently inspected her arm with a strong grip, then tried to look at her leg's injury, Aurelia untrustingly thrusting it away from their quick hands. They extended their palms as if attempting to pet an injured dog, and one of the men looked her in the eye as if to calm her. They had just brought her to their home about thirty minutes before, and yet the strange girl's wounds had already begun congealing.

All three of the strangers left the room, frantically and without explanation, leaving Aurelia wondering what to do. Should she stay here for a few days to let herself heal? Or should she leave now, taking her chances to hopefully find the portal somewhere outside?

Grabbing her coat in her hands and standing up once again, Aurelia marched out of the stone house. The people that were in the house a few minutes before were now nowhere to be found. It was nighttime, and the sounds of bugs swarming let her ears know that she wasn't alone. The darkness was overwhelming, only eased by the immense starlight above, every single speckled star in the night sky acting as a guide that brilliantly lit the night. She was in a sort of village or town it seemed. The small homes, some made of packed mud, others of stone, stood just barely taller than her head, and most doorways were even shorter at only four feet tall. Tropical plants interspersed the homes, growing wild with red flowers and untamed greenery. She waded through the humid air, her breath filled with moisture. Aurelia quickly navigated through the homes, without a clue what it was she was looking for. Perhaps just a stairwell amongst the houses? It seemed stupid. But then she saw it.

A pyramid, just beyond all of the single story homes, in an open, empty square. The tallest thing for miles, perhaps she could orient herself more effectively by climbing to the top - or, she hoped, that it was the portal. She raced to it, the pain almost debilitating in her leg as she moved. But she had to get back. She made it to the bottom of the pyramid, its square top and unique stairs built into the side with amazingly, similarly shaped stones all the way up. She began to step up, slowly, the discomfort in her leg keeping her from running. Behind her, someone shouted. She turned to see the same two men calling for her to stop, now with even more men around them, near the houses that she had just come from. She couldn't. She had to keep going. She had to get home. The fear of the moment rushing through her, shooting pains making her nauseous, she continued to step up. Dizzying, she realized the sky above her moved quickly as she walked - the stars shifting their positions in the night sky. Was she traveling in time?

Exhausted from only a few steps, she stopped and looked behind her. Where the few men had stood, now it seemed dozens of villagers gathered under the moonlight. Now, some of them held pine torches, while others were simply seated in prayer. She had definitely traveled in time - only slightly, she realized. One of the villagers looked up at the temple and spied her - the mystery God on their sacred temple. Shouting with a mania Aurelia thought was only reserved for the Beatles, the villagers all rushed to the bottom of the stairs to get a closer look. Aurelia turned and continued running up the stairs. This must have been the portal where the villagers had found her, and the portal was still open, she thought. She could get back.

The sky above her shifted into day as she stepped through time, and she breathed heavily as she noticed her head spinning. She couldn't continue. She had barely traveled through a day - how would she make it through centuries? Collapsing on the steps, breathless, she looked behind her yet again. Now in the midday sun, the plaza was filled with people. People of all classes it seemed; from slaves, to villagers, to merchants, warriors, priests, and even royalty, seated on raised pedestals at the end of the square.

Upon the sight of the *Teotl*, or God, returning, the people of the city erupted in celebration. The royalty standing with widened eyes, to see the blond girl appear out of nothing. People rushed to the temple's steps with flowers, food, jewels and other household items to give to their new God. Aurelia watched in awe as the people below her practically worshipped her.

'This is very bad,' Aurelia thought to herself, as she stood on the temple steps. 'So much for remaining hidden.'

Calmly, she walked down the temple's steps - surprisingly not traveling in time now. Had the portal closed, Aurelia wondered? Perhaps that was why it was so difficult to travel no more than a day. The adoring Aztec people all bowed their heads at Aurelia as she walked towards them. Now on the dirt of the plaza, the people nervously held their offerings at her, wanting her to accept them. Reaching up to the tall girl, the villagers touched her back and shoulders as she walked through, hoping to feel divinity for themselves. One of them touched her bullet wound, and she gasped in pain, grabbing her arm - the villager collapsing to the ground in apology, muttering in her language.

"It's OK," Aurelia said to the shaking woman, whose life was surely over for hurting a *Teotl.*

She continued walking, unsure as to where she was going, but soon coming to the end of the square, where the high priests and royalty stood in wait. Aurelia looked at them all, adorned in handwoven, embroidered clothes and capes. Headpieces stretching up with feathers and gems. Some warriors stood at the steps of them with spears and other weapons, tattooed to look like jaguars, and wearing minimal cloths, just to cover their hips. As she stared, they all began to bow to Aurelia.

They thought she was a deity, she realized. Royalty and priests certainly wouldn't be bowing otherwise. In their own language, they asked her who she was and why she had come to bless them with her presence. Aurelia of course, didn't understand a word they had said and simply looked at them with doe eyes. She motioned to her arm, where her blood had now soaked through the blue fabric significantly. Their leader, as she assumed the man in the middle was, barked at his noblemen to call for a healer.

All around her, the people showered her with gifts where she stood. They hoped to lead her back to the top of the pyramid, where a small room that served as a temple could be put to use, but the blonde God didn't want to move elsewhere. So, the villagers quickly constructed a palm leaf, woven shade above her, and placed reed mats at her feet for her to stand on. Bringing her a wooden stool for her to rest, and gently placing offerings around her.

She had waved them away as they tried to fan her, and so far had only accepted one bowl of maize and beans from a small boy. The healers tended to her wounds, carefully opening the cashmere fabric of her sweater, and the denim of her jeans, to reveal more of the injured skin. Somehow, the blood on her skin had already dried around the wound, healing extremely fast. Aurelia thought back to her time in the future - the nanobots. No wonder she hadn't experienced so much as a cold since their travels - she remembered Will telling her they had given her permanent bots. They must be able to heal injuries, as well as protect her from known microscopic pathogens.

But to the Aztec healers, the wet, bloodstained fabric didn't match up to the already dried wounds. It proved to them that she was not human.

Carrying a large cage, eight men placed a gigantic animal at her feet, bowing to Aurelia. It was a Jaguar. It's teeth bared, it paced back and forth in the few feet it had to move in. Stunning and majestic, it seemed a travesty to contain its greatness. Its spotted fur shiny and unique, its lips pulsing with warning. Holding up a spear, one of the warriors stabbed the beast in sacrifice, hoping to please Aurelia with this abundant offering. Aurelia screamed, standing up to stop him, the injured Jaguar's stomach now bleeding as he screeched in agony. She couldn't bare the sight. The cat swatted at the people around him, hissing with his ears pinned to his head.

The warriors looked at Aurelia, confused at why she was so upset - this was meant to be a gift for her.

She stepped towards the cage, the beast panting and collapsing onto its side. Why had they done that, she wondered? Tears streamed down her face as she watched the once marvelous animal sink from life. She sat holding the bars of the cage, the gorgeous jaguar's breath already gone.

Sitting back down in defeat, Aurelia wiped the tears from her face as they carried the animal away.

Only a few hours had gone by, and Aurelia's wounds were almost completely healed. The priests marveled at the sight - the impenetrable God healing magically.

The villagers and slaves had lined up to sacrifice themselves to this magnificent God, a tradition they felt necessary if she was to bless their families with good fortune, fertility, food or good weather. Unsure what this new God would bring them - as each deity they worshipped was responsible for some part of their lives.

Aurelia, skeptical as to what was happening, watched silently as the first man, adorned in paints and costume, stood near the stone altar at the top of the temple above her. Swatting away the mosquitoes in the air around her, she watched on. The villagers around the plaza began playing percussive music, and some of them pierced their skin with blades as they watched the man atop the temple, Aurelia gasping at the horror of them cutting themselves. What happened next made Aurelia's stomach drop.

The man at the top of the temple laid down on the stone slab, adorned priests surrounding him. Raising a sacrificial knife above the man, Aurelia realized what was about to happen. She screamed for them to stop, but the knife had already pierced the willing man - and they proceeded to carve it through his chest. Aurelia, her limbs shaking and jaw dropped, watched as the priest took out the man's heart and placed it in a gold dish. It was too much for her. She passed out in shock from the barbarity of the ritual.

Her eyes fluttering open to see the dozens of people surrounding her, Aurelia sat up quickly. She had to get out of there. Swatting the palm leaves out of her face that they fanned her with, she stood up, her breath frantic and overwhelmed. Her leg hardly hurting at the movement, she glanced at it to see that only redness remained, the wound all but healed.

'Thank God for technology,' she thought to herself.

She grabbed her puffy jacket once again, this time putting it on. The villagers all tried to speak to her, still throwing themselves at her with gifts, but she was done with it all. The priests and healers chased after her through the crowd, but she moved quickly, and the villagers moved with her, surrounding her while unintentionally blocking anyone from stopping her. Coming to the steps of the pyramid, she raced up them, praying the portal would work again.

Much faster than before, the sky turned around her. She was traveling in time again. The days flashed by in milliseconds, a strobing day and night surrounding her. She must have traveled years in just a few steps. Stopping for a brief moment - she realized the top of the temple now held a slightly abstract stone picture of a woman. It was her. Two painted indents where her bullet holes had been depicted injury, and her long hair and tall figure stood feet above the bowed villagers in the painted carving. This was bad. She had influenced history. She continued walking up the steps, time not moving quite as fast now, but still moving, and she reached the top of the temple shortly - the carving now finished further forward in time.

She knew what she had to do, although it seemed sad. She had to destroy it.

A family on the steps of the temple in the morning sun slumped to their knees to worship the God that had finally appeared again. She had returned to see the city's art that they had created for her, depicting the first time she had shown herself to the mortals. But instead of seeming happy, the tall God found a loose stone, and flung it at the large stone carving of herself, scratching her image. Other villagers began to gather at the bottom of the pyramid, staring in wonder at what the God did. Perhaps she hated the way they had depicted her. Perhaps she didn't want to be depicted.

Aurelia destroyed as much of herself as possible on the carving, hoping it would be a hint to them not to carve her again. Turning around, she realized she had an audience, and slowly walked down the stairs, hoping not to move backwards in time. Somehow, she didn't. Then, about halfway down the temple stairs, she raced back up them, once again moving in time.

How did this portal work, she wondered? It seemed different than all of the others. It seemed unstable, like it would stop working any second. She felt exhausted from traveling, the sickness building up in her stomach as she ran up. Her legs aching from the countless steps, she remembered her nana had always told her to keep in shape, although she never listened. Suddenly, the surroundings of Mexico shifted around her, the temple dissolving from view. What was happening? Where or when was she going?

CHAPTER 16

Grand Duchess Natalia

Appearing out of the changing surroundings as she walked up the stairs through time, a young girl, perhaps six or seven years old, rammed into Aurelia, sending them both tumbling down the staircase - the stairwell morphing into a new place.

The two of them quickly reorienting themselves, they were both in a new location, and new time. The young girl screamed in Russian at Aurelia, asking her what had just happened and where she was. Aurelia, not understanding a word, looked around at where they had ended up. The staircase they had fallen down seemed to be a small wooden bridge, with only a few steps up for pedestrians to walk. Their surroundings were filled with fields of flowers, a sunny, summer day upon them.

The young girl looked down at her gorgeous embroidered, purple gown with remorse, noticing the large tear in its fabric from the fall. The gown had long, adorned fabric, frilly at the sleeves, with delicate shoes that held her small feet. Dainty jewelry adorned her neck and wrist. A glint of sun next to her caught Aurelia's eye, and she realized a tiara in the dirt. Who was this tiny girl, Aurelia wondered, and why was she out in a field? Only, she wasn't out in a field before she had run into Aurelia traveling through time. She was at her family's new Catherine Palace, just south of St. Petersburg, during a ball they had held to entertain visiting royalty.

"Are you OK?" Aurelia asked the girl in English, sure she wouldn't understand.

The girl looked at her with a scowl, then switched to English with a strong Russian accent to match her, "No. My dress," the young girl said, looking away from her with her arms crossed in disdain.

"I'm sorry. I didn't see you walking here," Aurelia said, pacifying the spoiled child.

"*Here?* Why would *I* walk *here*?" she whined, impetuous with disgust. "I was in my palace."

"OK. Where's your family's palace? Nearby?" Aurelia asked, confused as to how the girl had ended up here with her.

The girl looked around, almost just now realizing the change in weather, and the endless rolling fields filled with wildflowers. She had never seen such beauty - but where was she?

"Who are you?" Aurelia asked the girl, picking up the tiara in the dirt.

The young girl snatched it from her hands with a scoff, and dusted it off with her hands before placing it atop her dark hair.

"Grand Duchess Natalia Petrovna of the House Romanov," expecting a response worthy of her title, she looked at the peasant, Aurelia, "who are *you*?"

"I am... Princess Isabelle... of England." Was there a Princess Isabelle of England? Aurelia had no idea, but it seemed fun.

Eliciting a hmph from the young girl, Natalia eyed Aurelia up and down, looking at her ridiculous outfit, a puffy coat with jeans and a blue sweater peeking through. She had never in her life seen an outfit like that. She was certainly no princess, Natalia thought. The young duchess stood up and began walking over the bridge, towards a farm home nearby.

"No, wait!" Aurelia said, chasing after the girl. If she was indeed a duchess who was just in her palace, Aurelia must have brought her here through the portal, somehow. "I have to bring you home."

The young girl swung around to face Aurelia, curious as to how she would accomplish that.

"I know it sounds crazy, but can you trust me?" Aurelia asked her.

"No," the young girl replied, turning back towards the house.

"Listen. What city are you from, Natalia?" Aurelia asked, the girl stopping yet again.

"It's 'Your Grace'," Natalia corrected.

Gritting her teeth with annoyance of this entitled child, "Sorry. What city are you from, *Your Grace*?"

"*Sankt-Peterburg*," she replied, with a look of obviousness.

"Russia?" Aurelia assumed. The girl looked at her waiting for Aurelia to get to the point. "Does this look like Russia, Nat- Your Grace?" she said, motioning to their surroundings. Natalia shook her head hesitantly, no. "Then, if you ever want to get back to your palace, you're going to have to listen to me."

Aurelia had held the girl's hand and attempted to walk up the stairs of the bridge - but absolutely nothing happened. It was just a normal bridge built over a trickling stream. But they had obviously traveled through a portal to get here. Why did it not work now? Aurelia tried it multiple times at different speeds, hoping that something might trigger it, but it was of no use. The portal must have closed.

They were stuck in time.

Defeated, the sun on the horizon about to disappear for the night, the two girls walked to the farmhouse in the distance, the duchess thinking this "Princess Isabelle" was so very strange. They knocked on the door of the quaint home covered in ivy, which was promptly opened by a woman in her mid-thirties, her face already worn and weathered from work, yet gently smiling nonetheless.

"Hello. We're just passing through and we wondered if you might be able to give us shelter for the night?" Aurelia said, doing her best to ask formally.

"*Désolé - Je ne vous comprends pas*," said the woman in French, not her commonly used dialect of Occitan, telling them that she didn't understand.

Speaking in French, the tiny duchess translated what Aurelia had tried to say, "*Pouvez-vous donner à mon ami et moi refuge pour la nuit ?*"

The woman looked at the young girl who seemed to be royalty, judging by her clothes and crown, and the young woman with her, wearing the most ludicrous clothes she had ever seen.

The sun already down, and the only house for kilometers, the woman responded, "*Bien-sûr*" to the young ladies, opening her door wider and allowing them inside.

"How do you speak French?" Aurelia whispered to the young girl.

"I am a duchess. Why do you not, *Princess*?" she said with a judgmental Russian accent.

'She really is a pill,' Aurelia thought to herself.

Aurelia took her coat off, revealing her tattered clothes underneath. The woman of the house rushed to see what was wrong, the large blood stains and torn clothes seeming like she was severely injured, although her skin was already healed from the nanobots.

"*Qu'est-ce qui est arrivé ?*" the woman asked Aurelia. "*Vous êtes blessée ?*"

The duchess translated, "She wants to know what happened. Are you hurt?"

"Oh. Um - non," Aurelia said, a single word of French popping into her mind, "but, could you ask her if she might have a change of clothes I could use?"

The duchess asked, and the woman nodded with a warm kindness towards the strangers, going into the other room to find some. They looked around at the modest home; a cauldron of leek pottage roasted over the roaring fireplace, filling the room with a unique smell, their eyes burning from the smoke that didn't vent out of a chimney, but rather concentrated itself in the room. A small wooden table and two stools occupied most of the room, and two wooden bowls sat at the ready for the woman and someone else to eat. Baskets of food and other items lined the floor, and a stack of firewood lay crumbling next to the hearth. This was a unique place for both Aurelia and Duchess Natalia. The duchess had never set foot in a peasant's house who wasn't even of the bourgeois class - she was always shielded from the commoners in gold adorned rooms filled with elaborate furniture and art. Her belly always full, her mind always occupied.

The woman returned with a dress for Aurelia, probably the only other one she had.

Aurelia thanked her profusely, remembering, "*Merci beaucoup !*"

She quickly changed in the woman's bedroom, which only held a straw bed on the floor, and a small trunk with the woman's things. The homemade, tan, wool dress she had given Aurelia, with a tie just above her waist, was crafted beautifully and carefully, she could tell. Aurelia walked back into the main room, where the duchess and the woman were already deep in conversation. Natalia laughed like she had just been told the most hysterical thing in the world.

"What is it?" Aurelia asked, sitting at the unoccupied seat at the table to join the duchess.

"She says we're in the Kingdom of France!" she laughed, knowing it was impossible to have ended up so far from home.

Aurelia, on the other hand, knew just how possible it was.

"Ask her what year it is."

The duchess chuckled, "Why? It's 1725."

Aurelia pursed her lips and waited for Natalia to ask the woman. She did, almost as a joke, and her face quickly fell at the answer.

"She says it's 1443."

The almost 7-year-old grand duchess wanted to believe Aurelia. She did love to be told a good *сказка*, or fairytale. But, surely this was a ruse? How could they have traveled in time to mid 15th century France? It wasn't possible, was it?

The kind French woman, as they came to find out, was named Amée. She lived a few days ride from the city of Toulouse, with her husband Piers, who shortly returned for dinner. He was a baker in the small village nearby, and every day rode one of their two horses to and from, bringing a loaf of bread back each night for them to enjoy. It was a quiet life in the country, their lives only as large as they could build themselves - from the home they lived in, the few farm animals they raised, and the garden out back for food. They had seven children, only one of which had survived into adulthood and was recently married to a local girl, with a child of their own on the way. All of the duties of the farmhouse now fell on Amée. Each morning awoken by birdsong and a calming draft in their bedroom, each night spent with laughter and stories. And now, they served royalty in their home.

Amée carefully scooped the hot pottage into the bowls for the two visitors, leaving only a few spoonfuls for herself and her husband. The Grand Duchess Natalia had never in her life tasted something so disgusting, and promptly spit it out, leaving Amée and Piers mortified at her behavior. Aurelia couldn't believe how this young girl acted - it made her never want to have children of her own - but then again, she thought, she wouldn't have raised them in such a spoiled, entitled manner. Aurelia finished her bowl gratefully, although the bland taste wasn't very appetizing, she knew she had to eat.

Soon, the plan was made that in the morning Piers would begin the journey with them into Toulouse, hopefully receiving an audience with the local aristocracy. After all - Aurelia had absolutely no idea how to get out of the 1400s, let alone get the grand duchess home to her time. And after what had happened to Johanna in Amsterdam - how could she get close to anyone again? No one would be safe around her. So, she figured, her best bet was to get her to the safety of another castle, where she could at least let Natalia continue her education and nobility.

Aurelia laid down on the dirt floor near the dying fire with a full belly.

"*Où est mon lit ?*" where was her bed, Natalia asked Amée in French. Motioning to the floor next to Aurelia, Natalia nearly fainted from the thought of dirtying her dress. "I can't sleep *there*!" she said to Aurelia in English.

"You can, and you will, *Your Highness*. We're lucky we're not sleeping outside tonight," Aurelia said condescendingly, shutting the duchess up promptly.

Her thoughts racing in the silence - Aurelia couldn't help but think about her life in Amsterdam with Will. His warm arms would be holding her now as she fell asleep, his breath on her neck. But he wasn't here. And perhaps it was a good thing - because she couldn't fathom the thought of losing him permanently. Being together meant risking his life everyday, in fear that whatever or whomever was haunting her from the future would destroy her present. At least apart, she knew he would be safe.

Soon, the two of them fell asleep to the sound of crackling embers.

Being shaken awake by the duchess, Aurelia jumped up to see what was wrong. The small girl sat back onto her heels and looked at Aurelia pitifully. It was barely dusk, the sunlight beginning to rise over the horizon and streaming through the holes in the house.

"I'm hungry..." Natalia groaned. She hadn't eaten the day before, as she had rudely declined the leek pottage.

Rolling her eyes and laying back down, Aurelia chuckled.

'Good,' she thought, 'maybe she'll learn not to be so picky next time.'

"Isabelle, please?"

'Who was Isabelle?' Aurelia thought, before remembering the lie of her fake identity she had concocted the day before.

Looking at the young girl, she could see a patch of innocence and light shining through from her soul - her kind eyes hidden beneath her entitled demeanor. Sighing, Aurelia got up.

"Come on," Aurelia said, walking outside of the farmhouse to see what they could forage in the garden.

Natalia ran after Aurelia, as she looked through the fresh

vegetables in the process of percolating to ripeness. She really didn't know a thing about gardening, and as her fingers brushed the green stalks, she thought about what life must be like here for a woman like Amée. A simple, hardworking existence, filled with sunlight and sweat, lacking the modern day comforts that a woman in the 21st century would have. Movement caught her eye and Aurelia saw a chicken fall from the garden fence. Gently reaching for the duchess's hand, a prospect the young girl wasn't used to but nervously accepted, they walked out of the garden to the side of the house. Just here, a few farm animals were fenced in. A small hutch was built for some chickens to lay eggs, four dirty, skinny pigs waited for their breakfast, and three goats attempted to climb out of their pen towards them. The duchess marveled at the animals, herself only ever seeing horses and dogs in person before, besides the wild animals they encountered during their hunting parties.

They wandered to the chicken hutch, where a loose fitting top allowed them to look inside, revealing dried grasses, and placed gently on top, three eggs. Aurelia carefully picked them up and handed one to Natalia, who squealed to dirty her hands.

"We're gonna take these inside for Amée and Piers, and then you can help me see if any of these goats are female," Aurelia said, walking back towards the house.

"Why does that matter?" Natalia asked with her harsh Russian accent.

"Because female goats make milk."

The duchess cringed at this statement - she was royalty - not someone who would *ever* touch a goat's udder.

Aurelia scrambled the fresh eggs in a cast iron pan above the fire, and managed to milk two of the three skinny goats - barely getting a quarter of a bucket full between the two. Piers was the first one up, and happily enjoyed this traveler's breakfast that Aurelia had made for them. Typically, they didn't afford the luxury of breakfast, and would only have a small midday snack, followed by dinner just after sundown, so this was a welcome surprise. Amée awoke shortly after, and began making the preparations for the three of them to journey to Toulouse. They had agreed to help get the duchess back to the aristocracy. They only had one saddle between the two horses that grazed in the fields behind them, which they called in to food before preparing them for riding. Although to the duchess it seemed they were extremely poor, they were actually very well-off for commoners, having many more luxuries than most of the townsfolk in the area.

The horses now tied to the fence around the house, Aurelia stood meters away just staring at the majestic creatures. She had never been this close to a horse before. They were both large draft horses, meant to help plow the fields when needed, but also conveniently ridden to and from town each day. One of them, an older chestnut boy, had a blaze just above his nose and relaxed eyes. The other, a dark grey stallion, kicked at the dirt in anticipation, his tail flicking and ears raised.

"*Beaux, non ?*" Piers said from behind Aurelia. They definitely were beautiful.

"*Oui...*" yes, Aurelia responded.

"*Pouvez-vous m'aider avec la selle ?*" he asked her.

"Huh?" Aurelia was lost in translation.

"*La selle... monter ?*" she still had no clue. The man smiled, and swiftly disappeared into the house, coming out with a heavy saddle and two bridles on his shoulder.

"*C'est une selle,*" this is a saddle, the man said slowly, holding it up, trying to teach Aurelia small words in French.

She smiled, walking closer to the horses, following just behind him. Riding should be easy, shouldn't it? But why was her heart racing so much? The man hauled the saddle up over the grey stallion, the horse shifting its weight in place.

He motioned to the dark grey horse, "*Je vous présente* Bijou," then pointed to the chestnut behind Bijou, "*et* Hugo."

Bijou and Hugo, two strong names for the large draft horses, both of them hearty and disciplined. Piers secured the girth underneath the saddle, and brought the stirrups down slightly to accommodate Aurelia's height. Piers placed the leather bridle over Bijou's ears, sliding a metal bit into his mouth. He unfastened the thin rope holding him to the fence in preparation to ride. Then, reaching the reins above Bijou's head and towards the saddle, he held the horse steady for Aurelia.

"*D'accord*," he motioned for her to get on.

She had never ridden a horse before.

Nearing the giant beast, Bijou neighed, sending Aurelia jumping. Piers laughed at her reaction, and patted the animal lovingly. Placing her left black boot in the stirrup, she kicked her leg over the tall creature gracelessly, thumping onto the horse's back.

Adjusting her dress, which she now awkwardly sat on, she grabbed for the front of the saddle for balance, unknowingly kicking her feet into Bijou's sides. The horse, mistaking the move for a strong command to go, tore away from Piers's grip and ran into the field. His long, deep canter quickly increasing to a full gallop, Aurelia held onto the saddle for dear life, squeezing her legs even tighter for grip, signaling Bijou to go faster. Screaming, she could feel the saddle slipping to the side, only one of her feet secured in the stirrups, unevenly weighing it down. She quickly lost her balance, and fell from the horse's back, landing roughly on her left side into the dirt of the field. The horse slowed, realizing it had lost its rider, and almost out of curiosity, trotted back towards her. Laughing, Aurelia rolled onto her back.

'Never a dull moment', she thought to herself.

Piers ran through the field after the horse, and Amée and Natalia came running up to Aurelia to make sure she was alright. Besides a bruised ego, she was fine.

Natalia chuckled as Aurelia stood up, brushing the dirt from her dress, "You're very bad at riding, *Princess*."

Aurelia made a face at the child when Amée turned, sticking her tongue out at her. Natalia copied her, sticking her tongue out back at her, laughing.

It took a bit longer than Aurelia thought it would to get a small lesson from the duchess as to how to ride. She didn't need to know much, only how to start, walk, steer and stop, but the duchess felt it was important to demonstrate all of them for her before she tried riding again. Then, carefully, Aurelia got on Bijou once more, this time very aware of her feet. Piers helped lift Natalia up to sit in front of Aurelia, and he hopped on Hugo bareback, since they only had one saddle. Slowly, the trio took off towards Toulouse, waving goodbye to Amée.

Their local village was the first stop on their journey, where Piers was able to buy some extra bread from his landlord's oven, and tell him he would be gone for a few days to bring the lost royal to Toulouse. This, of course, peaked the lord's interest, and he told Piers to tell the royal family how much he had helped them on their way - although he did nothing more than allow them leave.

After a few hours of riding, Aurelia's legs had nearly melted. How did people journey like this every day? Stopping for a short rest to let the horses graze and drink from a stream, Natalia jumped off easily from the front of Aurelia's saddle, and Aurelia weakly stepped down. Her legs shook from exhaustion, and her inner thighs burned with a vengeance.

"Can you ask him how much further Toulouse is?" Aurelia asked the duchess, who promptly translated.

"He says we should reach it in three days. Tonight we will stop in Còrdas with a friend," Natalia relayed.

How could she ride for three more days? Her legs already like jello? The duchess and Piers were conditioned to riding, their muscles primed for the journey. They filled up their two water skins in the stream, and ate half of a loaf of bread before continuing on their way.

The bastide of Còrdas was stunning. An exhausting ride, they had to navigate up through the hills to reach the small town perched atop their surroundings - but the views made it all worth while. An angelic town, still recovering and rebuilding from pillagers of the ongoing Hundred Years' War, fractured, yet still alive. Just on the edge of town was a small tavern, with a barn around the back for the horses to rest. Handing off the reins to a stable boy, they walked inside the already bustling tavern.

Probably the only place to drink or eat for kilometers, the tavern was filled with regulars. Not used to anyone of stature joining them, the room grew silent as the duchess walked through the crowd - her purple, adorned gown and glistening tiara still upon her head, despite Aurelia trying to convince her to place it in the safety of a satchel.

"*Papa !*" a voice from behind the bar said warmly.

A young man, probably younger than Aurelia, stepped under the bar and greeted them. He had long, dirty blond hair, and wore a large, dark tan, linen shirt, at the forefront of fashion of the time for commoners, apparently. The boy hugged Piers with a happy greeting, and they began to speak back and forth in Occitan, before Piers switched to French to introduce his traveling companions.

"*Je vous présente La Grande-Duchesse* Natalia Petrovna," Piers motioned to the tiny girl, who held out her hand for him to kiss.

"*Enchanté de faire votre connaissance*," the young man responded, formally telling her it was lovely to meet her.

"*Et qui êtes-vous ?*" the duchess quipped, asking him who he was.

"*Je m'appelle* Henri, *son fils*," he was Henri, Piers's son.

"*Et voici Isabelle*," Piers continued - Aurelia had skipped the "Princess" part of her lie when she introduced herself to Piers and Amée.

"*Enchantée*," it was lovely to meet him, she replied with a nod.

"*De même*," Henri smiled, telling her likewise.

After Piers explained why they were in town, Henri offered them to spend the night in the spare room next to his, above the tavern. While he wasn't the owner, he could bend the rules slightly on occasion.

They filled their bellies with stew and hearty bread, and Aurelia and Piers indulged in a homemade wine. They talked briefly to Henri each time he passed their table, yet were preoccupied with the warmth of the food. Then, exhausted from the day, they retired to their room, where a single, tiny wooden bed was crammed against the wall. The duchess immediately sat on it, and without hesitation, claimed the bed for herself, placing her crown next to her and quickly falling asleep. Henri introduced them to his pregnant wife Francine, who kindly brought them each a blanket. Laying on the hard, wooden floor, sleep soon overcame them.

Waking just before dawn, the duchess was ready to leave this unruly place for somewhere of higher standards. Her traveling companions still asleep on the ground, she crept out of the room to get some air and find some company. Despite her small weight, the wooden, rotting stairs creaked as she walked down into the tavern, waking Henri. She snuck outside, and was baffled to see the magnificence before her. A fog draped the landscape below them like an ocean, the city of Còrdas floating above the clouds. The light that barely tickled the horizon made the view magical - the mystery of the landscape instilling wonder.

From just behind her, a man emerged from the shadows, still reeking of alcohol from the night before. He drunkenly threw himself at the young duchess, and she shrieked in horror, attempting to escape his grip. He was much stronger than her, and her attempts seemed futile as she wiggled. His large hands wrapped around her arms effortlessly. He mumbled incoherently, and then noticed the dainty gold necklace hanging on her neck, which he promptly grabbed and tore off for himself, the metal clasp breaking.

"*Aidez-moi !*" Natalia cried for help, the voice barely escaping her throat, as the man held her arm tightly, inspecting the necklace.

Swiftly knocking the drunkard over with a push and a reprimand, Henri scooped Natalia up and brought the crying girl inside. Plopping her on the bar, he lifted her chin to check that she was alright. Whimpering, shaking, and scared - but no harm had come to her. Hearing the commotion outside, Aurelia and Piers rushed down the stairs, and quickly came to the young girl's side.

"What happened?" Aurelia asked frantically.

"A man... grabbed me... and... and..." sobbing, Natalia couldn't finish.

"And what?" Aurelia asked, thinking the worst.

"He broke my necklace."

After all of that, her necklace breaking was the most important part of the story to her. Not that something worse was bound to happen if Henri hadn't heard her footsteps - not the feeling of being trapped by someone - not the fear for her life that had flashed through her mind - the necklace. Aurelia couldn't help but smile for a fleeting moment at the thought. This 6-year-old, materialistic girl had more emotional strength than Aurelia had even now at 19.

Hugging Natalia tightly, Aurelia thought about how bad that encounter could've been. It would've been her fault if something had happened to the duchess - because if not for her traveling in time, she wouldn't have gotten stuck here with her. She had to get her somewhere safe, and then get as far away from her as possible - fearing the impending threat that the people chasing her from the future would bring harm to Natalia too.

CHAPTER 17

TOULOUSE

It had been a long, hard ride the past few days, but at least now Aurelia felt more than comfortable riding. Her hips had relaxed into the movement, and her hands became loose at the reins. Her horse, the feisty Bijou, was calm, now that he was worn out from the journey. His usual alert stance now replaced with a low slung head and supple ears. Besides their night in Còrdas, they camped under the stars with the horses - much to Natalia's dismay.

The sun was just overhead as they approached the city of Toulouse. The grassy path they had followed quickly turned to a slippery cobblestone, and before they knew it, they had to dismount and walk the rest of the way, since the horses weren't shoed for such a slick surface. The dank smells of sewage and horse manure wafted to their noses, a harsh halt from the calming smells of nature they had enjoyed on their ride. Young boys, their faces and pants covered in dirt, ran up to them. Some speaking in French, others in Occitan, hoping to entice the travelers into buying things, or spending the night at the inn nearby. Piers shooed them away like an incessant fly, and held tight to his reins so that they wouldn't reach for them.

Continuing on, they marveled at the architecture engulfing them. The buildings around them were tickled pink, most of them built with rose colored bricks. Before reaching the *Château Narbonnaise*, where they hoped to gain an audience, they passed a gorgeous cathedral, painted ornately and welcomingly. The duchess stopped walking, and stared in awe at the design. Aurelia slowed to a stop with her.

"May I pray first?" Natalia asked, nervous to meet the local aristocracy.

Aurelia nodded, and Piers took the reins from her so they could both go in together. In a way, stepping into the church felt like stepping through her memories.

Aurelia had never been very religious, merely dragged to church with her grandparents on some Sundays. Not that she didn't believe in God - only, she just despised how much work it was to be a part of the whole ordeal. Additionally, after losing both of her parents at such a young age, it felt like God didn't care about her, though every sermon tried to convince her to believe that He did.

She hadn't been to church since Christmas Eve of 2018 with her nana. They had just recently put her grandfather to rest, and she remembered the way her nana looked at her through tear-filled eyes - almost as if she couldn't stand the sight of the church anymore. In the months after that visit, for the first time in her life, Sundays would pass without so much of a mention of going to sermon. Aurelia wondered if her nana had gone back to church after Aurelia disappeared. Would she once again be comforted by His grace?

Colored lights seeped through the painted glass high above, and a few people gathered to silently pray, although it was midweek. The duchess lunged with a deep seated bow before entering, dipping her hand in a bowl of holy water, then motioned the sign of the cross with a whispered mantra. Aurelia blessed herself in the same motion, following her lead.

Natalia reached for Aurelia's hand, and guided her up the aisle to where a priest stood reading, in between sermons. The priest promptly looked up, and realizing he was in the presence of someone royal, bowed. The duchess introduced herself and Aurelia, or as she knew her, Isabelle, and asked if he would pray with them. They sat in the pews and silently prayed. Asking for strength, courage and acceptance from the local royals, the duchess clasped her hands tightly in prayer.

Aurelia silently watched the priest and duchess, herself unsure what to pray for. Closing her eyes gently, she thought only of Will. She missed him, deeply. But perhaps it was better to be apart, she told herself. After all - she couldn't put someone she loved in harm's way. As of now, it wasn't even possible to get back to him - the only portal she knew of hadn't worked. But where would she go after the duchess was safe with the aristocracy? Would she live here in this time forever? At least here, she could easily remain hidden and live out her life. Perhaps on a farm like Piers and Amée's, or as a seamstress to some entitled royal. She would be OK alone. So she prayed for Will - that *he* would be alright without *her* - and hopefully, maybe, one day, find someone else to love. A love that was gentle, a love that he didn't have to risk his life everyday to be with.

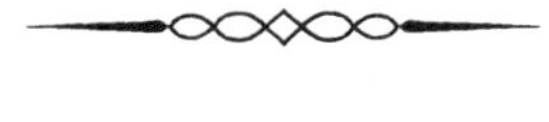

They waited outside the *Château Narbonnaise*, the main castle of the time in Toulouse, as the guards relayed the information to the royals inside. A Russian duchess had arrived seeking shelter. To the aristocracy inside, this information was heavier than Aurelia thought. In 1443, French relations with Russia had barely begun, and to deny or accept her may influence what was to come. Plus, The Kingdom of France was balancing an already divided court among themselves and England. So they consulted with the members of the court, discussing what they should do. After deliberation, they invited the group of travelers inside the castle walls for an audience with them.

The Great Hall was beautiful. Supported by brilliantly carved stone beams, the immense ceiling stretched high above them, illuminated with some windows letting in residual light as the sun went down, and a few grand candelabras that had just been lit and raised for their arrival. Stepping inside, Natalia bowed deeply, with Aurelia and Piers following her lead. Then, they walked towards the single throne where Margaret of Savoy, also known as The Duchess of Anjou, sat in wait of them, surrounded by men of the court, yet she held her own.

The squire introduced the group, The Grand Duchess Natalia Petrovna of the house Romanov, her governess, The Lady Isabelle, and Piers Fournier, who had helped them on their journey.

"Why have you come?" Margaret of Savoy asked, surprisingly in English, perhaps as a test to see if the young girl was indeed learned, as they claimed.

Natalia looked at Aurelia to explain for her, "We have come to seek shelter for the Grand Duchess Natalia. We hoped you would give her refuge and continue her education," Aurelia explained.

"Why is she here and not with her family?" Margaret questioned.

"Because..."

Why was she here? What was their excuse?

"Because my family is in trouble and I have claim to the throne. My mother was scared I would be killed. So she sent me with my governess to seek shelter until I was old enough to get my title," the tiny duchess lied effortlessly.

Margaret of Savoy fell silent, weighing her options. Should she allow this girl refuge in a time of war themselves? But how could she deny her - a helpless child. Nodding with authority, she said yes.

"See to it that the baker is rewarded for his aid," Margaret, the Duchess of Anjou, barked, and a satchel of coins was thrust at Piers.

They had made it. Natalia would be safe.

Natalia's new room was fit for a princess. With stained glass windows overlooking the city, and a plush bed with fabric slung above it from a wooden frame. Nothing like her room at home in 1725, but much more comfortable than the nights before.

Piers would go home in the morning, for tonight he was offered a commoner's room to rest, which he now retired to. Aurelia accompanied the young Natalia to her room with the handmaiden they had selected to care for her. Then, finally undressing from her purple dress, a seamstress had come to take her measurements. She promised to have a new dress by morning, which excited Natalia with a passion. The festivities concluded, and two large plates of luscious food were brought to her table to eat in privacy, so Aurelia and Natalia could share a meal in peace after their long journey.

"Nat?" Aurelia prompted, Natalia looking up. "You know I have to leave tomorrow, right?"

"What? Why?" the young girl asked, flabbergasted.

"Because you won't be safe until I'm gone."

"I don't understand. You can't leave me!"

"There are some very bad people after me... they'll hurt the people I love. They *have* hurt the people I love," Aurelia said, the memory of Johanna painful on her tongue.

"You are in love? What happened?" the intrigued duchess asked.

"I...I lost him..."

"In the future?"

"Oh, now you believe me?" Aurelia chuckled.

"Well, one minute I'm at my palace in 1725, and the next I'm in The Kingdom of France in 1443. Either I'm a witch, or you're really from the future. Either way is impossible."

"How old are you again?"

"I'm almost 7," the duchess smiled, proudly.

Aurelia laughed. At 7 years old, Aurelia was playing with barbies and worried about her imaginary friend disappearing for good. This young girl was already fluent in three languages, and had the wits of a 20-year-old.

"Yes. I lost him in the future. But I can't go back."

"And you love him?"

Aurelia looked at the young girl with sadness, "Yes."

"Then you have to find him again," Natalia proclaimed.

"Nat... I can't even if I wanted to. The portal - my way back, is closed."

"Then make a new one!"

'If only it were that simple,' Aurelia thought. Something had caused that portal to briefly remain open, although she had no idea what.

Natalia read Aurelia's expression. She couldn't get back to him, could she?

"Then, if not home, where will you go?"

"Maybe just travel around France a bit. I don't know."

"Isabelle, you don't speak French or Occitan, you don't have any money, you don't know anyone. Stay with me, please? We'll be safe together," the young girl bargained.

It was true. Where would she go? The duchess did have a point - at least together, two girls from the future could look out for each other. Plus, as much as her first impression of the duchess was that she was a brat - she had grown fond of the young girl, almost like the younger sister she had always wanted.

Aurelia nodded, "OK. I'll stay."

Natalia jumped out of her chair, excitedly wrapping her small arms around Aurelia in a hug.

"Nat?"

"*Да?*"

"My name's not Isabelle. It's Aurelia."

Aurelia dreamt of her parents. The time they had all gone to Disneyland when she was 5. She was dressed as a princess, taking photos with the characters, in absolute heaven. They had swung her between them in their arms, birdsong and delightful music filling her ears like a soundtrack to life.

Then, she woke up abruptly, for no apparent reason. Her breath tremulous, her heart palpitating, her stomach twisted. The castle was completely silent, although the sun was just above the horizon. She got up to drink some water from the wooden pitcher on her side table. Attempting to pour it into a glass, the water wouldn't pour. Perhaps it was empty, although it felt heavy. Defeated, she got dressed and began to walk to the castle's kitchen, where she could refill her pitcher.

It was eerily quiet. She had been here about a week with Natalia, and every day, without fail, was awoken to the sounds around her - horse's hooves stomping on stone, blacksmiths hammering blocks away, the bustle of the servants outside her door. But as she walked the hall, she couldn't hear a single familiar sound.

She turned a corner and skid back in confusion. Two servants passing each other mid-walk, were completely stopped and almost frozen in place. Dropping the empty water pitcher in shock, yet not hearing its thud, she realized that although she had let go of the pitcher, it still hung suspended in the air. She tapped the pitcher, and it moved slightly, still floating. What was happening?

Aurelia walked over to the two servants, both of them young girls carrying various items. Their faces unmoving, their draping clothes perfectly preserved. It was as if time had stopped.

Then, like a switch was flicked back on, the servants began moving as if nothing had happened, the bustling sounds returned to the castle, and the water pitcher fell from its floating position, startling the servants and Aurelia.

The pitcher was indeed full, and water flooded the hallway. Aurelia rushed to clean it up, but was shooed away by one of the servants who insisted she would do it. Carrying the now empty pitcher to the kitchen, Aurelia turned over what had just happened in her mind.

Why had everything around her stopped? And how?

CHAPTER 18

Courted At Court

Fresh, white roses sat on Aurelia's bed as she walked into her room. She didn't know why Louis XI, dauphin of France, and son of Charles VII, king of France, was courting her. She was only a lady of the court, of no royal blood. Perhaps it had something to do with the fact that she constantly disregarded all of his efforts, uninterested in finding love. This made Aurelia, or as he knew her, The Lady Isabelle, all the more desirable. Despite already having a gorgeous wife about her age, whom he hadn't seen in ages, Louis wanted what he couldn't have - the stunning Aurelia.

It had been just less than a year since the duchess and Aurelia arrived in Toulouse, and they had since traveled with the royal court to the *Château de Vincennes* just outside of Paris. The journey was long, but at least being part of the aristocracy, they were able to just sit in a carriage, and not have to actively ride a horse all the way there. Over the course of the previous months, Aurelia and Natalia had grown extremely close, like sisters. Before their travels to Paris, Natalia studied constantly, learning English and Dutch from Aurelia, and was further tutored by esteemed professors from the local *l'Université de Toulouse*. Aurelia attended some of these private studies with her, helping the young duchess navigate her new life in France. In turn, Natalia began to teach Aurelia French and Russian, along with Occitan, which they slowly learned together in Toulouse, at the time, the Occitan literary culture center of the country. Their days consisted of hobnobbing with royals, reading, immersing themselves in culture, and the occasional horse ride through the French countryside.

Now in Paris, life had become ever so complicated. After briefly meeting the Dauphin Louis XI at a dinner in Toulouse, when he was just passing through, he quickly grew enamored with The Lady Isabelle. A stunning blonde vision of culture and wit, in a way, a challenge he hoped to conquer, not unlike his victorious battles in the ongoing war. But besides Aurelia being emotionally unavailable, the dauphin was not even remotely her type. Arrogant, conniving, and constantly at odds with his family - even *if* he was the most handsome man alive, which he definitely wasn't, it would be impossible to overlook his horrid personality. But, when Aurelia and the duchess were summoned to court in Paris, it was out of the question to turn down the heir to the throne.

Aurelia grabbed the flowers and rushed to the now 7 1/2-year-old Natalia's room, although young, she was her only truly trusted ally who knew the whole truth about her.

"*Я так больше не могу*, Nat," she couldn't do it anymore, Aurelia said in broken Russian, bursting through the door to a reading Natalia. She switched back to English, "I just have to say no."

"Why? What happened, Ari?" the duchess asked, slamming her book shut for the scuttlebutt about the latest excitement of the dauphin's exclamations of love.

Aurelia ranted, "He's married, and he wants me to be his mistress. That's what all of this is," she paced back and forth, feeling the soft rose petals in her fingers. "But I don't love him. I never will," she paused to look at the smirking Natalia. "This isn't funny! He wants me to have dinner tonight. Do you know what that means?"

"That you will eat with him?" she quipped.

"Ha. Ha. 'Dinner' is code," Aurelia shivered.

"What does 'code' mean?"

"It means he wants me. It means he's not gonna stop until I've submitted to him. It means he wants to have..." remembering the young age of her gossip friend, she cut herself off.

"Well then, say no?" Natalia asked meekly.

"*No?* No. It's more complicated than that. I say 'no', and he could kick you out of court as revenge. That's who he is, I assure you."

"So then... say yes?"

"But I can't! If I say yes, he's won!" Aurelia plopped on Natalia's bed and laid back in misery.

All she could think of was Will. Centuries away, yet still always at the precipice of her mind. His kind, thoughtful gestures towards all of those around him. But he wasn't here.

Saying "no" would bring about an onslaught of wrath, which would not only endanger the duchess, but also perhaps make waves to the future, causing the people after her to find them. So, despite her wants - she could not be selfish. She had to say yes.

A private room was prepared, and Aurelia waltzed in, dressed in a long, red, off-the-shoulder gown with a slight V neckline, her blonde hair pinned into elegance and rouge adorning her cheeks. Even Valentino himself would take notes from this designer from the Middle Ages. To match her dress, the dauphin had given her a necklace to wear, a large ruby, encrusted with smaller stones around it, which framed her neck like a painting. Tonight, she looked more beautiful than any of the ladies at court, the perfect Princess.

The Dauphin Louis stood at the waiting, kissing her hand as she bowed to him. They sat across from each other at the large table, shrouded by vases and food. Not necessarily private, four different servants stood at the ready to pour wine, water and anything else they required.

Speaking in French, Louis shattered the silence from across the room, telling her she was stunning, "*Vous êtes magnifique, Dame* Isabelle."

"*Non, non. C'est très aimable à vous, Dauphin* Louis," it was very kind of him, she replied softly, not fully taking the compliment as the local French culture had taught her.

"*S'il vous plaît, appelle-moi* Louis," said Louis, telling her she could drop the title and call him Louis intimately.

"*Si telle est votre volonté*, Louis," as he wished, Aurelia smiled gently, already easing the conversation shut. What else was there to talk about?

Not soon enough, dinner was served and quickly eaten. The dinner conversation was drier than the venison, lacking warmth and happiness. But apparently Louis thought it had gone quite well, for when they finally stood up to retire for the night, he made his way towards Aurelia confidently. Sloppily, he pressed his lips to hers.

A stunned Aurelia asked what he was doing, as she pushed his body from hers, "*Qu'est-ce que vous faites ?*"

"*Allez... n'est-ce pas évident ?*" wasn't it obvious, he wondered? "Nous sommes parfaits l'un pour l'autre," in his opinion, they were perfect for each other.

Coming in for another kiss, Aurelia stopped him - she couldn't, "*Je suis désolée*, Louis. *Je ne peux pas.*"

"*Pourquoi ? Je suis l'héritier du trône !*" Louis shouted like a child, how could she turn down the heir to the throne? The future king of France?

She knew what a big decision it was, "*Je sais*," but it had gone far enough, her heart belonged to Will. "*Parce que... mon cœur appartient à un autre.*"

She had fessed up. She loved someone else.

Louis flew into a tyrannical wrath, whipping a vase from the table near where a servant stood, trembling.

"*Arrêtez, Dauphin* Louis !" she begged him to stop, but that only made it worse. He slapped her across the cheek, leaving a red, stinging mark where his dry fingers had been.

"*Désolée*," Aurelia whimpered, her eyes blurring with tears.

"*Partez !*" he told her to leave, and she hesitantly backed away. "*Maintenant !*" now, he yelled.

Running from Louis, she bolted down the long corridor to get to her room upstairs. She couldn't believe he had struck her, her cheek still burning from the action. Will would have never laid a finger on her. She missed his soft, gentle demeanor. His kind eyes.

What would this mean for the duchess? Would Louis throw them out on the street for her actions? Tears streamed down her face. If only she had hidden her feelings from Louis. This was all her fault.

Coming to the small stone stairway up to her room, she looked back to see the dauphin rushing after her.

"*Attendez, Dame* Isabelle !" he called for her to wait, perhaps regretting his reaction.

She couldn't see him again tonight. Aurelia rushed up the stairs, her chest hurting from heartache, tears shrouding her view. She sobbed, wiping her closed eyes, wishing she could lament about her woes to someone. She didn't love him. She never would. Her heart would always be Will's. Collapsing in emotion, she blindly reached for the stone wall beside her. Her hands unexpectedly cold at the touch, she opened her eyes to see what she had leaned on.

But she wasn't in the castle at all. No - she was in a smooth metal stairwell.

CHAPTER 19

GET BACK

Gasping at the sight, Aurelia pulled back from the metal wall. Where was she? How had she stumbled upon another portal hidden in a stairwell she had used countless times in the past months?

She ran back down, hoping to go back to 1444, but nothing happened. Natalia was alone. She had to get back to her. The young girl would never know what had become of her closest friend. They were closer than that even - more like family. She couldn't just abandon her in time.

How had this happened? The portal that took her from Amsterdam to Mexico, then France was a fluke - wasn't it? You needed an Okliot to travel in time. That was a known fact to everyone who traveled.

But, here she was - yet again traveling in time without a device.

Still upset from the dinner with Louis, she wiped her tears away and walked up the stairs to the doorway at the top landing. Opening the heavy door, she almost couldn't believe her eyes.

She was in the future. Will's future. Headquarters zoomed with a midday bustle of tourists wanting to see the world. Stepping into her new surroundings, the door slammed behind her and she looked at what it was labeled as. But she hadn't come out of Gira's portal, nor one of the tourist's portals - she had come out of a bathroom. Opening the door once again to confirm, the portal was gone as quickly as it had appeared - replaced by a large, multiple stall, women's bathroom.

How? Aurelia hadn't realized portals could vanish like that. Weren't they permanently wedged open somehow? She walked into the crowd, actually fitting right in with her medieval red dress amongst the costumed tourists. She bumped into a girl about 16 or 17 years old, dressed in avant-garde fashion, with a model figure to match. Her dark chocolate skin flawless beneath the bright orange of her dress and large matching hat, with her hair voluminous and styled in a wide afro. Aurelia looked at her face more closely - no, it couldn't be.

"Tess?"

It certainly looked like the girl she had met in London, only slightly younger.

"Sorry, do I know you?" she asked, her distinctive smile confirming it was indeed her.

"Oh. We've um... met before, I guess, in another time," Aurelia said, stumbling.

"Oh! Isn't all of this confusing? So I guess I like it then!"

"Like what?"

"Time travel! If we've met in another time, then I must love it, because today is only my first trip!" Tess exclaimed, bubbly and high pitched.

"Really? Wow! Yes, you do. Love it, I mean. Supposedly you've lived in a bunch of times!" Aurelia realized that she had just given her a spoiler about her future - was that OK?

"So, what's your name?" Tess asked.

Tess would one day know her as Aurelia, but here in B-udo, she was known as Miana.

"Call me Miana," she said, remembering how to send a flurry, minus the actual bracelet that facilitated it. "Hey, what year did I come back to?" luckily a perfectly normal question here.

"It's 44-0!"

She was four years earlier than the last time she was here. They must have just launched the company, Adventures In Time, about a year or two before. Will would only be 14 years old here - so he wouldn't know Aurelia yet. Should she try to find her way to the '70s portal again so she could try to find future Will? But it would be years until the party. Should she wait for him? The concept was extremely enticing, but her mind wouldn't rest worrying about the young Natalia alone in France. She had to get back to her first.

"Are you going on another trip?" Tess asked. "I didn't really want to travel alone... wanna go somewhere together?"

Weighing her options, at least traveling with someone would be easier to navigate, but she couldn't enter a portal here in public without first scanning an Okliot as her ticket.

"I would love that! But first I was gonna visit a friend here to pick something up."

Tess followed her new friend Aurelia to the back of Headquarters' main atrium, where a locked, unmarked door blended with the wall. Aurelia remembered it from one of her last times here, when Aleksander led them secretly through the back tunnels of B-udo. Swiping in a Z pattern back and forth like Will had once done, then adding taps where the numbers "4", "8" and "9" should be, as Aleksander had demonstrated. The door opened, and the two stepped into the hall. There were two people who knew Aurelia here in this time - Aleksander, who she had no idea how to find, and Eloise, who she hoped was still working in the hospital. Since Eloise was apprenticing under Aleksander a few years ago, she also hoped that Eloise would have access to a spare Okliot that Aurelia could use to get out of this time.

"What is this place?" Tess asked quietly, as they snaked through the hidden tunnels, normally reserved for the executives and royals to come and go as they pleased.

"It's a quick, secret way to get around B-udo," Aurelia briefly explained.

"How do *you* know about it?" Tess inquired.

"I know some people," Aurelia chuckled.

Within a few minutes, they entered into the hospital. Outside of each patient's room was a projected screen with the patient's current vitals, name, and personal information; and at the bottom, the current doctor treating them. Aurelia scoured the screens as they walked through the pristine white hall, hoping to see Eloise's name. Coming to a room with an older patient apparently about to have a heart replacement, she spotted a familiar name on the screen, "MD Eloise Blaise Sūn-Weiß". Could it be her? She tapped the name on the screen and the image shifted to show the doctor's information. An image of the platinum blonde girl she remembered appeared, and she knew she had the right person. She tapped a button that said, "Call Doctor", and was almost immediately connected to a video call, where Eloise, now ever so slightly older with her hair in a braided ponytail, and her suit a calming yellow mixed with paisley patterned pinks, answered.

Her face grew white at the familiar sight of Aurelia, seeing her again after all of these years.

"Miana? What are you...? Are you OK?" she asked, wondering why she was in the hospital calling her.

"Yeah, yeah - I'm great! How are you?" Aurelia asked.

"Uh... great?"

"Hey, is there somewhere we could talk?"

"I'll be right there," Eloise said, a bright smile across her face.

Tess waited just outside of an empty hospital room as Aurelia and Eloise talked inside. Aurelia explained that she had once again gotten stuck here in the future, briefly recounting her past year and a half. First going to Amsterdam with Will in 1993, then the people that were after her that sent her somewhere in Mexico, to ending up stuck in France in 1443 with a young duchess from the 1700s. It all percolated when she had suddenly ended up in a portal here in 44-0 - all without an Okliot.

How was it possible, she asked Eloise? But, it shouldn't be possible. Eloise could think of no logical explanation for how she was able to time travel without an Okliot - after all, it was a technological discovery that Aleksander had invented.

Skipping right to the point, Aurelia asked if Eloise could get her hands on an Okliot so she could leave 44-0. She nodded tentatively. It was possible, but she would surely be caught if they discovered any missing. The only way that she could avoid it was if she were to travel with them and then bring the Okliots back before someone were to notice they were gone, which was still risky. But Eloise had never traveled before, despite her longing to see the world. So a mini stolen adventure seemed like the most excitement she would have in years and she agreed to help.

The instructions were to wait in the main terminal near the secret tunnels, until she could swipe some newly made Okliots in the lab, then she would meet them there and quickly travel through a portal - getting Aurelia to safety, out of 44-0. Then Eloise would return home a few hours later, under the secrecy of night, to bring the stolen Okliots back. It seemed like a flawless plan.

Tess and Aurelia made their way back through the hidden tunnels of B-udo, coming out into the crowded terminal once again.

Aurelia had to get back to the duchess in 1444, but how? Near the front of the lines of tourists stood a virtual information stand. The girls stepped over to it and Aurelia began swiping through locations and times displayed on the projected screen.

"What're you looking for?" Tess asked.

"Paris in 1444," Aurelia answered uninhibitedly.

"Sounds amazing! Here, try this," Tess opened her hand in front of the projection, and a grey pulsing dot appeared, showing her it was listening, "show me trips in the 15th century."

Instantly, the screen auto populated with three different excursions in the 1400s, filled with photos and ideas of things to do. You could travel to 1488 Great Britain, too late. 1402 Italian countryside, too soon. And 1451 Morocco.

"Huh."

Morocco wasn't *that* far from Paris, was it? 1451 was seven years ahead of when she had just left Natalia in 1444, but at least she could get back to her, right?

"What?" asked Tess, hoping to get a glimpse inside her mind.

"How do you feel about a trip across Spain?"

Tess was more than excited to go on an extended trip - it had been her dream to travel out of B-udo since long before the possibility of time travel had even been announced. She hadn't realized you were able to stay longer than a week in time, but Aurelia explained that she had found a workaround, and Eloise would help them facilitate it. Tess wouldn't have to use her Okliot this trip until the return, which would allow her to remain undetected in the 1400s until she was ready to come home. It honestly seemed like the perfect scenario for her.

Eloise, who had changed into a short, light blue sundress with a white knit bag, unaware of when they would travel to, promptly met Tess and Aurelia in the terminal, and she dispersed three A Class Okliots amongst them. Eloise and Tess placed their futuristic bracelets in their bags, in preparation for travel. They rushed to the portal that would take them to Morocco, and after easily scanning their Okliots without issue, stepped back in time.

CHAPTER 20

TANGIER

Morocco's official visitor's portal entered into a shop filled with textiles. Crumbling stone held the walls up, and strong musty smells from the fabric, mixed with salt, filled the air. They all placed their Okliots in Eloise's small purse for safekeeping, now that they had finished traveling.

The three girls looked around, and their attention focused on a man wearing a long tunic, who had quickly begun walking up to them as they had arrived. Taking one good look at them, he nearly fainted.

"*Māthā tartadīna?*" the man asked in Arabic.

Aurelia looked at Eloise and Tess, hoping they understood, but they both seemed as bewildered as her.

"Do you speak English?" Aurelia asked, to which the man gave a scowl. "*Russki?*" Russian? Nope. "*Nederlands? Français ?*"

"*J'ai dit,*" the man said, picking up in French where he left off, "*qu'est-ce que vous portez ?*" Aurelia laughed, realizing the question.

"What did he say?" Tess whispered, hoping to get in on the joke.

"He wants to know what we're wearing," Aurelia motioned to their eclectic clothes, Tess in her bright orange layered dress with a giant hat, Eloise in a blue sundress that belonged in the 21st century, and Aurelia, still wearing her red medieval style dress - probably the one fitting into time the most.

"*Suivez-moi, les filles,*" with an eye roll, he motioned for them to follow him to his back room. "*Vous ne pouvez pas voyager dans le temps habillée ainsi,*" they couldn't pass for locals dressed like that. A small smile occupied the side of his face as he mentioned time travel, in lieu of his original harsh demeanor.

"He knows we're from the future," Aurelia whispered, as they began following him, "I think he might be one of the tour guides who can give us a welcome package."

This had to be Aurelia's favorite part of the company.

"Ooh... I've heard about this part!" Tess giddily replied.

"What's in a welcome package?" asked Eloise.

"It depends... money, clothes, jewelry, maps and pamphlets - each one is different based on when and where you are. But basically they're meant to help you blend in with the time you're in," Aurelia explained, realizing she was once the one with these same questions.

Passing through a doorway with dangling beads shrouding the entrance, they found themselves in a tailor's room, where women's dresses were displayed on wooden busts. A petite woman, wearing a dark purple hijab and matching dress that covered most of her body, walked up to the three tall girls, silently. The man barked an order at her, and she immediately began rifling through the shop to find appropriate clothes for them.

He stepped up to them as the seamstress was occupied and in a lowered voice, asked them for their proof of membership, "*Votre confirmation ?*"

Aurelia, knowing he meant to scan their Okliots, reached into Eloise's bag and got them out, handing one each to Tess and Eloise. Aurelia held hers out, with the inscribed "A" pointed towards him. The newbies, Tess and Eloise, followed suit and held theirs out as well. With a quick look behind him to make sure the lady wasn't watching, as she was probably a permanent, the typical red laser scanned the Okliots from his eye. Aurelia shuddered - she would never get used to that.

"*Tout l'honneur est pour moi,*" what an honor to assist them today, the man said, suddenly smiling nervously, realizing he had three top level travelers with him today - this was both a treat and a test.

If he wanted to keep his job, he would need to impress them. After all, the A Class Okliots were only reserved for the executives and nobles of ZhēnZhū, and they had more power in the future than God, it seemed.

They had been in Morocco for about an hour, and yet still hadn't left the shop. They now sat on the large, vibrantly dyed and carefully hand-woven rug that filled the floor, with a few cushions placed on top. They gathered around a small hammered metal table holding their delicious fresh mint Moroccan teas and some finger foods - mostly nut filled treats and pastries. The man had pulled out all the stops for them. He had his seamstress run to enlist the help of seven other girls nearby in town, all of whom rushed to perfect the three new, tailored outfits that the girls would wear.

After learning they wished to travel across the Strait of Gibraltar, he summoned a boy he knew from Aragon to accompany them, who would see to it that they would be safe on their journey. Luckily, the boy was fluent in Arabic, Castilian, Aragonese, and some French, so he would be able to also serve as a translator. He entrusted the boy with a satchel filled with both gold dinars and doblas, so they would have a working currency here and within Spain. Morocco's visitor's guide also knew of a trusted sailor with a ship that would be able to take them across the Strait, and he promptly paid a runner to go and have the ship prepaid and readied.

Although she needed to return to B-udo soon to return the borrowed Okliots, Eloise would take the ship with them and then stay on the boat to return to Morocco - the thrill of sailing on the ocean too great an opportunity to pass up. The man who served as their visitor's guide remained nameless through his escapades, and soon the dresses were completed for the girls.

Tess's outfit was stunning. Her deep, effervescent skin complemented with the bright greens and golds of her dress, her slim figure allowing the fabric to drape flawlessly. A large, matching green shawl covered her head, and tight fabric shoes held her feet. Eloise's dress was a dark, royal purple, the blue of her eyes amplified with the color. Her platinum hair hidden beneath the purple hijab. Her white knit purse now replaced by a leather satchel. Aurelia's dress was a deep, hot pink, embroidered with elaborate gold, and also matched perfectly with a woven shawl over her head for modesty. She left her gorgeous red dress behind, but kept the ruby necklace Louis had given her, its jewels fit for a queen.

They thanked the older man in the shop, who still wouldn't reveal his name - perhaps in case he thought he had done a poor job at helping them. Then, they were officially introduced to their traveling companion, Daví, a slightly suntanned young boy with dark brown hair and almond eyes. His brown clothes plain and diffident, and his skinny figure held together with a rope at his waist. He seemed to be about 16, perhaps serving as an apprentice or squire somewhere. Because he was skinny as a rod, they could tell he had distinctive bone structure, his cheeks and jaw his strongest features. He was cute, Tess thought. Without saying a word, he bowed to the ladies, perhaps told they were royals he would escort, and they were quickly on their way.

The girls finally exited the shop that they had spent the past hour in, and both Tess and Eloise very nearly fainted at what awaited them outside.

"No way," Tess whispered, while Eloise was speechless at the beauty.

The bright sun streamed into their eyes, a great ball of fire in the center of the blue sky, endlessly tall above them. It couldn't be real, Tess and Eloise thought. The sky above them was just a projection, wasn't it? But they could feel the warmth on their faces, the breeze swaying their clothes. After an entire life lived in an underground city, they were outside.

Immediately, the noise outside of the shop was deafening, and Daví led the group of girls through the outdoor market in Tangier. Fabrics and carpets surrounded them here, with vendors all vying to sell them their work, but they walked briskly through the crowd of needy people. Soon, they found themselves out of the textile market, walking through winding white walled alleyways that quickly disoriented them like a maze. Flea-ridden, skinny stray cats roamed freely here, respected for the good fortune they brought. Following the confident Daví, they once again cut through another market, where pungent, nauseating smells hit their noses with distinct spices, seafood and salt, mixed with unrefrigerated meats and mildew. Each stand was different, yet all had a vile harshness about them - plucked chickens hung upside down at one stand, fully intact lamb's heads lay on display in another. Dead fish sprawled on wooden tables, the fishermen actively chopping them in anticipation of customers. They quickly walked through, and turning a sharp corner, were thrust into stunning views of the mixing waters of the Mediterranean and Atlantic ocean. The wind instantly whipped in their ears, and their dresses turned into sails that felt like they could be carried away with. In the distance, beyond the clear blue waters, they could see a tickle of Spain. Still above a small cliff, they walked down a path to the dock, where a relatively large cog was tied.

Even from a distance, you could tell the choppy waters rocked the boat, and as they approached, a man whistled to his crew, who all stopped preparing the mast and bowed to the girls.

'OK,' Aurelia thought to herself, 'they definitely think we're royalty.'

The captain stepped up to them, and greeted them speaking Arabic, "*As-salamu alaykum.*"

Daví translated to Aurelia in French, telling her he said hello - peace be upon you. Unclear what the customs here were, she refrained from holding out her hand or kissing his cheeks, and simply told Daví to reply, "Hello, and peace be with you as well."

Tess, on the other hand, was not yet used to the concept of using other greetings, and waved her hand to the ground happily, as if sending a flurry to the man.

Aurelia whispered under her breath to her with a chuckle, when the captain looked at her strangely, "They don't use that greeting in the past," Tess grew flushed with embarrassment and put her hand down. "Just smile softly and nod - that's the best way when you don't know how to greet someone," Aurelia explained softly, through a smile with tight lips.

The captain proceeded to speak to Daví in Arabic, discussing the journey and where the ladies would sit. They were whisked under the bridge into the captain's stateroom, where cushions had already been prepared for them. Two small portholes showed the bobbing horizon, and Aurelia thought back to growing up in California. Despite living no more than fifteen minutes from the ocean, Aurelia had never been on an actual boat before, unlike her mom who was a marine biologist and had practically lived on boats. The memories flooded into her mind of her hot, sandy summers on the golden beach. Always a loner in large social settings, Aurelia would only ever be seen with one or two of her friends.

A single vision entered her mind of the time she and her friend Sarah had spent the whole day on the scalding beach. They had come across two boys from out of town who were dying to play volleyball, and although Sarah was a player in high school, Aurelia had never been remotely good at sports. But, the boys insisted, wanting more than anything to hang out with two gorgeous California girls. The teams split, and with one of the boys on Aurelia's team, they actually did well - several points up from Sarah and the other boy. Her confidence building, she lunged for the ball, and missing it completely, landed straight on her left wrist, breaking her bone. She played it off as being fine to the boys, and simply spent the rest of the day just lounging on the sand with them - her wrist throbbing and swollen, but hoping not to ruin the day. Then, as night fell and the boys left, Aurelia got into Sarah's car and finally fessed up to her embarrassing injury. They drove straight to the hospital, where a cast was put on, and summer fun quickly came to a close. It seemed like a lifetime ago. The fragile high schooler with intangible dreams of being a fashion designer, poor grades in English and History, feeling that failure would dictate the rest of her life.

Now, she was an insurgent of the future, traversing through the timelines, and making her own destiny. She had found people she could count on, and a guy she loved. Each day was an adventure, filled with new experiences and cultures. It really was amazing, she thought. It had been over a year and a half since the moment she went through the first portal in 2019, and now, finally accepting of her wild life, the 20-year-old Aurelia wouldn't change that moment for anything.

"I think I'm gonna be sick..." Eloise rushed out of the cabin to the deck outside.

They were close to landing, more than half of the sailing already behind them, when a dense fog rolled in over the choppy waters, a tempestuous wind rocking the boat with a constant lurching. Aurelia rushed to Daví to find out what was wrong, but he replied with a giggle - apparently the crossing was known for its dynamic, ever-changing weather. But despite the calm attitudes of the crew as they navigated through the thick fog, the girls were stressed out - not a single one of them ever having been on a boat before.

Tess and Aurelia followed after Eloise, and the three made their way to the bow, where they could all focus on the horizon, and hopefully help their seasickness. From here, it felt as if they were jumping on the water, the boat sinking and rising with each wave it encountered.

"What was that?" Eloise asked, pointing to the water on the port side, where a tiny cloud of white smoke held in the air.

"I think it's just the fog, Eloise," Tess said, squinting her eyes to try and see.

Then, with a sudden puff from the water about a ships distance away, another spray of white emerged.

"It's a whale!" Aurelia exclaimed, remembering the distinct puff of breath that she had seen from a distance so many times before.

Just near where the last puff had been, a huge, smooth, brownish-grey whale flipped its tail, the water dripping off of its body as it swam. Eloise and Tess were absolutely speechless. Whales had been extinct for over a millennium in their future. They had no idea of their sheer size and grace until seeing one in person. Now that they knew it was there, they could trace parts of its body under the waves. Not yet returning to a deep dive, it slowed to swim along with their boat for a moment. The fin whale had to be at least sixty feet long. Flipping over slightly as it swam, its eye emerged from the water, a gentle soul inside.

"It's so... beautiful," Eloise said, her eyes wet with tears. How had humans destroyed such an epic species?

The whale took one final breath, before it dipped further underwater away from them. Glued to the view, they scanned the surroundings wondering where it had gone. Then, further away, just as if to say goodbye, the whale jumped from the water, flipping its body in a spin, and collapsed into the ocean with a splash.

Eloise laughed, shouting to the whale as if it could hear her, "OK, showoff!"

It had never felt so good to stand on solid ground. Their bodies still acclimated to the swaying of the boat, they sat on a stone wall just near the dock to readjust. It was time for Eloise to return to the future, and before the ship took off once again, the three girls shared a warm goodbye between newfound friends. Something about Eloise was comfortable to Aurelia, like a synergy between their souls. She knew she would always have a friend in the future, should she ever need her again.

Daví saw to it that Eloise would be safe traveling back, paying one of the crew members that he knew well to be her guide back to the shop in Tangier. Then, with one final wave goodbye, Eloise boarded the ship again and Aurelia and Tess continued on their journey.

Nearby was a farm that Daví knew of through mutual friends, where with the help of a handful of rare gold doblas, they were able to buy three horses. Aurelia, now a confident rider, showed Tess the ropes. She made sure to remind her not to lean too much to one side, not to kick or press on the horse's belly if you didn't want to take off, and that if all else failed, the most surefire way to slow a runaway horse was tightening up the reins, and turning the horse's head to one side to steer to a stop with a tight circle. All lessons she wished she had known the first time she rode.

Their horses' names were Pablo, a young, fiery, all black steed with long hair, Mincho, a gentle bay with a soft, somewhat lazy disposition, and Dionysius, a large, stunning, light grey horse with a black mane. All Andalusian stallions of the highest grade, intelligently trained for princes and kings. It was quite a difference for Aurelia, being in the 15th century again, this time with her own riches.

Helping Tess onto the kind Mincho's back, Aurelia demonstrated the basics. Then, when Tess felt she was comfortable enough, Daví held his hands out for Aurelia to step onto the grand Dionysius. Daví quickly hopped on the spritely Pablo, and they were off. Their new horses beneath them, they rode to a nearby village, where they loaded up on supplies they would need for the next week or so. Buying mats and blankets to sleep on, flint for fire, bread and other food, water skins and liquor, they were ready to make their way across Spain.

CHAPTER 21

TAPAS AND TIME

"Can you ask him what his favorite food is?" Tess asked Aurelia, who translated her conversation with Daví.

She waited for his response, "He says he doesn't have a favorite," Aurelia said, the beating of hooves beneath them dulled only by their speech.

"What? That's impossible. Everyone has a favorite. What about ice cream? Everyone loves ice cream," Tess said, flabbergasted at his answer.

Aurelia translated yet again, "He wants to know what 'ice cream' is."

"No wonder you don't have a favorite!" the girls laughed. "Ice cream is like eating cold, flavored heaven."

Daví laughed at this description when Aurelia translated it in French.

"Well, then it sounds delicious, he says!"

Aurelia had been translating Tess and Daví's little flirtatious conversations for the past few days - her brain fatigued from the constant switch between languages, but happy to be facilitating a budding romance. There wasn't much excitement beyond their conversation as they rode across the effervescent Spanish terrain. Although it was February, the weather was still somewhat mild here - with a nip in the air that was best solved by riding with blankets over their shoulders.

Besides Tess and Daví's attempts to flirt through Aurelia's translating, the girls had Daví teach them small words and phrases in Castilian Spanish on their journey. It came rather easily to Aurelia - the language similar to the South American Spanish she had previously studied in school, however, filled with different pronunciations and many emphasized "th's". Then, just as she thought she knew where a sentence was headed, a word would be different and stump her. Aurelia never thought she would come to love the art of language learning as much as she did now, but it was in fact, hard to remember a time when all she spoke was English. Not only useful to travel with, but also somewhat of a magical connecting force between once divided cultures.

Dusk was almost upon them, so stopping for the night in the wilderness somewhere near Ciudad Real, they prepared to make camp. Daví tied the horses, Tess began unloading the mats and blankets, and Aurelia followed the sound of water to a trickling stream. She helped herself with handfuls of water, and took the opportunity to fill her water skin.

Walking back to her traveling companions, her eyes widened. Thinking they were alone, Tess and Daví were passionately kissing. Trying to silently walk away and let them have their moment, Aurelia's foot crunched on a small branch, which caused Tess to immediately pull away from Daví and spot Aurelia.

"Shit! Sorry Miana," Tess said, rushing after her, Daví slinking back towards the horses in embarrassment.

"Why?" Aurelia grinned. "No need to apologize! I'm the one that walked up at an inopportune time!"

She continued blithely walking away, but Tess ran up and grabbed her hand, turning Aurelia back to face her.

"So you're... OK with it?"

"Of course! Why wouldn't I be? You guys are so cute together!" Aurelia smiled.

Tess sighed with relief, "OK good. I just wasn't sure what you meant by the fact that we were 'friends' in my future."

"*What?* No! Definitely not anything more than friends," Aurelia laughed. "I mean you're gorgeous, don't get me wrong - but I'm with someone - a... a guy."

"You *are*? Oh my God! You have to tell me everything about him! Would I know him?" Tess grabbed her other hand and sat on a fallen tree nearby to gossip.

"Um..."

What could she tell her? Apparently from their first meeting, Tess was oblivious as to who her Will actually was, so she would have to omit some parts.

"I don't think you'd know him," she lied, knowing full well that they were cousins and close friends. "He's from B-udo, of course, um... he loves to travel... and he's kind, and generous, and loving... protective and... really handsome."

"Oooh! What does he look like? Is he tall? Blonde? Chinese?

Black?"

Aurelia chuckled thinking about him, his brown hair, blue eyes - the dimples on his cheeks that appeared when he was happy.

"He's white... brunette... and he's tall... and he has these teeth that aren't *quite* straight but he didn't want to fix them. He said that everything in B-udo was too perfect, so he wanted something to himself that was truly *him*. And he has this way about him with strangers - like he's always, reserved and proper, and cautious - but then when we're alone, he'll dance with this... *stupid* grin on his face, or... make these little asides that just make you laugh your ass off."

Tess squealed with excitement, "Awwwww! Oh my God he sounds soooo sweet! He sounds like the perfect guy! Is he rich too?" Tess said jokingly.

Aurelia laughed - that had never been important for her. However, he was definitely well-off. She nodded.

"OK, you'd better let me be your maid of honor at the wedding," Tess joked.

"Deal," Aurelia laughed.

She wondered what their wedding would be like in her future. Although she had pried with Will about what was to come for her, he would always shut her up with a kiss, like she had done so many times before to him in his past.

She hoped it was on a beach, somewhere warm, with her all of her friends and family around her. In a stunning off-the-shoulder chiffon dress, her hair wrapped in flowers. In her mind, she pretended that her parents would be there, her dad walking her down the sandy aisle. She imagined that they danced and drank all night, blissful and unthinking about the people from the future finding them. It was a nice dream. But, in her heart of hearts, she knew that they had probably just eloped in secret - hidden somewhere in time.

"What's his name?" Tess bubbled.

"Um... it's Will."

"Aww that's my younger cousin's name too! Well, he goes by 'William' now because he thinks it makes him sound much more 'professional'. Like *please* - you're 14, you're not supposed to be professional at anything."

"Oh? That's cute. It's a great name."

Nodding yes, Tess crinkled her nose, thinking about her now 14-year-old cousin back in B-udo, a once shy boy who had suddenly found himself at the center of society. Aurelia sighed in relief that Tess seemed to obliviously skip over any assumptions that her cousin Will could be the same Will that Aurelia was with - after all, B-udo was a large sector with thousands of residents, what were the odds that they both knew the same Will?

"So why isn't he here with us? I wanna meet him!" Tess said enthusiastically.

What was her reason that he wasn't there? She couldn't say the truth, that she was protecting him by being apart.

"He's gonna meet me."

Although it was true, he would be meeting her where they had their first kiss, the onus was on Aurelia to first find him in his past.

"Awwww! Is that why you're going to Paris? That's so romantic!"

She still hadn't told her about Natalia, "No, actually! Um... why I'm going to Paris is a long story."

"Well it's not like I have anything better to do! Splosh!"

"Splosh?"

"You know - jaunder - tell me the deets!" Tess's colloquialisms confused Aurelia, but she knew she basically just wanted her to spill the tea.

"Well... I sort of... accidentally... time traveled with a permanent and lost her in time."

Tess grew silent. A first for her.

"Yeah... um... so I stayed with her for about a year, and got her back to the royals nearby-"

"Wait - so, she was royalty?"

Aurelia nodded, "From Russia."

"Oh my God - was it the lost Princess Anastasia?"

Aurelia laughed. She wondered what history had written of the lost duchess.

"No. She's the Grand Duchess Natalia Petrovna," Tess had no response, she obviously had never heard of her. "She's a Romanov. Daughter of the Tsar, Peter The Great."

"Well, shit. How did that happen?" Tess's eyes bulged.

Aurelia began babbling, "I was using this portal that... well... I don't know, it was weird. It shouldn't have even been there. And I didn't even have my Okliot so it must have made it very unstable-"

"Wait. What? What do you mean?"

"Huh?"

What had she said?

"You... time traveled without an Okliot?" Tess knew that was impossible.

"Well... yeah. But, there was this group of people that all had Okliots, so I think I just piggybacked off of theirs."

"Miana - but, that's not how it works at all. Every person has to be holding a device - that's literally the *one* rule that they teach you before you travel, so you don't get stuck in time."

"Well then how is it possible? I definitely used the portal! A few times, actually. And then I used another one that accidentally brought me into the future," Aurelia thought back to her very first trip - she hadn't used an Okliot to go to the '70s either, a fact that she just now remembered.

"It's not. It's not possible," Tess floundered. How could Aurelia travel without technology? "Are you sure you didn't have an Okliot?"

"I don't know... no... I mean... I didn't."

She had just assumed it had something to do with residual energy in the air that allowed her to time travel - but now that Tess had blown her theory, what else could it be? Each time, she had been wearing different clothes, and not holding any advanced technology. It didn't make sense. Something had allowed her to time travel. It wasn't like humans could do it on their own. Could they? No. *That* was impossible. Maybe it was the nanobots? But no, she had time traveled before that. Maybe it had something to do with Will? After all, his dad was the inventor of the Okliots. Was it possible that he had done something in her past to allow her to time travel?

They had been riding every day for almost three weeks, their pace now slowed significantly with the sudden onslaught of cold March rain, as they approached the mountainous terrain. Although it wasn't a torrential downpour, it wore on them after not stopping for the past two days. The horses and themselves exhausted from the long, laborious journey. They had almost reached Aragon, their halfway point, but it was nearly impossible to make headway when the mud began to build underneath the horses' feet, each step now a struggle. Their hooves squished and pulled away from the sinking ground, as they made their way to a city nearby to regroup and get some rest.

Daví had found himself sick from the wetness, his body trembling in the rain. It was when he began to cough incessantly that the girls found themselves worried. Tess and Aurelia, although cold and dreary, both had decontamination nanobots that prevented them from catching a chill. They would be fine, but Daví was fragile, they realized. All of their clothes completely soaked through, they soon neared the grand stone walls of Cuenca.

Hidden amongst the mountains, balancing atop the hills, lay a city of great stature. Buildings here clung to the sides of cliffs as if they were cairns stacked with finesse. Water rushed beneath them in a river bed, and they followed a precarious bridge into the city. One day the city would, like most, become more commercialized, a tourist hotspot just a stones throw from Madrid. Filled with paved roads, schools and stores. But now, in the 1400s, the town had a sort of quaint, medieval, fairytale magic about it.

Passing through the open gatehouse, they entered the city, happy to finally be somewhere other than the wilderness. Reminiscent of Aurelia's first time in Toulouse, children ran up to them here, hoping to guide them to the local *auberge* for a tip, which they gladly accepted. They dismounted from their slick leather saddles with a squish into the mud. Aurelia and Tess's once delicate shoes were utterly destroyed from the ride, their elaborate dresses torn and tattered. It was nearly impossible to ride in flats, but they hadn't come across a single town since leaving the tip of Spain, hoping to cut straight through and not dilly dally. Their feet throbbing and blistered, legs chaffed, and backs aching, they hobbled inside the inn.

Not unlike some taverns Aurelia had been in before, the first room was bursting with conversation. Some folks found themselves sloshed with ale, while others gambled their fortunes away. Walking straight through the crowd, the young boys guiding them brought them to an older woman. Daví negotiated rooms for the girls with the crusty, jaded old woman, her soul hardened from years of running the place.

"Daví, *Trouvez-vous une chambre je la réglerai*," Aurelia told Daví they would give him a room as well.

His eyes widened. What kindness these girls had, he thought, "*Merci, Votre Grâce !*"

Perking up at the sound that the girl was royalty, the inn's owner increased her price. Daví tried to whittle her down, but she had made up her mind. He begrudgingly handed her a single gold dobla from the girls pouch, which she quickly stuffed into her bosom and traded back a handful of copper maravedís. They had five nights here to rest and recover.

They were quickly shown to their three rooms upstairs, privacy usually a rarity in the 1400s. Surrounding the hearth's chimney from downstairs, the rooms were slightly warmer than outside.

Sticking together in Aurelia's room, they hung out their mud laden blankets and shawls, keeping on the bare minimum of wet clothes.

"I would kill for a hot shower right now," Tess joked, finger combing the crud of riding from her rain soaked, textured hair that had been tightly pulled back for days.

"Ughh me too! I haven't had a proper shower in almost a year!" Aurelia laughed.

That was certainly something she had to get used to being in the Middle Ages. Everyone here smelled of ripeness and manure. Being a lady of the court in France with Natalia, she had enjoyed a few warm baths, but not many. Usually, she would simply walk down to the well in town and splash cold water upon herself as needed for modesty, or on rare occasion, if she was feeling cheeky, go to the public bathhouse.

"How did you do this for *so* long, Miana?"

"Do what?"

"Live in the Middle Ages!"

"Well, I didn't really have a choice. I thought I was stuck here."

"Right. So then how *did* you get back?"

Aurelia shrugged, "I dunno. I guess I just stumbled upon a portal somehow."

"OK, but that's what doesn't make sense to me. I mean, so like, you found a portal - but you still didn't have an Okliot to use it? *Right?* I just think there's more to it that we're not seeing," Tess speculated.

"And what would that be?"

"That maybe you don't need an Okliot to travel. What if you have, like, superpowers, or something?"

Aurelia laughed, time travel she could wrap her head around, superpowers, not so much, "I definitely don't have superpowers!"

"Ok but like - *that's* what someone *with* powers would say. Maybe you just don't know how to use them yet," Tess stated, matter-of-factly.

"And how do you propose I got these 'powers' then?"

Tess paused, "Hmm. Well actually - maybe it's built in you! Maybe you're an augment."

"A what?" Aurelia looked at her unknowingly.

"An augment. You know - an AI?"

She was most certainly born and raised in the 21st century.

"Oh, I'm definitely not a robot."

Tess sharply inhaled, "Miana, don't say that!"

"What?"

Tess whispered like someone would hear them, "*Robot?*"

Aurelia chuckled, "Why not?"

Tess's mouth dropped, "It's *so* derogatory! You've been away from ZhēnZhū too long! You know they don't like that term anymore!"

"Right..." there were so many things that had changed in the future. "OK, but I'm definitely human, not an... augment."

Tess sighed. There had to be something they weren't thinking of.

Aurelia thought about her working theory about Will or his dad having done something, "Do you think it's possible that Aleksander could've done something to allow me to travel without a device?"

"As in Aleksander Kovachev?" Tess asked. Aurelia nodded. "You know my Uncle?"

Sometimes Aurelia forgot that Tess hadn't had their encounter in 1993 London yet, and she still didn't know Will was her love.

"Yes... for a while now. He's a friend... through Eloise. But, what do you think? Is it possible?"

Tess rolled it over in her mind, "Yeah. I mean, I don't know how his inventions work, but I'd assume that he'd be constantly trying to improve his work. Maybe he figured out how to make the device microscopic? Did he ever test anything out on you?"

"No... I mean, not that I know of."

"Hmm..."

"It makes the most sense though, doesn't it? I mean, how else can I travel in time without an Okliot?"

Tess shrugged, it did seem the most likely of all the theories, "Have you tried it out? Like actually tested the extent of what you can do?"

"Not really," each time she had been running from something - she hadn't had time to experiment with it. She gasped, "I think I might've just realized how it works."

"How?"

"Well... every single time I've traveled... I was rushed, or stressed, or scared. What if my emotions are somehow triggering the portal or some sort of microscopic Okliot to work?"

"Huh. So your endorphins activate some technology in your body that allows you to travel?"

"Something like that... maybe?" Aurelia shrugged. She couldn't believe how strange her life had become.

"Maybe...? Well once you check on your friend Natalia, and we head back to Morocco, you should try giving me your Okliot and see if you can still travel in the portal to test it out!"

Aurelia didn't have another Okliot with her. She wasn't planning on going back. It wasn't safe for her.

"I'm not going back... I'm staying in France, Tess."

"What? For how long?"

Aurelia's silence spoke words.

Daví, sick with a slight flu from the cold weather, remained in his room to recover as the girls walked through town, although he tried to insist otherwise. The weather had calmed itself now, but they enjoyed their small hiatus from the constant riding they had grown accustomed to.

They quickly found a cordwainer's shop in town, where their feet were fit for new boots, appropriate for riding. Down the street, they happened upon a local dressmaker, where they each ordered new dresses. Each of them would have two new outfits rushed, one utilitarian dress for the rest of their journey, and another, more grandiose for their arrival in court, which they would store in a protected saddle bag until they were close.

It was wild for Aurelia to watch the differing techniques of designers through the years and places - each one of them unique. Here, a white *camisa* was worn underneath a kirtle, then the actual adorned sleeved dress would be layered on top. The small selection of silk fabrics here were apparently bought from a frequent traveler, and the wools, linens and hemps all woven locally. Ever since first traveling to the 15th century, Aurelia was amazed at the care that went into each individual piece.

Growing up in the 21st century, she could go to a fabric store to get the exact color and amount of fabric she wanted, drive home in less than ten minutes, search for a pre-made pattern or idea online, and hem it with her electronic sewing machine, all in less than a day. Here, wool had to be sheered, spun and dyed, fabric had to be made, which would take days, and each piece had to be carefully planned. Then, they would hand sew the piece for days or sometimes weeks, before finally delivering it to their customer, all for a measly price.

After their fitting with the dressmaker, they continued on their way. The town was alive with energy - merchants lined the streets in little markets filled with food, art and music, all competing for attention. The locals here were standoffish, especially to Tess, that is until they realized that the girls were loaded. It was sad, and spoke to the character of the world, but no matter the time or place, it seemed like money was always a door opener.

A tempting smell of meat and spices wafted in the air, and the girls followed their noses to a small restaurant buried amongst the madness. Each seat already filled, the chef hurrying to serve everyone. A server rushed past them holding a large cast iron pan, sizzling and filled with some sort of food.

"*¡Pasen! ¡Sientense!*" the friendly woman motioned for them to sit at the end of a long table, where they could squeeze into a bench amongst the other customers, asking them what they'd like. "*¿Qué les gustaría?*"

"*Dos vinos, por favor,*" two wines, Aurelia said, her high school Spanish classes finally paying off - although she had learned South American Spanish, a much different dialect than the Castilian Spanish spoken here.

The woman nodded and briskly returned with two mugs of wine, topped with meat. Tess lifted it off and inspected it, it seemed to be salami. Why was there salami on their wine?

"*¿Perdón?*" Aurelia asked, grabbing the busy servers attention. "*¿Qué es esto?*"

The server looked at her like it was obvious, "Chorizo."

"*¿Por qué viene con el vino?*" why did it come with the wine, they wondered?

The woman laughed, "*¿De donde es usted?*" Aurelia's accent was much different than the locals nearby.

Where *were* they from, Aurelia wondered? Growing up in California, then Amsterdam with Will, France for a while, and Tess from the future in ZhēnZhū.

They were not from here, that was for sure, "*¡Lejos!*" Aurelia chuckled.

"*Esto se llama, 'tapa',*" the meat was called a tapa. "*Aquí, Cubrimos nuestras bebidas con pan o carne,*" the woman explained that here, they covered their drinks with bread or meat.

Aurelia could decipher a bit of what she was saying, and realized that this tradition would one day expand into what Spain's cuisine was known for, tapas. Tess took a small bite of the spiced meat, and her eyes bulged with satisfaction.

"Oh my God! *¡Delicioso!*" Tess said, her mouth watering from the salty, smoked meat. She quickly finished it off with another bite, "Can we have more?"

"*¿Mas, por favor?*" Aurelia translated, placing a few maravedís on the table for the woman, unclear as to how much it would be, but showing her that they could afford it.

The server smiled and walked away. Within a few minutes, the woman returned holding a large plate filled with small samplings of cold cheeses, meats and bread. Small clay bowls atop the platter held fresh olives stuffed with bell peppers.

The girls dove into the plate, the buttery, yet crisp flavor of the sheep milk manchego cheese coating their tongues. Then the gentle salt of the olives changed their palate, thinking of an ocean day. Aurelia placed a slice of Iberian ham on top of a piece of warm, homemade bread, the flavors melding perfectly. The server once again returned with more food, this time a cast iron pan, similar to the one they had seen when they first entered the tavern. Visibly hot, and hearing the sizzle, they awaited the incredible, unknown taste. A saucy mixture of chopped chorizo, with paprika, spicy pepper and salt. They ate it quickly, and soon realized that the watery, yet oily sauce itself was the best part, dipping their bread to soak it. The woman yet again returned with a small plate filled with sliced potatoes, and seafood on top of it.

"*El especial del chef... esto fue traído todo el camino desde Valencia,*" proud of the special dish, the woman told them that it had come all the way from the seaside town of Valencia.

It was octopus, reddened with paprika and grilled to perfection. They tasted it, unsure of what to expect. Unlike some octopus, this one was smooth to eat, not the chewy, spongy texture you would expect. It definitely was a delicacy, and they savored each piece.

Now, despite the small portions of each plate, they were absolutely stuffed, their bellies finally satisfied after weeks of travel. At this point, most of the other customers had already left, themselves now able to stretch out more. The server returned with a pitcher of wine, and filled their cups.

"*¿Les gustó, chicas?*"

"*¡Sí! ¡Todo fue incredíble! ¡Estuvo muy rico!*" Aurelia replied, everything was all so incredibly delicious.

They came to find out that the woman's name was Margalida, wife to the chef. They thanked her and her husband profusely for the incredible lunch, and soon made their way back to the inn. It was surprisingly quiet midday, and just as they thought they were alone in the building, they heard a symphony of soft snores from one of the rooms which housed a group of travelers. It was time for the town to take a mid day *siesta*, they realized, which sounded delightful to the tired, full girls. Retiring to their rooms to join in on the tradition, they soon nodded off.

Their horses loaded, Daví feeling much improved, and new dresses finished for the girls, the group was ready to continue their journey. After eating just about every meal the past few days at the local tavern, Aurelia and Tess said farewell to Margalida, tipping her and her husband for their cooking talents with two gold doblas. Initially, she declined out of pride, but Aurelia closed the coins in her hand with a smile, insisting the gesture. Sometimes subconsciously, Aurelia gave a little extra to the kind people she came across on her journey through time.

Tess and Aurelia began walking back towards the horses, where Daví would be waiting, when suddenly the sounds stopped. Aurelia looked around to see the entire town stopped around her. It had happened again. Where the merchants' calls once scratched her ears, was silence. The shifting trees nearby stood still as a glass lake, the wind held everything in place like an invisible hand. The horses were more like stuffed statues in a history museum than alive and rearing to go. Aurelia turned to Tess, her vibrant friend, who had now paused midwalk, about to say something.

What was this?

Aurelia panicked. It had happened once before in France, almost passed off in her mind like a dream or delusion - but this was no hallucination. Time had stopped again, and she was the only one aware of it.

"Tess?" Aurelia called, waving her hands in front of her face to see if she moved. She didn't. "Can you hear me?" Tess was paralyzed in a fragment of a moment.

Aurelia walked around, almost as if to find something that could end this nightmare, but she had no idea what to look for. Was it somehow her fault? Was her theory right? Had she triggered the time travel technology in her body somehow? But if so, how? She had been calm, her emotions stable. They were only walking.

As if an ice pick lurched into her bicep, a sharp pain debilitated Aurelia out of nowhere. What was wrong? She turned around, as if expecting to see someone who had inflicted her injury, but she was alone. She shimmied her sleeve up over the painful spot to reveal her bare skin, but absolutely nothing was there. She was unharmed. Why had she felt such a strong, sudden pain?

Around her, as if watching a picture fade, the colors of the town began to drain from view. The townspeople sucked of their bright, rosy cheeks, the sky's bright cobalt blue waining to a whitish blue. What was happening? It was as if life itself was being wrung out of the town like water in a sponge.

"STOP!" Aurelia screamed into the empty air. She rushed back to Tess, "WAKE UP!"

Shaking her shoulders, Tess resumed her sentence, stunned that Aurelia was now suddenly in front of her, shaking her body, "-ke that... How did you...? Weren't you just behind me?"

She was awake. Tess was OK. But time around them continued to stand still. Somehow, touching Tess had caused her to enter this moment between moments with Aurelia.

"Why... why is everything...stopped?" somehow Tess's voice seemed muted, as if the sound wasn't quite strong enough to reach Aurelia's ears.

"I don't know," Aurelia whimpered.

What if this was permanent? What if time never started again? It seemed like Tess's vibrant color had returned, gently fading back from sepia, however, the surroundings still seemed devoid of life.

Tess began hyperventilating, "This... something's wrong. It's hard to breathe..." Tess's dark skin began to turn a grayish color - somehow she wasn't getting enough oxygen.

"What? What do I do?"

Tess began to clutch her chest, gasping for air.

The molecules around them were still stopped in time, including the oxygen - now not as easily assimilated into her lungs and skin. Although the constant gasping helped, her body wasn't strong enough to pull the molecules frozen in time throughout her bloodstream, in a sense, starving her body of air.

"TESS?"

"Can't... breathe... help..." Tess said between wheezes. She collapsed onto the dirt, struggling to find air.

Aurelia sat down next to her on the ground, what could she do? She didn't know how to perform CPR, didn't know what was causing time to stop, and didn't know why Tess couldn't breathe. Aurelia started sobbing as her friend passed out. Catching her and placing her head gently on the ground, Aurelia began trying CPR to keep Tess breathing. Pushing the breath into her lungs, her face drenched in tears. Why had this happened? What had happened? Tess couldn't die. This couldn't be happening.

Shaking, Aurelia pulled back from Tess, nothing was working. Somehow, she knew she was still alive, although it was fleeting.

If Aurelia could indeed use a portal without an Okliot, maybe there was something she could do to start time again. Maybe.

A complete shot in the dark, Aurelia sat back and closed her eyes. Placing her hands on the dirt to ground herself, she attempted to go inwards. She began to imagine the world around her - the man selling carved wooden toys to her left, the pregnant woman just down the street, watching her young toddlers play, the small bird above her sitting in the olive tree, the dust about to rise from underneath a horse's hoof. Somehow, they were all connected. She imagined the outskirts of town, frozen rivers, flowing into an endless ocean that stretched around the earth like a blanket. Cities, countries and continents all paling in comparison to the immense water teeming with life. Almost like seeing Earth from space, everything began to zoom out, and suddenly she could envision the other planets in the solar system, all of them frozen in time.

Overwhelmed by this vision, Aurelia brought her thoughts back to the town. Back to Tess, and Daví, and Margalida. Back to the weathered old innkeeper, and the drunkards in the tavern. Back to their horses, Pablo, Mincho and Dionysius. She imagined the sounds filling her ears once again, the movement resuming. The people moving, walking, breathing. The sun shining.

This was her last resort. She prayed, begging for her vision to become reality. Time had to start again.

As if someone had heard her prayer, the town exploded back to life, the sounds and light overpowering and hostile, like a band all tuning their instruments at once.

Aurelia leapt to Tess's side, and began shaking her in the hopes she would wake up. Taking her fingers, she felt her neck for a pulse. It was there, but weak.

"Tess! Wake up, Tess!" by now, people around them had gathered and quieted out of respect, thinking the girl was dead. "TESS!" Aurelia screamed.

Tess gasped for air, coughing from the sudden onslaught of

oxygen. Her eyes popped open, her vision blurry and unfocused.

“What happened?”

“You passed out. You’re OK. You’re OK,” Aurelia hugged her friend on the ground, both of them shaking from the moment.

“Time was... everything was...”

“I know. I know,” Aurelia hushed, tempering their conversation just in case someone spoke English, since most of the townspeople around them were still listening nearby.

“It was like I was breathing underwater, like the air was liquid,” Tess whispered. “Why did that happen? And how did everything start again?”

“I... I don’t know.”

CHAPTER 22

PROMISES

The weary travelers stopped off in Toulouse to speak to Aurelia's old friends at court, in her once home, the *Château Narbonnaise*. They got the scoop on everything that had gone down the past few years. Apparently, the Dauphin Louis had become an even greater prude, constantly plotting against his father, King Charles VII. He had been sent away from his father to his own Province of Dauphiné, shortly after the death of his first wife.

News had just spread that the Dauphin Louis XI had gone against the wishes of the court and married again - this time to the eight-year-old Charlotte of Savoy. To Tess and Aurelia, that news seemed idiotic - it couldn't possibly be true, could it? But, times were different in the Middle Ages, marriages were less for love, than strategic alliances and economic gain. Apparently, the marriage would only be consummated once Charlotte came of age. But, with the lifespan of the average bloke here hardly reaching forty or fifty - that is *if* you were one of the lucky few to survive past childhood, you had to get on with things quickly if you wanted to procreate and create an heir.

In the Hundred Years' War, it seemed hopeful that the conflict between France and England was finally seeing the French victorious, although it was hard to tell definitively. Each battle brought destruction on both sides, not only for the soldiers, but to the towns nearby - each town pillaged from the entitled soldiers, who carried disease and death with them. The country was tired, fatigued not only from war, but from the harshness of life.

In other news, supposedly the Grand Duchess Natalia had been back in Toulouse for a while, and recently this month, journeyed back to Paris, where she was engaged to be wed to an older Nobleman. After Aurelia had mysteriously vanished years ago, Natalia faced the wrath of the heartbroken Dauphin Louis, who just as expected, cast her from court onto the streets. News of Natalia's expulsion from court reached one of her former private tutors in Toulouse. He had her summoned and promptly took her in, resuming her place in court and private studies with the professor and his peers.

Supposedly, as the years passed, Natalia had grown to be a whip smart, piercing brunette with deep almond eyes, who captured the heart of every man studying at the Toulouse College, where she frequented with her custodian, the professor. News of her beauty began to spread like a tree sowing seeds in spring throughout Christendom, and soon a marriage proposal was set between the 14-year-old Natalia and a visiting Lord, who had offered a decent sum to the professor for the arrangement.

Aurelia nearly collapsed with worry over what the young girl had gone through because of her. She could barely begin to imagine what it had been like - still a child, all alone, cast from the palace to beg for food on the streets. She wished she could thank the professor that had taken her under his wing, but he had apparently traveled to Paris with her for the wedding. Natalia was meant to marry in a week.

Although they wished to rest and regroup, they couldn't let Natalia marry. She was too young, too innocent, to be thrust into marriage, especially to a middle aged nobleman. It was wrong. Plus, it was Aurelia's fault, she convinced herself. It would be a long, difficult ride to make the normally two week trip to Paris in only one week, but Tess and Daví agreed to help Aurelia in her quest.

Spending a single night in Toulouse, and waking before dawn, they continued their journey to Paris.

The smell of sweet bread filled the village that they rode through. Stopping for a brief time to load themselves up on food and also feed the exhausted horses, they were about a two days ride from the palace in Paris.

Aurelia looked around at the merchants' stands. She had been to countless markets over the past year, but none were quite like this one. Quaint, unassuming, yet filled with expensive tastes and rare treats. The smell of cinnamon found its way to Aurelia's nose, and she followed it to a stand just steps away. Here, warm cinnamon apple pies were placed on a table. It was the first time she had seen one since Johanna's recipe. Gasping for breath, her memories overwhelmed her. Amsterdam. The rain. The blood. The sound of the gunshot. Will.

Collapsing to her knees in shock, she held back tears.

"What's wrong? Moya?" Tess questioned, calling Aurelia by her nickname, and rushing to her side.

The sound of Tess's voice barely reached Aurelia's ears. Tess's words were muted and replaced by the ringing of the gunshot in Aurelia's memory. What had her life become?

Almost as if the floodgates had opened, she thought of everyone she missed - most of them gone permanently. Will, her greatest love, her small, dwindling family - her nana, papa, mom and dad. Her friends in 2019. All she wanted was to see them all again. She knew Will would be waiting for her somewhere. But how could she endanger him again? She realized that in trying to protect Will, she had in turn become close to more people that could get hurt. Natalia, Tess, Daví. Why did she keep caring for people, when she knew she would have to eventually distance herself from them, to keep them safe?

A few panic attacks like this had ensued in the past year, but none quite as debilitating as this one. It felt as if the air had been sucked out of her lungs, the sobs overwhelming.

Tess crouched on the ground to hold Aurelia's head, hoping to soothe her, but in truth she didn't know why she was so upset, so there wasn't much she could say that would help. Catching her breath, the merchant of the pie stand shooed them away for loitering, assuming they were begging for scraps.

"*Psss - du vent !*" the street vendor said to them, telling them to scram.

"Are you OK?" Tess asked, knowing she wasn't, holding up her friend with an arm under her shoulders.

Aurelia nodded and forced herself to smile through tear stained cheeks. She had to be OK.

The Grand Duchess Natalia readied herself for her wedding, with a handmaiden she knew at the *Château de Vincennes*. She would be married to Lord John of Luxembourg, apparently in his twenties or thirties, although to the 14-year-old Natalia, he seemed like a grandpa. Her light blue gown, embroidered with browns and golds, suited her white skin tone with the subtlety of nobility. She wished her father could've seen her in her wedding gown, finally a true woman.

Her small tiara from Russia was pinned in her hair, at this point her only remaining token from home. Her bosom laced, her hair loosely braided, she was ready. They walked out of the castle, hopping atop their horses. Natalia and her handmaiden would now make their way to the church, *Église des Billettes*, situated about seven kilometers away. Just a few blocks away from the Château de Vincennes, a familiar face in town stopped her in her tracks.

"Aure- Isabelle?" she gasped - it wasn't possible - was it?

Breaking from the scenery of commoners and merchants was Aurelia, wearing an adorned, deep purple gown, and her red ruby necklace upon her neck that Natalia remembered the Dauphin Louis had given her. Natalia jumped from her horse, for the moment completely forgetting about getting to the church for her impending wedding.

"Nat?" Aurelia flung herself at the duchess, embracing her in a long awaited hug. "I'm so sorry."

Natalia broke into tears, holding her friend, "Why did you leave me?" she sobbed, the harsh memories flooding in of the court casting her out like a rat in a kitchen, almost seven years ago.

"I didn't mean to, Nat. I promise... I'm sorry..." Aurelia cried, pulling away gently and grasping her shoulders to look at Natalia, now almost five feet tall, with the hints of womanhood showing through. "You're so beautiful..."

Natalia giggled through tears, "I'm to be married," she sniffled.

"I heard... Do you want to marry him?"

Natalia paused, "It has been my dream to one day marry. So yes. I suppose so."

Her Russian accent had almost all but disappeared, now replaced by a French one.

Aurelia nodded, "Do you love him?"

"I'm not supposed to love him. He's only to be my husband."

"No, no," Aurelia shook her head, "that's not how it should be. You should marry the person that you think of every time you're emotional. Someone you want to share every good or bad moment with. Not out of obligation... out of longing... out of love."

"I want to find someone like you did - you know I have always wanted that," Natalia straightened herself, "but, you're just lucky. It's not like that for me. And I've already been betrothed. I can't back out of a promise. I have nowhere else to go."

Stepping from behind Aurelia, a dark beauty wearing a deep blue gown dripping with elegance joined the conversation, "We can take you to the future," Tess said, a glimmer of mischief hidden in her voice.

CHAPTER 23

THE KING

"We don't know that it'll work, Tess. I'm still not even sure how to travel on my own, let alone take someone with me!" Aurelia whispered to Tess as they trailed behind Natalia and her handmaiden on horseback, with Daví leading their tired horses without riders.

Natalia had lied to her handmaiden and said she had forgotten something crucial to the wedding in the castle, so now they all walked towards the portal hidden in a stairwell in the center of the *Château De Vincennes*, that Aurelia had used seven years ago, about a half-mile away.

Aurelia continued, "And what about Daví? Do we bring him too? I know you love him-"

"Pfft. I do not!" Tess exclaimed vehemently.

"Really?"

"Trust me, if it *was* love, I would've told him about who we were. I could never keep secrets like that from someone I'm close to."

A pang of guilt hit Aurelia like a brick - she still hadn't revealed who she was to Tess; not the fact that she was on the run, not Will, not where, or rather *when*, she was from, not even her true name. Tess still knew her as Miana from B-udo.

"So, you're just gonna say goodbye... and that's it? You never see him again? You're OK with that?" Aurelia pried - she could never be so quick to give her heart away.

"I mean, I haven't really thought about it. He's a permanent. It was just a fling. He's not '*the one*', you know?" Tess explained flippantly. "I always knew it had to end, at some point."

"Oh. Yeah, no, I get it, I guess I just read it wrong between you two."

"Don't get me wrong - he's *hot*. If he wasn't a permanent, maybe things would be different - but I can't see myself settling with *one of them*. They're all so... uncivilized."

"Who... the permanents?" Tess nodded, and Aurelia continued.

"You know - they're not all bad... they get much better in time - it's just... the Middle Ages were very... dirty," it was strange for Aurelia to be referring to herself in third person, after all, she herself *was* a permanent.

"No... I've seen the history. They're all this way, in their own right. I mean, take the war in the 2000s."

"Wait, 2000s? Which one?"

That was Aurelia's time. A war was going to happen?

"Ha. Right? Too many conflicts to count," Tess mistook her legitimate question for sarcasm. "We're elite, Miana. Sure - we can have a little fun in the past, but it's not like we would settle down here. Not when we have somewhere so advanced and peaceful as our home. The permanents here... they're all such dullards. Really just... narrow-minded, barbarous people."

This didn't sound like the same Tess that Aurelia had met in London of 1993. That girl hated B-udo. She definitely didn't think it was "peaceful" - for some reason, Tess hadn't been "home" in years, and she certainly didn't refer to the permanents as a people so vile. Aurelia didn't think the people here were *that* harsh and terrible.

Sure, things were harder because of the lack of technology and medicine, and people were weathered from hard work - but they were still people. Like any place or time - some were beautiful souls, and some were cruel. But, their trip across Spain and France had been good, hadn't it? Why did Tess have such strong, negative views about the people in the past? And what had changed so drastically for her in the future?

"Sorry, Maya."

"Huh?" Aurelia said, breaking her spinning thoughts.

"I know you care about Natalia. And she's a permanent, right? I shouldn't have said that about them."

"Thank you..." Aurelia continued, "I know this is your first trip, and there have been some challenges we've had to overcome, but there's still a lot more amazing culture in this world for you to see. And the people out there - they may speak a different language, or have different values, education, or privilege than us, but really we're all the same. Don't just focus on the ugly personalities - focus on the beauty all around us here... like... Margalida. She was kind, and generous, and I think she and her husband might've been the best chefs I've ever met."

Tess laughed, "That food was pretty amazing, I'm not gonna

lie. But her life is so... small. How can you even compare her to us?"

"Her life is just as important as ours. Don't you see? Just because we're lucky enough to be born in the future, doesn't make us better than her, or anyone. And you don't know the impact that one person can have on the world. It only takes one person to spark a revolution, or make peace with an enemy. And who knows the ripple effects that one person can make that have shaped the future to be what it is? For all we know, Margalida could be your distant ancestor, and if her life didn't exist - you might not be here either."

"I know... I guess it's just... hard, to see people waste their lives on such shitty things. Like, who would actually want to be a swineherd or shoe shiner?"

Aurelia chuckled, it definitely seemed like Tess never had to work a crappy job like everyone Aurelia knew in 2019, including herself.

"Can I ask you a question?" Aurelia slowed to a stop, as their group in front of them continued.

"Yeah. Of course," Tess replied, stopping with her.

"Look around us," the dirt road swarmed with people of all statures. Most of them worn from an already long day, despite it only being the early afternoon. "What do you see?" Aurelia asked.

"Um... a lot of tired people."

"OK..." Aurelia chuckled, she could see that part, although that was not her only perception of the town. "Do they look happy?"

Tess studied their faces. Despite the constant work, most of them smiled at each other in passing, and little moments shared seemed to brighten their day. Her eyes wandered to the side of a building, where a young, skinny mother, covered in ash and soot, openly breastfed her baby. As the harsh town buzzed around her, she was focused solely on her child, with a bright smile across her face.

"...Yes. Most of them seem happy," Tess confessed.

"Sure - they're naive and ignorant about the things that we have in life - but they make the best of what they're given. No matter the time or place, at the end of the night, humans come together to eat, and drink, and toast. They have friends, and children - they work hard for their home and country. They play music, create art, play games and make love. Even though people here are plagued with sicknesses and uncertainties - they still smile and love their life. In French, they have a saying, '*La vie est faite de petits bonheurs,*' which means 'life is full of the little pleasures'. That is why we, *manger bien, rier souvent, et aimer beaucoup...* Eat well, laugh often and love a lot. How is that any different than you and I? How are we any better than them?"

Tess's nostrils flared with emotion. She knew she was right. Why had she been so cruel?

"We're not. Better than them," she wiped a tear out of the inside of her eye. "I guess I didn't think about how hard they have it in the past... maybe I've been judging them too harshly. But, you're right, you can't choose where or when you were born... Thank you."

"For what?"

"For being so wise and putting up with my shit."

Aurelia laughed, putting her arm through Tess's, "I would put up with your shit any day."

"I'm really glad I met you, Miana."

A wave of guilt overwhelming, she couldn't keep up the ruse a second longer. She missed hearing the sound of her name out loud.

"Tess? I have to tell you a secret. But you can't ask why I kept it from you... it's too... complicated and... dangerous. And you can't tell anyone. But, I just can't keep lying to you about it."

"Uhhh... OK...? What is it?"

"My name isn't Miana. It's Aurelia Quinn."

Tess gently punched her shoulder, "Why would you lie about that, silly?" Aurelia chuckled nervously, she had good reason. "Of course I'll keep your secret! Besides, who am I gonna tell? It's nice to finally meet you, Aurelia."

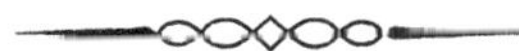

Aurelia couldn't believe how close she had become to her horse, Dionysius. His regal, fortified, yet gentle disposition had created an unbreakable bond between them. He was the most stunning horse Aurelia had ever seen, with his long, coal black mane and grey body - and she was sure she'd never have another horse like him. He had made the long, arduous journey across Spain seem easy. Most horses would have certainly grown lame or tiresome after the onerous ride, and needed to be traded to continue the rest of the distance - but their horses had somehow been raised with an intense fighting spirit and desire to please, and had made it all the way to the *Château de Vincennes*, on the edge of Paris.

She had already patted Pablo and Mincho goodbye, but now that they had finally arrived outside the majestic castle, it was time to part with her traveling companion. Saying goodbye to Dionysius proved harder than she ever thought. Whispering "I love you", and giving him a final kiss on the side of his face, she sadly handed the reins to Daví. She hated goodbyes.

She kissed Daví's cheeks twice, and tearfully said goodbye to him as well. About to turn and follow Natalia and Tess, she remembered the coins she still held in her satchel. Pulling out the black bag filled with gold, she placed it lovingly in her friend Daví's hand. Although confused, he hesitantly accepted the gift. She knew that amount of money would allow him and his future family to live comfortably for a long time.

Tess didn't feel the same level of attachment and empathy that Aurelia did. It was obvious from the surprisingly nonchalant goodbye to her lover, Daví. But perhaps the difference between them was, for Aurelia, each one of her travels in time had become her new home. For Tess, she always had somewhere to go back to. Aurelia could never go back to her family in 2019, so each new companion became a part of her new family, in a sense.

The guards allowed them passage into the palace with Natalia's handmaiden explaining that they had guests. Walking into the familiar halls of the *Château de Vincennes*, the girls made their way towards the stairwell, unassumingly. Tess was in awe at the gorgeous architecture surrounding them - it was Tess's first time inside of a castle.

Turning a corner, they were stunned that they nearly ran into King Charles VII, The Dauphin Louis's father. He was actually in the castle? Aurelia had only met him once, briefly, with Louis. Curtsying into a deep seat, they profusely apologized for being in the way and stepped to the side. Not acknowledging them, he continued on his way with his crowd of people, but slowed to a stop to look at Aurelia.

"*Oú as-tu eu ça ?*" the king asked in French, pointing to her red ruby necklace hanging from her neck, asking where she got it.

"*C'était un cadeau, votre altesse royale,*" it was a gift, she told him, keeping her head slung low when addressing him.

"*Tu es une des maîtresses de Louis ?*" she was one of Louis's mistresses? She nodded. That was all she had become here. He lifted her chin, inspecting her features. He could see why his son liked her, and who wouldn't? She was stunning. "*Je comprends pourquoi vous l'intéréssez.*"

Aurelia gently scoffed at his remark, humbly disregarding his complement, "*Non, je ne sais pas, Votre Majesté.*" No, I don't think so, Your Majesty, she said.

His eyes slim, he released her chin.

"*Tu sais que Louis n'est pas là ? Je l'ai envoyé au Sud,*" did she know that Louis was not here?

"*Oui, Votre Majesté,*" yes, she knew Louis was not there.

Then why was she not with him? Why was she here? "*Alors, pourquoi tu n'es pas avec lui ?*"

Aurelia stumbling to find the words, Natalia jumped in, "*Pardonnez-moi, votre altesse royale. Dame* Isabelle *est ici pour assister à mon mariage aujourd'hui,*" The Lady Isabelle, as Aurelia was known here, was here for Natalia's wedding, she explained.

"*Vous êtes Isabelle ?*" she was the infamous Isabelle, the king asked? "*Mon fils a dit que tu étais l'amour de sa vie. Après l'avoir quitté, il était misérable pendant des mois,*" Louis told his father that she was the love of his life and her leaving really left him miserable for months? Wasn't she just one of many mistresses? "*Tu vas aller vers le dauphin dés maintenant, comme une offre de paix de ma part,*" the king instantly concocted an idea; He would send Aurelia to Louis as a peace offering between him and his son, "*Peut-être qu'il regrettera d'avoir épousé* Charlotte," he laughed, his son would surely regret marrying the 8-year-old Charlotte Of Savoy when he saw his love, Isabelle, again. "*Vous repartez immédiatement,*" he ordered her to leave at once to go to the Dauphin Louis.

But Aurelia couldn't leave the castle - she had to get to the portal with her friends, "*Votre Majesté... je ne peux pas... je dois rester avec La Grande Duchesse* Natalia... *pour son mariage...*" she fibbed about the importance that she had to attend Natalia's wedding.

Louis had spoken to his father about how the Dame Isabelle disappeared on him and had a strong mind of her own - but how dare she question a direct order of the king?

"*Il m'a dit que vous étiez volage. Vous n'avez rien d'autre à faire que ce que votre roi vous dit de faire,*" he would see to it that she would get to Louis. "*Gardes ! Accompagnez-la jusqu'au Dauphin Louis à Grenoble. Partez maintenant,*" he instructed his guards to accompany her to his son in Grenoble.

Two guards stepped forward and grabbed Aurelia's slender arms. They would take her to Louis by force, if necessary.

"*Non ! S'il vous plaît, Votre Majesté !*" No, please, Your Majesty, she said.

What could she do? The stairwell was just down the hall. They were so close!

"*Laissez moi au moins offrir un cadeau de mariage à La Grande-Duchesse* Natalia !" she lied to the king, begging him to let her at least give the grand duchess her wedding gift. Perhaps she could convince them to let her go upstairs once more. "*C'est seulement à l'étage ! S'il vous plaît, Votre Majesté très Chrétienne,*" it was only upstairs, she lied, tugging on his religious heartstrings.

It did seem sad that the duchess would not get her wedding gift, Charles thought, and he didn't want to send his olive branch to his son in a foul mood. He motioned to his guards to ease their grip on her arms, and they released her.

"*Bon. Vous pouvez le lui donner, puis partir,*" she could go upstairs to give her wedding gift to Natalia, then she would leave.

"*Merci ! Merci, Votre Excellence ! Vous êtes le plus généreux !*" she thanked him profusely for his generosity.

"*...Dites à mon fils... qu'il me manque,*" the king told Aurelia to tell his son that he missed him.

"*Je n'y manquerai pas,*" she promised, although she knew she wouldn't be able to tell him.

The king walked off, and the girls all curtseyed as he passed. The guards stayed close to Aurelia, if indeed she was a deserter, as the king had implied, they would keep close watch of her. The girls began walking towards the stairwell, staying close.

"Get your Okliot out now," Aurelia whispered to Tess, who promptly slipped it out of her satchel, Tess's eyebrows furrowed.

"We only have one Okliot, Aurelia. Will you be able to get Natalia through too?"

Aurelia wasn't sure. If indeed their theory was right, that Aurelia didn't need an Okliot to travel through a portal - maybe she could get Natalia through as well. It was a risk that could very well fail, but all she knew was that they had to at least try to escape.

Natalia told her handmaiden to stay downstairs, promising they would only be a minute upstairs, "*Reste ici, Jeanette, nous serons de retour dans une minute.*"

They reached the stairwell. It was time.

"Hold my hand tight, Nat. Don't let go," Aurelia whispered.

The girls stopped at the stairway, nervous about whether or not the portal would work. If it didn't, the guards would take Aurelia to Louis, Natalia would be married into a loveless marriage, and Tess would be alone, months away from the nearest portal, with their horses and all of their money already given to Daví, who was probably already gone. The portal *had* to work.

"*Après vous,* Tess," Aurelia motioned for Tess to go first, a shakiness building in her voice.

Tess nodded, and began walking up the winding stone stairwell. Aurelia held Natalia's hand and followed closely behind Tess. This had to work. The guards were mere steps behind them. One wrong move and they could grab Aurelia, maybe keeping her and Natalia from traveling. They kept walking up the stairs. Why was nothing happening? Then she remembered her theory. She had to tap into her emotions. She thought of Johanna. The sight of the red rain in the street. She thought of the fear of losing Will. Of the sadness she had felt when he told her she could never go home. The pain building, somehow she could tell it was working. Her stomach dropped like she was on a roller coaster, her palms sweating. She had to keep going. She thought of the heartbreak and misery she was in the last time she used this portal - she had just left dinner with the dauphin. He had slapped her. She thought of the harsh ceremonies she had witnessed in Ancient Mexico - the sacrifice of the jaguar - the... human sacrifice. The empathetic pain she had felt for all of the deaths she had witnessed. She thought of Tess when time had stopped in the town of Cuenca. Tess had almost died.

It was working, the stone walls began to blur and morph. The guards behind them began to yell at the disappearing girls. How were they vanishing into thin air? It shouldn't be possible. They must be witches. They had to tell the king. The guards ran back down, partially in fear, and partially to get aid to stop the witches.

The girls increased their speed, running up the stairs as the portal activated. Natalia looked around in wonder at the magical walls. She hadn't seen what it was like to travel in a portal - the first time she traveled, she was thrust back in time from the 1700s, falling down the staircase with Aurelia, suddenly in a new location. But now, she marveled at the dynamic, changing surroundings - it was truly incredible.

Aurelia looked ahead at Tess, who somehow looked like she was fading from view. Was the portal taking her somewhere else?

"Tess! Grab my hand!" Aurelia screamed at the disappearing girl.

Tess looked back, her image a faded, see-through mirage. Somehow she was traveling somewhere different than Aurelia and Natalia, or perhaps not at all. The portal wasn't stable. She reached for Aurelia's hand, but her hand passed through like a ghost.

"What do I do?" she screamed, but the sound barely breached

the invisible barrier between them.

Aurelia focused her energy. They had to stay together. Reaching for Tess with determination, her hand grasped Tess's. The surroundings around Aurelia and Natalia shifted again, combining with Tess's.

Aurelia was learning. She could somehow control this, it seemed. Keeping a firm grip, they all continued running up - now single file in a tightly wound, black metal, circular staircase. Aurelia was exhausted. She hadn't traveled in months. She stopped for a moment, the girls stopping with her.

"Are you OK?" Natalia asked Aurelia, noticing how winded she was.

Aurelia nodded, a feeling of a lurching exhaustion overwhelming her. Maybe it was so severe this time because she had traveled with an extra person, Natalia. Before, it had just been herself traveling - and even then, it was tiresome to travel.

"Aren't you guys tired from that?" Aurelia asked.

"No, not really," Tess replied spiritedly.

"OK. I'm fine, let's keep going," Aurelia continued up, really not fine, but insistent to keep moving - although this time only walking, not running.

The materials ever-changing around them, the staircase suddenly settled on an all white - almost cloud like surface. The stairs hard, yet wispy with fog. The fresco painted walls disappeared, as if a gust of wind blew their particles into space, and it was replaced by a pure, brightly lit white that stretched as far as the eye could see. The only variance in the engulfing, never-ending white were the stairs - a material that seemed impossible. It was like standing on a cloud in the shape of a straight staircase leading up.

What kind of place was this? When were they? Was this the future, or the distant past?

They reached a floating door with no handle at the top of the staircase, apparently attached to nothing but the white air around them. Looking behind them where they had just come from, the rest of the stairs had faded from view, now replaced by white. It was calming, yet terrifying. Like standing on a cloud above a white washed earth.

"Did we die?" Natalia asked, tears in her eyes.

"What? No! This is... normal! Right, Miana - I mean... Aurelia? I'm sure this happens all the time," Tess backpedaled.

It was most certainly not normal. Aurelia had never seen anything like this in all of her travels. Something was wrong. They needed to get out. But there was only one place to go. The floating door.

Back in 1451 France, the guards responsible for taking Dame Isabelle to the Dauphin Louis XI hurried to King Charles VII, bursting into his chambers with an angst about themselves.

"*Sorcières ! Ce sont des sorcières, Votre Majesté !*" one of the guards breathlessly shook, bowing quickly and telling their king that they had come across witches.

"*Qui ?*" the king said, hastily standing from his desk. Who were they?

"*Dame* Isabelle, *La Grande Duchesse* Natalia Petrovna, *et la Dame d'Isabelle ! Ils ont utilisé la sorcellerie pour nous échapper !*" the guards dropped to their knees, begging for forgiveness for letting the witches escape, "*Pardonnez-nous, mon roi.*"

This was very bad. Not one, but *three*, sorcerers within the castle's walls? And one of them had bewitched his son, the Dauphin Louis XI. It was no wonder he had been so tormented with his love for the Lady Isabelle - he was under her witch's spell. If news spread that his heir had been manipulated by a witch - the entire monarchy could be compromised.

"*À qui avez-vous parlé de ça ?*" who had they already told about this?

They hadn't told a soul, "*À personne, seulement toi.*"

"*Bon,*" Charles breathlessly rolled the situation over in his mind. No one else knew. He could contain this. "*Nous devons effacer les archives royales de toute mention de Dame* Isabelle *ou de La Grande-Duchesse* Natalia Petrovna," they would expunge all of the court records that mentioned they had ever broken bread with the girls. They would tell no one. "*Vous ne raconterez à personne ce que vous avez vu. Comprenez vous ?*" would the guards be sworn to secrecy?

"*Oui,*" they answered in unison.

"*Elles sont, à partir d'aujourd'hui, ennemis de la Couronne,*" from this day forward, the "witches" Aurelia and Natalia, were enemies of the French crown.

CHAPTER 24

SPACE BETWEEN TIME

The floating white door with no handle loomed above the girls. With the staircase behind them mostly vanished, there was nowhere else to go but in. Letting go of Natalia and Tess's hands, since they seemed to be in a stable part of the portal, Aurelia approached the ominous door. She attempted to push it, but it was securely locked. Reaching where a handle should be for no reason, almost as if by muscle memory, her hands settled on a cold metal object. Gasping at the touch, she looked to see what her hand had found, but it seemed to be wrapped around air. There wasn't a handle there, but why could she feel one? How had she known that there would be a door handle there? Long and smooth, she pushed the invisible handle down, and the door clicked open.

Inside was blackness. Devoid of any light, the exact opposite of the great expanse of the lit, white, cloudy stairway they now stood in. It was almost as if the darkness slowly began to suck the lightness into its void, consuming it hungrily for itself.

Aurelia looked back at her terrified friends.

'What have I gotten them into now?' she asked herself.

Where were they? What was this?

The darkness was monstrously scary, but for some reason it drew her in like a siren. Her soul told her it was OK, although her head filled her with logic to be afraid of an endless dark void. But something was nagging at her - telling her this was a safe place for her. Her hands shaking, she stepped inside the darkness.

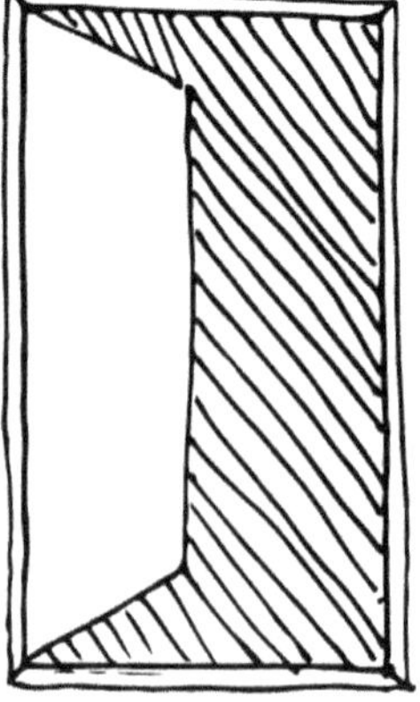

Expecting there to be a surface to step on, her foot plummeted into nothingness, and she began to fall - no, spin - no, float. It seemed like gravity was missing here. She spun into the darkness, screaming, her arms flailing to try and stop herself. But she was disoriented. Everything was dark, except for the white door behind her that appeared in her vision on every spin, where she could see Tess and Natalia standing, calling for her frantically as she disappeared into the darkness.

It felt as if she was in the vacuum of space - that is, if space was a breathable place that had been sucked dry of any starlight. Everything was black around her, consuming her into its emptiness. Was this purgatory? Was this her punishment for putting her friends in danger? Would she eternally be forced to spin in darkness, alone?

Pulling herself from the negative, dark thoughts that overwhelmed her psyche, she took a deep breath. This wasn't that. Feeling her heart beating in her throat from stress, she knew that they were all still very much alive. She wasn't some helpless girl. She had been so strong in every time she'd accidentally traveled to - holding her own. Now she knew definitively that she could travel without an Okliot. She had learned so much already, touched so many lives. But she still had a lot to do in this life. She wouldn't let this beat her. Aurelia Quinn was a fighter. She could figure this out.

Settling her mind, she reached her arm out instinctively, hoping to find something in the darkness to grasp. After a few seconds, what felt like a string, lightly brushed her finger, and she excitedly reached her pinky around it, barely grabbing it before she spun away from it and it slipped from her fingers. But something had happened when she touched it - a pulse of golden light. From that brief pulse, she could see that the string continued on through the darkness. She could grab it on her next spin. Coming around, she flung her body at the string, grasping it with her left hand and holding tightly. She hoped it would hold her - it seemed more delicate than a strand of hair.

Her body whipped to a stop as she held fast to the string. Now, the glowing golden light emanated from the string, lighting up the surroundings like a gorgeous 3D spider web that expanded as far as the eye could see. Growing like water trickling down a dry creek bed, the sparkling gold traced its way around what looked like photographs - but they couldn't be. Each photo sprung to life, suddenly moving as if life had returned to them and she was now watching a video.

She looked back at the white door in the far distance - she could still see two distinct figures standing waiting for her. She had to get back to them, but this magical place suddenly held her mind from leaving.

Aurelia, still holding the sinew-like string tightly, walked her hands up to the nearest video - it was of an old man sitting in a wheelchair. But it seemed to be like no other video - Aurelia could feel the moment as if she was living it - but not just as him - as the energy that surrounded him, breathing life into every object.

The smells of antiseptic, medicine and mustiness filling the air. The hospital room beeped with his dwindling vitals, and the steady flow of cold oxygen crept into his dry nose. She could tell that the man was thinking about a newspaper article he had just read. She remembered his life to a T - his children, his grandchildren, his pets through the years, his passions and hobbies, his job and education. But in this present moment, he was still, soaking in the bliss of a life well lived, although with a few regrets. He gently looked outside his window, and suddenly the moment stopped. A string of light led from his window to a bird, apparently what the man was looking at outside.

Consumed with intrigue, somehow forgetting about her friends at the white door, she followed the newly emerged string of light that led to the bird. This time, the direction of the bird's moment was reversed in time, flying backwards from its perch on the swaying oak tree. She followed the stream of moving pictures, watching the blue bird's life as it went backwards from adulthood, to taking its first flight. Its mother gently feeding it as a baby, and the eggshell reassembling itself around the tiny bird. Suddenly shifting her attention to the now empty nest, she noticed a string of light coming from it as well.

She grasped the new string in the bird's nest, pulling herself towards the next moment. Here, she could see one of the stick's "life" in reverse. From the moment the expecting mother bird placed it in her nest, to it flying through the air in her mouth, being picked up from where it had fallen on the ground, and then the moment the wind detached the stick from the spruce tree. From here, the tree was alive with golden strings, showing all of the animals, insects, people, and even rocks amidst its roots that it had touched. Everything was connected.

Calling out from a white spec in the distance, she could suddenly hear the sounds of someone yelling, "Aurelia!"

Who was Aurelia, she wondered?

Taking her attention yet again, like a constant lulling temptress drifting her into submission, she focused on the rock in the ground in the moving picture, wrapped in the roots of the tree. Tracing its origins back through time, following the golden, interwoven strings, she could see the day and night cycles pass by as if they were milliseconds. The rock had traveled a long way to eventually be covered underneath the tree in the ground. Washed over by rain and slowly eroded by time, she followed the history of the single rock, she could see how it had journeyed miles to end up in its current spot in the world. Sometimes carried by humans, stepped on by animals, knocked over mountains only to land and shatter. Then finally, the origin of the rock on earth was revealed, when she traced its story to a large asteroid, burning through the atmosphere millions - if not billions of years ago. Tracing back even further, she followed the giant, hurdling asteroid back in time. Its journey through the expanse of space - across the Milky Way, redirecting past planets and stars, being pulled back further and further. It had condensed itself into a large size over the millions of years, as smaller fragments of dust and rock were pulled into its gravity - but in the end, it separated back into atoms. Everything seemed to gather around the tiny fragment of the rock's atoms back in time, as if all of the debris in the universe was once one.

Still holding on to the string, following it deeper and deeper into the void, she reached the end of the delicate golden rope. It couldn't be over. What else was the string supposed to be attached to? There was more - there had to be. It was intoxicating, as if she herself could even feel the emotions of the atoms in the rock, the concept like a drug. She had to learn more - she needed to.

A strong hand on her shoulder shocked her, and she spun to see who or what was touching her. The girl holding her shoulder was a young woman with chocolate skin and a worried expression. She had a deep, royal blue gown on, the fabric floating in midair from the lack of gravity.

"Aurelia? Are you OK?" the girl asked.

Who was this "Aurelia"? Why did the name sound so familiar? It was almost as if the name - and the stranger in front of her - was from a far away dream that she had once had.

Noticing the confused look in Aurelia's eyes, Tess took her hand and looked at her intently.

"It's me, Aurelia. It's Tess. What's wrong? Can you not hear me?"

Tess. The name rung in her head, and she searched for a matching memory - but her mind was overwhelmed after seeing even just an infinitesimal glimpse into the timeline. She knew a girl named Tess. Somehow.

"Talk to me. AURELIA?"

Aurelia couldn't speak. The concept of words seemed so far away. She couldn't remember how to even form the sound in her mouth. How long had she been here, a few years? A few centuries? More?

"We have to get you out of here."

Tess pulled her hand, but Aurelia couldn't leave. No, this was where she belonged, wasn't it? It felt so natural here. She needed to stay.

"Aurelia! Come *on*! Something is seriously wrong with this place, it's doing something to you. We *have* to get out!" should she follow this person? "NOW!"

Something in the back of her mind instinctively told her that this person was safe, what was it? Trusting the stranger, Aurelia let go of her firm grip on the string, instead holding steadily to Tess's shoulder. Tess began moving towards the white door in the distance, hopping her hands across the now dimmed string as they gained speed floating in the dark void.

The door seemed less like it was getting closer, but rather just getting bigger as they approached it. Who was the brunette standing in its frame? Why did she also look so familiar to Aurelia?

Reaching the frame of bright white, Aurelia looked behind her once more. She didn't want to leave. She wanted to soak herself in the moments of time, living them vicariously and watching as they unfolded themselves - each object and living being connected in some way. It was breathtaking. Addictive.

Two pairs of arms pulled her out of the darkness, and suddenly a wash of reality hit her as she collapsed on the white cloudy floor.

Tess. Natalia. And *she* was Aurelia.

Will. Her life in 2019 - growing up with her friends - her family. How had she forgotten herself? Everything that made her, *her* gone from her mind, like waking up from a dream that you soon forget all about, although it's still buried deep in your subconscious.

"Aurelia, can you speak?" Tess gently slapped her cheek as if to wake her. "Come on."

Natalia was sobbing at this point, "What's happened to her? What's wrong?"

"I don't know. It's like she was in a trance or something in there..."

Aurelia rolled onto her back from exhaustion, still speechless. She remembered every memory she had experienced in the void. The man and his life, the bird growing, the tree blooming, the rock traveling across the universe. It warped her mind, the sheer greatness of it all. And that was only a tiny sliver of time. Like a single grain of sand on earth.

"HEY!" Tess screamed at Aurelia, shaking her shoulders.

"I'm... OK..." Aurelia croaked, the experience of how to speak still coming back into her memory.

"Oh my God! What happened? What were you doing in there?" Tess rambled.

"...It's all connected."

"What? What is?"

"...Everything."

The girls sat in the almost heavenly white, misty stairwell for about an hour, readjusting Aurelia back into normalcy. Although she had only been inside the space between time, as they came to refer to the dark void as, for no more than ten minutes, for Aurelia it felt like years. She felt different, changed somehow, more in tune with her surroundings. She couldn't believe how every single thing was connected to the universe in some way. Maybe seeing what she had seen was enlightenment, or an awful curse bestowed upon her. Somehow she had a greater understanding for the way things worked, and getting caught up in the unimportant, trivial things in life seemed so useless now. Human life was too short to wait or to be unhappy.

Thinking of the old man she had seen inside the space between time, she had felt his life as if it were her own. Stuck in a job he hated, being a doctor, he had a realization that he didn't like it halfway through med school. But at that point, he had already invested so much of his time, energy and money into his career, that instead of changing his life's trajectory right then and there, he kept studying, not wanting to be a college dropout. Eventually opening his own orthopedic practice - but still unhappy with his consuming career. He had spent the next forty-six years of his life practicing medicine, until he finally retired. He hated every minute of it. Although his life was happy in other ways, with his family and life outside of his job - he had spent over 112,000 hours - or condensed into the waking hours of the day, 7,500 days - or rather over twenty straight years of his waking life, doing something that made him unhappy. Twenty years out of a life that would end at 87 years old. The man had wasted over twenty-three percent of his precious life following a career that he despised. He could've taken that time to find what truly made him happy, Aurelia thought.

It seemed life's biggest crime - to be unhappy when you have the ability to change it. Sure - there are other things out of people's control, and sometimes you have to do things you hate to survive, but the trick was to make unhappiness a temporary state - not a constant drain.

Aurelia had to live life to the fullest, and experience everything she had dreamed of - be who she wanted to be. She couldn't waste time being scared of the future catching up with her. There was always going to be a reason to be scared - but being unsure of what the future may hold was better than regretting not having lived life to its fullest capacity.

She had to stop fearing what would happen if she let her guards down and jumped headfirst for love. Will knew the risk he took being with Aurelia - yet he still followed her and chose to be by her side through it all. The fragile, glass heart that lets itself love, even with the unceasing fear of being broken, is the bravest heart of all. Understanding her regrets beginning to bubble, she knew she had to go back to Will. How could she not? She loved him, and he loved her. Everything was clear now.

Tess had also seen the photos, connected by the lit golden strings in the space between time, but for some reason hadn't seen or felt them move like Aurelia had. In a way, she wished she had experienced what Aurelia had too - her newfound lease on life was contagious. She seemed different - awakened, lively and at peace, unburdened by her usual demons. But, Tess felt unchanged - Aurelia seemed to be the only one affected by the drug-like experience inside the space between time.

Convincing the girls that she would be fine, Aurelia stood up gently and began to make an escape plan of how they would get out of this strange portal. The stairs still faded into nothingness at the bottom, and at the top, only led to the floating white door. Going back into the space between time wasn't an option anymore, so the only way out had to be back down.

Grasping Tess and Natalia's hands tightly, they began to walk down the stairs. Stopping as they reached the last visible step, Aurelia squeezed her friends hands even tighter. She would either fall into the white nothingness, or perhaps this was another instance of the invisible door handle. Terrified to test her theory, yet confident enough to jump if need be, she alone took the step of trust into oblivion.

Her foot found a step where her eyes couldn't see one, and she laughed in relief. It worked. Still holding hands, Tess and Natalia followed suit, and the three began slowly stepping down the invisible stairs. As they walked, tan painted, fresco walls began to reconstruct around them, particles flying through the air to find their rightful space. The stone stairs began to fade into view, and looking behind them, the endless white had vanished completely, only replaced by the same fresco walls and stone steps all the way up to a corner landing.

Continuing down, initially the stairwell merged into a stopped escalator, then passing the escalator's landing and door, the stairwell turned into a pure grey marble, on the steps and walls. Whenever this was, it seemed high end and very nice - perhaps it would be a good place to stop.

Coming to the darkly stained, pressed bamboo door, they opened it.

CHAPTER 25

THE ATRIUM HOUSE

Tess, Aurelia and Natalia stepped into the dimly lit hallway, not sure what to expect. It was completely empty, and silent. Filled with the same luxury finishings as the stairwell, they followed the marble floor down the hall, where the light grew stronger. Turning a corner, a glass atrium to the left filled the space with light and greenery. A garden, now overgrown, but obviously once beautifully maintained with roses, pink blooming cherry and willow trees, with floor-to-ceiling, black paned windows. To their right was the kitchen, a technologically advanced one, completely clutter free. The marble floors flowed effortlessly into the countertops, and the cabinets were the same dark bamboo as the doors. They were in someone's home. It seemed whoever had designed the house had wanted the materials in each room to match, keeping a similar theme throughout.

"What is this place?" Natalia asked loudly, which garnered a frantic hush from Tess and Aurelia.

"It seems like a house... but we might not be alone," Aurelia explained with a whisper.

"If this is a home - let's find some food - I'm so hungry, Ari!"

"I think that might be the kitchen," Aurelia said, referring to their right.

"*That's* a kitchen? It looks like art," Natalia began walking towards it in search of food.

"Wait..." Tess interrupted, stopping Natalia, "Aurelia's right, we might not be alone"

Aurelia jumped in, "We need to check the rest of the house before we get caught eating someone's food like Goldilocks." Natalia wondered who Goldilocks was, but nodded sadly in agreeance, disappointed that she couldn't eat something right away. "Alright then, let's split up."

The house was completely empty, and perhaps had been for a while. The closets and cabinets were full, but it seemed the people who lived here had left in a rush, as the signs pointed to. A broken suitcase, covered in dust, was sprawled out on an ottoman, unmade beds seemed untouched since the sleepers had frantically jumped from their dreams, and a door was left open to one of the many atriums, causing the inside of the room to now be piled with leaves. They wondered why the family had left. What had happened to cause them to abandon their life here?

Whoever had lived here had great taste, and a lot of money to spend. The house was seemingly never ending, it was so huge. Natalia found an extensive library and lounge, four bedrooms, and a gigantic indoor pool and spa. Aurelia came across the stunning master bedroom, gym, recording studio, private movie theater, arcade, game rooms and even a private bowling alley. Tess discovered four other kids bedrooms, a playroom, traditional dining room, bar, extensive pantries and breakfast room, and finally the center atrium which seemed to be the spot for outdoor entertaining. The rooms were all built in a circular manner surrounding the heart of the home; the kitchen and center atrium. Every atrium in the house had a tinted, fogged plexiglass top to it that blocked the sun and stars from view - perhaps keeping the bugs and outside air out, and just letting the light in. Additionally, the entire house was windowless to the outside, only flooded with light from the inner atriums. Because of that, their surroundings outside of the house were a mystery to them. It was almost designed like a bunker, although not at all claustrophobic or restraining - as it had to be over 30,000 square feet, with soaring ceilings - more so a hotel resort than a house.

It all seemed somewhat more advanced than Aurelia's time, with so many flawless automations and unrecognizable tech, but they couldn't be *that* far ahead in the future from 2019, she thought. Perhaps fifty or a hundred years?

Finally coming back near the kitchen, Aurelia checked another door and found a stunning garage. The sports cars were out of this world - easily a few million dollars worth just sitting in the abandoned garage. There were quite a few different types, only one of them seemed recognizable as a Porsche - perhaps now considered vintage, although it still seemed more advanced than the 2019 models she had seen. The other cars shimmered with a metal material unknown to Aurelia, and the wheels seemed to have holes in them, purposefully.

They had full glass doors, and one of them seemed to be more carriage-like than anything - lacking a driver's seat, more like a kitchenette table inside of a car with a tall roof.

"I think whoever lived here is long gone," Tess said, approaching Aurelia, who closed the garage door.

"Well then, I guess we'll have to enjoy it for them?" Aurelia coyly responded.

Sarcastically, Tess responded, "Ughh... I guess it will do. I mean I'm used to higher standards but I suppose I can compromise, just this once..."

Natalia caught up with Tess and Aurelia back in the kitchen, where the girls had already started cooking. Natalia was completely dumbfounded by the futuristic house. Growing up in the 18th and 15th century, it seemed like everything was new to her here; the style, the advanced technology, the artificial lighting, even the toilets. Luckily, Tess knew how to work the technology that was too advanced for Natalia and Aurelia, although she wondered why Aurelia, being from B-udo herself, was so stumped by it all. Aurelia knew how to manually chop and cook the hydroponically grown, canned vegetables in the pantry, so they worked together to create a meal.

Any ingredients they were missing were easily ordered through the service 美食去 (*Měishí Qù*), roughly translated to "Foody" or "Delicacies To Go". All you had to do was tap the touchscreen device in the pantry, that hung above what looked like a giant glass tube in the floor, and choose your ingredients by scrolling through the photos. They had a similar service in B-udo, where practically anything your heart desired could be delivered straight into your home. Tapping that they wanted filet mignon, within a single minute, three lab grown steaks were whisked through the underground tunnels, straight into the kitchen.

Ordering each ingredient as needed, Aurelia made side recipes of buttered mushrooms with garlic, freshly chopped sautéed spinach, and to start, a light butterhead lettuce salad to aid digestion. Preparing ahead a cheese and fruit plate to finish the meal off, the food would be spectacular. Her unique cooking had influences of her grandfather's cooking that he learned from his Italian-born, New York raised family, Dutch inspired food from her time in Amsterdam with Will, and now all of the influences she had picked up in France and Spain.

Tess focused her energy on cooking the filets perfectly, and for the first time in her life, used a stovetop to cook. Plating the food as Natalia watched them without a clue as to how the girls prepared the food, dinner was served.

"Oh! We need wine!" Aurelia said, placing one of the plates on the dining table in front of the kitchen island.

"There's a cellar down the hall!" Tess recalled.

The girls made their way to the cellar door, a castle-like wood that marked the distinguished feel that was to come. Opening the door, the moody lights dimmed on, illuminating the vintage wines and liquors stacked high in the room. Tess confidently walked inside, starting her search through the bottles for the perfect red. Aurelia joined her, but was stumped on how to read the labels. It seemed every bottle was written in Chinese.

"How can you tell which one will be good?" Aurelia asked Tess, looking at the labels dumbfounded.

"Well it seems like they have them sorted by vintages - the ones at the top are the oldest... so maybe those are the best?"

"You can read Chinese?"

Tess turned to her with a puzzled look, "Can't you?"

Everyone in ZhēnZhū was fluent in Mandarin and English, it was one of the first things you downloaded as a child.

Aurelia chuckled, "No! I wish! Sometimes I think it would be a whole lot easier traveling, if I knew every language."

Something was nagging at Tess, telling her that Aurelia was still hiding something from her. It wasn't apparent in their time in the Middle Ages, but now, coming further along into sophistication, she wondered why Aurelia seemed so surprised by the antiquated technology here.

"You're from ZhēnZhū, right?" asked Tess, directly.

Aurelia turned to her, her forehead crinkling in a lie, "Yeah... of course. Why?"

"Which level did you live on again?"

"Um..."

Wasn't B-udo the level? No, it was the sector. There were other cities on the same level.

"B level - same as you."

"When are you from, Aurelia?" What was Aurelia omitting from her?

"I was born in 43-1," she remembered the year that she and Will had first traveled to. "Why are you asking me these questions, Tess?"

"No reason... I'm just being nosy," Tess bottled up her feelings. It was obvious Aurelia was hiding something, and if she wanted to tell her - she would.

After a few days of throughly enjoying their time in the resort-like atrium house - utilizing the indoor spa, game rooms, kitchen and bowling alley the most, they sat at the breakfast table, dressed in their borrowed linen clothes from the abandoned closets. They could get used to this life of relaxation and full bellies.

Tess could see why Aurelia spent so much time and energy traveling halfway across Christendom to return to Natalia; The two of them were kindred spirits with an unbreakable sisterly bond. Although she was still tinted with entitlement, Natalia had been through hell since Aurelia disappeared, and was now humbly happy to be in their situation, out of the 1400s.

Breaking the silence, a piercing siren rang through the house, with a repeating, blaring message in Chinese, "现在撤离安全起见 (*Xiàn zài chè lí ān quán qǐ jiàn*)"

"What's happening?" Natalia screamed, covering her ears with her hands.

"It says we have to 'evacuate and get to safety'? Where do we go?" Tess screamed.

"The portal. Come on!" Aurelia said, grabbing Natalia's hand and running back towards where the stairwell was.

"I need my Okliot!" Tess screamed over the sirens.

"Just hold my hand in the portal like Natalia!"

"NO! Wait! I have to get my crown - please, it's all I have left of my family!" Natalia sobbed, pulling back towards the room she had been sleeping in.

Aurelia shot Tess a glance, "Fine. Both of you go get them. Hurry! We don't know what this is, or how much time we have!"

Letting Natalia's hand go and running back with them to all stay together, they ran to their rooms, Aurelia standing outside of hers. The ruby necklace. She had time to get it. Rushing inside to her bedside table, she grabbed it, clasping it to her neck as she ran down the hall.

Where was Tess, and Natalia? She called for them over the blaring alarm, her voice barely audible amongst the sound. She was at the portal, were they already inside? She opened the door, but the portal was gone, replaced by a coat closet. Did she have the right door? Looking around, it was the only one in the hall. They were stuck here in this time. Running from around the corner, Tess and Natalia came skidding to Aurelia.

"The portal's gone! We have to find another way out!" Aurelia screamed over the sound of the warning alert. "Go to the garage!"

They all ran to the garage as fast as they could, unsure which car to drive.

"Grab the keys, Tess!"

"SHIT!" Tess screamed.

"What?" Aurelia asked.

"They're all biometric!"

They couldn't get out. The cars would only work for their designated drivers, or passengers.

The vintage Porsche. It seemed the oldest. Maybe it still used a key? Aurelia looked around, opening every garage cabinet she could in search of it. Opening one of the top ones, she hit the lottery. Thrown in, probably just before the family living here had left, was the Porsche's key. She grabbed it, clicked the unlock button, and the car's two doors opened automatically.

"Get in!" Aurelia screamed, getting in the passenger seat. "You have to drive, Tess!"

"What's drive?"

Both Tess and Natalia had never even been in a car before. Every mode of transportation in the future was automated.

"Crap!"

Aurelia hurried out of the passenger's seat and into the driver's seat. She was the most equipped, mostly through secondhand experience, as she still hadn't gotten her license in the 21st century. Her grandparents only had one car growing up, and in most cases her friends would drive her places, or she would just use a rideshare app. She had driven once, maybe twice, before the infamous party on her 19th birthday. Although she had gotten her learner's permit months before, her nana had been too preoccupied to give her lessons. Even in Amsterdam, Will had always done the driving.

Natalia scooted into the middle of the two seat vehicle, where she straddled her legs over the gearshift. Tess got in, while Aurelia looked for the keyhole - there was none.

"There's a button!" Tess screamed, reaching over to press the start button on the car.

It was keyless. The keys only had to be inside for the car to work. Her hands shaking, the car roared to life, and the car doors automatically shut, sealing with an airlock. As if sensing the engine, the garage doors rolled open, finally revealing their surroundings, outside of the atrium house.

Everything was red with smoke. The sirens outside were just as loud as inside, luckily somewhat muted by the car's sound dampening technology. Across the street, a large mansion was ablaze with fire, slightly burned out, as if the flames had been going for hours, if not days. The streets were completely empty, save for the flying embers that crossed their path. They hadn't been able to tell what was happening outside the house at all. Little did they know, but the fireproof house had noise canceling walls, full insulation covering the artificially lit atriums, and its own air supply to sustain the people inside for years.

Aurelia shifted the manual gearshift into place - lower gears were for going slow, right? The customized car was especially made for whoever the family was that owned it - utilizing more manual, human touch features for racing, that had since become passé. Placing her right foot on the gas, they lurched forward, the car plummeting towards the neighbor's burning house. Natalia screamed, the sound piercing in Tess and Aurelia's ears. Quickly releasing the gas and slamming her left foot on the clutch to stop, nothing happened. The car wouldn't slow down. Frantically, she looked down to her feet - why were there three pedals? Trying the middle one instead of the left, slamming on the brake, they stopped abruptly just feet away from the house, nearly sending the girls flying into the dash.

'This car had some serious pickup,' Aurelia thought.

"Everyone OK?" The girls nodded. "Now would be a good time to put your seatbelt on, Tess. Nat - sit on her lap."

Natalia complied, and Tess pulled the seatbelt over the two of them.

'What was this wild beast of the future,' Natalia wondered?

Shifting into reverse, Aurelia gently pressed the gas again, moving backwards just enough to turn out of the neighbor's driveway. Shifting back into first gear, she began driving, cautiously.

'OK, I can do this,' she thought to herself.

Slightly increasing her speed, the engine revved, and she remembered she had to shift into a higher gear since it wasn't an automatic. Grinding the pristine gears as she failed to use the clutch, she shifted into third gear, probably much too high for the slow speed she was going.

Everything was on fire outside. The neighborhood was indiscernible from the grandiosity that it once was, but they could tell that every house was originally stunning. Some houses, similar to the atrium house they had been in, seemed fireproof, and only burned on the exterior, probably due to some fallen debris on top. The road was covered with ash and scattered with large pieces of partially burned objects, which Aurelia navigated around as best as she could. The blaring sound of the alarm pulsated as they drove - playing in every home's speaker system, although apparently to no one. Besides them, the neighborhood was completely deserted.

Navigating out of the once gated neighborhood and into the city, the buildings slowly became tighter and taller, all of them wrecked with damage and continuous fire. Detouring themselves onto another street to avoid a fallen building, they continued through the city slowly, unsure as to where they were going, but the warning sirens continued even here.

Squished between the new, grey, straight-lined architecture, a giant, colorful building from centuries ago lay practically untouched. With stacked, curved roofs and probably a once welcoming garden, the girls wanted nothing more than to stop and look inside the anomaly. The city encircling the old world like it was either trying to smudge out the light, or protect the building from harm.

Speeding up again as they passed the building, they continued through the smog and ash. It was hard to see further than a few blocks away, and if not for the car's excellent ventilation system, they would all certainly be coughing from the air quality.

Turning to avoid another fallen building, hidden from the smog, just a few blocks in front of them seemed to be a giant fence, at least forty feet tall - a boundary keeping something in, or perhaps something out. Coming from the top of the fence, a blinding spotlight illuminated their car. Someone had seen them. Aurelia braked.

"What should I do?" she asked the girls.

"赶快 (*Gǎn kuài*)," hurry up, an amplified voice called from the wall, "另一个来了 (*Lìng yī gè lái le*)."

"He says another one's coming?" Tess translated.

"Another what?"

"...I don't know. Keep going, Aurelia. Get to the fence."

Aurelia stepped on the gas, navigating through the fallen debris, her heart pounding.

"快一点 (*Kuài yī diǎn*)," the voice echoed from the loudspeakers atop the fence.

"He says go faster," Tess relayed.

Aurelia sped up, now rolling over some of the smaller objects in the road, rather than avoiding them.

"在你后面 (*Zài nǐ hòu miàn*)!" the voice yelled, and Tess turned in her seat to try and see what the voice meant. What was behind them?

Natalia squeezed the seatbelt, "I'm scared, Ari."

Me too, she wanted to say, but the words wouldn't come, "We're OK. Don't worr-"

A boom from behind them sent the car plummeting sideways through the air. There was a bomb near one of the buildings. With a severe impact, the car rolled violently, crushing the top and sides. The airbags deployed, but they were barely of any use with a crash so bad.

Shrapnel metal of the frame of the building flew through the air from the bomb's shockwave, a piece of metal slicing into the driver's seat, cutting through the side of Aurelia's stomach and pressing on her spine. As the car rolled to a stop, ending upside down, Aurelia gasped for air, blood filling her lungs and mouth. Her ruby necklace rested on her chin, pulled down from her neck by gravity. Her arms hung above her, and she tried to move them to pull the metal out of her, but they wouldn't move on her command. Her arms were paralyzed.

She turned her head to look at her friends - Natalia's forehead was bleeding, and her body hung from the chair unconsciously. Tess was awake, seemingly unharmed, pounding at the windows to try and get out.

She turned to see Aurelia, and Tess's face dropped with anxiety, seeing the metal protruding from her body.

"Oh my God, Aurelia..."

The blood in her lungs suffocating, the pain of the shrapnel in her body unbearable, Aurelia passed out.

CHAPTER 26

JĪQÌRÉN

Will's voice filled Aurelia's mind. Although he wasn't actually there - she imagined he was. Just like how he had rescued her in B-udo when they attempted to leave 43-1 through Gira's portal, he would save her now.

Slipping in and out of consciousness, she watched Natalia get pulled from the wreckage. Tess, right before she was helped out of the upside down car, placed a hand on Aurelia's cheek, trying to tell her that she would be alright, but her words were muffled - Aurelia's ears still ringing from the bomb. Her vision was blurred from the blood oozing down her face, worsened by the constant choking cough.

Awoken again from pain, she screamed out as the metal in her stomach was moved.

"她还活着 (*Tā hái huó zhe*)," a voice from above her said excitedly. She was still holding onto life, just barely.

Her body kept trying to wake up. Lights flashed above her. She was out of the car. How had she gotten out? She looked down, she was being rolled on a gurney, the metal now cut enough to move her, but still protruding from her stomach. She was surrounded by doctors. A man with brown hair morphed into a friendly face.

"...Will?" she croaked with a whisper.

Was it...? No. Her mind was playing tricks on her.

"她醒来了 (*Tā xǐng lái le*)," a woman said above her.

Aurelia looked down through her warped vision, they were performing surgery.

"给她更多麻醉 (*Gěi tā gèng duō má zuì*)," one of the doctors

spoke. What were they saying?

The woman above her placed a mask over her nose and mouth filled with gas, "你会好起来的 (*Nǐ huì hǎo qǐ lái de*)," she said in a comforting tone to Aurelia, who quickly fell back to sleep.

Hours later, the anesthesia wore off, and Aurelia woke up in a large convention center, surrounded by hundreds, if not thousands, of injured people laying in cots. A young man above her changed her IV fluids, and she tried to sit up, but her body wouldn't move.

"Help..." she wheezed.

What had happened to Natalia and Tess? Where were they?

"已经起来了 (*Yí jīng qǐ lái lè*)," the young man smiled.

"I need..." Aurelia coughed, everything hurt, "I need to find... my friends."

"You speak English?" the Chinese man asked, genuinely intrigued. Aurelia nodded. "I bring... 宝华大夫 (*Bǎo Huā dà fu*)... your doctor... with you," he said in broken English.

Minutes later, the young man returned with a middle aged Chinese woman with dyed red hair, apparently Doctor BǎoHuā.

"I have to get up. I have to find my friends," Aurelia said, cranking her neck to try and move the rest of her body, "Why can't I move?"

"You in serious accident," the doctor explained, trying to translate into English. "Spine severed. You are, how you say? 瘫痪 (*Tānhuàn*). No walk. Sorry."

She was paralyzed? No. That couldn't be. Besides, even if she was now, wouldn't the nanobots heal her? She would be alright. She was sure of it.

"No. I'm OK, I'll heal. But my friends-"

"You friends good. I treat. Tess very worried you."

"Where are they? Can I see them?"

"They at camp. They safe."

"Camp? Where... what is this place? Where am I? ...What year is it?"

The doctor shot the nurse a look - Aurelia was obviously confused from the accident and still in shock, "It July 17, 2167. You in Tianjin."

The doctor reached in her lab coat and pulled out a metal band, placing it over Aurelia's flinching head.

"Wha- What is that?"

"I check your head," the doctor slid open a scroll-like tablet and connected a wire to the head band on Aurelia. "You remember name?"

"My name? I'm Aure-" stopping herself - she wasn't supposed to use her real name. "Where's Tianjin? What's happening here?"

"Tianjin in China. You remember the war?"

"What war?"

"We in the 机器人战争 (*Jīqìrén ZhànZhēng*). We fight for freedom and life, they fight for control."

"Freedom? From who?"

"From the 机器人 (*Jīqìrén*) - you say in English... droids."

"Droids? As in, AI? Robots?" Doctor BǎoHuā nodded. "But, isn't that technology?" Aurelia motioned with her head to the tablet in the doctor's hands. "Couldn't robots hack into something like that?"

"This closed circuit. No communication. Your car have maps, they see you easy, that why you crash," the doctor looked at the nurse, "她的头很好。她可能只是感到震惊 (*Tā de tóu hěn hǎo. Tā kě néng zhǐ shì gǎn dào zhèn jīng*)."

"What?" Aurelia asked as the doctor slipped the headband off of her.

"You head fine. You rest," the doctor began to walk away.

"Wait! What about my friends?"

"Visit tomorrow."

The night passed by glacially, and Aurelia was kept awake by the glaring convention center lights overhead and the incessant painful moans of the injured, sick people inside. New patients continued to stream in constantly - it seemed like the *Jīqìrén* War didn't sleep either.

Unlike other nights in uncomfortable places, Aurelia couldn't turn onto her side and block out the noise with her arm like she would normally do, as she still couldn't move her limbs. Every minute that passed worried her more and more that the nanobots weren't working, and she was actually permanently paralyzed. So, instead of sleeping, since it didn't seem possible anyway, she spent the night focusing on trying to move her fingers. Staring at her unmoving hand, impaled by a tiny IV tube taped on top, she imagined what it would be like for her hand to move again.

Any bit of movement would make her happy, she thought, just a tiny flinch, a glimmer of hope. In her mind, she could feel her fingers opening and closing, the movement natural and easy, but the second she would open her eyes to check if her imagination had become reality and her fingers had actually moved, she would again be disappointed by the stillness her hands displayed.

A few hours later, the nurse visited her once again, checking her limbs with the light touch of a pen to see if any feeling had returned to them at all. There was a lack of feeling in her body - only her head, to halfway down her chest, felt the cold, drafty air circulating the convention center, but the rest of her body just felt empty. But then, after a few more hours, the painful tingling started. Almost like every nerve in her body was on fire, but the pain was more comforting than the lack of feeling - perhaps it meant that the nanobots were working, she hoped. In a way, it felt similar to when you had sat too long in a strange position and your leg had fallen asleep - only the painful feeling was tenfold and amplified throughout her entire body. She kept attempting to move her fingers, with no luck.

She couldn't quite tell how long it had been when Tess and Natalia came to visit, but she burst into tears of relief to see that they were both alright. They had changed clothes, Tess now wearing army green cargo pants and a black T-shirt with a crossbody fanny pack across her shoulder, and Natalia wearing faded black pants and a short sleeved, asymmetrical, button-down shirt - probably the first time in her life she had ever worn pants, coming from the Middle Ages.

Spotting Aurelia in the hospital bed, Natalia rushed to hug her.

"Ari!"

"Are you hurt? How's your head?" Aurelia said, remembering Natalia's unconscious body in the car.

"*Je vais bien.* Don't worry. It was just a cut. But you... I'm so sorry Aurelia... I heard... They said you won't ever walk on your own again."

"No. They're wrong. I'll be fine," switching to a whisper she continued, "I have a friend in the future who gave me nanobots."

Tess sat further down the bed in worry, placing her hand on Aurelia's shin, although she still couldn't feel it, "But, aren't the decontamination nanobots just for known pathogens? The type we have can't heal these kind of injuries on their own, you'd need new ones that were programmed by a doctor. We have to get you home."

Tess knew Aurelia would have to get back to B-udo if she even wanted to have a shot at walking again. But how would they? The portal was gone, and the company wouldn't have a visitor's portal anytime near a war.

“They’ve worked before. I must have gotten another type of nanobot,” Aurelia said, recalling her bullet wounds in Amsterdam that had healed magically.

“But I’ve heard that only the royals have access to the A Class nanobots... oh my God. Wait - is that your secret? Is that why you didn’t tell me your name for so long?”

“Huh?” What was Tess talking about?

“And, you had access to those weird tunnels in B-udo! Ughh of course! It makes sense! No wonder you’re so secretive! You’re not from B-udo at all are you?” She knew she was a permanent. The ruse was up. “No wonder you hardly talk about your family!” She didn’t talk about her family to anyone - she was protecting them. “...You’re one of the Lapites!”

Aurelia burst into a laugh, “What? You think I’m a Lapite?”

“Yes! It’s OK, you don’t have to hide it from me anymore!” Tess grinned.

“What is a Lapite?” Natalia asked, confused by the conversation.

“They’re one of the royal families in the future, so to speak,” Aurelia explained, before Tess jumped in.

“They’re not just one of them - they *are* them. The top. Everything that happens in all of ZhēnZhū is first decided by them. But I still don’t understand why you don’t speak Chinese,” Tess gasped. “Did you run away? Is that why you didn’t want me to tell anyone your name? Are they looking for you?”

“Tess. I’m not-“

She gasped again, really thinking she had nailed who Aurelia was, “You’re the heir, aren’t you? You’re supposed to take over the company. No wonder you ran... you didn’t want that life, so you left!”

“I’m not a La-“

“And no wonder you can travel without an Okliot! I’ll bet you royals get every prototype years before us normal folk.”

“Look. I’m not-“

“No, it’s OK, Aurelia. You don’t have to hide it from me anymo-“

“TESS!” finally she quieted. “That sounds like a really great story, but I’m not a Lapite.”

“But...” she really thought she had figured it out. It would explain everything. “Then, who are you?”

Who was she? A question she had pondered many a night. She had been thrust into a life that shouldn’t have been hers, but that she loved every second of, despite its constant danger.

"Just a girl. A normal, impossible girl, with a crazy, unconventional life."

Tess and Natalia had briefly gone back to the camp, only allowed to visit Aurelia for twenty minutes, since the convention center was already so crowded with patients. They would return just after dinner, to check on her again.

The minutes and hours slipping together in boredom, Aurelia perpetually attempted to move her body, but at this point, it seemed helpless. Maybe the nanobots wouldn't heal her like they had once before. Maybe Tess was right and they would only work to keep her safe from microscopic viruses. Maybe the bullet holes healing were an anomaly.

Tears streamed down her face, unable to be wiped away. She didn't want to be paralyzed. Then again, who would? She hated how helpless she felt; the nurse having to feed her, empty her waste basins, and occasionally move her limbs to prevent blood clots. It was humiliating. She didn't want to accept this as her life from now on. She couldn't.

Faster than expected, Natalia and Tess returned, sitting on either side of her on the hospital cot - this time with news. Apparently they could flee to a city just north of Beijing that was a safe zone. The war between the *Jīqìrén* and humans was raging worldwide, but there were tiny pockets of civilization that had been rebuilt secretly amongst the destruction, serving as refuge for some. This particular city they would escape to had been untouched, due to a disarmed bomb and a false signal back to the droids that the bomb had leveled the city.

Tess remembered downloading some broad information about the *Jīqìrén* Wars - little did the people here know, but it would last for the next thirty years, and nearly wipe out the human race in the process. The tides would only be turned after a small group of *Jīqìrén* renegades managed to take down a pack of the droid's leaders, rendering the rest of their followers purposeless. The renegades turned to peace, garnering followers on both sides that also just wanted to live. Eventually, humans had to learn to coexist with the evolving, sentient technology. After many years and many more struggles, they would one day be completely liberated and integrated into society - most augments in the 43's indistinguishable from humans.

But here - now, the conflicts ran high and human life was

dispensable. Every major city worldwide was now a war zone with few survivors. They had to get to safety if they even wanted a chance at surviving this.

"How are we supposed to get there with me like this?" Aurelia asked, reality setting in.

"I'm working on getting you an EXO. They don't have any available yet, but as soon as we can get one we can leave."

"What's an EXO?" asked Aurelia.

"You've never heard of them? They stopped using them a few hundred years from now when nanobot technology improved so much, but they were what every disabled person used for a while."

Disabled. It was the first time she had heard that term implied for her.

Tess continued, "It's kind of like a suit you wear that you can use to walk again."

Aurelia quieted. How had this happened? Why had they left France? Aurelia looked at Natalia, she seemed drained and tired from the events of the past day. They should've kept their horses, attended Natalia's wedding and settled down where and when it was somewhat safe in 1451, not ended up in a time of war. But then Natalia would've suffered by being in an unwanted marriage, and Tess wouldn't have been happy staying in the Middle Ages - she wanted to go home to B-udo. She missed the regularity and safety it provided, and she even missed her parents, although they weren't necessarily close.

"I'm sorry," Aurelia said, a tear quickly rolling down the side of her face.

"You're sorry? I'm sorry. I'm sorry this happened to you," Tess picked up Aurelia's hand to hold.

Aurelia gasped. The feeling wasn't strong, more of a tickle than a handshake - but she could feel Tess's hand in hers.

"What? What is it?"

"I feel that!" Aurelia proclaimed.

"My hand?" Tess squeezed tighter. Aurelia nodded.

Natalia perked up from her silent, slouched position sitting next to Aurelia.

"Can you feel this?" Natalia poked her thigh forcefully.

She could feel it lightly, like a light tap rather than the strong poke.

"Let me check your wound - maybe the nanobots are working after all!" Tess said, lifting the bloodstained, tan linen shirt that Aurelia had worn since the crash.

Aurelia nodded, crying with happiness involuntarily. The large wound was bandaged with a blue, sticky fabric connected with wires that led out to a panel wedged in the side of the hospital bed - a technology for monitoring the wound for infection. The bandage wrapped around her stomach, across to her back. Peeling it back carefully, revealing a gel like substance on the inside of the fabric, Tess gasped.

"What is it?" Natalia said, jumping off her side of the bed and coming around to see the wound.

Tess was at a loss for words. The wound was closed - now only a red scratch remaining where a gaping hole had been, the sight of the thick metal protruding from the car crash still in her mind.

"How bad is it?" Aurelia asked, lifting her head to try and see.

"Let me in, let me see!" Natalia begged, hopping over Tess's shoulder to try and get a look.

"It's healing," Tess said, her pursed, worried lips twitching into a smile. "You're healing, Ari!"

Aurelia was alone yet again, but this time with a newfound hope. She was healing. The nanobots were working. Continuing with her attempts to try and move her hand, after a few tiring hours, she finally saw a twitch. Just the tiniest move from her thumb and index finger - but it moved nonetheless. It felt like the greatest relief in the world, just seeing the minuscule movement in her fingers. It made her appreciate all of the times she had taken for granted - the simple pleasures like brushing her hair, scratching an itch, or holding someone's hand.

But, she would heal. This was temporary. Thanking God for this immense blessing, she finally let herself sleep.

Aurelia was awakened by Tess and Natalia's voices. She had rolled onto her side in her bed during the night, a simple movement that she had so missed, even just for the few days she had been without it.

Tess's loud whispers filled the air, "Look, if not now, then later tonight. But that means she has to be a damn good actress for the next eight hours."

"Who has to be a good actress?" Aurelia asked, gently stretching her arm out for the first time, a pinpricking feeling filling her arm as she moved.

Tess hurried to Aurelia's side, holding her arm as if it was Tess stretching it, and not Aurelia herself, "*You* have to be a good actress. Do you think you can walk yet?" Tess whispered.

"Uhhh... last night I was just starting to move my fingers... but maybe...? Why?"

"They don't *have* healing nanobots here yet. They're not mainstream for at least another century or two - and even then they still use incubators and programming. People don't just miraculously heal from being paralyzed - and you're the *only* white person here besides Natalia, so you already stick out like a sore thumb."

"So...?"

"So, we have to sneak you out before somebody realizes that you're some miracle case."

Tess was right. She couldn't have another experience like ancient Mexico, where the people thought she was a deity. They needed to stay under the radar.

"If you can walk now - we found a back entrance that we can sneak you out of," Tess explained.

Natalia jumped in, "Then we can walk-" Natalia cleared her throat briefly with a small cough, "we can walk to a part of town where nobody knows you."

Could Aurelia move well enough yet?

"Help me sit up, let me see how I feel," Aurelia instructed, the girls coming to her side to assist her.

Sitting up was a whole other level than the micro movements she had done with her hand. She couldn't do it - not yet at least, her muscles wouldn't allow it. They helped lay her back down as Aurelia caught her breath from exertion.

From the act of sitting up, she remembered that she was wired into the bed and technology around her - her stomach wound's bandage connected to a tablet to check for possible infection, her hand hooked into an IV for fluids, a band on her wrist monitoring vitals, and even a catheter. They would have a lot to disconnect and prepare before she could leave.

"Tonight then. Be ready," Tess said under her breath, just as the nurse walked over to check on the patient next to Aurelia.

As Tess expected, it definitely took some good acting to pretend that Aurelia was still paralyzed. Especially when the nurse came to feed her lunch and change her bedsheets. It felt crass to be allowing someone to waste time to care for someone who didn't need help anymore. But, she knew why she had to keep up the ruse. Under normal circumstances, she would've remained paralyzed, not magically healed from futuristic nanobots.

When Natalia and Tess arrived, Aurelia quickly ripped off the bandages and wires connecting her to the bed, the feeling of tape ripping off stinging her hand. Looking around to make sure the coast was clear of any doctors or nurses, she nonchalantly stood up, her legs nearly buckling from the sudden pressure. Grabbing Tess's shoulder for stability, she wobbled upright. It was painful to stand - her muscles ached on every inch of her body, but they had to get her out of the hospital. She could do this. She would fight through the pain. Natalia offered her small body to steady Aurelia's tall one, while Tess wrapped a scarf around Aurelia's blonde hair and half of her face, spreading the scarf's fabric out over her chest to hide the bloodstains and gaping hole in her shirt. Then, Aurelia still holding onto Natalia, they made their way through the makeshift hospital inside the convention center.

It seemed every other patient had a serious injury from the war - amputated limbs, burns, or energy blast injuries similar to bullet holes. Some of them groaned in pain, others held their loved one's hands during the visiting hours. There were even the few that had already passed away - the hospital too busy to notice yet. It was horrific.

Aurelia widened her eyes as they passed her doctor treating another patient - would she recognize them? Tilting her head away from Doctor BǎoHuā, hoping she hadn't seen her face, they kept walking. Had she seen them? Looking behind her, her eyes caught the doctor's briefly. Her pulse elevated, they continued walking. Had they just been compromised? But to the doctor, Aurelia's familiar face was just someone in the crowd. She had treated hundreds of patients the past few days, and at this point, each face blended together, not able to remember which patient was suffering from which injury.

They reached the emergency exit doors at the back of the convention center, and hustled through them into a wide concrete hallway. Natalia and Tess let Aurelia sit along the concrete wall, where part of it sloped out, forming a sort of bench. Here, the lights were finally dimmed from the harsh LEDs in the convention center, and Aurelia already felt more relaxed. Looking at her friends, it seemed to Aurelia that Natalia looked especially pale, but maybe it was just from the lighting. Tess pulled out three clear, full face masks and dispersed them.

"What are these for?" Aurelia asked, examining the mask in her hand.

"We have to walk outside for a few blocks. Trust me, you don't wanna breathe the air in the 2100s, not to mention with all of the fires going nearby."

Aurelia put the mask over her face. In the past century, the earth's air had become toxic - after the human-caused global warming accelerated at an exponential rate. Ice sheets had melted, releasing large amounts of methane into the atmosphere, further accelerating global warming, among other things. It had reached a tipping point where deep frosts and extreme heatwaves were so severe across the globe that trees and crops soon couldn't survive the harsh weather, and people began to starve. At some point, most people came to see reason - that human's actions were suffocating the planet - but it was too little too late, the damage was already done.

Aurelia thought about what it would've been like to live through that - after all, they were only 148 years in the future from 2019 - if she had children and grandchildren, perhaps they would've still been alive today and had to live through Earth's decline. Life had seemed so carefree in 2019 - most people weren't concerned about Earth's legacy that they were leaving their future generations to deal with. If only things were different and everyone cared about the planet - perhaps the future wouldn't have become what it was.

Opening the heavy metal doors, they navigated through a tiny air-locked corridor, filled with sheets of thick plastic - vinyl flaps hanging down from the door frames, meant to keep as much of the outside air from seeping into the building. They opened the final door and stepped outside.

The sky remained a deep, cloudy red, and dark ash seemed to drizzle from above. They were still inside of the fenced area of town it seemed, so none of the buildings here suffered the same level of destruction as the ones in the rest of the city, besides the occasional spot fire from falling embers that was quickly extinguished. The streets were completely empty, since most people used underground tunnels to get from building to building now. But those tunnels were closely monitored and regulated, and patients leaving the hospital needed a doctor's approval, as Tess had found out, hence why they used the streets instead.

They made their way through the apocalyptic deserted streets, passing the once epic street markets in town and cutting through alleyways that seemed frozen in time - lit signs still flashing despite the stores and restaurants being empty for years. The only movement in the streets, besides them, was the occasional feral cat or dog, barely hanging onto life.

Aurelia thought about what it would've been like here in its prime. She imagined people stretching as far as the eye could see, all with somewhere to go. Mopeds piled high with crates racing amongst pedestrians, a sort of frantic energy from people navigating the town. The street merchants yelling in solicitation for customers and unique foods filling the air. It would've been amazing to see it then.

Natalia coughed frequently as they walked - maybe her mask wasn't on properly, Aurelia wondered? Pausing to check it, it seemed fine - the filters showed a green light implying they worked. It must just be from the cold, filtered air irritating her. But in the back of Aurelia's mind, she was worried. What if she was sick?

They quickly reached a giant plexiglass building, which seemed to protect and cover a historical market or village, sort of like a plastic dome covering this part of the city. Coming to one of the entrances, they went through another airlock with sheets of plastic blocking the doors. This one had a decontamination process in order to enter. The exterior door sealed shut with the girls inside, then blew a strong, cold, damp air mixture from above them, helping to rid their hair and clothes of the toxins outside before entering.

Just inside of the door was a young, slim yet buffed Chinese man with jet black hair tipped with bleached ends, wearing a rolled up fatigue jumpsuit with silver chained dog tags around his neck. Tess immediately whipped her full face mask off and ran up to the young, tall man, placing his hands in hers with the space between them shrinking. They kissed, with Aurelia watching, completely shocked, and Natalia scrunching her nose in mild disgust at their public intimacy.

"你在使用我的方向有设么麻烦吗 (*Nǐ zài shǐ yòng wǒ de fāng xiàng yǒu shé me má fan ma?*)" the young man asked Tess, pulling away to look at her, lightly brushing a wisp of her dark, curly hair from her face.

"没有。很容易 (*Méi yǒu. Hěn róng yì*)," Tess replied with an intimate smile. They spoke only of directions, but the sensual nature of their word's inflections was all that could be translated.

Aurelia's jaw was practically on the floor, "I'm sorry - *What?*" Aurelia interrupted, dumbfounded at what had transpired. "How long was I in that hospital?"

Natalia laughed at Aurelia's reaction - obviously she had been feeling the same way.

Tess smiled and opened her body language back towards the girls, "*Miana*, this is Qi-Chen."

"Please, call me Chi," the man said in a completely unexpected New Zealand accent, holding out his hand to Aurelia.

She hesitantly shook his hand, "You're Australian?"

"No'r, I'm a kiwi - well technically mum's a local here so I'm a bit of both."

"So this war then... is it... everywhere? How bad is it?"

"Ya must'a had some head trauma if you don't remember."

Aurelia chuckled, "Yeah - that's probably it."

'Or,' she thought to herself, 'I'm from almost a hundred and fifty years ago and I have no idea what's going on.'

"Some'a the island bunkers have managed to isolate, and obviously the colonists are untouched - but mostly, yeah. The fuckers are everywhere. I was explaining to Tess that I know'r of a city nearby that's been a safe place... The *Jìgīrén* thought they flattened it with their nuke, but the thing about technology without eyes, is they can be easily be manipulated into thinking their bomb was successful. So we've been sending some people there as a refuge - even my mum and sister are there now."

Tess jumped in, "So Chi is gonna get us on the bullet train today. He says we'll be able to stay with his family there," turning to Chi, she continued with a whisper, "I still don't understand why you can't come with us... It's not safe here - you said it yourself."

"You know'r why, Tess. I'm enlisted. They need me here."

"I know... I just don't wanna lose you days after we met each other in this crazy world," Tess professed, suddenly the romantic.

"You won't lose me. I'll meet you there after we've won..." Chi's mouth melted into a side smile, and he lightly kissed Tess yet again, obviously wanting to jump head over heels into a relationship with her.

Aurelia looked at Natalia with widened eyes, pursing her lips into a smile. At least one of the girls was enjoying herself here.

Clearing her throat in an obvious manner to pause their drawn-out kiss, Aurelia interrupted, "So... which way is the bullet train?"

CHAPTER 27

CLUB SHELTER

Today's train wouldn't depart for at least another few hours, so Chi guided them to his apartment, the entrance to his building shielded inside the covered plexiglass that seemed to cover most of this part of town. They would stay for a few hours while they waited for the train, in the small, well-loved hole in the wall.

Although Chi's apartment was tiny, it was well appointed. Here, the walls were used as storage to keep the apartment clutter free, but also for fold-out furniture, enabling each room to have a dual purpose to save space. The kitchen island could easily be lowered to a dining table, the couch in the wall could be flipped up into the wall for a desk. The bedroom had the same type of features, with the closet all around them in built-in cabinets, rather than a separate room, and three separate pull-out beds that easily transformed the room for sleeping, where Chi, his sister and brother had slept since they were little.

Connecting two apartment units, a door in the wall opened into a reversed, identical apartment, where Chi's parents had lived. In Chinese culture, your parents would provide for you until you were grown up enough, then the tides would turn and it would be your responsibility and honor to care for them as they grew old, in a sense, your way of thanking your parents for the sacrifices they made by raising you. So for Chi, family was everything. But now, the memory-filled apartment sat empty; his mum and sister were refugees in a hidden city nearby, and his father and brother had unfortunately recently passed away from sickness.

Aurelia had changed out of her bloodstained clothes into some of Chi's sister's clothes, which were snug and short for Aurelia's tall body, yet usable. Choosing a tight, red, printed T-shirt with a cartoon bunny on it, some cargo pants, which seemed to be all the rage here in the 2100s, a faded green, oversized, cotton jacket, and a bag, similar to Tess's, reminiscent of a sort of fanny pack that you would instead wear as a crossbody, with pockets up the strap. Aurelia placed her ruby necklace inside for safekeeping, the only sentimental item she had kept from all of her travels, somewhat a reminder of the past few years.

The group of weary travelers sat in Chi's living room, finally enjoying some food, which had been promptly delivered through the *Měishí Qù* food delivery service, that despite the war, was still running in full effect.

Aurelia was utterly exhausted and not quite fully recovered, her legs painful and strained. Even the young, vibrant Natalia looked spent from the events of the past few days, her eyes sleepy and normally rosy cheeks drained of color. Tess seemed like the only one out of the girls that wasn't outwardly tired, as she was distracted and enraptured with her new boy toy, Chi. Either way, they were all grateful for their full bellies and a moment of respite.

But, in the time of war, comforts of the past were short lived, and it was barely an hour before a loud bang erupted and the apartment shook as if a strong, short earthquake had ensued.

"What was that?" Natalia asked, jumping out of her chair.

The same repeating, blaring message that they had heard in the atrium house a few days ago, telling them to evacuate and get to safety, began again, "现在撤离安全起见 (*Xiàn zài chè lí ān quán qǐ jiàn*)."

"They're bombing us again," Chi said somewhat nonchalantly, standing up calmly and putting on a coat.

"Well, what do we do?" Aurelia yelled over the sirens. Another bang, and the apartment shook violently - this one seemed closer to them.

"We'll go down to the shelter," Chi motioned to his front door, and the group followed his lead.

It seemed like the apartment building was somewhat empty, the halls that they expected to be packed full of terrified people running for safety, were instead only speckled with a few groups. Perhaps people had been through enough bombings to understand that the shelters didn't work effectively enough, and if a bomb was indeed going to hit the building, there wasn't much that they could do. But, Chi still figured it was better to try something than just stand by and wait for the bomb to hit.

Reaching the elevators, and waiting a few minutes for one to open up, they loaded inside and pressed the button for the basement floor. Whipping them effortlessly down 67 floors and dinging open, the sounds and lights of the basement shelter flooded their senses.

As if they had entered into a nightclub, the music blasted,

replacing the sirens with its own raging beat, played by a DJ, complete with his own booth and mixing board. The dimmed colorful lights danced across the moving crowd, who screamed the lyrics of the hit dance song playing from the mid 2020s, a sound that was now way past vintage, but still a favorite. The mix of steel and concrete walls of the basement seemed somewhat fortified, yet not impenetrable.

Was this the safest place around? *This* was the bomb shelter?

"What is this place?" Aurelia screamed over the deafening music filling her ears.

"What?" Chi asked, leaning in closer.

"WHERE ARE WE?" Aurelia screamed louder.

Chi smiled, "Welcome to 'Club Shelter'!"

"Why is everyone so happy? Aren't they bombing us?" asked Tess, looking around at the neon lights and dancing crowd.

"If we're all gonna kick it in a bomb anyway, we might as well live our last minutes *like* they're our last!" Chi responded, walking over to one of the unmanned bars and grabbing a bottle of baijiu for them, pouring a healthy serving of the strong alcohol into four glasses.

"This is crazy!" Tess wasn't sure what to think.

"I know'r! But what else is there to do? Sit and wait for one to hit? Why not dance and drink?" Chi picked up the four freshly poured glasses and handed them to the girls, with Aurelia quickly snatching the glass back from Natalia's young hand, which prompted an annoyed look back from Natalia.

"Wine's one thing, but you're 13, Nat!" Aurelia yelled over the thumping music as she set Natalia's glass back on the bar.

"I'm 14!"

"Exactly!"

Tess handed the glass back to her, defying Aurelia's protective instincts, "I don't see the problem with *one* sip," Tess said with a wink, smiling at Aurelia with a coy look. "I'll be the bad influence."

"Fine. *One* sip. What is this, tequila? Vodka?" Aurelia asked Chi, who chuckled, avoiding her question.

"干杯 (*Gānbēi*)!" he shouted, holding up his glass in cheers.

The girls raised their glasses to join him in his toast, mirroring him yelling, "干杯 (*Gānbēi*)!" in response.

The liquor tasted like rocket fuel, and Natalia tried a tiny sip, a disgusted look appearing on her face, while Aurelia laughed.

"You *drink* that?" Natalia cringed, handing the glass back to her friends.

Chi took Natalia's glass from her and downed it in a single sip, tapping the empty glass upside down over his head with a smile, "Yeah, we do!"

The fear of dying mixed with alcohol made dancing feel like nothing else in the world mattered but the rhythm of the music. With nothing they could do, no escape and no hope, their lives basically hung in the balance of a roulette game, guessing where the *Jīqìrén* would bomb next. Each bomb that dropped nearby, shaking the shelter and causing clouds of concrete dust to fill the air from the walls around them, eliciting an elated yell from the crowd, and a drinking game where everyone would down another shot of baijiu.

After a few hours, the alarms finally stopped, and the club seemed to lose its electricity - the blaring music now reduced to the background, the drinking games no longer fueled by bombs, but rather by random people making proclamations in Mandarin about people they had already lost in the war.

Aurelia's legs hurt even worse now from dancing, but she had enjoyed every second of it, grateful to even be *able* to dance after almost being permanently paralyzed from the car accident. Realizing the constant bombing had finally eased, the group of friends decided to join the tired Natalia, who had left the dance floor after a few songs. They sat next to her in a ripped, worn couch in the corner of the shelter. Chi and Tess's heads spinning from liquor, Aurelia drunk only from the palpable energy of their surroundings.

Something seemed off with Natalia to Aurelia. Why hadn't she felt like dancing? Giving her a side hug as she sat on the couch next to Chi and Tess, she noticed the expression on Natalia's face, the lights finally bright enough to see clearly. She looked miserable. Coughing just under her breath, Natalia laid onto Aurelia's lap.

"*Ça va*, Nat?" Aurelia asked her if she was OK.

"Mmhmm," Natalia groaned.

"Did you drink that alcohol?"

"No. None."

Natalia began coughing excessively from the new position of laying down, exhausting herself. Aurelia rubbed her back hoping to soothe her - why was her cough so deep? Sitting up, and calming herself, Natalia nodded with a feeble smile, still coughing under her breath.

"Did you wear your mask the whole time you were outside?"

Chi asked her, joining the conversation, also worried. Natalia nodded. "You had the virus yet?"

Tess shot him a sharp, concerned look, "What virus?"

"The Nantong virus? H7N9?" Natalia's eyes widened - she had lived through many outbreaks of sicknesses in the 18th *and* 15th centuries but thus far had been quite lucky herself. "Well?" Chi asked, and Natalia nodded no - of course she hadn't had the virus. She had never even heard of it. "It's probably nothing. You feel alright then? No fever? Stomachaches?"

Natalia glanced at Aurelia, unsure what to say. She didn't want to be sick - in France they would have had her thrown into isolation so as not to spread the sickness.

"Nat? Are you feeling sick?" Aurelia asked, judging the look on her face. "You have to tell us. Please."

Natalia didn't have nanobots to protect her from viruses like Aurelia and Tess did. What if her body couldn't handle fighting an evolved futuristic virus?

"I mean... I'm well I think... my throat is just a little sore."

Aurelia reached her palm to Natalia's forehead to check her temperature.

"Shit. You're burning up too."

Chi reached over Aurelia to feel for himself, her temperature had to be at least over 102.0 degrees.

Aurelia stood up, pulling Chi and Tess aside so she could whisper privately from Natalia, "How bad is this 'Nantong virus'?"

Chi looked at Aurelia with pain, "I lost my little brother and dad to it a few months ago'r. They say it's been modified by the *Jīqìrén* to become as deadly as it is."

Tess wrapped her hand around his for comfort, "I'm so sorry, Chi. That must have been terrible." He nodded.

Aurelia couldn't find comforting words, "Well... and there's no cure? And it doesn't mean that's what she has, right? We can't jump to conclusions."

Chi answered, "No'r... they've been working on a treatment but with the war it's been impossible to manufacture... I'm sure it's not that though. We have to stay positive."

"If it is that... what's the... death rate?" Aurelia asked, unsure if she wanted the answer.

"It's high, Miana. Sixty percent maybe? Seventy? It's hard to tell. And so many people have died from the war, that it's hard to keep track."

Seventy percent death rate. No. It couldn't be that. Aurelia felt a lump in her throat.

"How will we know that's what she has?"

"You'll know'r. It's fairly quick. I guess that's the only good part. Wait - what about you both? Have you not had it? You shouldn't be near Natalia just in case."

"No... um... we're immune," Tess lied - although technically they *were* immune to known viruses from the decontamination nanobots in their systems.

"Good..."

"So, what should we do? Take her back to the hospital?" Tess guessed.

"No'r! Definitely not! If she has the virus they might put her down to stop another outbreak. And if she does have it, everyone that was in the shelter with us would be taken care of too, even *if* they're immune. They've just got it under control here a few weeks ago."

"WHAT? They would... *kill* her? They would kill *all* of these people?" Aurelia said, baffled. "Then how will she get any treatment?"

Chi hesitated to answer, "She... won't. Let's take her back to my place so she can rest."

Tess recalled the reason they had come to this part of town in the first place, "What about the train? Shouldn't we get to safety?"

"If she has the Nantong virus, they won't let you in unless she survives it. They're virus free there - that's partially why I sent *my* family there, so they wouldn't get exposed. Our safest option is to get her out of public and just pray she recovers."

CHAPTER 28

The Virus

Natalia's labored breathing in Chi's bedroom could be heard through the closed door, all the way into the kitchen. She worsened by the minute, as the virus began to build up and fill her lungs like a slow drip. Supposedly, there was a tell-tale sign of whether your body would fight it or succumb to the sickness - if your fingers and toes began to turn a greyish blue, your body wasn't getting enough oxygen, and you would soon die. Luckily, so far, her limbs were still a whitish, skin-tone pink and seemed fine.

Natalia was resting while Aurelia watched her by her side, while Chi and Tess spoke privately in the kitchen about further options and remedies that they could try. Chi had gone through this twice already - and watching his kind little brother and strong father be taken down by the Nantong virus was almost unbearable. Now, Natalia lay in the same room Chi's brother had been in when he fell ill, his brother almost the same age as Natalia was now. Like a repeating nightmare that continues to appear every time you fall asleep, Chi couldn't stand the actual sight of seeing Natalia suffer the same fate, so he stayed a room away while Aurelia cared for the young girl.

"Ari?" Natalia coughed softly, breaking the unspoken tension in the room. Aurelia leaned in from the bed next to her where she sat. "Am I going to die?"

Aurelia's twitching face held back from breaking down, "No. No I won't let you. You have a Russian fighting spirit. You've survived much worse than this... being ripped away from your family so young, only to end up in a foreign palace surrounded by arrogant royals? Not everyone could handle that the way you did, Nat," Natalia smiled through her tremulous breaths, but her face quickly saddened. "What is it?"

"I wanted to do so much more in my life Ari. Like you."

"And you still will! You're gonna beat this."

"I wanted to go to college like you told me about and learn about everything. I was lucky that they taught me so much in France - I wouldn't have gotten that opportunity in Russia. You know that most of the women in my time couldn't even read?"

"What? Why not?"

"Women were just meant to be mothers. Not leaders like you."

Aurelia chuckled, "I'm not much of a leader."

"Of course you are! Being a leader doesn't mean you have to have people to rule like a king. It's your confidence. Your manner. You inspire greatness in others. They want to be better people because of you..." Natalia coughed. "You inspired me. *That* is a leader."

At this point, Aurelia couldn't hold back her tears, "Stop saying goodbye, Nat!"

"I'm not. I'm just telling you that I love you."

"I love you too," Aurelia grabbed Natalia's small hand and squeezed tightly. "...What will you go to college for?"

"Maybe... theology... or medicine... I want to help people. And I want to find a husband that I love, and have children. Maybe we have a house... but I have a full life. And you're there... as my children's Auntie, with kids of your own so they can play together-" Natalia continued coughing, a deep chested, hoarse sound.

"It sounds perfect... and you're *going* to help people, and have an epic love story, and have kids, and grandkids. It's going to happen... OK? I promise you."

Aurelia closed the door to let Natalia sleep. Tess and Chi sat at the kitchen island, sipping a hot liquid that looked like coffee but smelled more like cinnamon.

"Tess, can I talk to you for a minute?" Aurelia motioned to the door to Chi's parents' apartment so they could speak privately. They slithered inside, the lights turning on automatically. "We have to do something. We can't just let her die, Tess. What if we gave her some of my blood? Or even yours? I mean, it has healing nanobots in it that fight viruses, right?"

"But they're programmed specifically to our body chemistries. They won't work for anyone else," Tess said in an obvious tone.

"Shit. OK... what about taking her back to the atrium house? What if the portal is back?"

"We don't have a car anymore, remember? And even *if* we had one, it wouldn't be safe driving through the city, now that we know we're in the middle of the *Jīqìrén* Wars!"

"I don't know what to do, Tess! I can't watch this happen to her!" Aurelia sobbed, her hands shaking. If the virus truly was as bad as Chi said, Natalia could be dead within the day.

"She needs to get to B-udo. That's the only way to make sure she survives this."

"HOW?" Aurelia said, emotionally loud. Tess grabbed her shaking hands to calm her.

"You," Tess whispered.

"What? *Me?*"

"You have some sort of power, or technology, that lets you travel without an Okliot. You even brought Natalia with you. What if you can open portals too? Didn't you say you just 'happened upon portals' before? That's not a thing. As far as I know there's really only *one* portal in each time. Not one in Tangier *and* one in Paris at the same time."

"What? So you're saying *I* opened that portal? How? I didn't... do anything."

"Maybe not consciously. But didn't you also say that you used one to get to ancient Mexico or something?"

"Yeah..."

"The company doesn't have portals that go to dangerous places like that - or like this one? In the middle of the *Jīqìrén* Wars? Why would they? They're a travel company. They *have* to keep their guests safe and happy in a controlled environment."

"So you think I can open a portal to get us back to B-udo? How would I even do that?"

"You need to learn. Fast."

Aurelia quickly found the emergency stairwell in Chi's apartment building and hustled inside.

Staring at the landing, thoughts flashed through her mind, 'What if it doesn't work? What if we're stuck here and Natalia dies? But, what if it does work and I *do* travel in time? What would that even mean? What if I can't control it and I can't get back? What if I end up stranding Tess and Natalia here in the *Jīqìrén* Wars?'

Casting the doubts and what if scenarios from her head - it *had* to work. It was the only option. She had to save Natalia.

Placing her hand on the sleek, metal handrail, she began her ascent, her body committed to travel in time. Stepping up the stairs with conviction, she had to make this work. Her legs were still slightly painful and sore from the car accident, but it didn't matter, she stepped through as if the pain wasn't there. Reaching the landing of the concrete stairwell - nothing had happened. She hadn't traveled. She walked back down, this time amping herself up before she tried again.

'This is it,' she thought, 'You're going to do it.'

Now with a running start, she headed back up the stairs, still set on opening a portal. She continued up past the landing, running up further and further. But again, nothing changed.

"Shit!" she yelled in frustration at the final top landing.

Seven floors and nothing. Not a single shifting step or even a slight feeling of wooziness.

Her thoughts casting doubt, she couldn't help but think negatively, 'Maybe Tess is wrong. How would I have powers? No. This is something else entirely. I'm not special, am I? I'm just a girl...'

Aurelia's mind was racing as she slowly made her way back down the stairs to try again, already panting from the exertion of running up the stairs, 'But why can I travel without an Okliot? It doesn't make sense. It's not like I'm a superhero. Something else is causing it. Right? Why would a normal girl from El Segundo have powers amidst a totally normal world? This is crazy. I went to that party in the '70s with Will by accident, didn't I? Or did I see their costumes and subconsciously want to go where they were going?'

She ran up the stairs yet again, scrunching her face in the hopes something would happen, but again, nothing did, and she yet again reached the top landing. Running back down, she gave herself even more floors to work with this time, running past the 67th floor where Chi's apartment was and down to the 60th. Running up, her legs burning from the sudden exercise after her extensive injuries, being paralyzed for days, and dancing the night away. The pain in her legs hurt worse from each step, almost like small ice picks were being shoved into her calves, tightening and cramping the muscles until she almost couldn't stand the agony.

Stopping for a moment in anxiety, Aurelia realized she hadn't let herself be emotional, bottling her fears for Natalia and trying to stay optimistic. It wasn't working. She had to get Natalia to B-udo or she would die.

'Natalia will die,' the image flashed in her mind. 'No. NO! Eloise. Eloise will save her.'

Her stomach clenching from nerves, she ran back up the stairs. Her mind fixated on getting to Eloise, the walls began to shift and morph around her.

She had opened a portal. She had done it.

For the first time, it was as if Aurelia could anticipate what would be on the other side of the door. She knew Eloise would be there.

Opening the sleek metal door with confidence, just as expected, the blonde haired, blue-eyed Eloise was in the hospital hallway, just leaving a patient's room. It seemed like Aurelia had come out of one of the hospital rooms herself, the stairwell portal spontaneously appearing inside.

"Miana!" Eloise hugged her friend, then noticed that Aurelia's face was twisted with worry. "What's wrong?"

"We need your help."

CHAPTER 29

NANOBOTS

"Tess, let's grab Natalia. We have to go," Aurelia said, bursting through the front door of Chi's apartment, with Eloise standing next to her.

"It worked?" Tess said, hopping out of the living room couch. "Eloise!"

Aurelia nodded, and Eloise smiled at her friend Tess warmly. Chi looked at the enthused girls.

"What worked?" he asked. "Who're you?" motioning to the strange girl Eloise, who wore a yellow, skintight suit sprinkled with pink patterns.

"No time to explain," Aurelia said, opening the door to get Natalia. Inside, Natalia was still asleep. "Nat! Wake up, we have a way to save you," Natalia didn't stir. "Nat?" Still nothing.

Aurelia pulled back the sheets and instantly realized her bluish-grey fingers, the symptom that Chi had warned her about.

"No. No, this can't be happening. I can't be too late," Aurelia rambled, placing her ear above her nose to listen for a breath.

"Oh my God," Eloise exclaimed as she watched in horror, "is she...?"

Natalia was breathing, barely.

"She's alive," Eloise sighed in relief, "just unconscious."

Aurelia scooped Natalia up, Eloise also noticing the fact that her fingers were greyish in color.

"Tess, you know'r she's not gonna make it, right? There's nothing you can do now. I watched this exact thing happen to my family," Chi said, preparing Tess for the worst.

But Tess knew that they could save her, just not here, not in this time. Kissing Chi a final time to say goodbye, she opened the door to allow Aurelia, holding Natalia, to get through. They could save her. They had to.

"Where're you going?" Chi asked as they all rushed towards the stairwell. "The elevator's the other way!"

"I know!" Aurelia answered as they ran.

Chi followed them in confusion. Where were they taking her?

"Are you sure you can bring two people without Okliots through the portal at once?" Tess asked Aurelia as they approached the stairwell.

"Yes."

Although she wasn't sure. It would be hard, no questioning, but she had no choice. They opened the stairwell door. They would make it.

Natalia began to choke involuntarily from phlegm, her lungs filled to the point where a simple breath was almost impossible.

"Put her head upside down!" Eloise barked as she sat down on the stairs, helping Aurelia maneuver her onto her lap.

"What can I do?" Chi called from the stairwell door.

"Go back to your apartment!" Tess yelled, realizing he was following them and would watch them use the portal in a minute.

"No'r, let me help!"

Eloise, holding Natalia face down, began to thrust her hand to her back repeatedly, hoping to potentially dislodge the phlegm stopping her breath. Hitting her back as forcefully as she could, Natalia coughed and seemed to resume breathing, although she was still somewhat unconscious.

"OK. Help me get her up!" Eloise called to the group, and Tess lifted Natalia, with a strain.

She was heavier than she seemed. Chi came up next to them and scooped Natalia from Tess's arms.

"No! You have to stay here, Chi!" Tess said, attempting to grab Natalia back from his arms and move him towards the stairwell door.

"There's no time! He's strong - just let him carry her!" Aurelia exclaimed.

Tess looked at the stubborn Chi and grunted in frustration, "Fine," she said through gritted teeth.

Aurelia was right. He was the strongest of them all and could carry Natalia through the portal.

"Get your Okliot out, Tess, and hold onto someone in case the portal's not stable! Eloise, Chi, don't let go of me," Aurelia instructed, linking her arm through Chi's and grabbing Eloise's hand firmly.

"What? Why?" Chi asked, as they began to walk up the stairs.

"Trust me," Aurelia said, pulling his arm to get him to move faster.

Could she even bring three people through the portal?

They all began to run up, and the concrete stairwell shifted around them - a terrifying experience for Chi.

"What's happening?" he slowed, almost to a stop, in fear.

"Don't stop! We have to keep moving!" Tess shouted, pushing his shoulder forward from behind.

The stairwell quickly settled into a sleek metal, and the group burst through the door and into an all-white hospital room in B-udo, slightly later in the year from the last time the girls were there in 44-0.

"Where are we? What is this place?" Chi said, completely confused.

"Put her down on the bed," Eloise pointed, closing the stairwell door behind them and opening it once again to reveal the hospital's hallway. "I'll be right back."

Chi laid the small girl on the plush bed, looking around at the pure white room they had entered, in amazement. Completely exhausted from traveling with four people and only one Okliot, Aurelia sat next to Natalia on the bed, holding her hand in somewhat of a prayer. They were so close to saving her. She had to make it.

Eloise came running back with a small insulated black box.

"Close the cradle," Eloise instructed, handing the glass tablet on the bedside table to Tess.

Aurelia stood up, backing away, slightly. With a few taps, the bed quickly enclosed a clear glass-like substance around Natalia, similar to a hyperbaric chamber. Eloise, with the black box now open, gently picked up a dark pink slide from inside the box, which she stuck like a sticker on the side of the glass cradle.

"What is that?" Chi asked Eloise as she worked.

"Decontamination nanobots," Eloise replied, reaching for the tablet Tess held.

With a few taps, the glass around the pink sticker flashed a bright neon red, signaling that it was receiving the bots. Microscopically, the bots floated through the compressed air and began to find Natalia's breath, being sucked into her lungs and assimilated into her body tissues, recognizing Natalia's DNA and performing a genetic lock onto their host. Immediately, the bots recognized the specific strain of the H7N9 virus and began blocking each of Natalia's cells from the insidious virus.

Each grouping of the nanobots had a different purpose - some of them were specifically meant to attach themselves to the virus particles and excrete them from the host's body, others were meant to rip through any viruses and foreign bacteria that the host had in their body, essentially "killing" the virus by tearing apart its genetic makeup and genomes inside. The nanobots, through their programming directives, were able to identify the differences between known, toxic sicknesses and the harmless, sometimes beneficial bacteria that lived symbiotically within the host.

"Now we wait," Eloise sighed, finishing up her coding for the bots. "Is he staying? Does he need some decontamination bots too?" she asked, motioning to Chi as if he wasn't in the room.

"No! He's going back," Tess answered abruptly, grabbing Chi's arm as if to leave right away.

"Back? But where even are we?" Chi asked, shooing Tess's efforts away.

"Ughhh," Tess grunted, "listen. You weren't supposed to come with us. You're a permanent. You shouldn't be here."

"I'm a what? Permanent?"

"Yes. Now let's *gooo...*" Tess said, motioning for Aurelia to reopen the stairwell.

Aurelia opened the door, and the stairwell reappeared where the hospital hallway was just moments ago. It was almost as if once a portal had been opened once, it could easily be accessed again just by thinking of it.

"She said the word 'portal' when we were walking up. Where are we?" Chi asked, planting himself in the doorway.

"Where I'm from. The future. OK? Happy?" Tess said condescendingly.

Why was he so headstrong? Why wouldn't he leave?

"The... future? ...You're time travelers?" Tess nodded with pursed lips. "Time travel's impossible. Isn't it?"

"Yep. You're right. It is. So let's walk back down to your apartment and you can just forget all about this, and... me."

"Tess!" Chi held her shoulders to look in her eyes. "You're serious? This is the future?" Tess sighed with annoyance - of course she was serious. "Do we win the war? Do we kill the *Jīqìrén*?"

"Look - we're really not supposed to tell permanents about their future."

Chi nodded, "Of course. The butterfly effect. But, I'm already here. You've already told me that *some* sort of future exists. What if you've already messed up the timeline? ...You might as well answer my questions."

Tess tried to think of a comeback that would stop him from knowing more, but it seemed futile - he was too persistent.

"And how do *you* know about the butterfly effect?" Tess asked, realizing he seemed to be way more OK with the concept of time travel than a permanent should be.

"It's only in every sci-fi 5D ever made. Not to mention the vintage movies and TV."

Tess sighed, he had a point, "Fine... I'll tell you. The war is long, and devastating. It takes time and finally both sides acquiesce to each other."

"So no one wins? It's all for nothing?"

"I mean, I wouldn't say 'nothing'. It's the start of a new, independent age for Augments - for *Jīqìrén*. They're finally accepted as a race and it's a turning point for inclusion. It takes a few centuries, but one day the segregation and hatred towards them will end."

"What about my family? How can I keep them safe?"

Tess looked at Aurelia, sort of for approval, to which she hesitantly nodded, "I think there was an underwater city in the Sea of Japan, near South Korea, that was always untouched. Maybe if you can get them there you'll all be safe. But I don't know exactly where it was or how to get there undetected. Now will you *please* go before someone sees you?"

It was already bad enough that they had brought one permanent back with them, Natalia.

"Will I ever see you again?"

"Not if I can help it," Tess smiled slightly, showing a crack in her tough facade she had put up.

"Thank you. So much," Chi gently placed his hands on Tess's head and kissed her forehead. "Goodbye, Tess. It was a pleasure knowing you."

"...Bye Chi."

Some secret part of Tess wanted nothing more than for Chi to stay in B-udo with them - but it was impossible. He was already part of the past's permanent timeline, wasn't he? He had to leave.

Aurelia felt drained from carrying so many people through the portal mere minutes before, and wanted to stay with Natalia to make sure she was alright, but Tess seemed adamant that Chi had to go back to China immediately. So, stepping down the single flight of stairs holding his shoulder, she guided him back in time.

"Why didn't she want me to stay? Did I do something wrong to Tess, Miana?" Chi asked, as they reached his time.

"No... Tess is just, how do I put this...? Set in her ways," Aurelia chuckled, thinking back at how easily she had let Daví go just weeks ago. Tess didn't seem to feel the same attachment to the people she met along the way that Aurelia did.

"I dunno - I felt like we had such a strong connection. Almost like she was..." Chi's sentence trailed off.

"Like she was what?" Aurelia pried, wanting to know his thoughts.

"No'r, it's stupid." Chi opened the stairwell door, stepping into his apartment building's hallway as he began to ramble, "We obviously don't know'r each other enough. I know'r that. It's just... almost like I felt we were instantly closer than we were, you know'r? Like I knew her, and trusted her instantly. Like we were already years into our relationship just from our first conversation in the camp. Maybe if we had met under different circumstances..."

Chi began to walk away, although it was a brand new relationship, he honestly felt heartbroken that Tess had just cast him aside, yet he tried not to show it.

Aurelia raised her voice to stop him and give him a moment of hope, "A few years ago, I met someone, at a... party. He was perfect. And I knew from that one happenchance meeting that I wanted to be with him... have kids and grow old with him... It seems illogical, I know." Chi shook his head no, it didn't sound strange to him. "But the heart is a fickle thing. Sometimes you just... know. And then, everything changed at the party, and we got separated in time - and I had no way to get back to him, and I thought I'd never see him...again..."

Suddenly the realization hit Aurelia. She had just discovered that she had the power to open new portals anywhere. She could open one directly to Will. She *could* see him again.

"Oh my God," she whispered under her breath.

"Did you? Ever see him again?" Chi asked, filling the sudden silence of her story abruptly stopping.

Aurelia's eyes began filling with happy tears and she held back a grin.

"Yes! I did! ...I will! I can!" Aurelia couldn't help but smile. "Love is powerful, Chi. The universe is rooting for happiness - and if it's meant to be, it perseveres. Now look, I don't know how Tess feels, so I can't speak for her, as much as I'd like to be an 'agent of love'. But just... don't give up hope. If it's meant to be, then maybe you *will* see her again, under different circumstances."

Aurelia's face was lit with a new, unwavering smile. She had healed from the car crash which should have left her paralyzed, they had saved Natalia, and now she could see Will again. Maybe the universe *was* actually rooting for her.

CHAPTER 30

THE TERRORIST

Natalia had never felt better. In her opinion, the nanotechnology of the 44's was the most incredible thing to ever exist. Even through explanation, she didn't quite understand how the science of it worked, as her education up until now had consisted of very antiquated, narrow-minded, 15th century viewpoints, mixed in with some of Aurelia's guidance. But the important thing to her was that it worked, and the debilitating virus was purged from her system.

With Natalia recovered, Aurelia began to plan and scheme in her own mind about how to get back to Will - the first thing was that she needed to make sure Natalia was safe somewhere in time. Maybe she could stay in B-udo with Tess's family - after all, besides Will and her grandparents, there was no one Aurelia trusted more than Tess.

So, Aurelia explained her exciting plan to her friends; She would open a portal to the '70s, meet Will just after the 19-year-old version of herself ran up the portal, and they would get to be together again, madly in love.

There were a few roadblocks with Aurelia's perfect, dream scenario. For one, Will had only just met Aurelia a few hours before. Just like how she herself had felt in 1950s Texas, when a future version of Will arrived on the doorstep, Aurelia would still be, in most ways, a stranger. Back then, Aurelia had felt so powerless knowing that he had already lived so many years of their life together and the future was set in stone. So perhaps she would have to approach it differently than he had, and keep Will unaware that she knew him in the future, letting him have a choice in his destiny.

Another issue to overcome was the fact that Aurelia had left the '70s for a reason. Some man that Will had called wanted Aurelia detained, which, for her, had started the entire cycle of her running from the infamous "them" - whoever "they" were. For all she knew, everyone at the party could be involved. Whoever they were or why they were after her, they were extremely dangerous, as they proved by killing Johanna in cold blood - which was partly why Aurelia wanted to make sure Tess and Natalia were far, far away, somewhere safe.

A part of Aurelia wished she didn't have to meet him in the '70s. There were so many unknowns. Perhaps she could go forward a few years in B-udo and wait until he returned - But Will was such a frequent traveler who rarely returned home, with dozens of tricks to avoid the public portals and rules of the company, that there was a chance their paths wouldn't cross for years, if ever.

Ironically, here in 44-0 B-udo, a younger version of Will was infuriatingly close geographically to Aurelia. It was a strange feeling knowing that a 14-year-old Will was in the same place and time as they were in now. It was tempting to just try and meet him now and perhaps change their future, if that was even possible - but here Aurelia was much older than him, and something about their first meeting at the party in the '70s seemed like it was meant to be, so she was determined to leave it intact.

So, the plan somewhat set, Aurelia and Tess decided to use the hidden tunnels in B-udo to navigate back to Tess's home and see her parents. They hoped that Natalia would be welcomed to temporarily stay with them in B-udo, and with Natalia safe, Aurelia would be able to go straight to Will.

Tess was never really close to her parents growing up per se, mostly because they were always hard at work living in a level much higher to the Earth's surface, P-yex. It wasn't until Tess had just turned 13, that her uncle, Aleksander, negotiated them a place in the coveted, lower level B-udo, where they all relocated to after extensive radiation therapy. Most people didn't move between the levels - when they did, it was a huge ordeal. But, Aleksander knew his wife would've wanted her sister's family to have a comfortable life, so he insisted that the company had to relocate them if they wanted Aleksander to keep making their precious Okliots. Suddenly her parents weren't of the working class anymore, and they threw themselves into merely enjoying life together.

Tess, on the other hand, spent her time on downloads - for the first time in her life with access to the top tier education that she had been deprived of in a "workforce centered" P level. With no specific leaning to any subject, she just wanted to know everything there was to know, experience everything the world had to offer.

The first few months were difficult for Tess adjusting to the spoiled, judgmental kids in B-udo, but luckily her younger cousin

Will took her under his wing. Since his dad was the talk of ZhēnZhū for his outstanding accomplishments, he was as popular as the children of the company's executives and royals, and Tess instantly became a small part of that elite crowd.

However, it was hard to be one of the cool kids when Tess's parents had forbidden her to become a Member of the company like them, and use the portals with her friends - afraid of what might happen to a young black girl back in time. What if her friends decided it would be "fun" to go to South Carolina in the 1700s, where the slave trade was booming and racism ran high? Although the company Adventures In Time assured everyone's safety, the past was riddled with horrible people, and they didn't trust that it wouldn't be a scarring experience for their young girl. Sometimes she hated her parents because of their seemingly controlling nature.

So, almost a year after they had forbidden her, mostly just wanting to prove them wrong that she would be safe alone, she had secretly bought herself a one-off ticket, which the company touted as a form of "membership" for anyone who could afford it, and then met Aurelia and embarked on their crazy adventure across Christendom in the 15th century. It had been about three months for Tess since she'd last seen her parents, but for them in B-udo, only about a month had passed. Even though they were distant, they still had seen each other every single day of Tess's sixteen years of life. What would their reaction be to her rebellious trip? Had they even missed her? Filled with a mix of dread and excitement, Tess was ready to find out.

Aurelia borrowed Eloise's bracelet so she would have a suit to blend into the times, and luckily Tess had held onto her original bracelet through their travels. The girls quickly tapped their bands to reveal the mesh-like colored suits, Aurelia with Eloise's yellow one and Tess with a mix of shades of purple, which Aurelia remembered meant she was open to possibilities romantically. It was strange just now realizing Tess's "gender", so to speak. Would she even be considered a "she" being a purple, Aurelia wondered? Three months and the subject had never even been mentioned. But to Aurelia, Tess was the same person she had always been, no matter the color suit she wore.

So, leaving Natalia in good hands with Eloise, the girls were off to see Tess's parents.

The hidden tunnels of B-udo were somewhat easy to navigate if you knew which general direction you were headed. Tracing around the Core and into each individual sector of residences, the tunnels warped underneath hallways and had several secret entrances to most of the executive's homes. Tess's family lived just next to Will's home, so avoiding the dreaded viral checkpoint altogether, they found a door that led into the correct hallway, conveniently just steps from Will's home. Aurelia wondered if this was perhaps the entrance that Aleksander had used so many times, to get from his home to his lab, in the middle of the night.

Walking through the eerie hallway pumped full of rose scented air, they quickly found Tess's door. Written on the projection were three names, Jemila Coleman, Farrah Imogene Branson, and Tess Coleman-Branson. Aurelia realized that Farrah Branson must be Will's aunt that he had mentioned, sister to his mom, Phoebe Branson. Tess still didn't know that Aurelia's Will was in fact also her cousin, and Aurelia would keep it that way until it was revealed in Tess's future, but it was odd meeting Will's extended family without him.

Hesitating for a moment, Tess wondered what would greet them on the other side of the door. Would her moms be happy to see her, or extremely mad that she had disobeyed them in such a blatant way?

"You OK?" Aurelia asked, slipping her hand into Tess's for comfort.

Tess cringed, "What if they hate me?"

"You're their daughter. They can't hate you even if they tried."

Nodding with reluctance, Tess opened the front door, the biometric door lock opening for her. Aurelia stayed just outside the open door, hoping to let them have a moment of privacy. Inside, the house was furnished in a mod, clean way. Boldly colored designer chairs stood out on a simple palette of whitewashed floors and walls. They had entered directly into the main parlor, a sitting room with a faux balcony overlooking a projection of the ocean, flawlessly outfitted with sea spray, sounds of seagulls and waves crashing to mimic the real thing. Aside from the two bedrooms, it was a completely open, loft-like floor plan. Just to their left was the kitchen, which flowed effortlessly into the download room, and to their right was the music and art room. It was one of the smaller floor plans of the sector, but to Tess and her parents, it felt like a castle, coming from their home in P-yex, the one room loft that they had lived in her entire life, up until three years ago.

"TESS? Baby?" a woman from the music room cried, running

towards them.

"Hi Mommy," Tess's face melted into tears.

Tess's mom, Jemila, grasped her arms and threw herself into a deep, shaking hug with her daughter, not able to contain herself.

"We thought you were dead. Oh my God. Are you hurt?" the gorgeous black woman pulled Tess's face into view from their hug to look at her, brushing her dark curly hair back from her forehead. Tess shook her head no. "Thank God," the woman sobbed, embracing her again. "Where were you baby? Were you safe? Was someone holding you?"

"What? No. I... went back in time. I'm so sorry Mommy. I know I disrespected you."

"It's OK, baby. I know you did. We tried to find you in Morocco."

"What? How did you know I was in Morocco?"

"You disappeared, Tess! We had the Guardians looking for you for weeks! They finally tracked your band to a scan at Headquarters and realized you left with undocumented Okliots. They sent a recovery team for you, but you were gone. Everyone thought the worst. And they said that the girl you were with... she..." her eyes shifted to look at the stranger that had come with Tess, standing just in the door frame. "It's you," Tess's mom finally acknowledged Aurelia, suddenly with a dark shift in her tone. "You're the girl, aren't you? You're the terrorist."

"What? No. I'm not a terrorist!" Aurelia's eyes darted to Tess's.

"Mom, this is my *friend*, Miana."

Jemila grabbed her daughter, holding her back from Aurelia as if she was here to hurt them, "You need to leave. Now!"

"MOM? What are you talking about?"

Jemila whispered into Tess's ears with a frantic energy, holding her tight with both arms, "Baby, she's dangerous. She's trying to destroy ZhēnZhū. They told us everything."

Aurelia stood with her palms out in a non threatening stance, "Look - I'm not who you think I am. I don't know what they told you about me, but I'm not here to hurt anyone."

"Mom, trust me, she's *not* trying to destroy ZhēnZhū. She's not a terrorist."

Tess's mom continued in her opinion, "They said that she'd get in your head. That's what they do. You're young, impressionable. This is what she does. They told me. She's done it before."

"She's not a bad person. She's my best friend," Tess wriggled out of her mom's grip, stepping to Aurelia and grasping her hand to show her mom she was harmless.

Jemila couldn't believe the sight. How had her daughter fallen prey to the extremist group? No. She was being brainwashed. It had to be. Reaching into her pocket, she pulled out a small clear tablet.

"Mom? What are you doing?"

Tapping her thumb to it, the screen lit up, "You're going to thank me for this one day, Tess."

"What are you doing, mom?" Tess asked, stepping over to her mom again.

"You need to trust me. I know what's best for you."

"Stop! Don't do this, mom!"

Jemila tapped on her screen yet again, and a small beep ensued, signaling it was listening.

"She's here!" she screamed, just as Tess ripped the tablet from her hands.

A chill rushed down Aurelia's spine. "They" knew she was here.

"What have you done?" Aurelia whispered.

Jemila paused for a moment, studying her daughter's face that was twisted in emotion, "They're going to help you. They *want* to help you."

"Mom...? Who did you send that to?"

"The Guardians."

CHAPTER 31

ESCAPING B-UDO

Tess stared at her mom in disbelief. She had really just alerted the authorities that Aurelia was here? Poor Aurelia was hiding from them, although she still didn't know why, somehow she trusted her friend explicitly. Aurelia was the kindest soul she knew. She couldn't be a terrorist, could she? That couldn't be the reason she was hiding her identity, was it?

"We have to go," Aurelia said sharply, realizing that within minutes she would be caught by the Guardians, finally putting a name to the infamous "them" chasing her.

Tess nodded, stepping away from her mom.

"What?" Jemila's face twisted, grabbing her daughter's arm. "You can't go with her!" Tess snapped her arm from her grip. "She's the enemy, Tess!"

"No. She's not. But you wouldn't even let me explain that," Tess quipped, walking out of the door with Aurelia, and quickly breaking into a run towards the hidden tunnel.

"No! Tess!" her mom called, running after them.

"Are you sure you want to come with me?" Aurelia asked breathlessly as they jogged away.

"I'm sure. I trust you, Ari."

From just behind them, a rumble of footsteps filled the hall.

Tess's mom called in the distance, "She's there! Aurelia Quinn is there! Stop her, please! She has my daughter! You promised you would protect her!"

Jemila even knew her real name. Looking back, they could see an onslaught of at least a dozen heavily armed personnel, all in generic, silver metal, full body, second skin suits.

They quickly approached Tess's mom, tackling her to the ground as she screamed, "What are you doing? I haven't done anything! I'm the one that called you! Stop!"

Tess stopped in her tracks, realizing her mom was being

detained.

"Mom?"

"Don't stop, Tess! Come on!" Aurelia called, jogging back a few steps and pulling her friend's arm to keep going, reminiscent of the feeling in Amsterdam, pulling Johanna's arm to keep moving.

Furthering Aurelia's feeling of déjà vu, the Guardians began firing their weapons at them, the immense sound like thunder in their ears. Tess screamed at the sound, jumping in shock. But they weren't shooting bullets this time - no, these were a kind of non-lethal, stun energy blasts. Regardless, the light ricocheted off of the metal walls and flew by their ears, barely missing them. The sounds of screams from both the girls and Jemila rang in the metal hallway. Springing into a sprint, the girls ran towards the tunnel they had come from, thankfully turning the gently bending corner and getting out of sight from the blasts behind them. Luckily keeping enough distance from the Guardians, themselves running for their lives, while the Guardians merely hunted their prey like a fox hunts a rabbit.

As they passed Will's front door, they quickly came to the hidden tunnel's entrance, an unmarked door with a small screen just next to it. Aurelia promptly swiped the secret code she had memorized from Will and Aleksander, and they hustled inside, continuing to run back the way they had come. Fully expecting the Guardians to follow them inside the tunnel, the sounds of shouting and slamming footsteps behind them seemed to fade. The Guardians didn't know that they knew about the tunnel, or perhaps they themselves didn't even know about it - after all, it was only supposed to be for the executives and royals. So why would Aurelia and Tess have access to it?

Despite losing the Guardians chasing them, they ran back the entire way, their clothes underneath their suits now soaked in sweat. They burst into the hospital and slithered into the room where Natalia and Eloise were, thankful to be safe. Tess was shaking from the events they had just witnessed, worried about what had transpired with her mom. Was she alright? Had the Guardians let her go or was she still being detained? Either way, Tess knew she couldn't stay to find out, unless she too wanted to be detained by the Guardians.

"Did your parents say yes? Can I stay with them?" young Natalia asked with an optimistic smile.

"Well... not exactly..." the girls almost didn't know what to say. The afternoon hadn't turned out at all as expected.

"Ah. That is fine," Natalia said, obviously saddened, and in her mind jumping to the conclusion that it was somehow her own fault.

"Listen..." Aurelia said, jumping straight to the point, "we have to leave - now, if possible. Eloise, do you still have access to those Okliots?"

Eloise had actually managed to stockpile a few "inoperable" A class Okliots over the course of the past few months, secretly hoping that Aurelia, Tess or even Will would return and want to go on another secret, extended trip with her. Since they were labeled as being discarded, the "inoperable" Okliots wouldn't be missed, and luckily wouldn't have to be brought back to the 44s like before. Eloise wanted nothing more than to join Aurelia, Natalia and Tess on their latest adventure, but Aurelia insisted that she should stay behind on this particular trip, avoiding the reason why - that they were on the run from the Guardians.

Although Aurelia had proved that she herself could carry multiple people through the portals, it was exhausting, and unpredictable, so it would be much safer to have Okliots with them, a surefire way to travel, just in case.

So, the girls said goodbye to Eloise as she gave them each a new Okliot, and Aurelia reopened the portal in the hospital room. Somehow the once daunting task of creating a portal had become second nature to her, now only needing a simple visualization that a portal would be there - and suddenly it was. Everything in life is hard, until it is understood. Just like how as a toddler you learn to stand, then walk, then run - and one day, you forget how difficult it was just to stand. Somehow Aurelia felt as if she finally understood how her power worked, although she still had no idea *why* it worked, but perhaps that was just one of the secrets of the universe.

Stepping into the stairwell, Aurelia thought about the ramifications of their day. Tess, who belonged here at home in the future with her friends and family, would now have to perpetually be on the run, because she had chosen to follow her friend instead of staying with her mom. But the future version of Tess that Aurelia had met years ago seemed happy. Had she ever been able to return home, Aurelia wondered? Or was today a turning point that caused her to be on the run hidden in time - just like Aurelia?

Now, going to Will seemed more like a pipe dream, since her friends hadn't found safety with Tess's parents. Aurelia knew that it would be egocentric to abandon her friends somewhere random in time just to go to Will, and bringing them along would be even worse, because the party in the '70s would soon be filled with Guardians looking for Aurelia.

They needed to play it extra cautious - especially since the Guardians now knew that Tess was with Aurelia. Wherever or whenever they went together, they decided to use Aurelia's trick of using aliases - Aurelia would switch it up to a new one - Valentina, and Natalia decided on a fake name of Natasha - similar to her own name, yet different enough.

Tess wasn't quite sure which name to use, but soon settled on Deja, like déjà vu, an ironic name since they were traveling back in time, reliving the history of events that had already happened. A fleeting memory flashed in Aurelia's mind - was that the first name Will had called Tess in 1993 London? Life was revealing itself more and more each day.

"So, where to?" Tess asked the girls as they stood on the top step of the stairwell.

"Whenever this portal takes us, I guess. Somewhere safe," Aurelia answered. "Just hopefully not back to the *Jīqìrén* Wars!"

"If you created the portal, can't you control where we end up?" Natalia asked, her light shining brightly again, now that she was healed from the Nantong virus.

"I'm not sure... maybe?" Aurelia turned it over in her mind, thinking back to her past travels - she *had* managed to open a portal right to Eloise at the perfect point in time. What if she *could* control where or when she was going? It made sense that she should be able to navigate somewhere specific - but how?

The last time, she had focused her mind on her memory of Eloise, and ended up exactly where she needed to go. Perhaps if she set her mind on going somewhere or to someone, it would work the same way. Her mind flashed back to her other travels, had she inadvertently thought of a place when she had used the portals?

"I have a feeling you can, Ari," Tess said reassuringly, a glimmer of excitement in her voice.

"Well... where do you want to try and go? Where would it be safe? Nat, do you want to go home to Russia?" Aurelia asked, realizing she might have the power to finally bring her back to her family after all this time. "You could go back to your family, and your life as a grand duchess! You'd be safe there, and you could live in your palace again."

Pausing for a moment to think about it, Natalia shook her head no, "One day, maybe. In my heart, I'll always be Russian, but I'm not the same delicate flower that left home. If I return, I would be offered up into yet another marriage, my education stopped. I'd rather continue on this amazing adventure in time with you. There, I would be treated as an object, not a person. So, I don't know if I even want to be a grand duchess anymore... Maybe it would be better to just be Natalia."

Aurelia smiled, somewhat selfishly happy that she didn't want to return, and quickly shifted the conversation in case she changed her mind, "So where should we go? Canada? Japan? A beach in Mexico?" she chuckled, honestly a beach somewhere secluded sounded divine.

Natalia smiled, cooking up a delicious idea... "What about Italy?"

The vision of Italy was probably less an actual place, than a feeling. A feeling of safety, of love, of her family. After all, Aurelia's own heritage was part Italian, on her grandfather's side. He had immigrated to New York with his parents, younger sisters and older brother as a child - thrust into a new language, new school, and new life. But his roots to Italy had always been strong, and he had raised Aurelia with an appreciation of her family's culture. She had always wished her grandfather would one day take her to Italy - back to meet his cousins and other relatives he spoke often of, most of whom unfortunately only wrote him by snail mail letters, since they were apparently deep in the countryside and didn't have access to modern conveniences. But before they were able to go to Italy, time had been cruel and taken her grandfather away from them too soon.

So in her mind, Aurelia dreamt up an image of a picturesque small town in Italy - pieced together from fragmented memories of epic TV shows and movies that were filmed in a stone villa with tall cypress trees lining the unnecessarily long, winding road. In the distance, rolling hills would stretch as far as the eye could see, sometimes aligning perfectly with the sun setting, to hold the glowing orange orb in mother nature's hand, just before disappearing over the horizon. There was a laid back attitude displayed in everything, yet despite it, the people had a strong work ethic, which melded together to create a perfect balance of 'work hard, play hard'.

Holding onto that feeling of the Italian countryside, Aurelia,

Natalia and Tess stepped through the portal, Natalia and Tess each holding an Okliot in one hand and Aurelia's hand in the other, staying together in case the portal wasn't entirely stable. The metallic walls around them shifted to stone, the steps beneath them turning to wood. The air musty from the rotting wood, yet crisp and smooth from a subtle smell, reminiscent of a pine tree. The feeling of traveling through time never got old - never quite knowing what would happen or where they would end up. The thrill of jumping headfirst into a new culture, exhilarating beyond belief.

It seemed to be sundown, judging by the dimming sunrays that seeped through the top of the bell tower they were in, and a gentle nip in the air pinched their cheeks. Stepping through the door at the bottom of the tower, they made their way into a small, empty church. Crammed with enough pews for the townspeople, the well-loved church was flooded with golden light from sunset, streaming through the windows and illuminating the building.

"*Chi sei?*" a voice from behind them asked, holding a gaslit candle in his hand, dressed in a black coat with a white necktie. "*Stavo per andare a casa, ma se hai bisogno di pregare, resterò con te.*"

The girls looked at each other in confusion. They had done it, they were definitely in Italy, their dream trip, with one major problem that they had forgotten about - none of them spoke Italian.

CHAPTER 32

THE TACCIONES

Unfortunately, Aurelia's grandfather hadn't taught her his first language, mostly because he rarely used it anymore living in an almost completely English speaking California city, El Segundo. She had never once heard her Nana Dottie speak it with him, and even his siblings in New York spoke English when they would visit, only shifting to Italian for small phrases that generally went unnoticed for Aurelia. The most that Aurelia remembered from her grandfather were the small words like, "*Ciao*", "*Buongiorno*" or "*Grazie*", which wouldn't be of much help in conversation.

So of course, the first phrase Aurelia asked the priest was, "Do you speak English?" to which he shook his head no to.

"*Sei Inglese?*" English - yes, they were English!

"Yes! Uh... *sì*," Tess responded.

"*Sei molto lontana de casa! Allora, cosa vi porta fin qui in Italia? Sei qui da sola?*"

"Huh?" just like that, Tess was lost.

His words weren't entirely pellucid to them, but Aurelia and Natalia could somewhat discern what he was talking about, since over the few years they had become fluent in some of the similar romance languages, French, Occitan, and Aurelia also conversationally adept in Spanish. The priest wondered what the three young girls were doing so far from home, all alone.

"*Ahh non importa, non capisci,*" the priest knew his words fell on somewhat deaf ears, "*Volete pregare? O avete fame?*"

Some words and phrases were easily translatable through the priest's descriptive hand movements as he motioned to his mouth - were they hungry? Always.

"*Sì... fame,*" Aurelia repeated. "I think," hopefully that meant what she thought it did.

"*E voi ragazze avete un posto dove dormire questa notte?*" the girls didn't quite understand his question through his fast accent.

"I don't, I don't know?" Aurelia asked in confusion.

"*Va bene, potete rimanere con la mia famiglia.*"

"Your family? *Famiglia?* We can eat with them? Is that what you're saying?"

"*Sì. Mangeremo con la mia famiglia a casa dei miei fratelli. E se avete bisogno di un letto per dormire, potete rimanere qui questa notte,*" the kind priest offered a meal and a bed to the girls at his brother's house, although they really had no idea what it was they were accepting.

"*OK! Grazie! Grazie mille!*" Aurelia thanked him.

"*Prego,*" the man began walking out of the church, motioning for them to follow him before the sun set and they would walk in the dark. "*Venite, camminiamo prima che fa'buio.*"

They walked down the long, winding dirt road towards the priest's family's home, where a steady stream of chimney smoke rose like a beacon in the dimming sky. The group strolled up to the stone house surrounded by a small garden of fragrant shrubs and flowers, the scents of rosemary and lavender wafting to their noses as they approached.

A bustling family of nearly a dozen were seated outside, about to take dinner underneath a pergola of vines ready to bloom. As the month of April came to a close, the sun warmed the surroundings a bit more each day, making it the perfect weather to sit outside.

A large grey, hearty dog with excess skin that drooped especially around his cheeks and eyes approached them, wagging his short tail as the priest patted him lovingly, then apprehensively sniffing the strangers to decide if he liked them. Aurelia bent down holding out her hand for the dog to sniff, and within a moment, the dog resumed wagging his tail and allowed them to pet him as well, walking in between them and the priest as they neared the house.

A woman, most likely in her late-thirties, wearing an almost floor skimming skirt that was muted in brown fabrics draping over her hips, came up to the priest.

"*Ciao caro,*" she greeted him while kissing his cheeks and smiling at the girls, "*e voi chi seite ragazze?*"

She eyed their strange clothes of pants and T-shirt's from the future, wondering where on earth they had gotten those hideous clothes - 'They must be extremely poor foreigners in need of charity,' she thought.

"*Abbiamo ospiti a cena,*" the priest explained that he had offered them dinner.

"*Ma certo!*" of course, that was no problem, the woman replied. "*Come vi chiamate, care?*" it seemed like she asked the girls a question, although they weren't sure what.

"*Ahh parlano solo inglese,*" they only spoke English, the priest explained, a phrase which Aurelia could understand.

"No! We do speak other languages! Just not Italian. Sorry," Aurelia extrapolated, "*Español, Occitan, Français-*"

"*Je parle un peu Français !*" the woman jumped in, telling them she spoke a little bit of French.

"*Excellent !*" Aurelia said, switching to French. "*Comment vous-appelez vous ?*" what was the woman's name, she asked.

"Giovanna Taccione. *Et vous ?*"

Aurelia quickly remembered the new aliases that the girls had settled on, Aurelia would be Valentina, Natalia Natasha, and Tess Deja, "*Je m'appelle* Valentina, *et ce sont mes amis,* Deja *et* Natasha."

Instead of taking their extended hands to shake, the woman kissed each of their cheeks to welcome them, "*Vienez manger, les filles !*" extending her hand to the table just waiting for them to join, she welcomed the girls to dinner, hoping to eat before the food grew cold.

The dinner was lovely and the company kind and generous. Padre Lorenzo, as they came to find out was the priest's name, had a large family, the Tacciones. They joined a table of eleven - the priest's mother and his two married brothers; the youngest brother had a 12-year-old daughter, Celia, and the priest's older brother, married to Giovanna, had two sons and two daughters. Giovanna's kids spanned in age, the girls aged 3 and 18, the boys 14 and 16.

Natalia was seated on the younger end of the table next to the boy her own age, Ricco, and the two of them began the dinner by only communicating with small smiles and hand motions, unable to speak the other's language. But as the night went on, instead of actually speaking about themselves or their lives, they found excitement in figuring out what some simple translations between English, French and Italian would be. Tess found herself in between the 18-year-old girl, Daniella, and the 16-year-old boy, Teodoro, themselves with a few words of broken French that barely carried a conversation. Aurelia was just next to them, speaking with the only person at the table that actually fluently spoke a language they understood, Giovanna, who translated Aurelia's French conversation to Italian for the others to hear, as her young daughter, Ilaria, went between sitting on her lap and running around the table.

Somehow, the food and red wine seemed endless. The meal had started with homemade bread and plates of antipasto, everything from thickly sliced meats and homegrown olives to the most delicious tartufo pecorino cheese they had ever tasted; the sheeps milk infused with small pieces of black truffle, found locally in the hillsides. Then moving to a hearty pottage soup with cannellini beans, kale, soaked bread and onion, called ribollita soup. Already full, a wide, yet long, thin, homemade pappardelle pasta tossed with a marinated wild hare ragu sauce was served, *pappardelle alla lepre*. A *secondi* of wine-braised rabbit meat was then brought out from the kitchen, and finally, a sweeter desert wine to drink with almond biscotti cookies, to end.

The family couldn't believe that the three young girls had traveled all the way to Italy by themselves - without reason or final destination. Of course, the Taccioni wanted to know everything about their journey. Had they taken a ship? Were they from England? Where was their family?

Aurelia was still unclear as to which year they had ended up in, although based on the family's fashions, it seemed to be sometime in the mid to late 1800s. Perhaps it wasn't completely recognizable to Tess, but it was obvious to Aurelia. They didn't wear the same extravagant hoop skirts and tight corsets as her fashion history course had taught years ago, but being that they were in the countryside, clothes would be much more practical than trendy, and subtleties of the times still stood out to her.

She knew some of the history of the 1800s, mostly scattered in her distant memory from a high school history class, with a teacher she had despised. The 1800s was a century obsessed with immigrating to the new world for a better life and to find work. Filled with such events as the abolition of slavery in the United States, civil wars, and a booming age of scientific discoveries and medicine - like Thomas Edison's invention of the lightbulb, and Louis Pasteur's vaccines. Unfortunately, her high school had been mostly focused on US history, and not necessarily details from the rest of the world.

So, lying imaginatively with learned information she knew, they were from America. They had come over on a large, crowded ship infested with rats, and were thankful to be on solid land again. All of their parents were gone, so they had found solace in each other's friendship. The Tacciones still couldn't believe their fashion choices of pants and shirts for girls - was that how people dressed in America, they asked? Aurelia chuckled at how out of place they seemed, answering that yes - it was indeed how Americans dressed, although in reality not for at least another century.

Why had they left America and what was it like there, the family wondered? An image of factories and soot came into Aurelia's mind, although in all honesty she had no idea what it would be like there in the 1800s. It made sense to her elaborate lie of a story that the reason they left was they wanted to get a fresh start somewhere, and Italy seemed the perfect place to do so. She explained that her grandfather was from central Italy originally, in the region of Tuscany. Although he had passed away, it felt Italy was an apropos place to start a new life. The Tacciones wondered who Aurelia's grandfather was, and if they would know him, since after all, they themselves lived in Tuscany, and although highly populated with hundreds of towns and cities, it was a small world with a tight community. Aurelia chuckled, knowing that he wouldn't even be born for at least another fifty or even hundred years, in the 1930s, but since they insisted, she told them his name, Federico Quinn. As expected, they had never heard of him - but were surprised at his surname, Quinn - it sounded like an Irish name to them, not Italian.

The darkness of night finally enveloping them, the dark stronger than the dim light of the gaslit candles illuminating the table outside, the family cleared the table and retreated inside. One part of the family split off to walk to another house located just a stones throw away, and the priest, his mother and Giovanna's family stayed here in their home, readying for bed. Their sweet, gigantic dog named Lupo followed them inside, plopping down in the center of the room for the night, immediately drooling a small pool on the tiled floor.

Kindly, Giovanna reiterated the priest's offer and insisted that the girls stay with them, and could sleep with her girls in the children's room. They happily accepted, Giovanna's daughters moving into one bed and allowing the three "American" girls to sleep in the other. It wasn't long before they all fell asleep, their eyes heavy from eating such copious amounts of meat, and their stomachs full from the delicious pasta.

The next morning, Aurelia woke gently to the sound of dishes clanging in the kitchen below them. Natalia was already awake yet still in bed, so they gently woke Tess and all headed downstairs.

The kitchen was bustling with the women of the family and young Ricco, all working in their own station, similar to an assembly line.

"Good morning!" the young boy said proudly, running up to his new friend Natalia.

"That was very good!" Natalia grinned, impressed that he had remembered a phrase she had taught him at dinner the night before. "*Buongiorno* Ricco!"

"*Buongiorno, ragazze!*" Giovanna said, greeting the girls with kisses on their cheeks. "*Vous avez bien dormi ?*" did they sleep well, she asked in French.

"*Oui ! C'était parfait. Merci,* Giovanna !"

"*De rien.*"

"*Que prépares-tu ? Que peut on-faire ?*" what were they making, Aurelia asked, and could they help?

"*...Oui ! Nous faisons du fromage burrata.*"

"She says they're making burrata cheese!"

"Yum!" Tess grinned, you could make cheese yourself, she wondered? "How?"

"*Je vous apprendrai !*" the woman happily offered to show them how to make the delicacy.

She explained how first, they had to make the cheese curds from scratch, heating fresh milk and animal rennet together, which they had been working on for the past hour or so and had just finished, now having plenty to work with.

They heated a large pot of salted water over the fire until boiling, and then, adding the cheese curds and salt to a large bowl, would pour enough of the hot water to submerge them, stirring and mashing the curds together constantly with a wooden spoon while they heated through.

Slowly, the curds would congeal and form into a single mass of smooth mozzarella, and you would keep adding hot water until every clump of the cheese was glossy and silky. Then you stretched the mound of cheese into rope and tore it into tiny pieces, which you would toss into another bowl of cream and salt, for them to absorb even more moisture, to be the gooey innards of the cheese. Every bit of the process was homemade, even the cream had been prepared by leaving fresh milk out for a day or so to separate the cream from the milk, skimming the cream off the top to use.

Finally, you would repeat the process to make the mozzarella. Taking a small ball of cheese in your hand, stretching it to make a little "pocket" which you filled with creamy innards. The last step was sealing off the pocket with your fingers and dipping it into cold water to solidify the outer layer of cheese. Once the burrata was finished, the girls each tasted the cheese. Creamy and mildly salty, it was unlike any cheese that they had ever tasted before - rich and soft in their mouths. Bursting with flavor, gentle tones hit their tongues. It was nothing like the pre-made, store bought cheese that Aurelia was used to eating growing up.

It felt a bit like alchemy, turning milk into cheese, now a delicious secret they could carry with them on their travels. Making a bit more food in addition to the surplus of burrata cheese, the family packed up a few baskets of food. Aurelia, Natalia and Tess somehow felt like part of the family during this little cooking lesson, their kind-hearted souls kindred spirits.

Stepping over to her eldest daughter Daniella, and her young niece, Celia, Giovanna lovingly ran her hands through her daughter's long, soft, dark hair which she still hadn't pinned up for the day.

"Daniella, Celia, *porta le ragazze di sopra, e prestagli alcuni dei tuoi vestiti per la chiesa,*" in Italian, she instructed her daughter and niece to go upstairs and lend Aurelia and her friends some of their dresses to wear, since they needed a change of clothes if they were to accompany them into town.

"*Zia... dobbiamo? Sono degli estranei...*" Celia whined, not wanting to give her clothes to the strangers, thinking they would surely ruin them, "*E se rovinano i nostri vestiti?*"

"*Attento a come parle,* Celia!" Giovanna snapped, telling her to watch her mouth. "*Sono nostri ospiti,*" they were their guests, and would be treated as such.

"*Ma certo, Mamma,*" Daniella replied, on behalf of herself and her cousin. Without warning, Daniella grabbed Tess's hand and began leading the three girls upstairs.

Tess, completely oblivious to the conversation in Italian, looked back at Giovanna, "Where are we going?" she asked.

Giovanna explained in French, "*Tes vêtements sont trop américaines. Vous pouvez utiliser les robes de ma fille jusqu'à ce que vous en aie.*"

Aurelia translated with a chuckle, "She says our clothes are a bit too 'American', so we can borrow her daughter's dresses until we get some new ones of our own."

Aurelia borrowed a brown, front button down dress from Daniella, meant to be floor-length, but on Aurelia, the fabric merely draped to her mid-shin, revealing her boots from the 2100s. Although they were in the Victorian age of fashion, luckily, they weren't in a highly fashionable city, where dresses would be extremely constricting, with tight corsets and gigantic hoop skirts. Here, the dresses were made simply to last. Tess easily fit into one of Daniella's dresses, almost like it was made for her skinny, model-esque figure. Natalia was luckily able to borrow one of Celia's dresses, which she begrudgingly walked down the road to her house to get, choosing her least favorite of her dresses, a dark grey, buttoned shift. It was slightly big for Natalia's small figure, but it worked nonetheless.

Hesitantly, Aurelia left their belongings under the bed upstairs; her bag with her ruby necklace, Tess's bag with her few things, and Natalia's tiara, but the girls decided it would be best to keep their Okliots with them, just in case. So they shoved them into pockets that were conveniently sewed into their skirts. With the girls like chameleons in their new environment, they were ready for town.

"*Bellissime, ragazze!*" Giovanna exclaimed as they walked down the stairs in their new garb, telling the girls they looked beautiful.

"*Gruzie!*" they replied in Italian.

"*Venite,*" Giovanna gathered the other children and men in Italian, then switching to French for the girls, "*allons à l'église !*" she explained they would go to church.

Walking down the same dirt path as the night before, they headed to the local church in the small village town nearby. Off on its own, yet surrounded by a few small buildings, the church seemed bigger than the night before, now fully illuminated with the bright, mid-morning sun. First greeting the priest, Padre Lorenzo, outside, the large group headed in, placing the baskets full of cheese just near the door. Aurelia expected the church to be somewhat empty, filled mostly with the large family that they were with, but instead the church was practically already full. The parishioners all spoke to each other while they waited for the service to begin, warmly greeting the family that had just arrived, who sat in the back row. It was barely a few seconds until the other parishioners realized Aurelia, Tess and Natalia's three new faces, and the conversation shifted to them. Who were they, they wondered?

Before Giovanna could explain who the girls were to the other parishioners, her brother-in-law, Padre Lorenzo, walked up the aisle to begin his service. The entire congregation held their questions in for the next hour, but with curiosity bubbling in their minds, they couldn't focus on the beautiful Catholic sermon. They had never had new visitors attend church with them, in their tiny, tight-knit town. Every few minutes, one of them would turn and look the girls up and down, then turn back to who they were seated next to and whisper about who they thought they were.

Aurelia smiled at being the subject of this little town's mystery. How intriguing they must seem to them just by appearance - a white, blonde young woman, gorgeous, tall, black teen, and small brunette, all dressed in borrowed clothes that they didn't quite feel comfortable in yet, making them stick out like a sore thumb.

It felt wonderful to Aurelia and Natalia to be in a church again after so long away. When Aurelia had lived in France months ago, she had become somewhat close to God. It was strange because something in her still cast doubt, but she had hid those feelings tightly in the 1400s - for fear of heresy. But being away from it for a while, it seemed like whether or not she believed in the entirety of the religion, praying for forgiveness, strength and wisdom seemed to clear her mind and help her soul.

The thing that she wished existed throughout the ages, was freedom to believe, and freedom to have your own unique divine relationship. It felt wrong to have so many holy wars and to hold judgement for people who didn't believe in the same God as you did. Perhaps she felt that way because she'd found perspective in her travels, always having to see things from a new point of view in order to fit in.

But one part of religion that she loved was how unifying it could be. Even right then and there, in a little stone church in the middle of Italy, the entire town was together. Bound by the music of the tiny choir, everyone put aside their strife and bickering to be as one.

As the service neared the end, the women of the family got up and headed towards the back of the church. Thinking they were going to leave early, the three girls followed them, but were surprised to see them instead unloading the burrata cheese from their baskets onto a small table with platters.

"*Que fais-tu ?*" Aurelia whispered, wondering what they were doing.

Giovanna responded that the burrata they had made wasn't for them to eat, as they had thought, but for anyone who may need it. It felt like such a huge gesture for such a small kindness. Why would they work so hard and not enjoy the fruits of their labors for themselves, or even sell the cheese? But, Giovanna explained, giving unconditionally had its own fulfilling reward; it fed your soul.

By the time the church service was over, everyone beelined to Aurelia, Tess and Natalia. Giovanna was protective of the girls in a motherly way, and explained the fake story to the townspeople; that the girls were from America, and had just arrived in their town last night, on foot, without a thing to their name, and Giovanna's family had kindly taken them in. How long would they be staying, the town wondered? Giovanna shifted the question to the girls, asking them instead, where did they plan on going as a final destination?

Speaking in English, Aurelia translated for Tess, "They're wondering where we're going after this."

"I don't know," Tess answered. "...Do they want us to leave, is that why they're asking? Should you ask her that?"

"*Voulez-vous que nous partions ?*" Aurelia whispered to

Giovanna in French.

"*Non ! Vous êtes trop jeunes pour être seules !*" no, Giovanna replied, they were too young to be out in the world all alone! "*Vous pouvez rester avec nous aussi longtemps que vous le souhaitez,*" they were welcome to stay with them as long as they wanted to.

"*Merci,* Giovanna!" Natalia smiled.

"*Ah bon ? Êtes-vous sûre ?*" really, was she sure, Aurelia asked? "*Nous ne voulons pas être un fardeau,*" they didn't want to be a burden.

They weren't a burden at all, "*Vous n'êtes pas du tout un fardeau ! Vous devez rester. Vraiment, j'insiste,*" they had to stay, she insisted.

Aurelia really couldn't believe what a kindhearted family they had stumbled upon, "*Grazie mille! Vous êtes trop gentille.*"

"So?" Tess asked Aurelia.

"She says we can stay as long as we want to!"

A few weeks had already passed staying with the family in Italy. They led a simple life, mostly revolving around family, friends and food. Everyday was a huge production in the kitchen, making enough food for an army, which Aurelia and Tess did their best to help with, although their cooking skills weren't quite as natural as the rest of the women. Natalia gave up trying after the first few days - she despised cooking above everything else. So instead, she would follow Ricco around the house and garden while he did his daily chores, barely helping, but rather just enjoying the other's company. When Ricco was needed in the kitchen, Natalia would sit and watch near them, practicing needlepoint.

Behind the house was a small barn where three cows, four sheep and three goats were kept at night, and next to it, a henhouse with a surplus of chickens. Each night's dinner rotated between Giovanna's large house, with her husband, Marco, then switched to his brother, Roberto, and his wife, Maria's house.

Learning a bit of Italian came pretty naturally to the girls. Luckily, already being fluent in a few different languages meant that learning something new wasn't as much of a shock to their system.

Now, Aurelia and Tess prepared a refreshing salad with Daniella, with fresh tomatoes, onions, cucumber and basil, all of which they had just picked from the garden. Then they added some soaked stale bread, seasoning it with olive oil, salt and pepper. The perfect recipe for a warm, spring day.

Unexpectedly, a sharp, electrifying pain stung Aurelia's inner forearm, and she screamed out from the pain. It reminded her of the sudden pain in her bicep she had felt in Spain months ago. Sort of like an ice pick lurching into her skin. Grasping her arm to try and see what was wrong with it - it looked unharmed. But then she noticed it.

The sound was gone. Tess and Daniella hadn't reacted to her scream.

Looking up, praying that she would see them moving in time, her face fell to see that the two of them were frozen in place.

Time had stopped again.

"No, no, no!" Aurelia stuttered. "This can't be happening."

Running outside, somehow in the hopes that time had only stopped inside the house, she scanned the horizon of rolling hills for movement - but nothing stirred. Everything was empty and devoid of life force. The color seemed drained around her, slowly turning to sepia.

Time was frozen.

CHAPTER 33

TIMESTOP

It was hard to keep track of time when the world around her was stopped. Had it been a few hours, or a few days? It was long enough to sit inside the house and wait for a while, merely staring at Tess and Daniella in the hopes that they would resume cooking and she could just jump back in as if nothing had happened. Then, seeing as that wasn't doing any good, she decided to walk into town to pray in church. Perhaps someone up there would hear her and time would start up again. So she prayed for a decent amount of time, with no luck, walking back to the house in defeat on the permanently sunny day.

But the sun didn't have the same warmth as it normally did, only the brightness, and eventually the beautiful golden hue faded to sepia, as well as the rest of her surroundings.

She thought one way to get out was to use a portal and travel to another time. So she attempted running up the stairs in the church. But it didn't work. It was just a staircase. She decided to try other staircases, but none of them did the trick either.

Aurelia tried to go into the same meditative state that she had been in when she saved Tess in Spain, imagining the entire earth resuming, but time still didn't budge.

Was she the one that had the power to start and stop time, she wondered? Or did it have something to do with the time travel technology of the future? Were there others who were awake during it? Or was she truly alone?

The silence was maddening. You don't realize just how many sounds you're surrounded with every second, until they're completely gone like the vacuum of space. The only noises she could hear was her heart beating, followed by the slosh of her blood through her veins and organs, and her breath. Somehow when every other sound is gone, your body's sounds seem amplified.

It was strange, normally she would feel hungry or thirsty after a while, but no such feelings came over her, as if she didn't *need* anything to sustain her here. Would she even age here? Or was her body also stuck in time?

What if this was permanent? What if time never started again? Would that be the end of the world? Sudden and swift, no one ever knowing that it was actually even over? It felt like it.

What if Aurelia was stuck forever, alone? In the back of her mind, she knew that she could wake someone up by touching them, just as she had shaken Tess awake in Spain, but she also knew the ramifications of that. Tess wasn't able to breathe for some reason. She needed time to be ticking in order to live. So waking someone up just to have someone to talk to for one minute wasn't an option. They would die. She was completely alone. But why could *she* survive without time?

At this point, Aurelia had been stuck in the moment of time in the 1800s for at least a few months. It honestly felt like years. With no variation from the sun, no real need to eat or sleep, and no company, the days felt like eons and were completely unmeasurable.

She had ventured to a few of the neighbor's houses, finding some books to read for entertainment in the largest home. The unfortunate thing was that they were all written in other languages, mainly Italian or Latin. It would take a while to decipher what they meant, but, after all, she had time. It was fun moving items here, since they were paused in time, normal things like gravity didn't have the same rules, and the moment Aurelia would stop touching an object, it would freeze mid-air. So for reading, she could position a book above her head while she laid in the sun, only having to lift her arm to turn the page.

Aurelia read through every sentence, in every book, in every house nearby, until her written knowledge of Italian was fluent. She loved reading aloud to hear her own voice amidst the silence - sometimes it felt like she was actually having a conversation with someone.

Then there were the days she spent hours daydreaming about Will. Coming up with fake scenarios, or reliving their epic moments together. How she would go to him when time started again. In her mind, she would find him just after she had left him in Amsterdam. He would be hers and she would be his. She missed him. It felt like a piece of her heart was missing being apart from him. She should've selfishly gone to him instead of getting Tess and Natalia to safety. Why hadn't she gone to him?

She had accidentally touched a moth on a doorknob, which sprung to life and flittered around for a few seconds of pure joy for Aurelia, until it suffocated and fell to the ground. It happened a few more times with tiny bugs like flies, but each time the same reaction ensued, and the insect would die in under a minute. Those few seconds of joy to see movement wasn't worth a life, as tiny as that life was. It solidified her theory that she couldn't wake anyone here.

After reading every book in every house, and fully exhausting the town for what it was, she decided to explore further. So Aurelia followed the barely used dirt road out of town, past the rolling hills that had made up her landscape for so many months. She made a point not to touch any woodland animals that she came across as she walked, like wild boars, porcupines, wolves, or even gentle deer, for fear they would die if she woke them into this paused moment. Sometimes a bird or butterfly would stun her as she nearly walked into them midair, but she walked slowly and cautiously for that exact reason.

Paying attention to the trees instead of her feet, she tripped over a protruding stone in the dirt road and fell, wrist first, into another, sharp rock. She should've bled. It should've hurt. Why didn't it hurt? It was the first time she had fallen or almost injured herself accidentally here in this paused moment in time. Taking her hand to the sharp edge of the rock in the road, she realized that no matter how hard she pressed, she couldn't pierce the skin. Somehow, she was impenetrable here. Perhaps her body was indeed also frozen in time.

After walking a long way, she crossed a wooden bridge over a still river, then came to another town, similar to the one she had lived in, with stone houses, and a little town square with a market and church. There were vineyards and other farms on the outskirts, and in town she found a dressmaker's shop and a cobbler. She spent a decent amount of time in the new town, staring at the unfamiliar faces and reading as many books as she could find, trying anything to get by and not lose her mind.

But there was only so much you could do alone. So she moved on to the next town, then the next. Finally, she came to a cliffside town overlooking the ocean. It was stunning. The frozen sight of the never-ending waters. She could swim in the still waters.

She hiked down the cliff, knowing that even if she slipped, she would be unharmed. Seeing the water up close was magical. Not even bothering to take off her clothes or boots, Aurelia ran towards the foaming water, overwhelmed with joy and anticipation to get to the water. But instead of stepping into the water, her foot stood on top of it.

How was it possible? Testing it out further, she stepped over the water, literally walking on top of the waves. She could walk on water, but she wanted to swim. But the water molecules were stopped in time, making a solid instead of a liquid, meaning that you couldn't step through or move, just like the water in her pitcher in Toulouse. She bent down and touched the solid surface, but unlike her feet which were impeded by her shoes, her hand was able to penetrate the water. It felt like goo, not water. Moveable with effort, but not at all the incredible feeling of a free ocean. It was disheartening.

She walked down the beach a bit, exploring the cliffs and caverns as she stepped where no one else could, on top of the rolling waves. But permanent things weren't as magical as a fleeting moment, and her surroundings didn't have the same vibrancy as when they were "awake", as she came to call it. Everything here was dormant, in a deep sleep. After a long while of sitting on the sand, looking out at the horizon, she decided to go back to the original town. There wasn't anything more that she wanted to see alone. She would go back and just wait for time to start again, if it was a day, a year, or a century. But this endless, aimless journeying had lost its meaning, alone.

Aurelia neared the small town where Tess and Natalia were, a town that even after all this time, since there weren't any signs, she still didn't know the name of. It felt wonderful to be back somewhere familiar after her journey away.

She found Natalia still in the garden, watching Ricco, who she was sure she had a crush on. It was obvious, even in this slice of a moment, just by her facial expression - a mix of nervousness, a tiny pursed smile, and a twinkle in her eye. Then she saw Tess and Daniella again, still in the kitchen making that same salad they were working on when time had stopped. A tiny sliver of white caught her eye from near the fireplace, and she stepped over to investigate. As her angle shifted, the white expanded, and she could see the door with no handle, floating just above the ground. It was the door that led to the space between time.

She looked around it, and it seemed to be completely flattened, and invisible from the other side. Was it here all along? Or had it just appeared? It was a way out of this nightmare. But going in meant she would lose herself - and with no one there to save her this time.

Aurelia couldn't bring herself to open the door to the space between time. Her thoughts and memories were all she had left. As the months passed, boredom and near madness took hold, and she yet again went exploring in other nearby towns. But the thought of the space between time kept creeping into her mind... 'There would be no more loneliness.'

Curiosity overwhelmed Aurelia with the idea that the space between time was just behind the white door with no handle. But what if it wasn't? What if the door led somewhere else, somewhere where time wasn't stopped? She ventured back to the door - just to look. Reaching where the handle should be, her fingers wrapped around the invisible knob, prying the door open.

It was different than Aurelia remembered. Instead of a pitch black, gaping void, it was illuminated with the most gorgeous golden light she had ever seen. Each photograph of moments connected with the same string, only this time it sparkled like a gold chain, the images all moving simultaneously as if watching a video. In the middle of the void, a massive glowing orb radiated like the sun. It was the source of the energy pulsing through each moment. Why had that golden nucleus not been there the first time she'd been in the space between time?

Holding the door frame so she didn't accidentally step fully inside, Aurelia looked further in. All around, the images of moments went as far as the eye could see, the void was endless, filled with every possible second experienced.

But she noticed something concerning; it seemed that the pictures below her were frozen, withered and faded to sepia, the pulsing golden light barely flickering through the string. Without the power connecting the moments in time, they became a shell of themselves. Was that the cause of time stopping here? Was the golden energy moving through the strings somehow the source of time moving? Could she fix it?

Above her, far in the distance, was another white door - an open door. Could it be a way out? But going in to try and investigate could mean forgetting everything, even the reason why she was trying to get to the other door. But what if there was someone else inside?

“Hello?” she screamed out, in the hopes someone would hear her. “Is anyone there?”

But no one answered.

In a town far from the frozen Tess and Natalia, Aurelia walked an unknown path, accidentally running into a bird mid-flight. The gorgeous little brown bird sprung to life, and found a tree branch nearby. It was alive. It had purpose.

Aurelia smiled, while tears streamed down her cheeks at the beautiful sight that would soon be gone. It would die without air, like every other tiny creature that she had accidentally touched here had. The small, brown bird swooped down to the ground, pecking at the dirt, tweeting. The sound was muted, since the sound waves couldn’t travel through the air normally here, but it was soft and sweet to hear regardless. Aurelia crouched down next to the bird, and could see its chest pumping for air.

“I’m sorry little one,” she whispered to it with a tear.

As the bird began to die and laid on its side, a little voice in her mind told her that it wasn’t right. This was her fault. Even though it was just a small creature, she couldn’t let the tiny, innocent bird die.

Scooping up the passed out bird in her hand, and closing her eyes, she imagined a tiny piece of her life force reaching out and sustaining it. Thinking of how the golden energy in the space between time flowed to the photographs. Like a golden thread that linked the two of them. There was something sustaining her here, perhaps a sort of energy within her linked to something similar to the energy in the space between time. If she could live in this moment paused in time, maybe she could share that force with something.

Keeping a strong hold on the vision of sharing her breath, her heartbeat, her soul, with the animal, the bird began to stir again.

Gasping, she opened her eyes. The bird now stood, upright, in the palm of her hands. Its tiny talons wrapped around her pinky. It had worked. It had worked?

The bird flew down to the ground again, and Aurelia couldn’t help but laugh and smile at the sight. She had done it. It was awake. The bird was alive.

Aurelia followed the tiny bird through the woods, running to keep up with it as it flew above her. She couldn't bear to lose the only creature in the world that was awake with her. But alas, the bird flew high into the sky and disappeared from Aurelia's sight, underneath the cover of the trees. At this point, she was lost, far from any trail or path, without the guide of sound or movement to show her the way, the sun in the middle of the sky, not much help to her either.

But if she had figured out how to wake an animal to be with her, maybe it would also work for larger creatures like humans too. She wouldn't have to be alone.

Being awake in a broken moment in time was a curse and a blessing. Here, she was invincible and immortal, she had all the time in the world to enjoy the world around her, but with no escape and no friends. Was there meaning to a life with no one to share it with?

In her heart, she didn't want to wake anyone up. It was a lot to take in, being stuck in a single second of time. But it had been years without hearing another voice. The selfish part of her *needed* someone to be here with her. But the selfless part reminded her that she wouldn't wish this way of life on anyone.

Instead of waking a human up, Aurelia decided to wake another animal. She had to make sure her newfound power was even stable enough that it could be repeated. So, finding a small roe deer grazing off on its own in the forest, she gently touched the creature to wake it. The color quickly returned to its fur, and it resumed eating, not even realizing that Aurelia stood silently behind it. She imagined the same string of life force reaching out from her to the animal, sustaining it here in this slice of time, linking the two of them. She wasn't sure if it worked, but the animal just continued to graze.

Shifting in her stance, the leaves underneath her feet crunched and the animal took off in a rapid leap, surprised that there was something just behind it. She watched in awe as the deer leapt through the forest, bouncing gracefully away from her without hesitation. It had worked. The bird wasn't just a fluke.

There were days when she came close to waking Tess or Natalia - but she knew that being stuck here was a bit like hell. If she was here with Will, then an eternity wouldn't be enough time, but alone - she almost couldn't bear it.

A long while had passed from the first time she had woken the bird, and since then, Aurelia had woken a beautiful all black monterufolino horse, the family's sweet dog Lupo, and a tiny kitten she found alone in town. She lived in Giovanna's house, near her friends, in case time decided to start again. Every so often, she would check the space between time, calling out in the hopes someone would hear her, although it seemed helpless. But why was there another door inside, and where did it lead?

Besides riding and training Knight, as she came to call her horse, she focused her time on meditation. In her heart, she believed that all those years ago in Spain with Tess when time had stopped, she had tapped into some sort of energy or force and pleaded with it to start time again. Perhaps her mind had reached out to the golden energy in the space between time. If she could focus her mind enough, she knew that she could learn it.

Deep in meditation, her mind focused yet empty, an overwhelming feeling of life within overcame Aurelia. Her heart beating, a flushed feeling in her cheeks. She grasped that feeling and pushed outwards, visualizing the feeling spreading through every facet of the vast universe. The piercing volume of sound around her pulled her from her trance, and instantly stopped as she lost focus.

But even if only for a split second, time had moved.

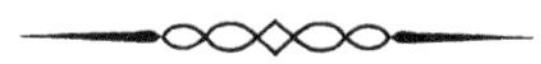

Slowly, Aurelia practiced time jumping in seconds, not yet fully able to stabilize time to start moving forward normally. She found that with concentration, she could move the seconds backwards and forwards in time, which was fun and scary. How was she able to control it? It literally seemed as if she had a direct phone number to the universe in her mind. But every day was now filled with excitement, as she grew to understand her abilities. She was close to escaping. She was sure of it.

Aurelia sat outside the farmhouse in the bright sun, in her daily meditation while Knight frolicked in the pasture. None of the animals, or herself, *had* to eat, drink or sleep, so everyday was filled instead with the in between moments that are normally taken for granted.

As she focused on that central feeling of life building in her, like an ember in her chest, time jumped forward a few fractions of a second. Tuning out the monstrous background sounds around her, and focusing on the fleeting feeling of warmth from the sun shining, time ticked forward a little further, before pausing again.

It felt as if the connection to time had been severed here. Like the energy in the space between time was somehow gone in this moment. But time had to start properly again, or life itself, all over the world, would end. Shifting her vision slightly, she thought of the golden energy in the space between time, hoping to reach some sort of consciousness within it and beg it to send its energy here once again. She imagined the feeling of the golden energy wrapping itself around this moment in time, filling every crevice on earth with time. The vision expanded past the atmosphere, into the solar system, far past the Milky Way. Time moving every rock, volcano and life, throughout the universe.

A hot, gasping feeling filled Aurelia's lungs from the vision, her skin bursting with sweat.

The sun suddenly seemed steadily warmer on Aurelia's face, and she opened her eyes, blinking away the colossal vision she had daydreamt. The gentle breeze whipped in her ears, flooding them with sound. The vibrant colors had returned to the landscape. It wasn't possible, was it? No. Her mind instantly chalked it up to a hallucination. But it was real.

Every gentle gust of wind felt like a hand on her skin, the subtle sway of grass around her tickling from movement. The deafening silence was gone. It had taken her years, but the world around her was finally awake.

Tess's voice broke the silence, "Valentina? Where'd you go?" she called from inside the house, using Aurelia's new alias she had been using here in Italy.

Time was moving. She had really done it.

Running inside the house as fast as humanly possible, Aurelia burst through the front door and hugged the startled Tess.

"OH MY GOD!"

Aurelia wasn't even sure what to think - only that it was the best feeling in the world to get to hug her friend after so many years in solitude.

It had felt like a seemingly inescapable prison.

"Weren't you just next to us? How'd you disappear so fast?" she asked as Aurelia squished her. "What's going on?"

Aurelia glanced at Daniella, not sure how much English she already understood just from listening to them in the past few weeks, "Do you remember what happened in Spain?"

"Huh?" Tess's face morphed from confusion to realization. "You mean time was...?" Aurelia nodded. "For how long?"

"*Long,*" Aurelia couldn't believe that time was moving again. It was a miracle. "I missed you so much! And Natali- I mean, Natasha!" remembering her fake name, Aurelia ran out of the house mid sentence to go see Natalia, with Tess and Daniella following just behind her.

She was right where she expected her to be, in the garden watching as Ricco plucked caterpillars from the cucumber leaves. Aurelia tackled her with a strong hug, ecstatic to finally be able to touch and hug people again.

"*Que fais-tu ?*" Natalia laughed, wondering what she was doing, her nose crinkling in embarrassment.

"*Je t'aime ma petite sœur !*" Aurelia told Natalia that she just loved her little sister, squeezing her tighter.

"I love you too," she chuckled, "but you're squishing me!"

"Sorry!" Aurelia released her, a grin plastered across Aurelia's face to see and talk to her friends again after so many years alone. But there was still one person missing for her heart to be full. She had to go to him. She couldn't wait another day. Her soul's missing piece, her love. Will.

CHAPTER 34

FOLLOW YOUR HEART

"Are you one hundred percent sure that you're OK with it?" Aurelia asked later that night, after she explained to the girls that she would leave them in Italy temporarily, so she could go to Will.

Once she met up with him in the 1970s and he had the chance to get to know Aurelia, she would bring him back with her to Italy.

Tess and Natalia trusted the Italian family, as they had seen their genuine kindness the past few weeks. But just in case, the girls still had their Okliots, if they needed to follow her for any reason.

"I'm sure. We'll be fine Ari. I'll take care of Natalia, I promise," Tess said, putting her arm around the still small Natalia.

"I don't need a governess anymore!" Natalia scowled.

"Alright, we'll look out for each other then, right?" Tess said, with a wink to Aurelia, Natalia nodded.

Aurelia looked at her friends as they stood supportingly at the bottom of the stairs in Giovanna's house, while the family was all out for dinner in the garden. It felt good to change out of her borrowed dress and into the t-shirt and cargo pants from the future, much more fitting for the 1970s than a floor skimming dress from a rural farmhouse in the 1800s. She decided to leave her bag with the girls for safekeeping, but of course would bring the Okliot with her, since she might need it to fit in with the group of time travelers.

But was this even the right decision, leaving her friends? After all, a bird in the hand is worth two in the bush. What if something happened and they lost each other in time?

"I think I changed my mind," Aurelia said, nervous about her plan.

"No. Nope. Not letting you. You are going! We're both fine here. We're safe. Really," Tess stated assuredly, walking with her to the first step. "Do your thingy. Come on," she motioned to the stairs for Aurelia to open the portal.

"But what if-"

“Would you stop?” Tess teased. “No more what ifs. Do you love this ‘Will’, yes or no?”

“Yes. I do.”

“Then you’re going. End of story.”

“I agree,” Natalia smiled. “You’ve sacrificed so much of your happiness for us already. You were miserable for years stuck in time. You deserve this happy ending!”

“Come ‘ere,” Aurelia opened her arms for the girls to come hug her. “You’re not my friends. You’re my sisters. And I want you to know that I love you guys so much. Promise me that you’ll be OK, and stick together while I’m gone?”

“Promise,” Natalia said, still squished in the hug.

“We will,” Tess swore.

Unfolding from their hug goodbye, Aurelia looked at the staircase in front of her. It was time. She was ready. She held her A class Okliot that she’d gotten from Eloise, although she didn’t need it. Then, smoothing her hair out, she walked up the stairs to go to meet Will.

PART
THREE

CHAPTER 35

THE 1970S

Aurelia thought of the first time she'd met Will. The live music playing at the party in the '70s. The atmosphere around them with dozens of costumed time travelers all dancing to an electric beat. The cliche '70s disco ball above them and colored lights that filled the room. It was an indelible image in her mind.

The stone stairs in the Italian farmhouse began to shift around her, the subtle pit in her stomach building as she traveled. But it wasn't nearly as bad as the first time she had traveled to the '70s. Now that she was a frequent traveler, it was an expected, mild, endurable wash of wooziness. The stairs underneath her feet shifted to a low pill grey carpet, similar to the stairwell she remembered from so many years ago, yet slightly different. Coming to the landing, she took a look around the stairwell she had ended up in. It wasn't the same one that she was aiming for, and no clock hung on the door, so it wasn't an official "Members portal" for the company. Opening the door, she found herself in a large, brightly lit room, on a small stage, while dozens of people buzzed around, hanging decorations. There was a band unloading from the street, and it seemed everyone was setting up for an event.

This was the place. This was where the party had been with Will. It took a moment to recognize it so many years later, standing on the stage with a different view than the dance floor, and without the decorations and dimmed colored lights, but this was definitely it.

However, it seemed she was too early.

Aurelia hopped down from the stage and approached the first person in front of her, a young girl frantically walking with covered platters of food.

"Um... excuse me?" Aurelia said, walking along with her. "Do you know who's in charge here?"

Without speaking, the girl motioned her head to an older woman standing near the front door of the place, who was speaking to the musicians as they carried their gear inside from a tiny parked car on the bustling street. Aurelia smiled in thanks to the girl, and headed over to the woman in charge. She seemed to be discussing the band's set list of songs they would play that night, curating it to her liking. Aurelia stood in wait, hoping not to interrupt her.

"I didn't hire you... Did I?"

"No," Aurelia smiled politely.

"Well, in case you didn't know, this is a *private* event," the woman informed Aurelia condescendingly, pausing her conversation with the band with an annoyed finger in wait.

"Oh, I know. That's what I'm here for. Sorry, I'm a bit early. Do you know what time the party starts?"

"You're with the company?" the woman's eyes narrowed, she didn't recognize Aurelia as someone who worked at the company's Headquarters.

"Yeah, sort of. I'm a Member," Aurelia lied.

The woman's face fell - how was a Member here so early?

She pulled Aurelia aside so they could speak privately, changing her tone to a kind whisper, "My apologies. The party won't start until 7 p.m. - I was told they wouldn't open it until then, so as you can see we're not yet equipped for our guests."

"That's fine. No worries. So it's just tonight then? A one night only type of thing?" Aurelia wanted to make sure she wasn't here on the wrong day.

"Tonight's *the* night," the woman boasted, with a phony smile, "but you're welcome to come back when we're not having an event just for our Members as well, of course."

"Right. So, how many hours until 7 o'clock, then?"

The woman looked at her watch on her wrist, "Well, it's only 7:50 a.m. now, so you've got about eleven hours 'till opening. You can either come back then, or I can certainly arrange a guide for you if you want to spend the day here."

"And, where is *here*?"

"New York City, of course! The city for dreamers and cynics alike. I'm sure you've seen the ads, no?"

"Oh, right! Duh!" Aurelia acted like she had of course seen the tourist information about New York. Knowing full well that she shouldn't leave and chance missing Will, she decided to stay. "I don't need a guide... but do you have welcome packages here?"

Aurelia's A class Okliot got her quite a few perks in the welcome package; a private limo service that would take her anywhere she wanted in the city, a fully loaded wallet, and a pamphlet highlighting the best things to do nearby. The woman quickly personalized the wallet and printed Aurelia a fake ID, with a bevy of nearly limitless credit cards to match. Asking her what her name was, Aurelia chose a random pseudonym, Polly Jones, to stay anonymous.

The woman recommended that Aurelia should see her style team down the street before hitting the town, commenting on how her t-shirt and cargo pants was a bit too grunge or punk versus the disco theme they would experience at the party.

So, hopping inside the limo that the woman arranged, Aurelia headed a few blocks away to an unassuming brownstone, with a storefront on street level. The driver rushed around to open the car door for her, but Aurelia was already out of the car and ready to see what awaited her.

There were two people standing outside to greet her, a skinny older woman with smoker's lines around her lips, who had an obvious jaded grit from the town, and a young brunette with tightly permed hair. They instantly gushed over Aurelia's beauty and what a breeze she would be to style, whooshing her inside the building, guiding her down the stairs underneath the storefront. Inside, the room was filled to the brim with racks of clothes. It seemed to be somewhat of a fashion warehouse. Sorted by size and gender, they quickly sized up Aurelia by eye and rolled out a few appropriate racks.

It was like Aurelia had just entered a candy shop. The sheer amount of clothes and fashions was overwhelming. Every single item on the rack was gorgeous, albeit extremely colorful and bold, which was fitting for the times. Aurelia ran her hands through the rack as the two girls pulled out dresses and jumpsuits to imagine what they would look like on her.

"You know who you remind me of?" the young brunette said in a strong Brooklyn accent, her speech somewhat impeded from the gum in her mouth.

"No..." Aurelia answered.

The girl continued, "That new girl poppin' up, you know who I mean, Cheryl? 'Member we saw her on Jeannie a few years ago, and she's in that show Charlie's Angels?"

"Farrah Fawcett! I could see that. You do look a bit like her, huh?" the older woman, apparently named Cheryl, responded in a thick New Yorker accent.

"Oh, thank you," although in all honesty, Aurelia had no idea who they were comparing her to.

"And her hairdo would be off the hook on you with your blond color and these new threads. Should we add some curtain bangs and layers? Give you that Fawcett flip?" the brunette twirled Aurelia's long hair in her hands, looking at the possibilities like an artist with a blank canvas.

It had been a while since Aurelia had changed her hair. Living back in time in the 1400s, her long locks of hair had been the perfect, treasured length. But it had been years of the same, and having fun and evolving yourself was a part of life.

"You know what, when in Rome! Let's do it!"

"Are you decent?" Cheryl asked just outside the dressing room.

She felt a bit like a fish out of water with the trendy colloquialisms and pop culture references that were so common here, but Aurelia loved every second of it. Looking in the mirror one last time, she stepped out from behind the curtain.

"Oh hun. You're a stone fox!" Cheryl said, her jaw dropped.

"Thank you!"

Aurelia couldn't lie, she felt amazing with her newly cut hair, styled with an absurd amount of volume and flip, which bounced as she talked. The girls had done her makeup, with a blue eyeliner and loads of foundation which covered her freckles. She ended up choosing an unexpected outfit, a bright red button-down shirt filled with floral patterns, with denim, high-waisted, flared, bellbottom pants and paired with ankle-height, vinyl, red platform boots. Casual, after all, the party wasn't until nighttime, and she had time to kill in town first. Regardless, the outfit was absolutely stunning on her tall, statuesque figure.

"So where are you planning on going looking like such a foxy mama?" the young girl asked her.

"This afternoon, I have no idea! But tonight, I'm meeting my boyfriend at a wild disco party..."

"Aww!" she smiled.

"Any ideas? What's your favorite thing to do in New York? I'm only in town for one day."

"One day? You'd need years to experience New York! Broadway shows, museums, fashion and stores, Tiffany's, The Plaza, Central Park, Times Square, carriage rides. If you were here in the winter, you could see the tree lighting or go ice skating, or the Macy's parade. The restaurants, the new clubs. Pick a direction to start moving in, and you'll experience some'ing."

So that was just what Aurelia did. Saying goodbye to the two ladies who helped her, she hopped in the limo out front and directed him to just drive.

Traffic was a bit congested mid-afternoon, but it was amazing to drive around the bustling city. New York was like a sandwich filled with every meat and topping ever created, some people eclectic and weird, others professional or hard at work. Women stood on street corners of the shadiest neighborhoods, already selling themselves despite it only being the middle of the afternoon. Parts of town were filled with vendors soliciting useless trinkets and souvenirs to the starry-eyed tourists. The cracked streets filled in with tar, grit and grime amongst the sparkly new buildings. It genuinely seemed like there was something for everyone here.

Her driver, Amir, narrated the entire experience through the small pulled down screen between them in the stretch limo, pointing out every divine restaurant, hole in the wall, iconic store or hotel.

Driving up through Hell's Kitchen and turning onto 57th street, he told her they were about to pass the Fifth Avenue jewelry store, Tiffany's. She had always dreamt of having something new and expensive from a store like Tiffany's, but the most she had been able to afford growing up was cheap, knockoff jewelry from the mall. What a treat, to buy herself anything she wanted with the credit cards she'd received in her welcome package! Telling him to let her out there, Amir promptly handed her his business card, knowing fairly well that she would be a while, and told her to give him a call as soon as she was done.

Hopping out of the short limousine, Aurelia stood in awe at the stone, clean facade of Tiffany's. Just above the outer metal doors, a large patina clock hung, held by the strong arms of a man's statue. She stepped up to the inner glass doors, where two security guards stood in wait, and promptly opened a door for her.

Somehow the air in the building felt expensive, and Aurelia was almost afraid to take a deep breath, or even speak a word aloud. She didn't belong in there, amidst the rich big shots and cavalier crowd. Especially with her new casual outfit; with flared jeans and young floral shirt. She should've chosen something more respectable to wear, but even if she had dressed dripping in elegance, a little voice in her head told her that she would always be the same girl in the background from El Segundo. She wasn't anyone special. But perhaps, just for the day, she could pretend.

The loft-like ground floor was grand, with open, giant ceilings. All around the room, glass display cabinets seemed to glisten from the jewels inside, while employees, dressed overly professionally, tended to their customer's every whim. The shiny, wooden paneled walls brought a slight warmth to the space, which helped to ease Aurelia's mind slightly.

Apparently, she hadn't moved since stepping inside, frozen in awe at the store in front of her, because another customer came inside the doors just behind her, bumping past her shoulders rudely. Aurelia casually followed the woman through the store, just wondering what someone so confident in here would buy. She seemed to be a very well-off lady, probably in her late-sixties or seventies, and she immediately beelined to a counter, where an employee greeted her, calling her by name.

"Hello Mrs. Richards, how can I help you today?" the woman behind the counter said in a pleasant voice.

"I need some gifts for my niece. She's visiting this weekend," Mrs. Richards responded with a deep voice that crackled like sandpaper.

"Certainly. Will another necklace work?"

The woman nodded. Obviously this was her go to place for gifts. Aurelia continued to eavesdrop while she stood just near her, looking longingly inside the glass cases, almost afraid to touch them and dirty the pristine glass with her fingerprints.

"So I see you're letting the riff raff in now?" Mrs. Richards said condescendingly to the saleswoman, blatantly referring to Aurelia, "Can she even afford to shop here?"

The saleswoman pursed her lips, not responding to the woman's insults. A flash of anger rushed through Aurelia's cheeks - how dare she?

Another saleswoman approached Aurelia, herself with frizzy black hair held back in a bun about to burst, "See anything you like?" the woman asked her.

“Yes, I see plenty I like... What’s your most expensive item in this case?”

“Hmmm... I would think our Schlumberger line’s broach would be the top, at least in this case. It has stunning white diamonds and black cultured pearls. Here, this is it,” the woman pointed to a gold broach in the case, encrusted with tiny black pearls clustered together, reminiscent of a blackberry. “That goes for just over fifteen thousand. And there’s clips to match.”

"OK.”

Without hesitation, and completely out of spite of the older woman next to her, Aurelia pulled out the wallet, that she was given just hours before in her welcome package. It was hard to tell which card would be best to use, as the only two brands she recognized were Visa and American Express.

She pulled out the American Express gold card, and held it up to the saleswoman, “Do you take American Express?” Aurelia said a little too loudly, so the woman next to her would undeniably hear her.

The first purchase was revenge, but the rest of the afternoon spent being fawned over while trying on diamonds was pure enjoyment. The store offered champagne on a silver platter, which instantly fizzed to Aurelia’s head and made every piece of jewelry seem even more divine. She fell in love with a large gold necklace, and a fun red enamel bangle bracelet, which she decided to buy for the party that night. The employees wrapped up her purchases in the infamous sea foam, mint blue boxes, tied with a perfect ivory bow. She had as much to spend as she wanted, so she decided to gift the ladies helping her each a bracelet of their choice, which they said technically wasn’t allowed, but Aurelia insisted.

Just as she was wrapping up her shopping spree, her eyes landed on a familiar item. It was a gold-rimmed wristwatch with a black leather band. It looked just like her grandfather’s watch that he had given her years ago. But her watch was still in their house in Amsterdam in 1993, probably sitting right where she had left it on her bedside table. Could it be the same model, if even, the exact same watch? What if Aurelia had actually given it to her grandfather? But didn’t he have it since he himself was a teenager - when his father gave it to him? Her original watch had to be from the ‘40s then, or earlier.

No, then it couldn't be the same exact watch, only one similar, a newer model. But still, it reminded her of her family, an image which faded more and more in her mind each day. So, adding that one final item to her order, Aurelia walked out of Tiffany's, dripping in her new jewelry, her hands full of little blue bags, happy as a clam.

Just across the street, a grandiose building seemed to call to her with its captivating windows, Bergdorf Goodman. She walked inside, unsure what to expect, but was instantly transported into the manifestation of her fashion fantasies. Racks of ready-to-wear couture items lined the rooms, each piece stunning and unique. It wasn't long until she found her way to the women's department, and she spotted it - a light pink, shiny, glimmering, floor-length jumpsuit. It was perfect. Iridescent in nature, with an almost lilac purple tinge to the pink, embroidered with sparkles mainly encrusted in the flared bell bottoms. She carried it through the store, holding the delicate fabric like a newborn, and quickly found some short, strappy heels in her size to match, and an adorable clutch bag. She was soon greeted by a saleswoman, who guided her to the dressing room.

It fit flawlessly, as if Aurelia's exact measurements had been used to design the outfit. This was how she wanted to meet Will. She looked undeniably stunning. She stepped out of the dressing room with her new outfit, leaving her jeans and button-down shirt inside, ready for the epic night to come.

"I'll take it."

Her feet sore, and her body heavy, Aurelia almost didn't remember what it was like to get tired. She hadn't slept since time had started again, heading straight to the '70s to go to Will that same night. But she was exhausted and hungry, two natural feelings that she had missed terribly all those years alone, but now hated because of the impediment they caused her.

She walked the streets confidently in her new pink, shiny jumpsuit, with Tiffany bags strung to her fingers, and her hair somehow still voluminous. Walking in New York was an experience unto itself; avoiding the metal grates that grabbed her small heels, and taking in so many sounds and smells that were all rolled together. What an enigma the people in this city were, with the men catcalling and wanting her, and women eyeing her in envy, wanting to be her.

She had wandered into a few more shops and bought some

trinkets, like perfume and lipstick to wear for the party, and a handful of useless items which she probably wouldn't even keep past the day, but shopping was fun regardless. Her favorite find had to be a pair of adorable round rose colored glasses, reminiscent of the great John Lennon.

She came upon a hot dog stand, where she satiated her ravenous hunger with a juicy, relish and mustard topped hot dog. It was almost too good - how had she not gotten hungry for so many years when time was stopped? In her mind, she could've eaten a dozen hot dogs right then and there, but her stomach wouldn't allow it, so she stuck to one for now, fully enjoying each incredible bite.

As the sun began to set in New York, she checked her new watch to make sure she wouldn't be late for Will, but surprisingly it was only just after 4 o'clock. She still had plenty of time. She wished she could've slept before meeting Will again, so she could feel her best, but she had almost forgotten what it was like to need to rest. When you live for years without the weight of tiredness, your mind acclimates to a new normal of being perpetually content. But she still had a few hours until the party, and there was no way she could stand on her feet a moment longer. So, taking her driver's business card out of her new clutch, she found a pay phone on the street and dialed him up, using some change stuffed in the wallet.

Amir pulled up within about ten minutes, spotting Aurelia on the opposite side of the street and making a very illegal U-turn to get to her. She nearly collapsed in the long leather seat, so happy to be somewhere comfortable and rest for a little while. She told him about her little shopping adventure, and he kindly complemented her new look. They got to talking as they drove through the city, and Amir told her about his journey to get to where he was today, immigrating from Pakistan with his family almost fifteen years ago. He was slowly making his way up through the world and building a better life for his children. It was an extremely interesting and compelling story, but unfortunately the constant pleasant tone of his voice slowly lulled the exhausted Aurelia to sleep.

CHAPTER 36

YOUNGER SELF

"Miss...? Excuse me, Miss Jones?" Amir said gently, holding the limousine's door open and standing over Aurelia.

Who was "Miss Jones"? Oh, that was *her* alias, which she'd received in her welcome package. Here, she was Polly Jones. But she really didn't want to wake up - it felt so amazing to nap after being awake for so long.

"Miss, my apologies to wake you, but you told me you wanted to be back for the event tonight."

Gasping, Aurelia sat up abruptly, "Yes! Thank you! What time is it?"

Had she missed the party?

"It's eight o'clock."

She was late.

Aurelia instinctively looked at her own watch to confirm the time, but it only read 6:07 p.m., "Are you sure? It's already eight?"

The man nodded. Her watch was behind. Thank God for Amir, otherwise after all these years, she would've missed her chance to meet Will again. Luckily, the party hadn't even started until seven, and then it had been at least an hour or two that Aurelia and Will spent dancing together, before the whole "portal disappearing" debacle would happen. She remembered asking the bouncer outside what time it was, and he had said it was almost 8:30 p.m., so truthfully, the timing couldn't be better.

She unwrapped her delicate Tiffany boxes, and put on her new necklace and bangle bracelet. Spritzing herself with Opium perfume by Yves Saint Laurent and blindly adding a layer of fresh pink lipstick, she stepped out, checking how she looked in the limo's side mirror. Her hair was slightly smushed to one side from sleeping, held in place from the product, but she was able to fluff it back into position. The last time she'd seen Will was the 26-year-old version of himself in Amsterdam, when she'd left him abruptly, because the Guardians had found her. But today, in a way, this was still the first time Will had ever met her, so she wanted to make a good first impression. It's not everyday you get to re-meet the love of your life.

"Do you have to get home now, Amir?"

"Not unless you're finished with my services, Miss Jones."

"So you're hired through tonight?" Amir nodded. "Then, will you wait for me here for a while? I have to pick someone up."

"Of course! I'll be here."

"Thank you!"

Putting on her rose colored glasses for slight anonymity, she walked up to the building where the party was, the familiar, muted music inside dancing through her memories. The security guard she had spoken to years ago stood just outside, and stopped her in her tracks as she attempted to walk in.

"Members only, Ma'am," he said with his arm extended to block her from entering.

Smiling with a slight nod, she fished in her clutch purse for her Okliot. Looking around to make sure no one was watching, she pulled it out, and the security guard eased his stance.

"Enjoy the party," he said with a slight smile, lowering his arm and instead opening the door for her.

"Thanks."

It was really happening. She was here. The rocking music, the colorful lights, the slight smell of cigarettes and cologne - everything was exactly as she remembered it. She looked to the center of the room, where the dance floor bopped to the music - there she was. Her 19-year-old self wore her little black dress, borrowed Halston sweater and crossbody bag, her long hair, straight and smooth, swaying to the music. At the time, years ago, she thought she had everything figured out, her identity somehow defined by her friends, fashion and school, but in reality, her outward appearance was insecure and somewhat awkward, unknowing of who she would become. Yet despite the lack of confidence and nerves from dancing with a cute guy she had just met, she seemed unburdened, innocent, happy.

'Oh my God,' she thought to herself, 'is that what I looked like dancing? Those are really bad moves,' she chuckled to herself. 'I was so naive and carefree. I hadn't even realized I was in the '70s yet.'

Then, through the ever-shifting holes in the crowd, she spotted Will.

He donned cobalt blue bellbottom pants, and a white and blue flower patterned shirt. Somehow Aurelia loved every bit about him - his hair, his eyes, his personality, but his most impressive feature was his dimpled smile. It had a bit of magic to it, no matter what she was thinking or how she was feeling, his smile had the power to change an entire bad day around in a second.

As much as she wanted to run up to him and have his arms wrap around her, she held herself back. He didn't know her like she did.

With the younger two of them still dancing, there was still time to fill. Looking around, she noticed Will's friends, Benji and Mason, hanging out in the opposite corner of the room, but other than them, luckily, she couldn't spot a single familiar face. Since she still had time, she needed to get out of sight for the time being, so someone didn't connect the dots that two versions of herself were in one place. Thankfully, her new haircut and ostentatious outfit drew away from her face's details, in a way, a disguise. But unfortunately, her current stunning outfit also drew every pair of eyes to her as she walked in. Luckily, Will seemed too enthralled with the younger version of herself to notice this version dripping in pink sparkles.

She wondered if there was another room she could hide out inside of until Will and Aurelia made their way to the stairwell, so she traced the room around, passing the stairwell door. Just out of curiosity, she opened the stairwell door to confirm it was indeed the stairwell. It was, but both the stairwell up, and the stairwell down were still there. Wouldn't the way down disappear soon? She looked back to the first version of herself and Will, trying to decipher where in their conversation they were at this point. It seemed like they had paused dancing and were talking. This had to be right before Aurelia stepped out to get some air - she was about to go to the stairwell, but both directions of the portal were still open.

As if a lightbulb went off in her mind, Aurelia realized it must have been *her* who closed the way home all those years ago. But how? She had never intentionally closed portals before, only opened them.

Stepping inside the stairwell, she tried to tap into the feeling of opening a portal, and attempted shifting her thoughts to instead close it, but nothing happened. She had less than a minute to figure it out, before her younger self saw that the stairwell had disappeared, sparking her thoughts about where or rather *when* she was.

So Aurelia *had* to learn how to close the portal - fast. It was strange, it felt like her mind and body wanted to close it, but there was something impeding her. Tuning into her abilities even more, it was as if something was pressing on an invisible arm, holding her back from shifting the portal. What was it?

Looking around, almost palpably feeling the energy in the stairwell, she was drawn to the corner of the first stairwell step down. Bending down to feel with her hand, she found a small metallic bead that seemed magnetically attached to the step. What was it? She pulled it off from the corner of the step, and noticed that the same thing was in the opposite corner as well. Pulling the other one off, the portal seemed to destabilize, the steps furthest down beginning to slowly disappear from view. Somehow, the magnetic beads were keeping the portal open.

What were they? They were obviously some sort of technology, but what? Was it something that Aleksander had invented? There wasn't enough time to investigate, so she popped the tiny beads in her clutch and started to head out, opening the door and spotting the younger version of herself finishing the conversation with Will, about to walk into the stairwell. Although, it seemed like the portal still wasn't disappearing fast enough. Closing her eyes in a last ditch effort, she focused on the same energy she had learned to tap into to open portals, and envisioned the portal wrapping itself up tightly, closing permanently. Opening her eyes, the lower portal had manifested into her vision, now only a wall where there was once a staircase down. She had done it.

Quickly exiting the stairwell, she hustled to the left of the door, away from where the younger version of herself would walk in, at any minute. Sure enough, the current day Aurelia watched as the 19-year-old version of herself walked away from Will, beelining to the stairwell. She observed another angle of Will, as he waited for Aurelia to return. His friend, Mason, walked just past the current Aurelia, giving her stunning body a double take, which she briskly turned away from so he wouldn't see her face, before he continued on. Mason made his way through the crowd to go talk to Will, a moment which she hadn't even realized had happened from her original point-of-view. Stepping a little bit closer, and grabbing a random red drink from a waitress walking by to occupy herself, she listened through the thumping music to overhear what they were talking about, careful to face the opposite direction so they wouldn't see her face.

"So, she's cute! Where has she been all this time?" Mason started, jokingly punching Will's shoulder.

"She really is, huh? She's definitely a mystery," Will answered.

Aurelia couldn't help but smile as she sipped her drink, he already liked her. "So you haven't seen her before either?"

"No... Is she from B-udo originally?"

"I don't know..."

"Doesn't matter. You should bang her anyway," Mason joked, and Aurelia almost choked on her drink at his comment.

Will laughed out loud, "Do you think she likes me?"

"Fuck yeah. Someone doesn't dance with you like that for an hour if they don't want you. You've got her if *you* want her, Will. But hey, I'll take her off your hands for you if you don't."

Aurelia scoffed at Mason's comments - who knew he was such a presumptuous prick?

Aurelia's eyes landed on movement to see the younger version of herself step out of the stairwell, checking around the wall to make sure that it was the only door, and looking inside the stairwell again. This was the moment she began to freak out and realize the impossible.

Tuning back into the conversation at hand, it seemed Will had also noticed the young Aurelia coming out of the portal, as she now walked towards the front door.

"Maybe I should ask her out," Will said with a nervous smile.

"Why would you do that? That implies commitment. You don't commit, Will, you play the field. I thought you learned your lesson with Bianca."

Who was Bianca, Aurelia wondered? Will's ex?

"She's not like those other girls, though," Will defended.

"Pfft. They're all clones. Every girl wants the same things."

"What's that?"

"Control, shoes and marriage," Aurelia chuckled, the middle one was pretty accurate. "I've seen this story before - you're gonna get attached, and she's gonna turn out to be a bitch and break your heart. You know it's much more fun to be single. Just fuck her and move on, man."

Every ounce of Aurelia's being wanted to throw her drink at Mason. What a douche. Besides, Will wasn't that kind of guy.

"Screw you, Mason," Will said, disgusted at the conversation, which Aurelia silently applauded.

"Hey - I'm just stating the obvious."

"So what, I get dumped *once* and I'm never supposed to date again, is that it? I should only stick to one night stands from now on, huh? Maybe that's what *you* want, but not me."

"I don't get it."

"What?"

"You meet some random girl, who I'm pretty sure doesn't even know who you are by the way, and you suddenly just... *decide* you're a different person?"

What was Mason even talking about? Will had always been such a gentleman to Aurelia. He didn't seem like a player.

"But I *like* that about her. She's not just trying to schmooze me up 'cause she knows who my dad is. Everyone's always so fake to me."

"Isn't that the best part *about* being *you*, though? You don't even have to try," Will scoffed at his opinion. "Look. All I'm saying is, what's better... a new flavor every day of the week, or vanilla - Every. Damn. Day?"

"...Whatever, man. You have fun with your flavors, but I'm gonna go get the girl."

Will walked away from Mason, heading towards the 19-year-old Aurelia, who had just walked back inside the party from the street.

'YES!' Aurelia shouted in her mind, so proud of Will for speaking up even though she knew how much he hated confrontations.

It felt like a massive victory had just been won, and even as a stranger, Will had stuck up for Aurelia. It felt good to know how he felt, and even sweeter to know that he was on his way to ask her out - although that part of the conversation would never ensue, seeing as the panic of the portal disappearing would take precedence.

Mason began to walk back to Benji with flushed cheeks, frankly, unsure why Will had gotten so defensive with him.

As Mason walked past Aurelia again, she felt his hand lightly brush her butt, "Hey babe, wanna dance?" he asked her, as she kept her face turned from his view.

"I have a boyfriend. So thanks, but no thanks," Aurelia said in a slightly higher, condescending tone than her own to stay as anonymous as possible.

Besides, even if she didn't have Will, Mason had just proven himself to be a dick.

Mason scoffed, moving on, and Aurelia focused her attention back on Will. Her eyes followed him, and the younger her, as they walked back to the stairwell, where within minutes, young Aurelia would steal his Okliot and run away, stranding him in 1977.

That would be her cue to meet him again.

As the stairwell door closed behind them, Aurelia casually

walked up just next to it, so she could somewhat listen through the door. Setting her drink on the ground next to her, she leaned against the wall as inconspicuously as she could. It was hard to make out the words through the closed door, but a slight mumble made its way through the wood to her ears, and the rest of the conversation was somewhat filled in by memory.

The pair talked about how it was possible that the portal could be closed, and Will proceeded to check his Okliot, shaking it to his ear. Strangely, the same fluttering feeling in her chest seemed to occur, as if her body was reliving the nervous sensation she had experienced years ago.

Then Will called his contact at Headquarters. Aurelia wondered who his contact was - was it someone she'd met along the way, in the past few years, and she would now recognize their voice? But through the closed door, it was impossible to make out any distinction on the other end of the call, the noise muted and muddled.

Within less than a minute, the conversation elevated, and she could clearly hear Will raise his voice.

"What? You mean Aurelia? Why would I do that?"

The man on the other end of the call had just told Will to detain Aurelia.

"William. Do it now. Do you understand me?" the voice on the hologram call actually did seem familiar, but hard to place - his voice's deep tone reverberating in the stairwell.

This was the exact moment that Aurelia had grabbed Will's Okliot from him, running up the stairs and back in time to the '50s.

"Aurelia! No! Wait!" Will yelled, as he rushed up the stairs after her.

It was time.

Opening the door to the stairwell, Aurelia looked up to see the younger version of herself disappear from view. Will ran after her, but came to a stop in the middle landing, realizing he wouldn't be able to follow her any further without an Okliot.

"Don't let them find you!" Will called out to the young Aurelia.

So many years of playing this exact moment in her head, yet Aurelia now felt at a loss for words.

"Will," Aurelia called softly, closing the stairwell door behind her.

"...Aurelia?" Will looked down at her with a double take, glancing up the stairs again to where the other version of her had just disappeared through the portal. "How did you...? Didn't you just...? Wait... how long has it been since... *that* you?" Will motioned up the stairs, wrapping his head around the dizzying parts of time travel.

"Not long," Aurelia lied, "well, long enough for *this*," Aurelia motioned to her new hairdo and outfit.

"What, your black dress wasn't cutting it for the '70s?"

"I figured I'd fully commit for the role."

"No, I love it. Very authentic."

"Thanks."

The small talk had abruptly reached a standstill, so they both attempted to continue the conversation, speaking over each other awkwardly.

"Do you-"

"We need-"

They paused.

"Should we-"

"Aren't they-"

Laughing at their equal eagerness, Aurelia stayed silent.

"Ladies first," Will smiled.

"Sorry. Um... look, we don't have much time before the Guardians come, but I guess... I was wondering if you'd like to come with me?"

"...Where?"

"Anywhere."

Will paused for a minute, wondering who this strange enigma of a girl was, and why the future was after her. She was obviously some kind of rebel, which excited and enticed him. He had never met someone like her. He wanted to know more.

"So?" Aurelia followed up, nervous about what he would say after all this time.

"Anywhere's my favorite place."

CHAPTER 37

Anywhere's My Favorite Place

Aurelia hushed him, avoiding Will's every question about why his contact at Headquarters wanted to detain her, so they could hurry out before the Guardians arrived. Taking Will's hand cautiously, Aurelia quickly led him back through the party, out onto the street and up the block, where Amir would be waiting with the limousine. Will's hand was a bit clammy and loose in hers, unlike his normal assuring grip that would usually be leading Aurelia. But Aurelia kept reminding herself, 'He doesn't know me yet, but he will soon.'

"Oh, hey, I don't mean to ruin the spontaneity of the moment, but could I have my Okliot back?" Will asked Aurelia.

She literally hadn't even thought about that part. The last time she'd seen his Okliot was with his future self, before he'd taken it to a friend in B-udo.

"Uhh... good news, bad news."

"What's the bad?"

"I don't have it."

"Didn't you just-"

"Yeah. I *did* have it," Aurelia was used to finishing his sentences by now. "I... well, I didn't really *lose* it, I just don't currently *have* it and... have... no idea where it is."

"So... you lost it."

Aurelia scrunched her face, not wanting to lie to him. Technically, it was with one of Will's friends in B-udo, although *which* friend, she had no idea.

"...Yeah. I lost it."

"So, what's the good news?"

"I... brought one back that you can use."

Truthfully, she hadn't brought the A class Okliot back for Will, but it was easier than explaining everything all at once - that she didn't even *need* an Okliot to travel in time.

They approached the limo, where Amir leaned against the hood. Noticing Aurelia walking back towards him, he promptly got up and opened the door for them in anticipation.

"How was the party, Miss Jones?"

"Very memorable," Aurelia smiled.

"So, where to next?"

"Can you take us to wherever your favorite spot is in the city? Surprise us?" Aurelia smiled, ready for wherever the journey may take them.

"Of course!"

Will nodded at Amir to say hello, and whispered to Aurelia as they crouched inside. "I thought your last name was Quinn?"

"It is. Polly Jones is my alias here."

"Your alias? Why do you need a fake name?"

"I always use one. You taught-" Aurelia interrupted herself, remembering that she didn't want to let on that they knew each other.

She wanted Will to like her because he fell for her naturally, not because he knew it was fated to happen.

"I taught, you? What do you mean?" Will said, much too perceptive to miss a beat.

"No, no. Sorry, *I* was taught that tip ages ago. It's just, much more fun."

"So it has nothing to do with the fact that you're..." Will whispered even softer, "*on the run?*"

"I'm not 'on the run' per-say," Aurelia lied, not wanting Will to be even more nervous, "they just don't like me 'cause I know how to open portals without the company."

She was sure that fact would be revealed to Will soon enough, so why hide it? It was better to use it as the excuse for why the Guardians were after her. It seemed like the most innocent thing she could think of as a reason, although in reality, after all this time running, she still had no idea why they were after her.

Will's eyes widened at her proclamation, "Wait, what? That's awesome! How?" Aurelia mimed zipping up her mouth and throwing the key away, which Will chuckled at. "So where all can your portals go?"

"I mean, everywhere, I guess."

"So, is it just random? Or can you pick a time?"

"I can... calibrate it, so to speak."

"Wow! I know you said you don't get out that much, but if I were you, I'd never go home!" a pang of sadness hit Aurelia's chest. But Will didn't know that would be a trigger, that she *couldn't* go home, because she was protecting her family. "So, are you even a Member then? You obviously don't need to follow the company's excursions."

"Sure I am. Who'd want to miss out on the welcome packages?"

Will laughed out loud, "You're funny."

"Looking?" Aurelia joked.

Will smiled, his dimples appearing. God, had she missed seeing his smile.

"What is it?" Will asked, noticing her stare.

"...You're cute, Will."

His cheeks turned beet red in embarrassment, something Aurelia had rarely seen before in him. He was normally so confident and assured.

"I think you're pretty cute too," he smiled.

New York City was giant, and every street was filled with a million possibilities, but Amir didn't have to drive too far to get to his favorite place. It was a street crammed with dozens of restaurants in red brick buildings with little awnings, buildings which seemed to live and breathe themselves, Mulberry Street. Some establishments were well worn and others had just arrived, but the ambience was irresistible. Amir pointed out his go-to restaurant, and dropped the pair out front.

Stepping inside, a hostess seated them promptly at a white linen table. The waiter took no more than a minute to attend to them, dressed in a white dress jacket and an old school bow tie.

"*Ciao!* Can I get you started with some drinks?" the waiter greeted them in a thick Italian accent.

"*Si, per favore,*" Aurelia said, immediately switching languages since the waiter obviously was Italian. "*Mi piacerebbe un po' di vino rosso... un vino leggero. Cosa mi consigli?*" she wondered if they had a good light red wine he would recommend.

The waiter had something perfect in mind, "*Io ho qualcosa che ti piacerà molto.* And you, Sir?"

"*Lo stesso, grazie,*" Will answered, and the waiter went on his way to get their wine. "So I see you opted for some language downloads too," he smiled.

"Huh?" Aurelia asked, before realizing he meant the educational downloads everyone took in the future. "Oh, no, I didn't, actually."

"Then, how do you speak Italian?"

"I... lived in Italy... for a few years. Did a *lot* of reading," and by lived, she of course meant she was stuck in a broken moment of time for years, alone. In fact, today was one of the first times she'd ever spoken Italian conversationally, not just to herself.

"So you just picked it up by yourself?"

"Yup."

"Wow! That's impressive. Do you speak any other languages?"

"I do... Dutch, French, Russian, Latin, Occitan, and I've dabbled in some others."

"Wait, so you mean you learned *all* of those *without* downloads?" Aurelia nodded. "I couldn't even imagine."

"You strike me as the kind of guy who's downloaded just about every language available in ZhēnZhū," Aurelia smiled, only pretending to guess, since she already knew that Will was exceptional with hundreds of languages and dialects, and it happened to be one of his favorite subjects.

"What, is my nerdiness that obvious?" Will laughed.

"No!" Aurelia chuckled. "Just a lucky guess, I suppose! But I happen to think nerds are cool."

"Really? You do?"

Will had always kept that "thirst for knowledge" part of himself somewhat of a secret from his friends, trying to keep his crisp "cool guy" exterior intact.

"Yeah!" Aurelia smiled. "I can't stand it when people hate learning. And I especially hate when people put intelligence down, making other people think that being passionate about something is... unhip or something, you know?"

"Yeah. Absolutely. So what about you then? What're your passions?" Will asked.

"Well... my life definitely hasn't gone the way I expected it to go, but at one point, I wanted to be a fashion designer... I loved... well, *everything* about it."

"So why'd you stop?"

She had stopped because she met Will at the party in the '70s, and was thrust into a life of traveling through time.

"I... well I... plans just, changed, that's all," she wished she didn't have to hide so much from him.

"Maybe you should pick it back up?"

"Maybe. I mean, traveling has its perks, and I definitely get to geek out on the fashion of the era that I'm in, but yeah. It'd be nice to have followed that dream and become some big, famous designer... but I just don't think it's possible anymore. My life is so... different now. I don't really have enough time to pursue that."

"Look. Aurelia. I agree, there's not enough time. But that's why you should follow your dreams, not why you *shouldn't*. Life is so short. I lost my mom when I was really young, but she had a saying that my dad would tell me about life - 'When you're running, there are much more important things than coming first in the race. Sure - you can finish first and get the gold, but the real winner is the person that smiled the whole track.' I take that as a reason to make every day worth living, and follow your passions to your heart's content."

"Your mom sounds like she was wise," Aurelia smiled sensitively.

"I think so. I didn't really get a chance to know her, but, I know she was special."

"I'm sorry. I lost my parents when I was young too. It's hard, 'cause I know that I miss them, but I was so little that I don't remember which *parts* of them I miss, you know?"

"Yeah. I do. How old were you when your parents... passed away?" Will asked.

"I was six."

"That's horrible. How, if I may ask?"

"Car accident."

"Car accident? Wait, so they died in the past?"

"...Yes," Aurelia had just gotten herself into a sticky conversation, talking about her childhood. She didn't want to reveal that she was once a permanent, for fear Will might have a stigma against it, as Tess had.

"So, they must have been some of the very first testers in the company if you were so young."

"Right..." Aurelia instantly went along with his theory, but immediately attempted to redirect the conversation. "What about your mom?" surprisingly, she didn't know how his mom had died.

"Radiation poisoning when I was 3," Will replied solemnly. "See, I'm not originally from B-udo, my dad and I moved levels from P-yex when I was 5."

"Oh? That's a big change. Why?" Aurelia pretended to be oblivious and let him tell her about his life.

"I know," Will didn't want Aurelia to know who his dad was, yet.

He liked that she wasn't interested in him just because of that. "Um... my dad got a job."

Aurelia wondered why Will was being so secretive and didn't immediately open up more about his dad, but decided not to push the subject.

Soon, the waiter returned with their wine and a beautiful antipasto plate. Aurelia decided on a rigatoni pasta with meatballs, and Will on a linguini with clams, which the kitchen whipped up quickly. The food was divine - the style completely different than what Aurelia had gotten used to in Tuscany, but perfect in its own unique way. Before long, the meal was finished and since Will didn't have any money that would work in the '70s, Aurelia paid, using some cash in her wallet from the welcome package.

The pair walked out of the restaurant, deciding to walk down the street a little, before they would call Amir to pick them up. There was something so freeing about walking in the crisp New York air after dark, with nowhere to be and no set plans. Almost like anything in the world was possible.

Will's tablet had been buzzing throughout dinner, but he had kept it hidden deep in his back pocket, since technically, as a member, not a guide, he wasn't even supposed to *have* his tablet in the past, a rule so that the futuristic technology wouldn't be spotted centuries before it was even invented. But, the company's rules hadn't always applied to Will. However, as they walked up the New York streets, the buzzing grew increasingly, until it seemed to be every few minutes. Will spotted an open pay phone booth on Canal street, and realized that it would be a good place to answer. No one would question hearing the other end of a phone call coming from a phone booth.

"I really should take this," Will said, picking up the pay phone to be away from prying eyes and hopefully avoid suspicion.

"Of course."

Will answered the call with audio only, and the volume down low, so as not to call any additional attention in case someone spotted him.

"Hi *Tatko,*" it was his dad calling.

"Where are you? Did you detain her? Are you alright?" Aleksander asked in a frantic voice. Why did he sound so stressed?

"I'm fine, dad. Look, she... went through the portal. I'm sorry, I tried."

"No you didn't."

"Huh?" Will glanced at Aurelia, hoping she would be able to explain what he meant, but she stayed silent.

"You didn't try. I know," Aleksander knew Aurelia from her past visits to B-udo. He knew that Will would protect her.

"What are you talking about? Of course I tried. She just, took my Okliot and ran!"

Will raised his eyebrows to Aurelia with mischief for her actions, to which she mouthed, "Sorry!" silently.

"She took your...? Are you still in the portal?"

"No."

"So you're home?"

"No, I'm still in the '70s."

"You're still-? Fine, I'm tracking your location now and I'll have someone bring you another Okliot. There are already teams there combing the city."

They were searching through the city and Aleksander was tracking their location? He could do that? Was it tracked through the tablet? Aurelia motioned to Will with a vehement head shake, no, in the hopes he could persuade his father otherwise. They would find Aurelia.

"Um... no, actually," Will backpedaled, going off of Aurelia's motions, "you don't have to do that."

"How else will you get home, William?"

"My friends. I'm fine, really, Dad."

"Who...? William, turn on your projection."

"I can't. I'm in public."

"I don't care. Who's there with you? Is it her? Is Aurelia there?"

Aurelia felt her breath grow stale. When she'd known Aleksander in his past, he'd called her Miana. But now, he knew her real name. Something had changed since the last time she'd seen him. He knew more about what would happen to her than even she did. Aurelia locked eyes with Will, the fear obvious in her face.

"No, no. Of course she's not here. Like I said, she went through the portal."

"You're lying to me. It's OK, son. We'll be there soon."

The tablet beeped pleasantly as Aleksander hung up.

CHAPTER 38

HELIOS

Aurelia felt the fear washing over her. They knew she was here. She'd made such a big mistake keeping Will in the '70s and not whisking him to another time immediately. But now they needed to find a way out. Aurelia needed to find a stairwell so they could leave.

"I'm sorry," Will said, his eyes tracing the worried expression on Aurelia's face. She hadn't moved since the phone call ended, almost just processing the information.

"It's fine... you didn't do anything wrong. Look, we need to find a stairwell, ASAP," Aurelia said, with a switch flipping in her mind for survival mode.

"A stairwell? You mean, to open a portal? Why not just a door?"

"When it's a new portal, I need stairs to kind of, kickstart it. I don't know why, actually. But a fire escape, stairs inside a building, something. It just has to be more than a few steps and I can make one to get us out of here."

"But, how? All you need is stairs and you can just, *make* a portal? Anywhere?"

"Yes. I mean, there's more to it than that but... look Will - there's no time to explain. We need to leave *now*."

Aurelia began walking briskly, her eyes darting above them at the occasional fire escapes, but unfortunately all of them were built much too high to reach the bottom ladder, probably to help prevent thieves from breaking in.

It seemed that every shop had already closed for the night, with iron gates out front sealed tightly, although they attempted to open every door with no luck. How would they get out? Every building was closed.

Nearby, they could hear police sirens growing closer, the magical city turning ominous in less than a few minutes. Then she spotted it, a block ahead of them. A stairwell down into a subway station.

"Come on!" Aurelia yelled, breaking into a jog.

They would make it.

The police sirens grew deafeningly loud, and Aurelia realized they were coming from not one, but three directions, all around them, getting closer. Just as they were about to run across the street, a police car zoomed in front of them, skidding to a stop.

A policeman jumped out behind the safety of his car, aiming his gun at them, "FREEZE! PUT YOUR HANDS WHERE I CAN SEE THEM!" he shouted at them.

Shaking, Will and Aurelia jerked their hands above their heads, terrified at the situation. The police were involved?

"We've got them," he spoke into his radio.

Just behind them, two more cop cars pulled up, with officers jumping out to surround them. A fleet of flashy, vintage cars proceeded to pull up next to the cops, and out of them, dozens of finely dressed men got out, who looked unmistakably like the quintessential mob. This crowd was obviously in cahoots with the dirty cops. Aurelia looked around, hoping for a way out, but the only stairwell she could see was the one going down into the subway station, behind the cop car.

A slow clap behind them broke out, and Will and Aurelia looked to see who it was. A sharply dressed man in a fitted suit with a green tie walked up.

It couldn't be. It was the man who killed Johanna. But seeing him dressed the way he was, it finally clicked and Aurelia realized she had known his face even before that. It was the man that Will had called in the stairwell. The man who instructed Will to detain Aurelia. Will knew him.

"You were close to slipping away, I'll give you that."

"Helios?" Will called out. Aurelia could finally put a name to her hatred.

"Hello William."

"I don't understand, what are you doing? *Why?*" Will asked with a slight quiver in his voice.

"I'm just following orders," Helios looked Aurelia dead in the eyes, and the pain of losing Johanna seemed just as fresh as if it had just happened. "Hello again, Aurelia."

No words would even form for the man, but a feeling of disgust and hate bubbled inside Aurelia.

"Men, take her," Helios motioned, and a small group of the mobsters stepped towards them.

"No," Will stepped in front of her in a protective stance, but was pushed and held down to the ground by two of them.

"Don't hurt him!" Aurelia cried out, stepping forward to let them take her, in the hopes that Will would be alright if she went easily.

Three of them grabbed her forcefully, their strong fingers clamping around her fragile arms, and they began to drag her towards one of their cars. Will struggled beneath the men's beefy arms, but couldn't make much headway with force alone. Luckily, Will hadn't stopped his downloads at just cerebral subjects.

Maneuvering with a twist underneath the men's grips, he pulled himself to a standing position where he could fight. Dodging the men's attempts to hit or grab him, he landed a few strong blows to the men, although they didn't seem fazed by his hits. They attempted to grab his quick hands, and one of them managed to for a split second, before Will circled his arms to break free and pushed him back. Although it was his first time attempting to fight, he seemed to quickly get the hang of it, the memories somewhere in his mind. They were big and clunky, but Will was quick and agile.

"Will, STOP!" Aurelia called out, she didn't want them to hurt him.

Shifting his fighting style for more power, he kicked at one of the men, but the man caught his foot and held him in place, off balance. Instead of giving in, Will shifted his weight upwards and pulled his foot free, going back for a strong punch, which finally knocked the man over. The other guy wrapped his arms around him from behind, to hold his arms in place, but Will was ready to play dirty. Kicking at his kneecap, the man let go, screaming in pain.

Will rushed towards Aurelia in an attempt to break her free as well, but as he neared them, the sound of bullets flew through the air. The police were shooting at Will.

"NO! NO STOP!" Aurelia shrieked, twisting her body to try and break free of the men.

Will writhed in pain, grasping his leg, where a bullet had just landed. An immense amount of worry emanated from her, hitting the men holding her like a wave, and she somehow broke free of them.

"STOP!" Helios screamed piercingly at his men, "WHAT THE BLOODY HELL DO YOU THINK YOU'RE DOING?"

Aurelia rushed to Will's side, as he shook in pain sitting down on the street, the blood sputtering from the front of his quad, darkening his blue bellbottoms.

"DO YOU EVEN *KNOW* WHO YOU JUST SHOT?" Helios

reprimanded, turning back to the car where his tablet rested, to call for a medic.

"You're OK. You're gonna be OK. Oh my God," Aurelia muttered, putting pressure on the wound.

"Who are you, really?" Will whispered to Aurelia, the reality of her predicament finally setting in. "Why do they want you?"

Aurelia looked at his blue eyes that searched her for the answer. But she didn't know why they wanted her. She didn't know why she could never be safe or go home.

"I don't know, Will... I haven't lived it yet."

Helios noticed Aurelia still crouched over Will and looked at his men who seemed to be standing in place, shocked by the situation.

"What are you doing? Take her!" he yelled. But the men didn't move.

"Aurelia... you need to go," Will said, still in a hushed voice.

"I'm not leaving you."

Aurelia looked behind her and somehow immediately understood why the three men weren't following orders. She had stopped them in time when she'd broken free of their grip. Aurelia hadn't even realized she could do that - isolate her powers to a small area? Everything else around them was moving, but they themselves were frozen in place. She couldn't let Will notice. He was already hesitant about the whole situation, and injured because of her. She didn't want to overwhelm or scare him any more.

Closing her eyes and focusing her energy like she'd been working on for years in Italy, she imagined the three men springing to life again. It was hard to focus when her thoughts wouldn't let her think about anything other than Will and his bleeding leg beneath her hands, but she attempted to tune everything out and think only about the three men she had stuck in time.

"What are you doing?" Helios screamed at his men who didn't seem to want to listen. "I GAVE YOU AN ORDER!"

Aurelia was able to wake the men up from their stance paused in time, although they were completely confused about how the girl they were just holding had escaped them in a split second. Looking around with stunned eyes, they spotted her behind them, next to Will.

"Aurelia. Go," Will pleaded.

"NO!"

She could see the men heading towards them.

"I'll be OK. Please."

Aurelia looked at Will's face one final time, his lower lip shaking in pain. He was terrified. This was all her fault. Every ounce of her soul wanted to tell him she loved him, stay, and fight to be together - but she was still a stranger in his eyes.

But Will knew Helios, so he would be OK if she left him, although in her mind Helios was the devil incarnate. She hated this. She hated having to leave Will.

"I'm sorry," she whispered, getting up from his side just as the men rushed to try and take her away.

She sprinted as fast as she could towards the subway station behind the armed police car.

"STOP HER!" Helios screamed, jogging towards her himself.

She wasn't even sure just how many bullets hit her, but the pain seemed to cover her body. She had been through worse. She would heal. But she had to keep running through the debilitating pain.

"NO - DON'T SHOOT! WE NEED HER ALIVE!" Helios screamed, the chaos spinning out of control.

She was just steps from the subway stairs. A policeman tackled her as she ran, knocking her to the ground, but she pushed him off of her, kicking at his face. Scrambling back up to her feet through the pain in her back, she hobbled to the stairs, the dozens of men chasing just behind her, not even steps away, grabbing for her arms, her hair - anything to stop her. The pain searing through her, she raced down the stairs, the surroundings beginning to shift and morph into an open stairwell. But they were still right behind her. They had Okliots.

One of them grabbed her shoulder, pulling her back, and she fell onto the stairs. No. She had to keep going. Pulling away from his grip, the adrenaline and pain actually propelling her forward even more, she pulled herself up and over the railing next to her, and jumped. The stairwell morphed even faster than she was used to, and she landed, very poorly, on the edge of two steps, rolling her ankle and plummeting herself down the remaining stairs onto the landing. She had to keep going. The pain now searing in her shins from the jump, she forced herself to stand up again, holding onto the shifting railing as she limped down the stairs.

She knew what she had to do, but was she strong enough? Could she even replicate it? Stopping at the next landing, with the men just above her closing in, she visualized the portal shutting just above her - a wall appearing in between herself and the men. Slumping down to the ground in pain, leaning against the back wall of an unknown stairwell, she watched as the stairwell above her faded from view, the men chasing her coming to a dead end.

Her powers were becoming clearer and easier to use, like second nature. Somehow now, all she had to do was hold the image of what she wanted in her mind, and it seemed her powers would listen. It should've felt like a win. She had done it. She had gotten away. But at what cost?

She still didn't have Will. She would easily heal from the bullet wounds, so she tried not to focus too much on the excruciating, temporary pain. She began crying, not even from the literal pain from the bullets in her back, but from the pain of losing Will again. Rolling into a ball, Aurelia sobbed herself to sleep, safe from further harm in her portal somewhere in time.

CHAPTER 39

TOMORROW

Honestly, Aurelia didn't want to move to get food or water, although the thirst was overwhelming. She had slept for quite a while, long enough for the three bullets in her back to be pushed out of her skin, the nanobots healing her from the inside out. The wounds hadn't completely finished healing, but slowly, the pain lessened. Her worry over Will permeated her thoughts, and she knew that she had to get to him. Was he OK? Had they healed him from his gunshot wound? What would he think of her now? What if Helios and the Guardians had poisoned his pure thoughts of her?

Eventually, Aurelia made her way down the stairs through the portal, the only way out, since she had closed the way back to the '70s to protect herself from getting caught. The first door, one flight down, seemed like she was entering into a busy train station, but anywhere public wasn't a good idea with her current outfit - a bloodstained, sparkly jumpsuit from the '70s.

So she continued down, imagining somewhere that would be safe and empty for a while, and the steps morphed into a thick carpet, opening into a random family's house somewhere in the 20th or 21st century. A labrador retriever greeted her with a few barks, confused where Aurelia had just appeared from, but quickly changed his nervous stance once he acclimated to her positive energy and promptly tried to lick her hands to clean them from the dried blood, which she shooed him away from doing. It was the perfect situation, it seemed like no one was home, and she could get some food and change into some clean clothes before moving on.

First, she downed a few glasses of water from the sink, a taste so refreshing it seemed to ease all of her woes. There was something miraculous about having access to clean, running water in such a simple way, such as just turning on a faucet. It was something that she had taken for granted growing up, but living in the past for so long, where there was so much effort involved just to get one pitcher of dirt and bacteria filled water, she found herself thankful for each filtered sip.

Remembering the other best part about having running water, she took a shower in the master bathroom, washing away the caked blood on her hands and back - the flowing water on her skin one of the best feelings in the world. She hadn't had a proper shower in years, being stuck in a slice of a moment in the 1800s. It felt epic.

She felt bad taking anything from the random family, but convinced herself that one sandwich, some jeans, converse, a crossbody purse and a T-shirt wouldn't be greatly missed. Still, the photographs of the happy family growing up through the years seemed to bother her - the carefree happiness of the parents and their young kids evident. Set on the coffee table were even more memories, stuffed in a photo book, which Aurelia flipped through while eating her bologna and cheese sandwich that she had just made herself, which tasted divine. The family had documented everything - their children's milestones and birthdays, their labrador when they first got him as a puppy, the dinners and events with grandparents, aunts and cousins. The sibling rivalry between the young girl and slightly older boy, yet the immense love they felt for each other at the end of the day. The parents, deeply in love, hard at work with steady nine-to-five jobs, yet easygoing and invested in their community. Almost like their entire life could be explained just by looking at the photos.

Aurelia could never have a life like theirs. A normal house, a fully stocked fridge, kids with a steady friend group at a school that they'd been to since first grade. It all seemed like more of a fantasy than her life traveling through time.

Closing the photo book and cleaning her plate in the kitchen, she left the house just as it was before her, minus one sandwich and one outfit, discarding her once beautiful, but now bloodstained, romper in the trash, but keeping the clutch and wallet from the '70s in her new crossbody bag as a token to remember the party.

Continuing through the portal, this time focusing her mind on a precise thought to pinpoint and control where she would end up. She thought of Will - the specific version of him in time just as she had left him, the image fresh in her mind - with his blue bellbottoms and racing thoughts. Since he was injured, she knew they would have taken him home to the hospital in B-udo, so even more explicitly, she thought of the white washed hospital rooms that all looked identical to each other. The cradle that would heal him, and the clean technology hidden beneath the surface of the walls.

The image firmly planted in her mind, she stepped up the stairs in the random family's house to, once again, get back to Will.

The portal entered into the hospital's hallway, a familiar sight that Aurelia had grown accustomed to, after being there so many times. Though it was hard to tell what year she had traveled to, she had been honing her powers so much lately that she had complete faith that Will would be somewhere nearby. Looking at the projections outside of each room for Will's name, she finally came to one labeled Mr. Kovachev, his dad's last name. It was him. Aurelia swung the door open, holding herself back from jumping straight into Will's arms.

Unexpectedly, the room was filled with people, Will's friends. It was a considerably larger room than all of the exact replica hospital rooms she'd been in before, and this one was outfitted with a sitting area in addition to the standard lounger next to the cradle. This was a room designated for the higher ups in the company - the more important people of B-udo. Everyone was dressed in ZhēnZhū's distinguishing full body second skin suits, Aurelia the only one dressed in clothes from the past.

A few familiar faces stuck out amidst the crowd, and Aurelia immediately recognized them as Mason and Benji. There was another guy, and a group of girls all floating around, who she didn't recognize, almost like it was a party, not a hospital. But the one person that stuck out, was a stunning brunette with freckles and an absolutely perfect figure, who stood just over Will, in a hot pink suit. Luckily, Will seemed recovered, and was seated upright on the bed with a bright smile, wearing his blue suit, this one different from the one she remembered him in. There was no white in the design. Remembering that having white in your suit here was almost the same thing as wearing an engagement ring in the 21st century, Aurelia finally felt what he had years ago - the symbolization of the fact that they weren't together yet.

Will hadn't even noticed Aurelia walk in. A pang of jealousy hit Aurelia in the stomach, seeing another girl trying to get with Will. But it was OK - he still didn't know Aurelia like that. She couldn't jump to any conclusions, after all, they could just be friends. But the brunette sure didn't act like just a friend, Aurelia felt. Her subtle movements, as she laughed and brushed her hand to Will's arm, were more than enough of an implication that she liked him. Plus, she looked flawless, her complexion smooth like a porcelain doll, her smile radiant and bright - how could Will *not* like her? Aurelia would never be that perfect.

Casting her jealousy aside, she walked past a few of the girls to get into Will's line of sight. Although he was mid-sentence, speaking to the beautiful brunette next to him, he took a double take at Aurelia and lost his train of thought.

"Hi," Aurelia smiled.

"...Hi! What are you...? Is it... OK for you to be here?" Will stuttered, obviously worried for her safety, since the last time he saw her she barely escaped from the Guardians.

"Yeah, no, it's fine! I'm here. I had to check that you were alright."

"I am. Good as new," Will smiled, patting his leg as if to show her. "You're OK, though? I thought they shot you too?"

"Um... no. I'm all good," Aurelia mildly lied. Even though she had been shot, she didn't want to go into it.

The brunette standing next to him jumped in, "Wait, you were with him when the permanents attacked? I thought you said you were alone?" she scolded, blatantly crinkling her forehead in mild envy.

The story had obviously been shifted for the public - claiming it was the permanents in the '70s that had attacked him, and not the Guardians.

"Um... yeah. She was there for part of it," Will replied, trying to untangle himself from his lie.

"And, apologies for not knowing. You are...?" the girl asked Aurelia.

"Oh, Bianca, this is Aurelia. Aurelia, Bianca," Will introduced, not used to the concept of using aliases yet.

Bianca. That was the name she had just overheard Mason mention was Will's ex-girlfriend.

"Hi," Aurelia smiled, trying her best to hide her worry, holding out her palm facing the ceiling and quickly twisting it towards the floor to greet her with a flurry, even though she didn't have a bracelet that facilitated the full sensation of the futuristic greeting.

Bianca sent back a quick flurry, with her eyes narrowed as she studied Aurelia.

"You're from here?" Bianca asked.

"Yes," Aurelia lied.

"That's so weird. I can't believe we've never met."

Will chuckled, "That's what I said when I met her. She's a recluse, apparently."

"Yup," Aurelia smiled.

"Well, I'm glad you weren't hurt," Will said to Aurelia with a twinge of doubt - he was certain she had been hit by the bullets.

"Thank you."

Bianca jumped in, "And thank God the Guardians showed up when they did. Who knows what would've happened if you didn't bring your tablet and call them!"

"Right..." Aurelia went along with the story. "Things could've been a lot different."

A twinge of regret passed through Aurelia's body. She should've made a portal out of 1977 immediately. They might have avoided all of this hassle if she had gone about things differently. But instead, the seed of doubt and fear had not only been planted, but watered, in Will's mind. Although intrigued by Aurelia, he wasn't sure if even being friends with someone surrounded by so much danger was such a good idea.

It definitely wasn't the safest place to be, while the Guardians were actively searching for her, but Aurelia stayed in Will's room for a few hours, floating around his friend group as Will and Bianca introduced her. As much as she was turned off by Mason from his rude comments she overheard at the party, she put on her best poker face and reacquainted herself with him and Benji to help pass the time, until she could get Will alone, so they could leave together.

As the hours passed, some friends left and others joined, and Aurelia could see his obvious popularity in B-udo. His friends definitely seemed nice, although it was clear that some of them were overly fake and *too* nice. Sure, a good portion of them seemed genuine, but there was an equal portion of fair weathered schmoozers and "yes men", who would most likely leave on a dime for a bigger, better deal. Somehow, even though Will was completely surrounded by a sea of people, Aurelia could sense his loneliness as he clung to conversations.

Finally, a doctor came in to discharge Will, and the "party" came to a close. Quicker than a dog to meat, the group of people left as the scene was no longer "hip", with only Aurelia and Bianca left as they gathered Will's few belongings and headed out.

The hardest part for Aurelia about being around Bianca was that there wasn't anything apparently hatable about her. At least if she was rude or petty, Aurelia would have no problem stealing Will away without a second thought. But unfortunately, she was kind and gentle, and a part of Aurelia almost felt like just leaving now and letting Bianca love Will. It seemed like it would be the best thing for him - not a dangerous life, running through time with Aurelia.

But then there was the other part of her, that knew how happy Will had been in the future with Aurelia. How could she take that future happiness away by giving up and leaving now?

The three of them navigated out of the hospital, which was the first time Aurelia had actually used the front entrance of it and not the hidden tunnels. They were in the Core of B-udo, a different area of it, with another center atrium filled with exotic animals. This atrium seemed to be winterized, with engineered snow falling from the ceiling. Carrying through the white washed design from the hospital, the wide, open hallways in this part of the Core donned white marble floors, and clean, zen finishings.

Aurelia was drawn to the glass, and remembering how to work the technology from her first time in B-udo with Will, tapped it to get a closer view of the animals down below. A screen instantly populated with a projection of the animals. There was a large family of polar bears in this particular atrium, with a deep, icy lake filled with fish for food. The microscopic cameras in the glass tracked the movement, and while Aurelia watched, she couldn't help but think how sad it was that the animals, and most likely their ancestors for dozens, if not hundreds of generations, had lived their lives in captivity - their natural environment above ground completely destroyed. But on the other hand, at least their species had been preserved from completely dying out on the Earth's surface.

"You like animals?" Will asked, stopping next to her to watch the zoomed live feed with Aurelia.

"Yeah. I love them. You?"

Will nodded, "And polar bears might just be my favorite," Will said with a smile, his eyes glued to the screen looking at the majestic white beasts below them.

"Hey," Bianca interrupted, "I've gotta get to Qiu's. I'm supposed to babysit Meiling tonight. You'll be good getting home alone? You feel OK?"

"Yeah, of course. I'll be good... Thank you for coming."

Bianca tilted her head, gesturing for him to step aside so they could speak privately from Aurelia. Although Aurelia wanted to be respectful and tune out what they were saying, she couldn't help but listen in as she nonchalantly watched the polar bears.

"Look," Bianca whispered to him, "I know I said I just wanted to be friends, but maybe... I don't know. Seeing you in the hospital today I just... maybe I was crazy... for letting you go. So, could we maybe have lunch?"

Aurelia could feel her heart racing. No. Will was *her* love, not Bianca's.

"I don't... I thought you said you didn't see a future together?" Will said a little louder than a whisper out of emotion.

"Well... what do I know? Maybe it's better that I don't know what's going to happen for us? I'd be willing to give it a try and see what happens," Bianca said.

"...Where is this even coming from?"

"You could've *died* from those permanents, Will! Maybe I just don't want to let you go."

"B... I don't know what to say."

"Look, just think about it, OK? You don't have to decide now... but if you want to, we can start over."

Bianca leaned in and kissed Will's cheek, before giving Aurelia a pursed smile goodbye and spiritedly walking off.

Will turned back to Aurelia, his head spinning. Aurelia wasn't sure what to say after witnessing Will's ex saying she wanted to get back together with him - right as *she* was trying to win him over.

"So... polar bears, huh?"

Will laughed out loud, "Yeah... nice *ice breaker*."

Aurelia walked with Will back through the Core, eliciting quite a few stares because of her outfit choice of jeans and a t-shirt from the past - not wearing one of the standard suits that everyone here in B-udo was accustomed to. She really shouldn't be drawing any additional attention to herself, but it felt so good to talk to Will, alone. It almost felt like they were back in Amsterdam, falling for each other all over again. But the longer Aurelia stayed here in B-udo, the more risk. As they walked, Aurelia kept her eyes peeled for a staircase, but B-udo was primarily designed with lifts and bullet trains. After walking through dozens of hallways in the Core, she finally spotted a beautiful, open, marble staircase that caressed itself down and around another glass animal enclosure.

"Will? It's time. I have to leave."

"Oh. You mean, *leave* leave? Back in time?" Aurelia nodded. "When are you coming back?"

"Honestly, I don't know... but listen, I haven't made good on my promise of taking you to your favorite place... anywhere. Do you still wanna come?" Aurelia asked.

"You mean, come with you?"

Aurelia nodded. After the events of last night in New York, Will wasn't sure anymore.

"If we stay off the grid, we'll be totally fine. I've done it for years with no issues. Maybe just don't bring your tablet this time," Aurelia chuckled nervously.

"Aurelia... they said you were dangerous. And that if you showed up again, I should steer clear and call Helios immediately, to turn you in."

"And... would you?"

"...I haven't called anyone yet, have I?"

"Look, I haven't done *anything* to them. If anything, they're the ones that have done horrible things."

Aurelia thought of Johanna bleeding to death in Amsterdam, the image burned into her mind.

"Like what?"

She couldn't tell him. She couldn't scare him even more.

"...It doesn't matter," but it did matter. It haunted her everyday. "Really, I don't know what's gonna happen that leads to them chasing me. Maybe we just have irrevocable differences. But I know that I can't live my life in fear of my future catching up with me."

"So that's what you do? Just stay hidden back in time?"

"Well, what's the alternative?"

"...Maybe you should try talking to them...?"

Aurelia cringed. If there was one thing she wouldn't do - it was have a conversation with the people that killed Johanna.

"So what, I just turn myself in? 'Hey guys! I'm sorry for what future me may or may not do, but hey - thanks for shooting at me and my friends - but let's have tea!'" Will had hit a sore subject. "... Sorry," she sighed.

"OK, so maybe not that," Will smiled, trying to ease the tension. "Look, if I'm seen with you again and I don't report it - I'm not so sure Helios will give me another pass."

"So then why are you still with me right now? We're literally in the lion's den," Aurelia pointed out, as they walked, in public, through the Core.

"I don't know. Maybe I don't believe them. You don't seem..."

"Bad?" Aurelia finished his sentence.

"No. You don't seem bad."

"I don't think I am. At least, I don't want to be. Then again, maybe there are no good or bad sides - maybe there are just opposing viewpoints, and no matter what you do, you'll always think you're fighting for the good, no matter what your opponent thinks of you. Maybe good and bad are only perceptions."

"No. You're wrong," Will objected. "There *are* bad people. But I think there are levels of good too. It's not cut and dry, but good is the side that always questions their morals and never settles in trying to better themselves, you know?"

Aurelia nodded, "So what am I then?"

"...I think you're good, but you're misunderstood. But look, I don't know you. Maybe I'm wrong."

"I hope you're not."

"What do you think of me?" Will asked with an insecure chuckle.

"Oh you're good. Through and through."

"Really? What makes you so sure?"

Aurelia couldn't tell him how he'd earned her trust as she'd fallen madly in love with him in Amsterdam.

"I just... know. You have that... face."

"That face?" Will laughed. "You get that vibe from my face?"

Aurelia joined in on his contagious laughter, "Yeah! You smile too much to be bad."

"So what if I stopped smiling altogether?" Will said, attempting to hold back his chuckle with a comically fierce frown.

"Oh! How did I not see that before? What? You're evil?" Aurelia jested sarcastically.

Will broke from his frown and bent over in a laugh, as the people walking near them stared even more intently, wondering what all the commotion was about. Aurelia's smile turned weary as the knot in her stomach tightened, noticing the attention coming their way.

"I think I could talk to you all day, Will, but... I really *do* need to go now."

"I know you do..."

"So... does that mean you're not coming?" Aurelia asked, a shakiness in her breath.

"I... can't," Will's eyes read Aurelia's disappointment. "...Not today, at least."

"What if we did this... I come back, right here, at the top of the stairs, tomorrow," Aurelia motioned to the open marble staircase, "and if you want to come with me, you show up. If you don't come... I guess we'll just... go our separate ways."

It was a huge leap of faith, but she definitely couldn't force him to come with her.

"Tomorrow..."

"Or the next day? Or next week? ...Or next month?" Aurelia laughed.

Will chuckled shallowly, deep in thought, "I just... maybe I need to..."

"Look, if you don't show up, I'll leave. No pressure. But if you do come... I would really love that. I want to know you, Will."

"...Tomorrow?"

"Tomorrow."

Aurelia reaffirmed with a smile, hopefully only a temporary goodbye, making her way to the stairwell. She took one last look at him, almost as if taking a picture in her mind of the moment. His young, carefree, contagious smile, his tousled brown hair, and his wise, blue eyes. To Aurelia, he was the epitome of perfection.

It took a few minutes to wait for the stairwell to be clear of anyone, for fear of being seen disappearing, but as soon as the coast was clear, Aurelia stepped down, creating a portal. Portals going to a different time but not a different place were surprisingly a bit more challenging to make, but she had managed to do it in ancient Mexico, when she hadn't even realized *what* she was doing, so she knew it was possible. It was important to focus on her current surroundings, and not let any other thoughts enter her mind, so she wouldn't accidentally shift it to a different place.

She stepped through as slowly, and steadily as possible, watching the people in B-udo shuffle about her like time-lapsed ghosts, until the lights in the metal walls were dimmed to blue for the night, and the nightly automated cleaning began. Before long, the lights shifted back to a yellow, golden hue, and the city was bustling once again. Aurelia stopped where she was, looking around to check for Will's face, before she turned around and headed back up, still going forward in time, slowly. She wasn't sure when he would come during the day, so she kept stepping up, being careful not to rush through the day so she didn't miss spotting him.

The crowds were constant throughout the day, but none of them seemed to hold Will. She had told him to wait for her at the top of the stairs. He would come. He had to. Aurelia kept holding out faith, even as the crowd began to thin and the lights shifted to blue for the night.

Maybe she had missed him. Stepping back down, reversing the day, she searched once again for his face. She still didn't spot him, even as she once again went forward in time to look for him. Thinking there had to be a reason why he couldn't get to her that particular day, Aurelia went through the next day, then the next, just searching for his face.

But he hadn't come to meet Aurelia. Will didn't come.

CHAPTER 40

ALWAYS

It felt like her lungs couldn't remember how to breathe. As if her heart didn't feel the need to beat anymore.

Will hadn't shown up. He didn't want to come with her.

Why had she told him that if he didn't come, it would be OK and they could just go their separate ways? She didn't want that. She only wanted to alleviate some of the pressure of their new relationship, that was off to quite a rocky start, by giving him the *choice*. But never in a million years did she think he would actually take the out she gave him.

Sure, the odds were against them, and in his eyes, they had only just met, so he wasn't giving up much - but there was a definite spark between them, even just from their first meeting. Hadn't Will felt it too? He wouldn't have let that spark go out without seeing where it may lead, would he?

There had to be a reason why he hadn't come. Was he alright, Aurelia wondered? What if something had happened?

Convincing herself to check on him one final time before leaving for good, Aurelia stopped the portal just as the blue light was turned on in the early evening, to remain unseen. It was a few days after she had seen Will last, so she hoped he would have had some time to think about everything. Retracing her steps and tiptoeing through the Core until she found the hospital, she snaked through the empty corridors, finding the entrance to one of the hidden tunnels that connected all of B-udo and following it to Will's house.

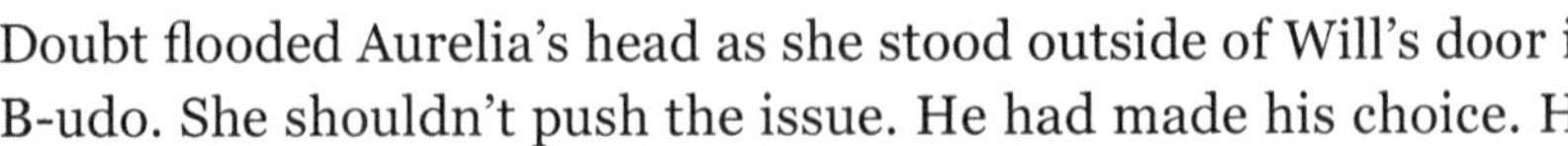

Doubt flooded Aurelia's head as she stood outside of Will's door in B-udo. She shouldn't push the issue. He had made his choice. He didn't want to know Aurelia.

But he had made a mistake. They were destined to know each other. The future was already written, wasn't it? Or had it changed because Aurelia had messed up the timeline somehow? Was that even possible? Could time be changed?

If she left now, without Will, the future would definitely change, Aurelia convinced herself. Will wouldn't know Aurelia any more than one crazy, dangerous night in the '70s. Maybe she had to push the future in the right direction.

Maybe she could still save their future together.

Maybe she was wrong to lie to him, and tell him that they didn't know each other past the party. Maybe that was partly why Aurelia had trusted Will so quickly when he came to get her in the '50s. She knew he knew her. Even though back then, she didn't know him well, in time, she came to love and trust him. Knowing a slice of your future and working towards it can make decisions easier. Maybe that was what Will was lacking. Maybe he needed to know that in his future, he trusted Aurelia.

Hovering her hand over the door handle, Aurelia thought through all of the possibilities that could be on the other side. Aleksander could be there and turn her in to the Guardians - the current version of him that now knew Aurelia's true identity, not the young, starry-eyed inventor she had met so many years ago. Will could feel any number of emotions for her being there - happiness, confusion, anger, or disappointment. Will might even call Helios and rat her out. What if she couldn't escape in time?

Opening the door would either be the most dangerous, reckless, stupid, or best decision of her life. But sometimes you have to take a leap of faith and jump headfirst for love.

Settling her fingers on the locked door handle, the technology in the metal recognized her biometrics and clicked open. At some point in the past, Will must have programmed his door to let her in. Aurelia smiled with hope - the door opening for her meant that sometime in Will's future, they would still know each other. Maybe the future hadn't changed. Maybe everything was happening the way it should. Maybe.

A gentle piano melody drifted to Aurelia's ears as she walked inside. Will's house looked a bit different than when she was here the first time, thirteen years ago. What was once an eerily empty ballroom, was now filled with a sitting room's furniture, a sign that Will and his dad had finally settled into life in B-udo. The same art hung on the walls as before, with the faux balcony overlooking a projection of Paris in the early 1900s. The familiarity of the house instantly brought back memories of her first kiss with Will here.

Following the sound of music to her right, Aurelia crept through the house, glancing inside dark rooms as she passed them, one used for downloads, which held two enormous reclining chairs, another for gaming, and a giant room with vaulted ceilings for an art studio. Coming to the end of the hall, the hallway's architecture curved into an open doorway, where the music seemed to be coming from. Peeking her head around the corner to check who was playing, she sighed a breath of relief to see that it was just Will, with his back to her, playing a natural wood, concert grand, Steinway piano. She couldn't see Aleksander anywhere, so she stepped inside.

Aurelia actually had no idea Will could play the piano so beautifully. His fingers seemed to move independently from his mind, finding the melody on their own. His playing was effortless, buoyant and confident. She stepped to his left, next to the piano, assuming he would see her instantly, but his eyes were closed, his mind lost in the melody. As the song came to a close, his eyes fluttered open, and he spotted her.

Gasping from shock, he jerked his hands back from the keys.

"Sorry!" Aurelia whispered loudly. "I didn't mean to scare you, it's just, I couldn't knock and risk your dad seeing me."

"Knock? What's knock?" Will said in a defensive voice, apparently no one knocked in the future. "But, how did you get in? The door's locked at night."

"To strangers, yes."

"But - so how-"

"Look. I lied to you," Aurelia sat down on the upholstered French chaise just next to the piano.

"What? What do you mean?"

Will's heart was racing. She had just broken into his house - maybe everyone was right and Aurelia was more dangerous than he thought.

"I know you - well, technically, I know the future you. After I took your Okliot at the party in the '70s, we met again. You helped me escape."

"I... what are you talking about? Me? I helped you?" Aurelia nodded. "But why?"

"Well... because we become close. We trust each other. That's how I got in tonight - you must have programmed your door to recognize my biometrics at some point."

"What?" Will took a deep breath, nervously brushing his hair back from his face with both hands. "I... so, how well do we know each other?"

"Very well."

"And... what... what are we in the future?" Aurelia looked at him, puzzled. "Are we... just friends?"

Will obviously felt the palpable tension between them.

Aurelia wasn't sure how to answer. To her, they were just dating, but she knew that eventually in their future, they would be married.

"We're a bit more than friends."

"I don't... then why would you lie about us not knowing each other?"

"Because I didn't want you to feel pressured. But when you didn't show up to meet me - I... I'm sorry. This isn't how I wanted any of this to go."

Will sighed, "Look. Everything here in my life is... complicated right now, and sure, it sounds like fun to come with you - but I can't just run off and leave all of that."

Aurelia thought about how she had felt in the early days of knowing Will. She was hesitant to leave her life too. But for her, she had no choice. She couldn't go home, otherwise she would risk her family's lives. Aurelia sighed, the tears inadvertently welling up in her eyes.

"I don't want this to be so complicated between us."

"I know," he didn't know, at least not yet. Will studied her face almost mechanically, unsure what the answer was that would alleviate the situation. "...How do I know I can trust you?"

Aurelia smiled briefly through her scrunched face, "What'd ya wanna know?"

Will wasn't sure what he wanted to know. He wasn't sure he would even believe her. But one thing he could believe in was himself.

"...What was the last thing I said to you?" Will asked.

"You mean, future you?" Aurelia clarified, Will nodded.

It had been so many years, but Aurelia remembered the moment well.

It was nearing Christmastime in Amsterdam, and Will was headed out into town early that morning. She had decided to sleep in, slightly, snuggled beneath the heavy blankets on the cold November morning. The rain drizzled on the canal outside, like white noise keeping her mind calm. Will stepped upstairs with a cup of coffee for

Aurelia, setting it on her bedside table with a kiss on her forehead.

"Don't go yet..." Aurelia had begged him with a coy smile.

"Don't tempt me, Lia..." sitting on top of the covers, his lips found hers, gently, and they shared a moment. "But I have to go..."

"Hmm... but what sounds better... staying here with me, or going into town on a rainy, miserable day?"

Will kissed her with his answer, "Is that even a question?" they were too close to see his lips, but she could see his eyes squint into a smile. "But I have some business with Sinterklaas today..."

"You know you don't need to get me anything, right?" Aurelia smiled in a mild lie - of course she *wanted* him to get her something for their first Christmas together.

"Of course I have to. I want you to know how much I love you, Lia," Will brushed Aurelia's blond hair from her face.

"But I already know. You're mine and I'm yours."

"Always."

Aurelia leaned up to kiss him goodbye, eternally happy.

"OK. Fine. Go, Go!" she laughed, pushing him away lovingly. "I'll see you for dinner. I'm making casserole," Will winced, jokingly. "Hey! So mean! My cooking's not *that* bad!" Will laughed, sarcastically shrugging his shoulders in question. "Shut uppp!" Aurelia laughed. "OK. Go. See you soon. Don't be too late, K?"

"OK... I love you!" Will said, backing up to the wooden staircase in their *rijtjeshuis*.

"I love you too... bye," Aurelia smiled, while she had watched him jump down the white, winding staircase from the safety of her warm, cozy bed.

The memory of Amsterdam still fresh, she zoned back into the actual current moment in B-udo.

She couldn't tell Will that his actual last words to her were "I love you". That would be too much, too fast. But just before that, his more poignant word had been something that Aurelia thought of often. Their phrase. He was hers and she was his - always.

"You told me 'always'," Aurelia said, looking across at a much younger version of Will than the one she had grown so accustomed to in Amsterdam.

"Always?" Will asked, and Aurelia nodded. Will scrunched his face, trying to decipher what "always" meant for them. He wouldn't have told someone "always", if he didn't trust them completely. What if she was lying though, he wondered?

"What does that even mean?"

It was like looking at a stranger. Every familiar, easygoing part of Will was hidden in this younger version of himself, instead replaced by fear and distrust. She knew he wouldn't remember their phrase - because for him, he hadn't lived it yet - but there was something so disheartening about the whole scenario of having to convince him to give her a chance.

"It's just part of a silly phrase we used to say," Aurelia managed a broken smile.

"What's the phrase?" Will seemed intrigued, yet somehow also disinterested in the tone he asked his questions.

Aurelia wasn't sure if she should reveal much more. What if she had already said too much and it would affect their future?

"I can't... I shouldn't tell you more."

"But, why, 'always'?" he wouldn't understand.

"It doesn't matter. Look, I'm sorry. I made a mistake coming back tonight. You made your decision when you didn't come meet me in the Core - I should've just left you alone like I promised," Aurelia got up, to hide as the tears began collecting in her eyes, heading towards the hallway.

"Aurelia, wait," Will got up from his piano bench and headed towards her, grabbing her arm gently to stop her. "I didn't show up because I can't be seen with you again."

Aurelia scoffed, knowing perfectly well that it was a valid point, but upset with the insensitive way he had put it, "I know."

"We really shouldn't see each other again. Helios, not to mention my dad, would have my ass for it."

"Fine," Aurelia said abruptly, a lump in her throat building up.

"But that doesn't mean I didn't *want* to come."

"...What are you saying, Will?"

"You can really control exactly where your portals go?"

"Yeah."

"So, theoretically, we could go somewhere in time for hours, or even days, and still come right back to the exact minute we left?"

Aurelia nodded, "I guess so..."

"So... what if we just took one trip - before we... never see each other again?"

He wanted to come with her. She had a chance to win him over.

"Where to?"

Will creased his forehead in thought, looking around at the room they stood in for inspiration, an idea bursting into his mind.

"What about here?"

"Here? What are you talking about?"

"Paris, in the 19th or 20th century - but the real thing?"

Aurelia smiled, Paris was the perfect, romantic place - not to mention how much she loved France from her time there with Natalia in the 1400s.

"One trip it is."

CHAPTER 41

PARIS

Aurelia couldn't hide her excitement. Even though the events of the past few hours were stressful and had her questioning their relationship, it was overshadowed by the happiness she felt, knowing that Will actually wanted to come with her on a trip.

Will had changed out of his standard second skin suit and into something a bit more appropriate for back in time, one of his father's fitted suits. Luckily, his dad was still at Headquarters pulling a late night, just like he did every night, so at the moment, Will's house was empty, and more importantly, safe, for a while.

Will personally didn't have any appropriate clothes for Aurelia to use, especially since in B-udo, most everyone just wore their second skin suits, but digging in his father's closet, he came across a trunk of his mom's old things from when they had lived in P-yex. Over a decade ago, they hadn't been able to afford the luxury of the radiation blocking, metal suits, so Will's mom had still worn regular, antiquated, fabric clothes. Will pretended not to let the fact that he was sifting through his mom's things faze him, but Aurelia was sure he was merely putting on a brave face.

Inside, besides an old digital sketchbook, a few delicate porcelain figurines and some other trinkets, the pieces of clothing that they found were mostly dirty, well-used shirts. However, they finally they came across a peachy pink, patterned, gently flared out dress in perfect condition, like a gem amidst the rest of the well-worn items, obviously something once special and prized. Will held it up to Aurelia to envision the fit on her, and with a melancholy smile, handed it to her to try on.

"You sure?" Aurelia asked, judging the look on his face.

"Yeah. See if it fits," Will said, looking back into the trunk as if to hide his face. "There're some extra rooms down the hall that you can change in."

Nodding, Aurelia left to change into the dress. Just to her left was the room she had slept in years ago, and she slipped inside its familiar walls. It seemed perfectly preserved in time, almost as if no one had stepped foot inside since the last time she had been in B-udo, over a decade ago in time. The faux balcony overlooking a projection of Paris at night dimmed on as she stepped inside, illuminating the large Victorian bed and bath that occupied most of the room. She couldn't help but remember the last time she was in the room - just two days after her 19th birthday, the thrill of time travel still making it seem like she was in a dream. Will had softly come into the room to wake her, sitting on the bed and gently brushing the hair from her cheek. It was an apprehensive kiss, just the beginning for her, that had slowly evolved itself through the months they spent together in Amsterdam. But somehow, this room symbolized the start of her feelings for Will, and now, years later for her, their relationship was about to start again.

Taking off her jeans, T-shirt and crossbody bag, and stuffing them inside an empty drawer to keep them hidden, she gently pulled the dress over her head. Woven inside the fabric, a hidden technology adjusted the size, the bunched layers automatically loosening to accommodate Aurelia's slightly larger bust and waist than the previous person who had worn the dress, Will's mom. She wondered how the technology inside the fabric worked - it was something she had never seen before, but it made perfect sense that it would be invented. It could make all clothes be "one-size-fits-all", just adjusting to each person's measurements.

Looking down at the well-cared-for dress with a nervous smile, she stepped out to show Will. Standing in wait, he briefly smiled at the sight, before tempering his emotions so as to keep himself from getting too invested.

"What do you think?" Aurelia asked, trying to read his complicated, conflicted mind.

"...Yeah! It works, no?"

She had expected more.

Nodding with a sinking smile, Aurelia began walking past him to the front door, "You ready to go?"

Will nodded and followed behind the enigma that was Aurelia.

They snuck through the empty corridors of Will's sector in B-udo, technically out past curfew, which would be a big violation if they were caught. But Will knew of a stairwell nearby that led to more houses just above them, still in B-udo, which Aurelia could use to make a portal. She decided it would be best to use a stairwell that hadn't been locked in place with what she assumed were Aleksander's devices, such as all of the ones she knew of in Headquarters, and rather go with a stairwell with a clean slate. Luckily, with the metal hallways so eerily empty and bathed in blue light, they remained unseen and made it to the stairwell without issue.

"You nervous?" Aurelia asked as they stood at the bottom of the stairwell.

"No," Will answered hastily.

It was obvious that he was. No amount of machismo could mask it.

"Here, take my hand," Aurelia said, reaching her hand out to his.

"Why?"

'It had never even been a question before,' Aurelia thought to herself.

"This one won't be like the other portals you've used - it's not stabilized. I'll keep us together in the portal - unless you *want* to go somewhere random in time, all alone?"

Will smirked at her sarcasm, tightly grabbing her hand, "You have your Okliot?" he asked, holding his newly acquired device tightly bound in his other hand.

"Of course," Aurelia still had the A class Okliot she had promised Will in the '70s, despite not needing it.

"And that's it? That's all you need? How do we open a portal?"

"I... have a device," Aurelia lied, quickly thinking up something that could be convincing. "See?" she held up her wrist, pointing to the watch that she had gotten from Tiffany's in the '70s that reminded her of her grandfather's.

"A watch?"

"Well, see, this isn't an ordinary watch. You might think it is, but, it's not."

"So, how does it work? You can calibrate it?"

Aurelia nodded, a poor liar, but so far Will seemed to think her lie was tenable. It was better than telling him the truth. The magic of technology is much more believable than something that's not discovered or understood.

"It's... very complicated. You probably wouldn't understand."

"I think I could follow. Try me," Will probed, hoping to figure out how it worked.

"Another time... I've already put in our destination. Come on, let's go," Aurelia smiled, gently pulling his hand and leading him up, to change the subject.

The two walked up the stairs, Aurelia focusing her mind on the feeling of Will's apartment in B-udo, the gilded chandeliers and Jazz Age inspired furnishings. In the apartment, the view had been focused on the Eiffel Tower, as if that was Paris's only defining feature, but for Aurelia, she had lived there centuries before the Eiffel Tower was even dreamt of, and to her it seemed like Paris was much more a feeling in the air than one specific piece of architecture. But it was hard to have an opinion, not seeing it for herself. So, she thought of the tower in her mind's eye as they traveled, hoping to land somewhere with a decent view so that she could finally have a more objective viewpoint.

Shifting around them, the metallic walls melted into patina and gold-laced, painted paneled walls, the detail in the wood darkened slightly to accentuate the framed carvings. The stairwell opened up into a small parlor room, fitted with wooden herringbone floors and plush, patterned, red lounge chairs. A fireplace crackled to their left, and floor-to-ceiling brocade curtains were draped across the closed windows, blocking the view. Aurelia couldn't help herself from going to look outside, so letting go of Will's hand, she beelined to the heavy drapes, pulling them across with some effort. Behind them, the vibrant city revealed itself.

Glistening with a hint of morning sun and dew, it was as if looking out onto a completely unrecognizable city. So much had changed since the 15th century. The city had thickened with new buildings, and seemed charged with mild industrialism. This particular building seemed perched along the Seine, and just across the murky river waters stood France's architectural achievement of the century, currently the tallest tower in the world, the Eiffel Tower.

"Wow," Will breathlessly exclaimed, now standing just behind Aurelia.

It was stunning. Surreal, as if it had been placed in its location from the hands of a God rather than built.

"So what year is it?" Will asked, looking around at the apartment they stood in.

"I dunno. Looks like we're in the 1900s at least."

"Looks like? Didn't you set your watch?"

"Right, yeah, I did, but it's not always exact."

Aurelia picked through the apartment, scanning the bookshelves framing the room's entrance and hoping to find evidence of what time they had landed in, but it was hard to tell. She picked up a small statue of a woman on the shelf to study its elegance, when she heard footsteps walking down the stairwell they had just used. A man dressed in a nightgown, smoking a pipe and reading a paper came down, immediately making eye contact with Aurelia and shouting in bloody murder.

"*Voleuse !*" he shouted at the apparent thief in his home, charging towards Aurelia.

"*Non, nous ne sommes pas des voleurs !*" they weren't thieves, Aurelia pleaded, putting down the statue and backing up to avoid the man's attempt to grab her. "Will, the stairs!"

Will raced towards them, the man just registering the fact that there was another person.

"*Qui croyez-vous être ? Entrer par effraction ?*" the man continued, as he swiped to grab Aurelia. "*Vous avez pris quoi ?*" what had they taken?

"*Rien. C'est un simple malentendu,*" they hadn't taken anything, it was just a misunderstanding.

Jumping over the red chaise, Aurelia darted behind the man, running after Will, down the stairs.

"*Désolés, Monsieur ! Nous partons,*" Aurelia backpedaled, apologizing for intruding, as she jumped down the stairs two, three at a time.

A few flights down, Aurelia burst out of the front door, catching a glimpse of Will's brown hair just turning the corner. She chased after him, the man of the house just behind her. Luckily, the street was almost empty, so she ran without hinderance and quickly increased the distance between herself and the man. But with the streets so empty, it would be hard to completely lose the tail of the man behind them, who continually shouted after the "thieves".

Ahead of her, Will turned another corner. As Aurelia turned, following in his footsteps, she realized he had disappeared from sight.

"Aurelia!" Will whispered loudly to her right, from behind a see through, wrought iron fence, inside a quaint garden. "Can you fit through?" he motioned to the bottom of the fence, where a large gap separated the dirt and iron.

Without hesitation, Aurelia crawled underneath, her borrowed pristine pink dress now brown from dust. Will helped her up, pulling her close to him behind a tree, as the man chasing them passed the garden, frantically. Will's breath was warm and fast on her cheek as they stayed pressed together, in hopes of not being seen. But the man didn't come back. They were OK. They slowly broke apart, realizing they had dodged the man. Unexpectedly, Will chuckled, his dimples appearing as he smiled.

"What's so funny?" Aurelia asked, studying his emotions.

"That was *amazing*!"

"What?"

"That was *so* much fun! And exhilarating! Right?"

"Weren't you scared?" Aurelia smiled, still catching her breath.

"Yeah, of course! But not like New York. This was more like a level of a game than real life! Is this what it's always like for you?"

"No... I mean, yes - sometimes. I don't know if I'd call it 'fun' though!" Aurelia laughed, brushing the dusty dirt from her dress. "It's not always so innocent as an uncoordinated man in his nighties running after you... Shall we?" Aurelia motioned to the gate so they could be on their way.

Just to the right of where they had shimmied under the fence, Aurelia noticed a door handle. Turning it just out of curiosity, she realized that the gate was actually unlocked.

Will smirked, looking sheepishly at Aurelia, "Well, I guess I should've tried the door first?"

Looming above them, the Eiffel Tower seemed almost like an illusion that couldn't be real. The morning sun glittered through the shaped metal, casting shadows that added to the mystery.

It only took a few minutes to figure out where to hop the fence to get onto the stairs, the policemen lackadaisical and scarce in the morning. Stepping up through the tower just a few flights, it seemed the metal staircase was never-ending. Shouts from below them reverberated through the metal, as the guards realized that the two had snuck past them. With haste, the guards unlocked the gate and began to run up the stairs to them.

"What should we do?" Will looked at Aurelia with furrowed eyebrows.

'It's not even worth stressing over,' Aurelia thought. She had been in much worse scenarios.

Smiling, she grabbed Will's hand, "Wanna see something cool?"

Will nodded, unassured. Aurelia gently nudged his hand forward,

pulling him just behind her as she increased her speed up the stairs.

The shouting quickly stopped, and the landscape morphed from morning to night, the sun reversing its direction in time.

"What...? Are we...?" Will stammered, looking in awe at the city around them as they traveled in time.

Aurelia nodded, equally taking in the beauty around them. He had never seen the full evolution of a free, unstable portal - every other portal he had used with the company had been from point A to point B, a straight and narrow path. Like stepping from 44-4, instantly to another time. But with the open air around them, he could see the flickering of day to night, the crowds blurring around them like foggy ghosts. Time seemed to move with them. Aurelia increased her speed back in time, and the buildings below them in the distance seemed to shrink and change as construction was unraveled, then new buildings appeared below them, some of them ostentatious and warped. The Eiffel Tower's metal turned a mustard, painted yellow. A huge globe and plaza appeared beneath them, obviously something temporary that was taken down after a while, but architecturally stunning.

"What are all of those for?" Aurelia asked, stopping them in time just before sunset, referring to the buildings that had popped up below them.

"I think it's a fair?"

Gasping, Aurelia realized what they had just stepped into, "It's not just that, I think it's the World's Fair! Isn't that why the Eiffel Tower was built to begin with?"

"Yeah, for one of the expositions, I think."

"Do you wanna go down?"

"Well, yeah, but we're dressed for the wrong decade," Will laughed, ever the practical thinker.

Looking down at the landscape, Aurelia could make out the figures below them, the women dressed extravagantly in layers of fabric draped to the floor, hardly a single one seen without a hat or parasol, the men with slightly longer curtails than the '20s. Fashion had changed remarkably quickly in the past few decades.

"Right..." Aurelia nodded, but luckily, it seemed that the Eiffel Tower was practically empty, perhaps due to the fact that it was nearing the days end. "Race you up!"

Aurelia ran up the stairs with a childlike fire in her eyes, staying stationary in time, as Will followed behind her.

The sun had just set beyond the horizon, the sky still streaked red with light, and by the time they reached the second floor of the tower, their legs shook like jello and their heart's pumped vigorously. But despite the inevitable exhaustion of running up stairs for almost twenty minutes, it felt like an immense accomplishment to have made it into the air so high above the city, almost like they were floating amongst the lowest clouds in the sky. They had hurtled past some conservative permanents walking on the stairs, who gasped in disdain at the reckless hooligans, but it made the prospect of racing up even more thrilling. But it didn't matter to them who had "won", just the rushing sound of blood pumping in their ears and the laughter that ensued, was what made the race worth it.

Aurelia enjoyed parts of this current youthful age of Will, although he had his immature tendencies, she felt free to be a kid again, to laugh and play without consequence or judgement. After such a heavy few years thrust into a life on the run, it felt nice to just let go. She wasn't sure just how many years she'd been stuck in that frozen moment in time in Italy, but before that, she guessed she was only 21, maybe 22 years old - it was hard to keep track of a linear count of age when moving back and forth in time. As an 18-year-old, Will was still learning and deciding who he would be in his life, and the weight of his reality hadn't quite set in yet. He seemed to smile more impetuously now, tossing around his emotions freely without protecting his soul. Aurelia equally felt happy to have the chance to be able to grow up with him, allowing herself to feel her own youthfulness, but she also felt slightly responsible to guide him, already aware of who he would one day become.

"God, I need to get in better shape if I'm gonna be hanging around with you!" Will chuckled, leaning onto the metal to rest from the journey up.

"Oh, you think *this* was tough? I once rode on horseback for over a month to get to Paris from the tip of Spain!"

"What? From Spain to get to Paris? That's insane. Why would you want to do that?"

"Well... it wasn't really a planned trip, my friend was here."

"So you came all that way to visit a friend?"

"It's a long story..."

Instantly, Aurelia regretted bringing up the aside. Conversation was so hard when you were trying to avoid specific details of your life to someone that you would one day trust explicitly.

"I actually lived here for a while. In Paris - and Toulouse, with my friend. And she... accidentally, got stuck here for a bit, without an Okliot. And at the time, I didn't know how to open a portal so easily to get right back to her. So hence, the journey across Christendom to get back to her."

"How... how did she get stuck here? Alone? For how long?"

"...A few years. But what matters is that she's safe now," Will's twisting stomach was apparent on his face. "Don't worry," Aurelia laughed, "I'm not gonna leave you somewhere in time. You saw how easily I can open portals now."

"You still haven't explained how that works," Will pointed to her watch, which she had pretended was the reason they were able to travel in time.

"Do you wanna... see it?" Aurelia played along, holding out her wrist, begging for an excuse to let Will touch her skin.

Taking the hint, his hand supported her wrist as he moved closer to look at the gold-rimmed watch. Studying it with slanted eyes, he watched as the clock hands moved steadily, hoping for some irregularity that could denote what technology was being used.

"I don't get it. It just looks like a watch," he said, still searching.

"Hmm... well it *is* a watch," Aurelia said, truthfully.

"Obviously. But how does it work?"

"Magic."

"Ha. Ha," Will rolled his eyes playfully. Aurelia smiled, keeping her lips sealed. "...Wait - Really? Is it?"

Laughing, Aurelia pulled her wrist away, "No. This is just a hunk of metal and cogs. But, sometimes it seems that way, huh? The whole prospect of traveling in time? It's a bit like magic."

"Yeah. I've begged my dad to tell me how it all works too, but he's just as secretive as you about it. He won't even tell his boss. Like it *is* some form of magic that only he knows how to cast. Well, him and you, I guess."

Aurelia wondered how Aleksander was able to create portals. Was it the same as her - some innate ability within herself that she was only just discovering? Or was there another way with science and technology?

"Here, gimme your wrist," Aurelia said, taking off her watch.

"What?"

"I want you to have this."

"But I just said I don't know how to use it!"

"Maybe one day I'll tell you all about how I open portals. We won't have to have any secrets. But until then, you can keep this safe for me."

Aurelia gently pulled his hand closer to her, placing the shiny leather band on his wrist, a symbol of trust and hope for their future.

"...You love me... don't you...?" Will said, his eyes shifting between her eyes, unsteady, yet wanting.

"Always," there was no hesitation for her.

Will grew uncomfortable from the intimate honesty. Turning away, retracting his hand from hers, he leaned against the railing to daze at the Parisian cityscape glowing a subtle orange from the sunset.

"I can't love you, Aurelia."

"Why?"

"Everything is so complicated. You're on the run... and who my dad is..." Will avoided saying more. "If I get caught, he could lose his job - we could lose our place in B-udo."

Aurelia knew he was right. He had everything to lose by choosing her. Tess had chosen her and in doing so, it meant that she couldn't go home. As much as she loved her friend - she hated that she had been forced to give up so much for her. It weighed heavy on her subconscious.

"Then don't love me. I don't want you to."

Will sighed with a smile, rolling his eyes, "Come on."

"No, I'm serious! If loving me is going to jeopardize your life... I don't want your love. We have to keep our feelings out of the equation."

"And what, just be friends?"

Sharply inhaling no in a light response, Aurelia continued, "We can be more than that, and not have... feelings, can't we?"

"I dunno, can we?"

"...Yes. Definitely. We have to," she smiled. "Besides - you only wanted to go on *one* trip with me - so how hard can that be?"

"Right. I did say that, didn't I?"

"You did."

Will scrunched his eyebrows together, "Fine, so one trip, no feelings, right?"

"Right. No feelings."

Stepping over to her, Will's hand slipped behind Aurelia's waist, pulling her body towards his unexpectedly. Almost as if he needed to unveil the mystery hidden between them, his lips found hers, searching and unsure. But she knew him; the exact spots where his lips fit with hers, his taste, his cadence. It wasn't a mystery for her - it was a long awaited memory.

Pulling away, Will took a sharp inhale, afraid to relish in the moment a second longer than he should.

"That was..."

"I think-"

"No, you go first," Aurelia blushed.

"You're gonna be hard to forget about after this 'one trip'."

"You too."

Trying to contain herself, Aurelia realized the significance of what had just happened. Their first kiss. They were in Paris, on the Eiffel Tower, above the World's Fair.

She knew where to one day meet Will.

She had to make plans that would stick in his mind for the future.

"One day - maybe we should come back here - actually go to this Exhibition. Opening day. Dressed appropriately of course. I mean technically, it's the same time and place - it could be counted as the same 'one' trip, couldn't it?"

"So just an extended trip..."

"Right... with multiple stops and locations. I mean, briefly going home could just be counted as a stop in the trip too, huh?"

"You need to pack appropriately and travel light for a trip, so that makes sense to just stop off for supplies," Will rationalized, going along with her.

"Sure - I mean some people go traveling the world for months-"

"-Years even," Will jumped in.

"And we have the world at our fingertips. Why should we waste such a great opportunity for an epic trip?"

"It makes no sense why we would. If we can time it out properly, no one even has to know that I'm gone."

"Sure. You can continue to live your life by day, and travel with me at night - or even once a week. No one will be the wiser," Aurelia gleamed, for the first time in years seeing a glimpse of the Will that she fell in love with.

"So it's settled... one trip."

CHAPTER 42

PERMANENT

After enjoying their time in 1900 atop the Eiffel Tower, the two walked back down through the portal she had created, coming back to the '20s. Will and Aurelia walked a few kilometers along the Seine, their minds spinning giddily from their day so far, still without a cent to their names, and not a clue as to where they were going. But luckily, conversation flowed, and Aurelia told Will of some of her travels up until now. How she had inadvertently become known as a deity in Ancient Mexico, and some stories of her life here in France in the 1400s, getting courted by the Dauphin Louis XI. How, like a fish out of water, she had embraced the culture and languages around her out of necessity. It felt liberating to tell him part of her story.

As the morning sun rose, filling the landscape with golden hues, the city slowly came alive. New cars filled the streets, scattered with only the occasional horse-drawn carriage, symbolizing the end of an era as modernization took hold. Peddlers and young boys selling newspapers and other trinkets occupied the street corners, which sparked in Will the idea to ask one of them the date.

"'*La Croix' ! Dix centimes !*" a young boy repeated loudly.

"Hey kid, what's the date on that paper you're selling?" Will asked in English, to which the boy blinked in confusion to. "What... day is it?"

Aurelia smiled, unsure why Will hadn't asked him in French.

"*Mon ami se demande si tu connais la date du journal que tu vends ?*" Aurelia asked, translating for him.

"*C'est le journal d'aujourd'hui. Mardi,*" the boy responded, telling her he was selling today's Tuesday newspaper.

But what day was today?

"*Et quel serait la date d'aujourd'hui ?*"

"*Le huit août,*" August 8th, the boy answered.

"*Et cette année ?*" and the year, she asked?

"*T'es stupide ?*" was she being silly, the boy laughed? "*On est en mille-neuf vingt-trois !*" it was 1923.

"*Merci,*" Aurelia began walking away, the boy following after them.

"*Hé ! Tu ne vas pas en acheter un ?*" weren't they going to buy a newspaper?

"*Non. Nous n'avons pas d'argent,*" they didn't have any money, Aurelia replied, the kid scoffing with a curse word under his breath and moving on to try and find someone else who wanted a paper.

"So, what year is it?" Will asked Aurelia.

"You don't speak French?" Aurelia was almost certain he had told her he did - but that was in his future.

"No... I didn't know I'd be coming with you to France. Normally I just download languages as I need 'em."

"Hmm," Aurelia nodded, realizing how young this Will was. He hadn't even discovered his insatiable love for languages yet.

"What?"

"No, nothing."

"Oh come on, there's obviously something," pried Will.

"No, it's just, I didn't know you only downloaded things out of necessity."

"I don't! It's just, well... most of my friends hate their downloads, like they're being forced to learn new things. So it's... hard to be inspired on your own when you don't have anyone to talk to about stuff."

"*Tu peux me parler. Toujours.*"

"What does that mean?"

Aurelia smiled, set on keeping him guessing on what she had said.

"I just think that you shouldn't let other people dictate what you love. If you enjoy something - learn it, or do it, even if just for yourself. And when you find *what* you love, *who* you love will come with it."

Aurelia's feet hurt from walking so much, and her body was heavy with exhaustion, but she was finally with Will. Trivial weaknesses didn't seem important. As the pair continued to walk along the Seine, they soon came to the Musée du Louvre, a stunning former royal residence that had now been transformed into a museum. Aurelia had visited the actual site a few times before, centuries ago, but the building itself had changed remarkably and was unrecognizable to her. They still didn't have any money for admission, and quite frankly, were unsure if they even needed it, but the security in the 1920s wasn't as well equipped as they would one day come to be, and it only took about ten minutes to slip past the policemen and into one of the buildings of the colossal museum.

Inside, grand ornamental rooms housed countless pieces of art, some of which were still hung frame to frame, paintings crammed along the walls as if in competition with themselves. The architecture almost as impressive as the actual art, with carved columns and gilded ceilings, skylights and windows flooding the space with light. Each room was unique unto itself, filled with the angst of creative minds. As they were moving through the rooms, one piece in particular seemed to catch Aurelia's eye, the statue *La Victoire de Samothrace*, a carved marble Goddess, draped in flowing fabrics with wings like an angel. Missing her head and arms, yet somehow still complete.

"I wonder what she was like when she was first carved. Look what time's done to her," Aurelia said, the broken statue symbolizing the fragility of life.

"Only time knows. That's what's so special about it all. It's ever changing."

"Like me," Aurelia laughed, remembering how different her life had been before Will.

"Have you changed a lot?"

"You could say that. Or maybe I've just realized who I was all along."

"And who might that be?"

Aurelia hadn't thought about that. Who was she, now, after surviving and thriving in so many scenarios? She had even seen into the space between time, giving her a mind numbing perspective on it all.

"I'm... confident, content. With myself, with what may happen. I've seen... life, from so many different viewpoints, and now I'm open to the future. When I was younger, I used to get so hung up with stupid little things in my life that would just stress me out, but something's changed since then. I've relinquished control. Growing up, I remember constantly worrying about what grades I would get in school, or what my friends would think about my latest post on social media - and now that seems so trivial."

"Wait... what? Social media...?" Will grew momentarily silent and pale as a ghost. "...Aurelia, is that why we hadn't met...? Are you a permanent?"

A flood of anxiety washed over Aurelia. She had slipped. Years of carefully avoiding revealing conversation with Tess, Natalia, Johanna, and everyone else she had met along the journey, and in one sentence she had blurted it out to Will. In Will's future, he would know everything, so it was hard to separate and filter out what he did or didn't know yet - constantly watching her words and actions so as not to give away their future. It was exhausting. She hated it. But it was necessary, wasn't it?

Aurelia hesitated for a moment, debating whether or not she should lie yet again, entangling herself even deeper. But Will would know eventually. She wanted him to know.

"...Yes. I guess I was."

CHAPTER 43

THE WATCH

Will raced out of the Louvre, onto the street along the Seine, retracing his steps towards the portal that had brought him to Paris. He knew it was a mistake coming. Aurelia walked just behind him, shell-shocked from his reaction about her being a permanent.

"Will, stop. Please. Let me explain!" Aurelia pleaded, grabbing for his hand, which he swatted away.

"I can't believe you lied to me about something so monumental!"

"I'm sorry. It wasn't my intention. Just stop and let's talk about this," Aurelia once again reached for him, but he avoided her touch.

"I have to go home," Will said, shortly.

"OK. I'll take you."

"No! I don't need your help. Just leave me alone."

"...What's wrong with you? All this because I was a permanent?"

Will turned around to face her, "*Was?* You ARE a permanent."

Aurelia could feel her face flush, "So what if I am? What makes you so special? You're from a specific time too. You're a permanent."

"It's different! You know it is."

"What makes you holier than thou? Huh? Explain it to me."

"Everyone here," Will motioned to the city around them, "is insignificant. We - *I* can't associate with that. Their viewpoints cause wars. We have perspective from all of this shit. We've evolved." It sounded like the same speech Tess had once given her, almost programmed.

"But, you're so wrong! Maybe you don't see it, but there's so much corruption in the future. You're basically in a prison in B-udo. You can't think for yourself, be who you want, or go where you want. You can't even stay for more than a few days in a portal without someone coming to escort you home. Everything is monitored. That's why you think there's no violence - there is - you just aren't allowed to see it, because they keep the levels and sectors so segregated!"

"You need to go back to where and *when* you came from. You're trying to take down my society by spreading these insane theories," Will exclaimed.

"No, I'm not. I'm just talking to *you*. But you can't get out of your own way and see past your viewpoints."

Aurelia could feel her heart rate elevating.

"Oh, so this is my fault? Everyone has to see things the way you see them, is that it? And what's funny about that is you're a liar! And here you are talking about *my* viewpoints when everything you've told me has been a lie since the minute we met. Like you're trying to manipulate me."

It was worse than a dagger in the heart. Was this what Will really thought of her?

Tears streamed down Aurelia's face, her vision blurry and mind foggy. All the time she had spent with Will in Amsterdam, and not once had they had a legitimate argument. He had loved her. She had loved him.

"It hasn't all been a lie. I mean - yes, I lied about when I'm from. I *had* to. But I was honest about everything else. I mean, I even told you that I knew you, future you!" but she *had* lied about how she was able to travel in time.

"Why did you have to? Huh? What aren't you telling me? Why do the Guardians really want you?"

It was hard to talk through the uncontrollable sobs, "I told you. I have a way to travel without the company. That's the *truth*."

Will scoffed, "Right. So what did you do, steal it?"

Will abrasively took off the watch she had given him, slapping it into her hand.

"No, I didn't steal it."

She attempted to hand it back to him, but he jerked away. Instead, she put it back on her own wrist.

"...Is that why you're trying to get close to me? Because you know who my dad is?"

"NO! Will, why are you doing this?"

"Because you're still lying! If I knew you were a permanent in the future - why would we still even be friends?"

He really didn't see it. His hate was too blinding.

"You really care that much about when I'm from? Can't you just see who I am? You're really letting society dictate who you can and can't be with? What's the difference with you coming back in time and meeting the permanents here?"

Will rolled his eyes, annoyed by the conversation, "There are boundaries we just don't cross. I probably don't even know you, do I? I'll bet you're lying about that too."

"I'm not. Why would I lie about that?"

"To get me to trust you."

"I know you, Will. I do. You love to draw, and paint, and learn. You hate strawberries - you won't even eat anything that touched them - why? I have no idea. Your favorite artist is Van Gogh-"

"Just stop! This isn't worth it."

"What isn't worth it? ...*Me?*"

"...All of it! I have a life in B-udo. A really good one. I don't need to jeopardize it by cavorting with you. You said it yourself - me loving you is a mistake."

"I didn't say it was a mistake. You know that's not what I meant."

"I just need to go home, Aurelia. I can't do this. We went on our 'one trip'."

At this point, even Will had begun tearing up. Even though she *was* a permanent, empathetically, he could feel the pain he had caused her.

"OK. You're right," he wasn't right. Her circumstance shouldn't dictate their relationship. "Just let me make sure you get home safely. Let me take you. Please."

Without saying more, Will motioned for her to walk first to guide him home.

The silence was unbearable. The full ten minutes that it took to find a staircase and make a portal back to B-udo was worse than the years of silence stuck in a broken moment of time. Every thought that popped into their minds was held back, creating an air of unspoken regret. But there was nothing more to say. Aurelia couldn't change who she was, and it seemed she couldn't change Will's mind.

Reaching the door to Will's home, Aurelia broke the silence, "I'm sorry, Will."

She wanted to hug him, cry onto his shoulder and have him ease her mind. She wasn't a bad person, as he had made her feel, was she?

But instead of a hug, he turned away to open his front door, and Will stepped inside.

"...Goodbye Aurelia. You should go home."

It was a sharper pain than he had meant to inflict. That dreaded thought - she couldn't go home and risk her family. Will closed the door. Her thoughts deafening, Aurelia realized her hypocrisy. She herself wouldn't risk her own family and friend's lives, yet she was asking everyone else around her to do so.

The regret made her stomach turn. She felt she had done so many things wrong, and Will was right - their relationship was too complicated. She wanted to forget about him. Forget that she had ever loved him. That would at least mean that he could be safe. Thinking about Tess and Natalia still in Italy, she came back to the thought that they too would be safer, and happier, without her. Maybe if she could find her way into the space between time again she could just float away into the abyss, and take the easy way out instead of drowning in all of her emotions. The life she led was too difficult.

Finally letting herself sob as she reached the stairwell, the toxic thoughts seemed to dissipate as each tear fell. She didn't want to forget Will, her friends, or herself. She wanted love, and happiness, and life. But life is not always governed by peace. Life is a constant battle between happiness and sorrow, great moments and painful ones, the balance always tipped to one end of the scale. As much as she hated the bad, dark moments, in order to also appreciate the light, you cannot have one without the other.

'And today is just a bad moment,' she thought.

She was finally about to go back to Italy, after waiting about an hour for the flood of emotions to pass, but looking at the watch on her wrist, Aurelia's mind drifted back to Will - why did her mind always do that, she wondered? All the time spent together in Amsterdam couldn't be erased by one fight. But it would be better to just leave. To let his goodbye be final.

Stepping out of the stairwell, Aurelia crept down the blue lit hallway once more, back to Will's house one last time, holding the watch in her hand. Instead of walking in, as she had done before, she decided to knock first. But despite trying twice, no one came to the door. She couldn't leave the watch on the ground to be stepped on, so she quietly opened the door and set the watch on a small table just inside the foyer. He would know what it meant.

Feeling some level of closure, she walked back towards the stairwell. A door clicked open behind her, and she looked back to see a brunette girl stepping out of Will's house, Will just behind her in the doorframe, both of them dressed in their metal, second skin suits. Jumping into one of the concave door frames to remain hidden from view, Aurelia waited for the girl to leave and Will to close the door. Unfortunately, their voices carried in the metal hallway, so as much as she honestly didn't want to know what was said, it was easy to tell.

"Thanks for coming over, B," Will whispered.

Wasn't "B" what he had nicknamed his ex-girlfriend, Bianca?

Aurelia peeked around the corner to look, but couldn't quite see her face from the angle, although she wore a hot pink suit just like she remembered Bianca had.

"It was nice," the girl smiled, running her hand down his chest.

It sounded like her too. It had to be her. He had called Bianca over just moments after Aurelia had left.

"It was."

Bianca leaned into the doorframe, kissing him, before she perkily walked away, and Will retreated inside. So that was the other "complication" Will had in his life. He still loved Bianca. He hadn't even waited a day to hook up with her after his time with Aurelia.

One tiny part of her felt happy for him - at least Will would be OK without her. But the overwhelming emotion was betrayal. Aurelia had told him that they were more than friends in the future. He knew she loved him. Even though he didn't feel the same way about her yet, wouldn't a small part of him have a conscience enough to think about all of that first, before calling his ex over for a late night booty call?

Aurelia walked to the stairwell, her body weak. How could she move past all of this? She didn't want to like him anymore, she wanted to hate him. She *did* hate him. She hated who he was today. But she loved who he would become, and that's what clouded her vision. The conflicting emotions were all she could focus on, her heart drumming in her ears - so much so, that she didn't even notice that she accidentally left the portal open behind her as she walked back in time to Italy.

CHAPTER 44

HEARTBREAK

Food genuinely didn't taste as good as it usually did. Aurelia was going on multiple days of horrible sleep, and a rollercoaster of emotions from meeting Will again. Somehow, she wound up coming back to Italy a few weeks later than she had attempted to travel to, perhaps because her mind and body was so off balance that it was hard to focus. At least the location had been right - she had aimed for the church just before sunrise, so as not to run into anyone. But Tess, Natalia, and the kind family they were with, the Tacciones, were just happy to see that she was alright. They didn't care that it had been a few weeks.

She almost didn't want to talk about what had transpired with Will. She was already over him, she told herself, lying even in her own thoughts. But he was right. She was a liar. She lied to the family they stayed with about every part of herself, even her name. She had lied to Johanna and everyone in Amsterdam about who she and Will were. She continued to lie to Tess about when she was from. The only one that knew the entire truth about her was Natalia.

So instead of talking about herself, Aurelia pivoted the conversations back to the family. They would be a bit confused as to how Aurelia, or as they knew her, Valentina, had become fluent in Italian since the last time they had seen her a few weeks ago, so Aurelia continued speaking to Giovanna in French, still pretending to be oblivious to most sentences in Italian, rather than try to explain her experience in the paused moment of time where she had actually learned. But once again, Aurelia realized she was lying. It was like a curse. Every conversation somehow led to a lie, and Aurelia had become such a good actress, that lying came effortlessly and thoughtlessly. Whenever there was something she shouldn't explain, it was as if a switch would go off, and her brain could automatically create an elaborate fabricated story to fill in the gaps of what shouldn't be known yet. What kind of person had she become, she wondered?

To her, it was obvious why Will didn't trust her. But even though he didn't trust her, why did he hate her so much for being a permanent? Looking around the breakfast table at the sweet-natured family they stayed with, she couldn't imagine hating them because of what year they were born in. Sure, they were ignorant about the future's technology and knowledge, but they were intelligent in their own right. What made Will, and everyone else in the future, believe that their lives were insignificant and dispensable? What if that mindset meant you inadvertently killed your own ancestor? Would you cease to exist? Didn't changing events in the past have some effect on the future? If so, why were the permanents regarded so lowly, when they in fact were the foundation upon which the future would be built? Aurelia's mind couldn't help but spin and twist into a headache.

All along, Will had been the person that she knew she could always rely on amidst an unsure life. Her mind had convinced itself that he would never hurt her, never throw daggers, never hate her. But he had done just that, and suddenly it felt like the beams holding up her fragile soul had crumbled, and she was left to fend for herself. She hadn't let Tess in completely yet, and Natalia would always be like a little sister that she was responsible for. Will was the only one that had been *her* support, and now she had to let him go.

"Come 'ere," Tess pulled Aurelia aside after breakfast, "so what happened?" her tone was calming - genuine.

"I..." Aurelia wanted to say something. She wanted to tell her every detail.

"It's OK," Tess pulled her into a hug. Somehow she already knew everything without knowing anything.

"It was different. Before, he was... familiar. Surefooted. And now, he's a stranger. He says things without thinking of the consequences... I don't understand how we fell in love in the first place."

"What did he say?"

"He said... I..." once again, she was guarding herself. She couldn't tell Tess what their fight was about - the fact that Aurelia was a permanent, at least not yet. "It's too hard to explain... right now. Can we just talk about something else? How are you?"

Tess nodded, trying to understand the hidden complexities, "...I think *I* might like someone."

"What? Who?"

"Dani."

"Daniella? But she's a permanent."

Aurelia felt the fresh wounds Will had torn in her chest about the stigma of being a permanent.

"I know, I know," Tess sighed, her eyebrows raised, creasing her flawless chocolate skin. "Is that bad?"

"What, liking her?" Tess nodded. "...No... I mean you liked Daví... and Chi, and they were both permanents, right?"

"But I *like* like Dani. I'm not supposed to feel so attached."

"Listen. I know it's totally different, because we're just friends, but I love Nat. I would do anything for her. And she's a permanent. So no. I don't think it's bad. If you love someone - or *like* someone, it shouldn't matter *when* they were born."

It was almost as if she was giving the advice to herself. Somehow she knew exactly how Tess felt and the inner dilemma she was going through. It was the exact thing she had just tried to convince Will of. Maybe she could tell Tess when she was from, maybe she'd understand.

Tess once again swung her arms around Aurelia, enveloping her in a hug.

"You're the best, I love you, Ari. That 'Will' is a fucking fool for hurting you."

"Thanks... I love you too," Aurelia couldn't help herself from crying.

The final resolution of how she felt hadn't settled in yet, everything was too fresh. But Tess's simple words had weight, and Aurelia felt comforted knowing she had a friend to count on.

The girls expected June in Italy to be sticky and hot, gearing up for an intolerable summer heat, but the weather was almost perfect - nearly eighty degrees during the day and dropping to a cool breeze at night. Daniella and Tess spent most of their days together, hiding from the family's prying eyes as they explored what "liking" each other could be like. Ricco and Natalia were also inseparable, almost like they were glued together. They were constantly finding things to do together, their young love evident, even if they didn't recognize it themselves yet. Whereas Aurelia found pleasure in solace, mainly sitting by the running stream nearby that she had wandered upon in the paused moment of time she was in, with her horse, Knight, grazing freely in her company.

Walking back from her favorite spot, with Knight following behind her, Aurelia came upon a solicitor at the family's door and smiled as he let her pass inside as he spoke to Giovanna. Who was he, and why was he here? Did unannounced guests often show up like this in such a small town?

"*Scusi*-" the man said in Italian, glaring intently at Aurelia.

Giovanna stopped him, telling him she would not understand what he was about to ask, even though she would, "*Parla Inglese o Francese.*"

"That's fine," the man continued, switching to English, "forgive me, you look very familiar. Have we met?"

Was it meant to be a pickup line, Aurelia wondered? She studied his face, darkened and wrinkled from the sun, and long, black hair curled like noodles, but he didn't seem to be someone she knew. It was odd though. Why would he know her?

"Umm... no, sorry, I don't think so."

"What's your name?"

"Valentina."

"Hmm," the man held out his hand. "Nice to meet you. I'm Raf." His hand was cold and slimy, like his personality.

"And you. You don't sound Italian, where're you from?"

"Oh, a little place in the Caribbean. You wouldn't know it."

The Caribbean. That was where ZhēnZhū would be in the future.

Aurelia faked a smile, her face twitching. What if he was from there? He said he knew her.

"Oh? I've been before. Maybe I know it," he was testing her, she was sure of it.

"You have? Hmm. It's a nice spot, huh? I'm from a lesser known area there that they call 'The Pearl'."

The Pearl. That was what ZhēnZhū meant in English. He was from the future. They had found her. He must be one of the Guardians.

"Hmm," Aurelia shook her head with pursed lips, hoping he hadn't realized who she was. "No. Don't think I've heard of that island... Anyway, sorry, I better go, hope you have a good day, Raf. Giovanna, *T'as faim ? Est-ce que tu veux prennent le dîner maintenant ?*" Aurelia hoped to get her to end her conversation early with a question of food.

"What's your rush, Val?" the man smiled eerily. He was onto her.

"It's Valentina. And no rush. Just hungry," she laughed.

Could he tell her stress from the slight waver in her laugh?

Maybe she wasn't as good of a liar as she had given herself credit for.

“You can stay for dinner if you'd like, I'm sure it would be alright,” Aurelia offered in the hopes he would decline and realize she wasn't who he thought she was - because who in their right mind would offer food to someone they were on the run from?

“...No, no. Thank you. I should be going. *Grazie* Giovanna,” he took the bait. He was leaving.

Aurelia watched with a fake smile as the man walked back down the dirt road into town, continually praying that he was indeed leaving. Who was he - really, Aurelia wondered, and how did he get there? But one thing had become clear - they were no longer safe there.

CHAPTER 45

DANIELLA

Running upstairs, Aurelia searched for Tess and Natalia, to no avail. Where had they gone? She combed the house, the garden, until she finally came across Natalia, Celia and Ricco in the barn.

"We have to leave. Now," Aurelia exclaimed breathlessly.

"*Ah bon ? Pourquoi ?*" Natalia jumped down from the wooden stall fence she had been sitting on.

"Someone found us - someone found me. I don't understand how, but we need to leave, it's not safe. Come on. Pack your things," Aurelia began walking back to the house, Natalia, Celia and Ricco following behind. "Celia, *adesso devi andare a casa - trova i tuoi genitori, e vai a casa del tuo amico nella città accanto. E dì a mamma e papà di restare dentro, qualunque cosa accada,*" Aurelia told young Celia to get her parents and go to their friend's house in the next town over - and not to leave.

"*Pensavo non parlassi Italiano?*" Celia thought Aurelia couldn't speak Italian, when had she gotten so good?

"*Imparo in fretta,*" she was a fast learner, Aurelia smiled, "*allora, puoi farlo per me? Non te lo chiederei se non fosse importante,*" would she listen?

"*Sì... lo farò,*" she would do as Aurelia asked.

"*OK. Puoi andare. Più velocemente possibile.*"

Celia took off in a run towards her house, unsure why Aurelia had been so adamant.

Natalia looked as if her world was crumbling before her eyes, "We can't just *leave*! What about our friends here?"

"They'll be fine here after we're gone. This is their home. We can't involve them anymore than this," Aurelia said sharply, "but, I need you to tell Giovanna and Marco to take everyone in the house away from here - temporarily. They've seen me with them, which means they're going to think they're harboring us - that they're our friends. That doesn't bode well for them."

Aurelia shivered at the thought before continuing with her plan, the image of Johanna's blood on the street flashing before her eyes, "If they're not here today, if they can't find them, I think they'll be safe."

Ricco grabbed Natalia's hand as they walked, speaking up, "I don't want you to leave," he mumbled to Natalia.

"I don't want to go either," Natalia whispered back, squeezing his hand tightly.

"Nat, where's Tess?" Aurelia interrupted.

"In town."

"In town? That's where that man went! What if he recognizes her?"

"Why would he?"

Aurelia stopped in her haste to look her in the eyes, "Natalia - he was from ZhēnZhū."

Natalia realized the severity of the situation, her eyes widening, "Oh. What do we do?"

"...OK. I'm going to go find her. You need to go gather anything you want to take with you and be ready to leave when we get back. Grab my bag and Tess's too, and anything from the future - and *make sure* you get the Okliots. OK? Understand?" Natalia nodded confidently. "OK. I love you."

Aurelia kissed Natalia's forehead, before whistling for Knight, who came cantering to her obediently from the nearby field. Jumping on bareback, Aurelia held onto his mane and broke into a full gallop towards town.

Screams rung in the air as the flames began to overwhelm the town. It was unnecessarily barbaric, but the Guardians had been instructed to destroy everything human-made in town near the unregistered portal. If someone from ZhēnZhū had been there, they may have been trying to change history by influencing the townsfolk. So everything, and everyone, nearby had to go. The traitors from the future would be found eventually and punished accordingly for their attempted treason, but until then, they had to leave no stone unturned.

A fire demolishing the town and townspeople would be easily explainable, especially in the 1800s, without cameras or local daily press. All it took was a little planning; they added in some extra obstacles at each door's exit, and made sure to set each building ablaze at the same time, so as not to cause premature panic, and then would step back and watch as the fire did the dirty work. Most people would die quickly of asphyxiation from smoke inhalation, and others who thought they could outsmart the fire would be gravely disappointed to find each exit sealed. Anyone able nearby would certainly run into town to help, like a moth to a flame, saving them the effort of finding them. Those too young, old or sick to help would stay in the safety of their home, the easiest prey to catch. It was only a matter of time until the screams in town would cease, and they could move on to the surrounding homes nearby.

"I think I found one," Raf said, walking up to his boss, Helios.

"How can you be sure?"

"They looked familiar... I could've sworn I've seen them before."

"And?"

"And they knew the name ZhēnZhū. I could see it in their eyes."

Helios sighed. He shouldn't waste resources investigating a hunch. They should just follow instructions and finish what needed to be done. But if he ignored it, the backlash could be worse.

"Take a team to detain them, as soon as we're done here."

"Yes, Sir."

Aurelia could see the black smoke billowing up from the town as she approached. The picturesque little town she adored was on fire. So many voices could be heard crying out, even from a mile away. Why was no one helping them? Her stomach dropped, what if Tess and Daniella were some of those screaming?

As soon as the burning town came into view, Knight slowed his pace, stomping and rearing slightly to indicate he didn't want to go further. Hopping off, Aurelia continued on foot, until she came close enough to the town that she could see what was happening, dropping to her stomach to hopefully not be seen. The town was swarming with unrecognizable people, all much too calm to be locals watching their lives and homes burn down. Stone buildings don't just randomly catch on fire. It was obvious, the fire was caused by the Guardians, and each of them had an exit blocked for each building. They wanted to kill everyone.

Heat seemed to fill Aurelia's head from her blood pressure

spiking. How many people were inside? How many people had already died? How could she save them? Where was Tess?

There were seven buildings - the doctor's house, woodworker, a small shop filled with food and books, two houses, a tavern and the church, the only building not on fire. It made sense that Tess and Daniella would've been in the shop to get or trade supplies. They were nowhere to be seen outside, or on the path home - what if they were still inside?

She counted at least twenty Guardians in town, all dressed in costumes of the times. There was no way she could get inside to rescue them without being seen. She needed to pause time.

She imagined everything around her stopping, the sound of the fire raging disappearing. The air freezing in place. But nothing happened. The fire kept burning.

'No. NO! Now I need you to listen! Stop!' she shouted in her mind.

Every second she waited could be the moment Tess or Daniella was overwhelmed with fire. She couldn't learn how to stop time now. She needed to be calm - in her meditative state, for it to work, she was sure of it. Her heart was beating too fast, her hands shaking. She needed to solve it another way.

Aurelia snuck up behind the burning shop, looking for any other way in. It seemed like the Guardians had begun to disperse from the town in teams, leaving only a few stationed at each building. There were small air vents along the sides of the stone building, which she looked in, calling out Tess's name, with no answer. The fire was too loud. The sound of the screams had stopped. After realizing there was only one door, she knew what had to be done.

Taking a rock from the ground, she snuck up behind the Guardian blocking the entrance and flung it at his head, knocking him to the ground. Pulling him aside with immense effort, so no one could see his unconscious body, she replaced his spot by the door. Not only was the entrance blocked with what looked like an extremely heavy beam, the wooden door itself was smoldering. They had used some type of violent accelerant. All hope seemed to be gone. Aurelia looked around at the Guardians still in town, luckily they seemed distracted and too involved in their own conversations to notice she had replaced one of them.

She wrapped her hands around the beam, wincing in pain as she touched its burning hot surface. She would heal from the nanobots in her system. The pain was temporary. But despite the knowledge that she would be alright, the sizzling flesh on her hands and arms, that seemed to melt to the wood, made her sick with searing pain unlike anything she'd ever felt. Finally shifting the beam out of place, she kicked open the burning door, stepping inside as the flames ate the extra oxygen she had just fed it.

It was impossible to breath. The black smoke roared through her lungs, burning her throat. She couldn't help but cough incessantly.

"TESS?" she screamed out coarsely through the deafening sound of the fire.

Even though it was a small building, she couldn't see anything inside from the thick smoke clouding her vision. Her eyes burned and watered so vigorously that she could barely keep them open. As she stepped through blindly, she could feel broken glass crunching beneath her feet, stabbing her even through her boots.

"*Aiuto,*" a small voice cried out from somewhere.

It was so disorienting. Where did it come from?

Aurelia dropped to her knees to crawl through, hoping she could see more clearly beneath the density of the smoke above her. The glass cut her arms as she crawled, and the wooden floors held burning embers that slowly began to ignite the ground, but it didn't matter. She had to find Tess. Just to the left of her, she could see slight movement. She rushed to see what it was, whose voice had been calling out. It was Daniella. Her body was limp, barely able to move, but her eyes looked directly into Aurelia's, and her mouth repeated help. She was alive.

"*Dov'è* Tess?" Aurelia remembered her alias here, "Deja?"

Daniella weakly moved her arm to the right of her, which Aurelia crawled towards to look. Sure enough, Tess was there, unconscious. She had to save them. She could feel the dizziness overwhelming her, her own body weakening by the second. She grabbed Tess's limp body, dragging and hoisting her with every ounce of strength she had left. Above them, the building creaked from instability.

"*Seguimi*, Dani!" she yelled out to Daniella, instructing her to follow. She waited for her answer, but no response came. "DANIELLA?"

Crawling just a few feet to look at her, she realized she too was now unconscious. She couldn't carry both of them. Tess would tell Aurelia to take Daniella. She was sure of it. But she couldn't leave Tess;

her closest friend, her confidant. She would come back for Daniella. She had to get Tess out first.

She couldn't breathe. The air in the building was gone, eaten by the flames. As the lightheadedness set in, it was harder and harder to pull Tess's heavy body through the rubble. But finally, after what seemed like a few minutes of struggling through it, she got her just outside. Aurelia gasped for air, slapping Tess on the cheek to wake her. Laying down next to her, she tried to feel for a pulse through the seared flesh on her hands, Aurelia's nerve endings all severely damaged. She barely felt it - weakly. Tess was unconscious, but alive.

Aurelia rolled onto her back, hyperventilating from the sudden onslaught of breathable air around them.

Daniella. She had to go back in. She had to save her. Attempting to stand up, Aurelia collapsed back down to the ground, the surroundings spinning viciously around her. But she couldn't just leave her. Aurelia took a deep breath, then crawled back inside. Retracing her path, she felt around for Daniella. A crashing sound came from just in front of her, and she realized the building was crumbling, the roof falling in on itself. She had to find Daniella and get out. Finally coming upon her, she began dragging her to safety as quickly as she could. But above them, tiles crashed down, barely missing them. With dragging Daniella, Aurelia wouldn't make it to the door before the entire roof came down.

Pausing for one second, Aurelia felt for a pulse on Daniella, praying that she was still alive. But she couldn't feel one. Maybe it was from the burns on her hands, but she couldn't find Daniella's pulse. She put her ear to her mouth, hoping to at least hear her breath, but she couldn't hear even the faintest sound, her ears instead filled with the raging crackling of the fire around them.

She was already gone. Aurelia had let her die by saving Tess.

Tess would never forgive her. Aurelia wasn't even sure she could forgive herself.

Her face soaked with tears, Aurelia crawled out of the building. A mixture of sobs and coughs, she breathed in the air as she laid down on the dirt, watching as the building folded in on itself. Daniella was gone. Daniella was gone.

CHAPTER 46

SURVIVAL

"Aurelia! Wake up!" Tess whispered in Aurelia's face, shaking her body to wake up.

She had passed out, the excruciating burning on her arms overwhelming. But Tess was alive, and awake. Sitting up to hug her, Aurelia wrapped her arms around her friend.

"I couldn't save her. I couldn't save Dani. I tried to get her out, but the building..."

"What...? She's... dead?" Tess's voice was grainy and course from the smoke.

Aurelia nodded, the sobs returning, "I'm so sorry. I killed her. I couldn't get her out!" Tess was silent, her face frozen in shock. "I'm so sorry. I'm so sorry, Tess."

Aurelia's face was twisted from pain. Daniella was gone. It was her fault. She continued her mix of coughs and gasps amidst her sobbing.

"We have to leave. Can you stand?" Tess hadn't let the emotions in.

"I'm so sorry, Tess."

Tess shook her head, coughing from the smoke still in her lungs, "It's OK. It's fine. It's not your fault."

"But it is! I couldn't save her! You should hate me!"

"I don't. Stand up."

"TESS!"

"Shhh!" Tess motioned to the other buildings in town around the corner. "They'll hear you."

Tess had apparently dragged Aurelia out of sight.

"I don't... I can't..."

"Aurelia!" Tess grabbed her shoulders to steady her, looking her deeply in the eyes. "We have to leave, now."

"...OK. Yeah," Aurelia sniffled, "we have to get to Nat."

Tess had hurt her leg from a bookshelf falling on her amidst the fire, so the path back was more a hobble than a run. But luckily, besides a few cuts from being dragged through the broken glass, Tess hadn't suffered any other major injuries. Aurelia could feel the burning sensation on her arms and hands start to ease, ever so slightly, but each gust of wind perpetuated the pain. It didn't matter. They had to get back to Natalia.

They took a slightly roundabout way back to the house, avoiding any footpaths where they assumed the Guardians would be. Then, once they were far enough out of town, Aurelia whistled for Knight, hoping he would hear them and come to their aid, but he was nowhere to be seen. After walking a bit more, she saw him in a field in the distance, pacing as he watched the smoke billowing. Somehow he knew that the smoke meant danger. Whistling once again, he came trotting hesitantly towards them, which Aurelia praised him profusely for. She first helped Tess onto his back, before jumping on herself. He wasn't as surefooted as he normally was, spooked from the smells and sounds in the air, but he trusted Aurelia, and listened when she led him back towards the house.

Finally reaching the house, Tess realized the imminent threat. Just in the distance, on the foot path they had avoided, was a group of people headed their way.

"They're coming here. They burned the town, now they have to finish the job," Tess said, almost emotionlessly.

Hopping down from Knight, Aurelia looked at him one final time. Her companion that had made life tolerable in the broken moment of time. She knew she would never see him again, his glossy black coat and wise eyes.

"Thank you," she whispered to him, before pushing him to go. "Go, Knight! Go! Get!" she yelled, but he didn't budge. He needed to get away from here. She clapped her hands in the hopes to scare him away, but he only shifted in his stance. "Knight, GO! Leave!"

"Aurelia, we have to get inside."

"I can't let them hurt him," Aurelia had never laid a hand on him, and in other cases never would, he was such a good boy, so she knew what would get him to run. "GO!"

Swatting at his hind, he kicked out, running off, stunned and confused as to why she had hit him. But it did the trick, and Knight ran away from them.

Going inside hastily, Aurelia locked the door behind them.

"NAT?" Aurelia called out, the family's dog, Lupo, barking at the loud startling tone.

Natalia jumped down the stairs, carrying everything Aurelia had instructed her to gather, with one addition - Ricco had also packed.

"You found her!" Natalia exclaimed. "Where's Dani?"

Aurelia shook her head solemnly.

"You couldn't find her?"

Aurelia couldn't sidestep the question, "Nat... she's dead."

Natalia stepped back as if she'd just been impaled, "...How?"

"The Guardians," Tess said coldly. "They killed her."

Aurelia looked at the small boy trying to follow the conversation in English, "Ricco, *dove sono tutti gli altri?*" where was the rest of his family, she asked him in Italian.

"*Di sopra,*" upstairs.

He needed to go get them, "*Vai a prendere tutti quanti e digli che è un'emergenza.*"

Ricco ran upstairs, calling for his parents, who came downstairs quickly, Giovanna carrying her young daughter, Ilaria.

"*Qu'y a-t-il ?*" what was happening, Giovanna asked.

"*Dov'è* Teodoro? *E* Padre Lorenzo?" Aurelia avoided her question.

"TEO?" Giovanna called, to which the boy came downstairs to, standing next to them, yet confidently on his own.

"Padre?" Aurelia asked.

"*Chez* Roberto *avec sa mère,*" Father Lorenzo was at Roberto's house with his mother. If Celia had done as she had instructed - they would all be safe for now - in the next town over.

They all needed to run, "OK. *Dovete correre tutti.*"

"*Stai parlando Italiano?*" Giovanna wondered why Aurelia was suddenly speaking Italian.

"*Sì. Mi hai sentito?*" did she hear her?

"*Cosa è successo alle tue mani?*" Giovanna asked what had happened to Aurelia's hands, just noticing the extensive red, blistering burns.

She would be fine, "*Me la caverò, non preoccuparti.*"

"Aurelia," Tess said, looking out the window, "it's too late, they won't get out in time."

The Guardians were here.

"Shit."

"We have to leave now," Tess said, motioning to the stairs. "We can't take them all with us."

"No. If they can't get out, we can't leave them."

Aurelia shoved a chair underneath the front door handle to buy them a few extra moments, in case the Guardians attempted to come in. Around them, the torches had begun to set the house on fire, slowly, hoping to draw everyone out so the team could question the traitor from ZhēnZhū. Some sort of burning material was thrown inside the house's stone air vents, which instantly began to melt everything it touched. Lupo barked at the unknown sounds coming from around the house, staying glued to Marco's side. As soon as the smell of smoke began to waft into the house, Marco and Giovanna held their children close and attempted to get out, but Aurelia and Tess stood in front of them, blocking the exit.

"*Per favore - Devi fidarti di noi! Se te ne vai, ti uccideranno,*" Aurelia pleaded with them, hoping to convince them of an impossible choice - that staying inside a burning building was safer than getting out.

Her pronunciation and grammar wasn't perfect, only guessing how the language would sound just from reading it in books for so many years, but luckily, the family could understand what she said - if they tried to get out, they would be killed.

"*Chi lo farà?*" who would, Marco asked, finally able to converse directly with Aurelia.

"*Ascolta - noi non siamo quelle persone che diciamo di essere. C'è troppo da spiegare e troppo poco tempo,*" they weren't who they had claimed to be, Aurelia explained, and there was too much to explain in too little time. But most importantly, there were some extremely dangerous people after them, who were outside now, "*Ci sono alcune persone molto pericolose che ci perseguitano. Quelle persone sono fuori.*"

"Valentina - *dobbiamo uscire!*" they had to get out, Giovanna yelled. "*Parleremo con loro. Spiega che si tratta di un malinteso. Ma non possiamo restare qui!*" they could talk to whomever was after them, explain that it was a misunderstanding, but they had no choice, they couldn't stay in a burning building. "DANIELLA?" Lupo barked again as Giovanna yelled, as Marco shushed him. "*Dov'è* Daniella?" Giovanna realized her daughter was missing. Was she still inside?

"*Lei è in città,*" Marco eased Giovanna's mind, telling her she had gone to town. Aurelia couldn't tell them what had actually happened to their daughter yet.

"*Ho un'altra via d'uscita. Sembrerà impossibile,*" she had another way out, Aurelia explained, but to them it would seem impossible. "*Ho bisogno che vi aggrappate a me, e non lasciare andare, non importa cosa succede,*" they would need to hold onto her and not let go, no matter what happened. "Tess, Nat, you have your Okliots?"

"Ari - you're already injured. How are you gonna carry everyone through the portal at once?" Tess pleaded, holding Aurelia's shoulder in place to talk to her out of her optimism.

"We have three Okliots. That'll help. Nat, give one to Ricco."

"Don't be stupid. You're talking about taking four people yourself - the most you've done was three, and you said you could barely manage that!"

The fire popped from behind them, taking hold, which the family jumped at. Teodoro shivered, "*Mamma, ho paura,*" he was scared.

"*Dobbiamo partire, adesso!*" Giovanna insisted that they had to leave now.

"Tess - it's not a debate. This is what's happening," adamantly, Aurelia turned to look at the family. "*L'importante è che ti fidi di noi. Ti porteremo in un posto sicuro. Ma devi stare calmo. Bene?*"

Crying, Giovanna or Marco wasn't sure who to trust. There was no other way out of the house, and yet the strangers they had so graciously let into their lives were blocking the exit to them while their lives were in danger. But someone outside had lit the home on fire. Could the foreigners be right, that it was more dangerous to get out?

The wooden front door shook with sound, as whomever was outside attempted to get in, the chair wedged just under the handle barely holding it. Tess leapt to the door to help hold it shut as the Guardians shoved on the other side.

"We have to go - NOW!" Tess shouted as she strained at the door, Natalia and Ricco coming to her aid.

"*Puoi tirarci fuori?*" the girls could really get them out another way, Giovanna asked?

"*Sì. Lo prometto,*" yes, Aurelia promised.

Giovanna nodded apprehensively, and Aurelia jumped into action, despite the searing pain of her burned hands, grabbing Giovanna and Marco's hands to guide them to the staircase. Giovanna still held Ilaria tightly on her hip, their giant dog following the family to safety.

"NAT, TESS - make sure you hold on to someone!"

Natalia ran towards Aurelia, Ricco just behind her, tightly holding her hand and the small golden ball Natalia had given him in his other hand. Natalia linked arms with Teodoro, instructing him to hold onto his mother, which he did quickly.

Aurelia began her ascension up the smoke-filled stairwell, instantly feeling the weight of traveling with so many people, like trying to swim in a riptide. But she had to get them out. She could take two trips, at the risk of the people she left behind getting stranded, or worse, killed by the Guardians. It wasn't an option.

Tess finally jumped away from the cracking door, which exploded open as two men and a woman broke it down, rushing inside after her. Tess sprinted to the staircase, holding onto Teodoro just as they began to disappear from view. Behind her, a woman grabbed at her dress, pulling Tess onto her knees, away from the group. Turning around, she kicked at the woman's chest, sending her plummeting down a few steps. Bear climbing up towards the shadow of the group, Tess reached for Natalia's open hand as they ran, grabbing her and pulling her into the shifting portal.

CHAPTER 47

Welcome To The Future

It was too much. Aurelia had found her limit. Sitting as she gasped for breath on a random landing of the portal she had created, Aurelia felt as if she had just sprinted through a marathon. Her heart thudded in her ears, her skin sticky with sweat. Trying to get so many people through the portal at once was a mistake. But everyone was accounted for. She had saved everyone in the house, the entire family, even their dog, Lupo. Except Daniella.

The family was in absolute disbelief. How had they gotten here? Where were they? Were the girls that they had sheltered all those months really angels, demons - witches? It didn't make sense. One minute they were in their house as it went up in flames, the next, in a stairwell filled with unknown substances - peeling linoleum floor tiles that smelled of mildew, sleek black metal railings, and canned electric lights in a popcorn ceiling.

As Aurelia rested, she let the family grill them with questions, being as truthful as she could.

They were from the future. They had been on the run for years. Their names weren't Valentina, Deja and Natasha. Padre Lorenzo, Celia, her parents, and Marco's mother were all safe, as far as she knew. But there was nothing and no one else left to go back to. Their town was gone. The Guardians had burned it down, and everyone in it.

It took a moment for Giovanna to realize what it meant. Daniella was in town. Her daughter, her baby girl. As it hit her, she gasped for breath, grabbing onto her husband's arm for stability, before she melted to the ground. Marco didn't understand until Giovanna said the words aloud and Aurelia nodded, crying. Daniella was gone.

Marco fell to his knees, holding his shaking wife in his arms as he too sobbed. Lupo came to Giovanna's side, trying to lick her face of tears. Teodoro cried, sitting by himself on one of the stairs. Ricco attempted to stay strong as Natalia hugged him, herself sobbing over the loss. But Tess still hadn't cried. Stepping up the stairs past Aurelia, Tess paced across the steps, almost annoyed by the inconvenience.

Aurelia limped up towards her, Aurelia's energy depleted and face sallow from traveling with so many people.

"Are you OK?" Aurelia asked Tess.

"Huh? Yeah. I'm fine, why?"

"Are you sure?"

"We need a plan. We've just displaced five permanents from the 1800s. We've told them too much. We can't just bring them back."

"Tess, if you need to talk about Dani-"

"That's not important right now," Tess was blocking it out. "What is, is figuring out what to do next. How did the Guardians even find us? We weren't written about, we weren't photographed."

"Do you think they were after *us*? It didn't seem targeted like before."

The man Aurelia met certainly seemed to recognize her, but not in the sense that he was actively searching for her.

"They just casually destroy towns? No, they had to know something. What about the portal in the church - was there a way they could've hacked into it?"

Aurelia's stomach twisted. It was her fault - it had to be, "I... Tess, I was in B-udo. What if they followed me back? What if this is all my fault?"

"But you wouldn't have left the portal open. There's no way they could've guessed where or when you were going," Tess cast aside the assumption.

"I... I was upset. What if I did leave the portal open? It's not like it's a switch I can flip to turn off a portal. It's all a subtle feeling - sometimes it's more obvious than other times, but I don't know. I think I did. I should've. I must have closed it. Like coming here - it was obvious - all I could think about was getting away and stopping them from following."

"And coming back from B-udo, did you feel that way?"

"...Yeah. I wanted to distance myself from Will, after everything that happened."

"But did you wish he would follow you?"

"Of course. But why should he?"

"Because you still love him," Tess let it hang in the air for a moment. Could it be true that everyone in town - including Daniella

- had died because of Aurelia's reckless heart? "Look. We don't know that's what happened. Maybe they have a way to reopen portals that are closed. It's not your fault. What's important now is that we find somewhere safe for everyone."

"Why can't they go back to Italy?"

"Aurelia. They don't have a single possession to their names, their town and everyone they knew is gone - and they know that time travel exists. We can't just dump them off somewhere and hope for the best."

Aurelia nodded. Tess was right - of course she was.

"...What if we got them welcome packages? They could start a new life somewhere in time," Aurelia said.

"We can't bring them through B-udo to find a guide."

"No, of course not. But what about somewhere we've already been?"

"Tangier?"

"No. Not after the attention we drew in Paris with the King. What if rumors spread about us?" Aurelia had only been to three other official portals, New York 1977, London 1993, and Texas 1958, in all of which her identity had been compromised. However, if *she* wasn't staying, any of them could theoretically work. "...What about the '50s?"

"Where's the company portal there?" Tess asked.

"In Texas. We could get them some money, IDs, whatever they may need."

"And what, they just stay in Texas? They're gonna stick out like a sore thumb there."

She could bring them to the family she had met years ago in Texas, John and Louise, but it would be a temporary solution. There was one place she knew they'd be safe, but if she wasn't careful, it would reveal too much to Tess.

"I have some friends in New York that'll be there in the '50s. They even speak Italian. It's the perfect scenario."

The Tacciones could befriend Aurelia's grandfather's family, the Quinns. She was sure that they'd look out for them, a family with such similar circumstance to themselves, moving into a strange new place from their homeland. It would take some finagling, but sometimes just putting someone in the right place with the right introduction is all that it takes. In the early 1950s, they would have already immigrated from Italy and be settled into their house in Queens, New York.

"Friends? Who? Do I know them? You're sure they'll be there?"

"You wouldn't know them, they live there. They're... permanents," the phrase seemed to attach more and more negativity unto itself as time went on.

Tess nodded, and you could visually see her concentration as she worked out the details in her mind, "It wouldn't be smart for us to stay with them. Someone could recognize us, and we'd be in the same scenario as what just happened-"

"I know. That can't happen again. Ever," Aurelia wouldn't risk endangering her family by staying in New York - not after what happened to Daniella. Even still, just the memory of Johanna kept her from sleeping at night.

Tess smiled apprehensively, her eyes glassy and expression distorted. No one she knew had ever died before, until Daniella.

"OK. I'm with you. If you think it's a safe place for them, I trust you."

Aurelia had wanted to hear someone say that for ages. Tess trusted her. Wrapping her arms around Tess delicately, she held her in a much needed hug. It didn't ease their aching hearts of all the pain they'd been through, but it helped to affirm that they weren't alone.

The plan set, Aurelia opened a portal to the diner she had visited so many years ago in the '50s, hoping to get there a bit earlier than her last visit in 1958. Opening a portal to a specific time wasn't a perfect science, and extremely hard to navigate, but it helped to have a distinct memory to fixate to. The red leather booths, black and white checkerboard floors, the fresh, bubbly waitress. Opening a back door, so to speak, into the mainstream portal, Aurelia came upon the door with the clock nailed to it. On it, it read century 20, year 52, day 28, hour 8, minute 9 - January 28th, 1952 at about 8 a.m. - six years earlier than her last visit.

Peeking inside briefly before going back for everyone, Aurelia could see the diner she remembered so clearly. The smell of burgers grilling wafted into the portal, the sounds of dishes clanging rang in the air. Instead of an empty restaurant like she had seen before, the place was filled with locals - or perhaps tourists - it was hard to tell. But darting around the restaurant was a familiar face dressed in the same mint green uniform that she would wear for years to come, the waitress, Sue. She seemed even more smiley than Aurelia remembered, maybe because she was younger, or maybe because she was newer in her job. But besides that subtle change in Sue, it was as if she had entered a snapshot of the same day she was in six years later.

If indeed things were the same, Sue would be eager to help them. It would work. It had to. Closing the door behind her, Aurelia went back through her backdoor portal for her friends, who would soon be plunged into their new lives.

Aurelia figured it best for her to stay in the portal while the Tacciones went in to speak to Sue, so she wouldn't be recognized by anyone inside, and she could keep their dog, Lupo, with her. She explained that all they had to do was ask the waitress for a welcome package with their new documentation, and hold up the golden, copper balls that she had handed them. Unfortunately, there were five of them and only three Okliots, so they decided to take two trips inside. Luckily, the Okliots could be used back to back, since they didn't have any identifiable markings, besides the A to designate which membership level they were. As Tess explained, maintaining privacy and anonymity was critical when time traveling, so the Okliots had been designed as inconspicuously as possible.

They figured it was best to mention that part of their family would be by later, and to give them the same credentials and surname, for ease in their journey. Tess would accompany Giovanna, Teodoro and Ilaria, and Natalia would go with Ricco and Marco, to be sure they got everything they needed, and to act as liaisons, or rather translators, in case Sue only spoke English.

The first group finally going inside, they almost couldn't believe their eyes. Sure, they had been magically transported to a random stairwell hours earlier, but now the culture shock kicked in. They were really in the future. Everything was different - the smell, the people, the language, the glossy floors, the bright flickering artificial lights, the drawn plastic blinds that covered the windows and even the metal rimmed tables. Still in shock, Tess pointed out a table and Giovanna rushed to sit down. Foreign eyes seemed to dart at them, prying for answers as they picked apart their appearance, judging every detail. They certainly looked like a motley crew, Tess's outfit tattered and soot ridden from the fire, all of their faces sallow and puffy from crying. Giovanna with her long, dark curly hair and olive skin, her teenage boy Teodoro and young daughter Ilaria slightly lighter skinned than their mother, but still with glossy dark hair. Additionally, the locals around them whispered about the young black girl sitting at the same table as them, acting as if she was their equal, defiantly in a whites only diner. Why were any of them in the diner, the locals wondered? Three apparent immigrants and a black in the south, sitting in their diner.

Tess had of course experienced hatred and racism before in her travels with Aurelia, but somehow the glaring daggers thrown at her here were worse than ever. The waitress hurried over to them nervously with menus, seeing which door they had come out of.

"Sweet thing, you shouldn't be in 'ere. Y'all know it's not safe. I'm so sorry they didn't warn you about the stigmas o' the time. I'm sure they'd let you exchange your trip for another if y'all explained," Sue whispered, mainly directing her conversation at Tess, referring to her skin color.

"They just need welcome packages and we'll be on our way," Tess smiled sweetly, hiding her bubbling despise for the company. People like the waitress, who worked for the same company, had killed Daniella.

"*I* have no problem with you in here, but Hun, these people 'round these parts don't take kind to people of your color sitting with them. Why don't ya wait outside for your friends and I'll get that sorted out for y'all?"

It made her stomach turn. At least the waitress was honest about it, Tess thought, although it didn't make it right. Of course Tess had downloaded the history of the '50s, with the civil rights movement which was just beginning to stir change, and learned about how people of color were treated so poorly here, but being in it was a whole other story. Here, now, she was looked down on, judged before she even spoke a word. Even the Tacciones were being judged harshly, albeit not enough to ask them to leave the diner as the waitress had with Tess.

B-udo wasn't like that with race, although people were still definitely classist in the future, the levels of ZhēnZhū had their own form of segregation, each one almost completely blocked off from the other. The only thing that had somewhat opened up travel between the levels was the company, Adventures In Time, opening their Headquarters. Everyone, on every level, wanted the chance to experience traveling. Temporary visas between the levels had become common, although to get approved, you had to first complete the expensive, extensive decontamination process and radiation therapy. Slowly, more and more people saved their allotted money to go, literally skipping meals and spending their last credit just to buy a ticket.

But even though visitors were slowly allowed in B-udo, didn't mean that they were respected or wanted. Tess herself had experienced a bit of it when she first moved to B-udo from P-yex as a 13-year-old, but luckily she had the clout of her family to help offset the harshness of judgement.

Looking at the waitress, and around at the rest of the diner, she wanted so badly to stay seated. To break the boundaries set for women of color like her here. She wasn't a soft spoken person. But right now wasn't the time to start a revolution or speak up about her human rights. She needed to get the family their welcome packages. They needed to stay safe, and under the radar. Now was the time to nod sweetly, to say she of course understood, and leave politely, as much as she hated it. So, briefly explaining to Sue what all the family needed, and that their other relatives would be joining them shortly, Tess left, secretly seething, and joined Aurelia and the others in the portal.

It wasn't a quick endeavor, each group of them inside for over an hour, picking at their food with lifeless enthusiasm while the waitress slipped in their new IDs and money, hidden amongst the other plates of covered food she brought them. But after a bit of a wait, each of them had a fake passport, a large stack of bills, a pamphlet for the upcoming events to see in 1952, and a personalized paper to-go bag filled with clothes and accessories of the time.

Once the second group finally came out of the restaurant, the family changed into their new clothes. Aurelia changed into the borrowed light pink dress from Will that Natalia had thankfully remembered to pack in Aurelia's bag. Stealing the tie from Marco's new suit, she tied it around their dog Lupo's large neck for a makeshift leash to bring him, his wrinkled skin inhibiting the tie's potential length. Natalia was the only girl who had gotten pants to wear, which in regards to fashion, she enjoyed immensely, yet also despised from their constraining nature.

"*È troppo corto,*" the dress was too short for her, Giovanna exclaimed, realizing that her dress only came to her knees.

"*Benvenuti nel futuro!*" welcome to the future, Aurelia laughed, thinking about how the fashions would only get shorter as the years went by.

It was a far cry from a simple day. Aurelia's small crack at humor made the group smile for the first time in hours. It felt hopeless. As if there was always going to be pain, an empty hole that could never be filled for those they'd lost.

Once everyone was dressed, they counted the large stacks of money the waitress had given them, because of their A class Okliots each receiving $40,000, for a grand total of $240,000 amongst the five members of the family, plus Natalia. They were extremely rich. It would be easy to blend in with such flexible funds. Most men only made a few thousand dollars with a full year of work in the '50s. The Tacciones would be able to live off of their money for years, if not decades, to come. For safety, they stuffed the funds inside Ricco's cloth bag and Aurelia and Tess's bags from Tianjin, which held what little remaining possessions they all had left.

She wasn't sure where her grandmother, Dottie Smith, would be in 1952 - had she already moved to Queens where she would meet her husband Federico in high school? Or was she still living in the Midwest with her mom? It would be more of a sure bet to look for her grandfather's side of the family first. Although Aurelia had never been to her great-grandparents' house where her grandfather grew up, she knew that is was located in Woodside, a neighborhood in Queens. They had immigrated there in the late 1940s, and her grandfather had told her often of his adventures there; his family's dear friends at Donovan's Pub down the street from their house, the overhead train running constantly above them just blocks away. Their church, St Sebastian's, with its community unto itself. Aurelia was sure that with the right amount of asking around, she could find her family. It was thrilling to think that within the day, she could actually re-meet her grandfather, Federico Quinn, as a teenager, and her great-grandparents, Arnaldo and Lili, for the first time.

Would they recognize her in some way, feel some kind of affinity towards her, or would it be like meeting a stranger?

She honestly wasn't even sure where Woodside was in relation to New York City. Unfortunately, she hadn't bothered to ask her family growing up, so she decided to aim for somewhere easy to navigate, Grand Central Terminal, and go from there. Finally ready to help her friends take on their new lives, Aurelia opened a portal to New York City, making a concerted effort to stay on the same time zone as they were currently in, January of 1952. Her family would have lived in

New York for at least three or four years, which made it a great time to find them, after they'd already settled into life a bit.

She would split her friends into two groups with the three Okliots, to ease in their travel through the portal, and after which make sure that the portal had indeed closed behind them, so no one would follow.

Ever since the first day she had time traveled, she had dreamt of meeting her family again. Although the day was clouded with the painful events that had just occurred, she couldn't help but feel excited, her stomach twisting with butterflies to go to meet her family, the Quinns.

CHAPTER 48

WOODSIDE

Grand Central was flooded with people, and it would be easy to get lost in the shuffle, so Giovanna insisted that they should all hold hands to get through. Aurelia held Lupo as they walked, guiding them, even though she was just as lost as they were. It was dizzying, being in such a massive crowd of people, so many of whom hurried past, bumping into them without the tiniest apology. How could people live in such a crowded place, the Tacciones wondered? It wasn't as bad for Tess and Aurelia, both having been raised in cities with plenty of crowds, but Natalia was also a bit taken aback by the hurried nature of the place.

It wasn't long until Aurelia spotted a board filled with an interconnected map of the trains, and perked up when she found a station literally labeled "Woodside", not far from them, in Queens. It would be a great place to start. Woodside couldn't be *that* large of a neighborhood, could it?

The group found a ticket counter, paying for tickets with their newly acquired money, and then beelined to the tracks to board the corresponding train that would take them to Woodside.

The family had heard of trains, of course, but had never once seen one in action. So as the monstrous machine pulled up to the tracks, their reactions were mixed; Giovanna jumping into her husbands arms, grabbing young Ilaria to shield her eyes of the impending doom about to crash into them, Teodoro standing frozen in awe, and Ricco and Natalia squeezing each other's hands as if they were witnessing their final moments together. Natalia breathlessly whimpered, not even knowing that such a machine existed until this very minute, having been born in the 1700s, and raised in the 1400s. Aurelia felt horrible for not preparing the family more, assuming that they would know what to expect from a train, the technology ancient to her. Apologizing, Aurelia showed them how to step onto the train car, guiding them on as most of them shook from fear. Teodoro seemed to be the only one who was fearless, instead marveling at the metal dragon they stepped inside of.

Giovanna muttered a prayer as the doorman abrasively closed them inside like sardines, giving the all clear to the conductor. The train roared to life, and the family was off. As the train exited the building, rain fell on its roof, the sound on the metal piercing and harsh, adding to the terror.

Arriving at Woodside station not many stops away, Aurelia hurried the group out of the train, Giovanna finally taking a full breath as she stepped outside. The rain instantly soaked them, and they ran to the overhang for cover, hoping it wouldn't soil their paper to-go bags from the diner too much. Before making their way out of the station, Aurelia randomly stopped a few people to ask for directions to Donovan's Pub, where she hoped to come across someone who knew her family. Unfortunately, despite Aurelia remembering her grandfather telling her it was one of the neighborhood's favorite places, no one had heard of the spot. What they didn't know was that the pub wouldn't even open until the mid '60s, more than a decade later.

Striking out on the pub, the group instead asked where they could find the fish market, a place she recalled her cousins had told her about, which apparently had the best french fries in the city. Luckily, someone knew the place they meant, Joe's Seafood, which was literally only a block away, just following the overhead train tracks.

Taking their instructions, they exited the station, coming onto the street, where countless cars wizzed past them.

"*Cosa sono quelle?*" what were those, Giovanna exclaimed, jumping back from the traffic.

Aurelia explained, telling them that they were just like horse-drawn carriages, only mechanical, and much faster. Cars hadn't existed until the late 1800s, and weren't made popular until the early 1900s, so the Tacciones had no idea such an invention would exist. With Giovanna's question, Aurelia realized what a ginormous learning curve they would have with everything here - phones, radios, television, records - even everyday conveniences like blenders, electric heaters and air conditioning were all foreign concepts to the family.

Keeping her explanation short since the rain was pouring down on them, they all walked the short distance to the fish market, covering their bags with their arms to keep as much water away from them as possible. If only Aurelia had her cell phone and could just type in exactly where she needed to go for directions - or if she knew her family's phone number, or even house number, they could get there much easier. Things would become much more accessible in time. Thankfully, the shop was barely a minute away, and the family crammed inside, avoiding the rain. Lupo shook off, his short fur soaked like a wet rag.

Inside, it reeked of fish, the place which Aurelia had assumed was a restaurant, based on her cousins' descriptions of the fries here, was instead an actual fresh fish market. The man behind the counter finished up with another customer, kindly sending them off with their goodies, before turning to the strangers to help them.

"How can I help ya?"

Aurelia smiled, taking the lead, "Hi! I'm wondering if you know of a family, they come in here all the time. Arnaldo and Lili?" the man shook his head, no. He hadn't heard of them. "Or maybe you know their kids? Federico and Bobby? Or Gwen and Mia?" the man looked puzzled, racking his brain for their names. "They're Italian, moved here a few years back?"

"Sorry, don't know 'em. Ya sure they come to *this* shop?"

Maybe they hadn't become regulars and discovered it as one of their favorite places yet.

"...Sorry to bother you. Any idea where St. Sebastian's is?"

Only a few blocks away, they walked to St. Sebastian's Parish, passing the Loew's Woodside theater, which would ironically one day soon become the church's new site. Going inside, Aurelia was relieved to see that the Monday mass had started, with a few scattered parishioners in attendance. They would be able to ask around once the service was over - someone was bound to know her family. Dogs were probably not allowed, so sitting at the very back and telling Lupo to lay down between them, their clothes now fully soaked, they listened to the sermon.

Giovanna sat with her eyes closed, silently sobbing over the loss of her daughter as the service went on. Why had God taken her from them? Why were they being punished? How would she be able to go on carrying such a heavy loss with her? They hadn't even laid Daniella to rest, didn't have a tombstone to visit. It was as if she had just suddenly ceased to exist.

Truthfully, they had been putting on a brave face out of necessity, but they all felt the same - a new emotion that had been slammed onto them - grief.

For Aurelia, she felt overwhelmed by emotions, the guilt and sadness suffocating, yet somehow she was numb to it all. After dealing with her parents death at a young age, then her grandfather, Johanna, feeling the life and deaths of others in the space between time, now Daniella, all of the townspeople they knew, and even in a sense losing Will, it had become a regular occurrence to lose the people she loved. She even had to say goodbye to her grandmother and friends in 2019, knowing she would never see them again.

As much as she hated it, she wasn't a stranger to letting go. She knew what to expect from her stages of grief. Although you can never replace or fully heal from loss, new memories and relationships would eventually help to ease the pain. Instead of your mind being filled constantly with reminders of those you lost, slowly, they would become fleeting, until hours, then days, and even months could pass without thinking of them. It was no use trying to delay or suppress the onslaught of grief, and Aurelia knew that each of them would have to deal with their own emotional journey as the months would pass by. Some would ultimately be alright sooner than others. But for now, it was fresh. There wasn't much difference in the emotions they all felt today - sadness, pain, anger, confusion and disbelief. They were scared, unsure and weak.

However, it was comforting to be able to take a moment and pray for Daniella's soul in God's house.

Once the sermon was over, the family headed into the reception hall, where the parishioners and clergy gathered. Immediately, Tess, Natalia and Aurelia began asking around if anyone knew Arnaldo or Lili, with no luck. Not a single person, not even the priest, had heard of them. But this was their church. Aurelia knew for a fact that this was the church her grandfather and his siblings grew up in. He often told her stories of his Sunday school here, and how involved his parents had been with the community. Why had no one heard of them?

Defeated, the family sat inside in prayer while Aurelia, Tess and Natalia strategized outside under the awning as the rain continued to fall, now slightly lighter.

"They should be here. It doesn't make sense," Aurelia said, shakily. Her family was here somewhere - they had to be.

Tess scrunched her eyebrows together, "Maybe we're too early.

Maybe they haven't immigrated here yet."

"No. They moved here in the late '40s. I'm sure of it. They would've been here for at least a few years already. It's definitely 1952, right? Maybe I accidentally skipped back in time when we traveled here."

"Let me go ask someone inside to check," Natalia offered, running back inside the church.

"You don't think..." Aurelia didn't want to finish her sentence. She didn't want to even think about the ramifications if she was right. "What if the timeline got... altered, somehow?"

If that had happened, and her great-grandparents never immigrated to New York, would that mean that her grandfather wouldn't meet her grandmother? Would her father cease to exist? Would she?

She almost couldn't breathe from the thought. What if she was never born? Would she disappear into nothingness eventually?

"There's still no proof that the timeline can be altered."

"What do you mean?"

Tess looked around to try and give an example, "I mean, it's all a paradox. If I went back in time, to let's say, change the name of this church from, 'St. Sebastian's' to... 'The Church of St. Tess', would you remember that it was ever called 'St. Sebastian's'? Or was it always 'St. Tess's' to you? And how would I have remembered it was called 'St. Sebastian's' in order to actually go back and change it to 'St. Tess's' in the first place? Maybe I wouldn't even be able to change it. Therefore, how can we definitively prove that events in time can change? Do you just take someone's word for it?"

"You're warping my brain, Tess. So you're saying everything that we do back in time... has, in a sense, already happened?"

"Theoretically."

"What about free will? What if I deliberately wanted to stop something from happening that I knew happened? Could we stop a war? Could we save a life?"

"I don't know. In that case, how would you know who to save from death, or when it would happen, if they had already been spared? Would your entire future be altered because of one intentional choice?"

Aurelia had wondered about it for so long - saving those she had lost, "So you're saying, if I went back to save Daniella, then this version of myself might cease to exist, because I wouldn't have been led down the same path to get to where I am today?"

Tess nodded, her face falling solemnly, "We can't change our past. Maybe there are other realities that we would create by doing so - and we fracture the timeline or something. Maybe nothing happens at all. Or maybe we cease to exist," Natalia and Ricco ran back outside, with news, "either way - we can't chance it."

"So?" Aurelia asked Natalia.

"It's 1952. You're right," Natalia smiled, proudly.

Then where was her family? Maybe Tess was wrong. Maybe someone *had* changed the timeline. They weren't here. But if they weren't here - what did that mean for the future? Would Aurelia still be born?

Aurelia decided to go out in the rain herself, to canvas the neighborhood for anything familiar. She had once seen photos of her family's home years ago, but the memory wasn't fresh. All she could remember was the bland, white painted exterior and a window box of flowers. She hoped that if she spotted it - she would know. But nothing seemed to strike her. Everything looked the same in the gloomy January rain. There were dozens - if not hundreds of white houses. After a while, the rain shifted to a slushy snow, and the cold set into her bones, wind whipping her arm's bare skin. Her hands had completely healed from the burns she had gotten just earlier in the day to save Tess, but the cold, wetness of the snow still felt soothing on them as she walked.

The Quinns were supposed to be here. They were supposed to help Aurelia and her friends. But they weren't here, and nothing seemed recognizable in real life, trying to remember something from a black and white photo she had seen ages ago, now warped in her memories.

Maybe she should look for her nana instead. But she hadn't shared the details with Aurelia of where she lived in the '50s with her mom. All she had was her name, Dottie Smith, and the stories about her life growing up in a small town in the Midwest filled with farms and bugs - all of which she despised - until her single mother moved them to Queens, where she quickly met Federico and they instantly fell for each other. It was intangible - not specific enough to be able to find her. Perhaps if they went further forward in time, they would have more luck finding the Quinns. It was possible that they just simply hadn't ingrained themselves into the community yet. Even with the hopeful scenarios she dreamt up, Aurelia couldn't help but jump to negative conclusions. Her family wasn't here. What did that mean for her?

But here, now, the Tacciones had money of the time and new identities. They could still start over in Woodside, with or without the help of Aurelia's family. They could be safe here. One issue would have to be solved at a time - first, the outstanding one was making sure that the family had a place for the night. Aurelia walked back to the church to tell them of her failure, and to figure out the next steps to starting over in 1952.

CHAPTER 49

SNOWBALLS

"Ari, look at the snow, isn't it beautiful?" Natalia yelled to her from the ground where she and Ricco had started gathering up the light covering of snow, as Aurelia walked back to the church.

"Mmhmm!"

"When I was little in Russia, my friends and I would sneak outside at night after the guards had left us to have a snow battle. We called it a '*битва снежками*'. Do you have that tradition here?"

Aurelia smiled, knowing exactly what Natalia meant, "Hmm. How do you say it? *Bitva snezhkami?*" Natalia nodded. "So you would have a snow battle? Interesting," she leaned down and packed together a tight ball of fresh snow, judging her surroundings for a good place to hide from the imminent attack. "And so you, what, would battle for the most snow?" Natalia shook her head no, still clueless as to Aurelia's strategy. "You would use swords?" Natalia shook her head again, just realizing Aurelia's hands filled with the first weapon. "Well here in America, we throw snowballs."

Aurelia flung her first attack at Natalia, then ducked behind the tree nearest her to gather more snow.

Laughing, Natalia threw a snowball back, showing Ricco how so he could aid her. Hearing the commotion and fearing the worst, Giovanna rushed outside holding Ilaria, followed by Marco with Lupo, Teodoro and Tess.

"I need more on my team!" Aurelia laughed playfully, distracted from the stress for a moment.

Giovanna sighed in relief that no one else was hurt, severely on edge from the day, sitting on the church steps and sending little Ilaria to play. Marco handed Lupo's makeshift leash to Giovanna, plopping his belongings next to her so he could join Ilaria's new team, and Giovanna motioned for Teodoro to join Ilaria and her husband.

"Come on Tess, give me the advantage!" Aurelia smiled, hoping to entice her friend to be on her team.

"I'm OK, you guys have fun, I'll just watch," Tess smiled back, proceeding to lean against the church.

Aurelia, on her own one man team, shifted to join Natalia and Ricco, smashing snowballs into their rivals, the cold thrilling, yet numbing her already cold hands. Something about it felt so comforting - being shoulder to shoulder with her friends, forgetting about all of the troubles of the day for a brief moment. Exhausted, mentally and physically, however strangely adrenaline filled. The snow had barely covered the ground more than an inch, yet it was just enough to pack and send flying. The trio ducked behind a tree to avoid any incoming snowballs, squished together to strategize.

"OK, Nat, you go for Ilaria - gently. Ricco, *vai per tuo fratello,*" Ricco would go for his brother, Teo. "I'll get Marco," Natalia and Ricco nodded, excitedly. The three bent down to make their snowballs, while waiting for Aurelia to give their cue. "Three, two, one - GO!"

Lunging out from behind the tree, the three threw their snowballs at the unsuspecting team, expecting perfect hits. But instead, the flung snowballs hung suspended in the air, perfectly preserved in space from the second they had let go.

Natalia turned worriedly towards Aurelia, "What's happening?"

Their warm breaths still hung in the cold air. Ricco looked stunned, silently tapping the floating snowballs in wonder, causing them to fall down slightly. Time had stopped. Natalia put her hand to her chest, wondering why it had suddenly become so difficult to breathe.

"Oh my God," Aurelia knew what it meant.

If she didn't hurry, unlike her, Ricco and Natalia would suffocate here in this paused moment of time.

Closing her eyes, Aurelia placed her hands on her friend's shoulders, trying to remember the exact visualization she had used in Italy to somehow connect her life force to the animals. Sharing the golden, glowing string of light in the space between time, that she imagined was somehow connected to her, allowing Aurelia to survive in paused moments.

"Ari - I can't breathe!" Natalia gasped for air, noticing Ricco had also become uncomfortable, gulping and scrunching his forehead nervously.

It wasn't working. It had been a long time since she had done it, and only on a few occasions, one animal at a time - most impressively on her horse Knight, the family's dog Lupo, a tiny kitten, the deer and her first animal, a bird. Never had she done it with a human - let alone two lives at once. But she had to.

As Ricco and Natalia gasped, falling to their knees, Aurelia tried to stay focused, dropping to the ground with them to keep them close.

"Aiuto!" Ricco squeaked.

"What do we do, Ari?" Natalia whispered, her breath weak.

Keeping her eyes squeezed shut, Aurelia tried to go into a meditative state, despite her pulse pounding and mind firing on all cylinders. She could do it. She had done it before, although the stakes had never been so high.

Breaking the silence, Lupo barked at the three of them, he had broken free from Giovanna's grip, concerned why Ricco and Natalia were acting strangely. Lupo was awake. How? She hadn't been touching him. Aurelia had woken him once in Italy, had he retained whatever essence could sustain Aurelia here? Trying not to question it too much, and rather focus on helping her friends first, Aurelia strained for the right thought that would work. She thought of her soul, her aura, expanding like a golden glow, wrapping itself around her friends like a bubble, preserving them and their own auras here with her in time. Aurelia instantly felt depleted, which almost signaled that she had been successful.

Their breaths finally steadying, they gasped for the air that now was available to their lungs. It had worked. Aurelia had saved them.

"What just happened?" Natalia asked breathlessly.

"...Time has stopped."

CHAPTER 50

THE QUINNS

Snowflakes hung in the air, unique ice crystals glittering like tiny stars all around them. Slowly, the color seemed to drain from the sky and surroundings, leaving everything somewhat monotone and white-washed with snow. Although the weather was freezing just moments ago, the feeling of coldness seemed to vanish as time stopped, perhaps because although they were able to move, their body's atoms themselves were stopped in time, so relatively, the snow didn't feel cold to them anymore.

Ricco walked around their surroundings in complete bewilderment, whispering "*Dio mio*" and gasping as he tapped snowflakes suspended in the air. Was it an act of God he wondered? It seemed too surreal to even be possible. But his eyes weren't deceiving him. The world around them had stopped.

"Is Tess OK? Is everyone? What does this mean, Ari?" Natalia asked, flabbergasted at the surroundings. But Aurelia didn't answer.

Unsure how long it would last, Aurelia could feel the panic set in. She couldn't be stuck here again. How many years had it been last time? One year? Two? Ten? No. It couldn't be happening again. Hyperventilating, Aurelia sat down in the snow, her hands shaking from stress. Why had it happened this time? Here, now? What had she done? Was it somehow her fault?

"Ari. Ari!" Natalia sat down next to her, attempting to shake her from her trance. "Are you OK?"

But Aurelia almost couldn't comprehend the words coming out of her mouth. Everything was stopped again. She couldn't do it.

"I - I can't be alone again. It's... I can't..."

"You're not alone. Take a breath," Natalia demonstrated taking a deep breath. "Is this what happened before?"

Aurelia nodded, attempting to slow her breathing as tears steamed down her face thoughtlessly. Lupo laid down next to Aurelia, resting his large head comfortingly on her lap.

"I'm sorry. You shouldn't be here. I didn't know time was gonna stop again and I must have touched you by accident-"

"It's fine. We're fine," Natalia looked back to try and prove that Ricco was just as OK as her, but he was preoccupied by the splendor of their surroundings, his jaw dropped and eyes bulging as he continued to tap the floating snowflakes. Perhaps he wasn't as OK with it all as Natalia had assumed, she realized.

Aurelia shook her head no. It wasn't OK, "It's not fine! What if time doesn't start again? What if we're all stuck here?"

"We won't be. How did you get out last time?"

"I was meditating. But I don't know if it was even because of me."

"So just take your time to calm down and we'll try it. If it doesn't work - then we can worry about it."

Aurelia nodded, squeezing her hands together out of nervous habit. Now that Aurelia had brought the two of them into the paused moment in time, she could explain what had happened, as best as she understood it. Of course, she had told Natalia about her experiences stuck in frozen moments, but verbally describing it was unequal to actually living it.

"I'm sure it's not all bad... right? Why don't you tell me what the best part about time stopping is," Natalia prodded, hoping to help Aurelia get out of her own head.

"...The water. You can walk on it here. And the peace and silence - but that's also the worst part. It's so silent. Listen," around them, not a sound could be heard, even their voices seemed dulled, barely audible only a few feet away.

"*J'adore,*" Natalia whispered that she in fact loved it.

'Why?' Aurelia wondered, "*Pourquoi?*"

"*Parce que* - it's familiar, somehow. Maybe it's the snow that makes me think of when I was a kid..." Aurelia chuckled at Natalia's comment, since she was, in fact, still a kid. "But it feels like home," Aurelia scoffed, stopping herself from saying something. "What?"

"No, nothing."

"What were you going to say?"

"It's just, before all of this happened, I was gonna tell you that I failed - I couldn't find my friends here. But I was gonna suggest that since Ricco and his family have everything they need to start a life here, maybe this could be *their* home for a while."

"Just for them?"

"Yeah. It's not safe to stay with them. Someone from ZhēnZhū could recognize us at any point."

Natalia looked at Ricco, who was completely lost in the conversation at this point, still pacing back and forth off on his own, whispering in awe at the frozen world, "...They wouldn't know me."

"No. No - but wait, Nat - you don't wanna come with Tess and I? You wanna stay with them?"

"...I don't... I don't know," it was not a decision Natalia made lightly.

"...But, we can't just leave you! You're... you're my sister."

"And that won't change, but what's the plan after this, Ari? Do we just keep starting over in new places all over time? I want to make an impact in my life, get an education, maybe have a house - start a family. How can we do that as we are?"

It was everything Aurelia wanted for her. Shaking her head no, Aurelia knew that a life on the run with her couldn't sustain her dreams. Plus, every extra minute spent with the "terrorists" Aurelia or Tess meant that Natalia could be flagged, and then would never have a chance at a normal life. As of now, no one from the future knew who she was. Natalia was a ghost, transplanted in time.

"OK," Aurelia could feel the tears begin to fall again, just minutes after her panic attack had eased.

"OK?"

"When time starts again, we'll go back to the diner to get you some documents and you can stay with Giovanna and Marco, wherever we set them up."

"We don't need to go back."

"Huh?"

"I already got a passport."

"What? You did?"

"At the diner," Natalia pulled out the papers from her back pocket to read them to her. "Apparently I was born in 1939 in 'Little Rock, Our Kansas'."

"You mean Arkansas?"

Natalia nodded, continuing, "Brown hair, brown eyes. Name, Dolores - Hmm. That doesn't seem like me... Maybe I can use Dolly - no - Dottie, instead? Yes. Dottie Smith."

"...What did you just say?"

"Dottie Smith."

Chills seemed to rush down Aurelia's spine. Dottie Smith. It was Aurelia's grandmother's name.

"That's... that's impossible... can I see that?" Natalia handed the thin booklet to Aurelia. Sure enough, it read Dolores Smith. "It must be a coincidence... it can't be..."

"What's wrong?" Natalia asked, trying to read Aurelia's shocked expression.

"Ricco - *Dove sono i tuoi documenti?*" where were his documents, she asked him, waking him from his trance of amazement.

Without a word, Ricco ran towards Giovanna, who was paused in time, searching through the bags just next to her to find the bundle of passports, eerily staring at his mother's unmoving figure. Running back to Natalia and Aurelia, he opened them up to find his, reading it aloud.

"*Penso che questo sia mio... Nato, Toscana, Italia - il 3 di novembre, mille novecento trentotto,*" his new identity was born in Tuscany, Italy, November 3rd, 1938.

What was his name?

"*Come ti chiami?*"

"*Va bene! È simile al mio!*" Ricco was happy - the name was similar to his own.

"*Che cos'è?*" what was it, Aurelia asked impatiently?

"*Mi chiamo* Federico Quinn."

"Oh my God," the blood had drained from Aurelia's face.

It wasn't possible. Was it? All along, Natalia had been her grandmother? Ricco was her grandfather? No. It couldn't be true. The Quinns had immigrated in the forties. They had two younger daughters, not just one - and no one ever spoke about losing a sister. Her nana and papa had met in high school. Her nana didn't speak other languages.

Grabbing the other passports from Ricco, she had to check.

Giovanna's new name was Lili Quinn, her great-grandmother. Marco was Arnaldo Quinn, her great-grandfather. Teodoro was Uncle Bobby, tiny Ilaria her Aunt Mia. Her Aunt Gwen must not have been born yet.

The entire time, Aurelia had come full circle to practically raising her own grandmother unknowingly? That meant that back home in 2019, her nana knew everything. She knew that Aurelia had traveled in time that fateful day. She knew it would change her life. But it also meant that her nana had expected Aurelia to disappear. Her nana was alright in 2019, and she knew Aurelia was also alright.

What else did her grandparents know? Had they been protecting Aurelia her entire life? Was that why, even growing up as a teen amongst the most public era, with every tiny detail shared online, Aurelia had been able to grow up safely? Despite social media and a generational obsession of sharing every nuance of life online, the Guardians hadn't come for her. Did she owe it all to her grandparents? But Aurelia remembered something future Will had said to her, in the very beginning of their relationship - that together, they had blocked all of the portals in the early 2000s through 2019, so Aurelia could grow up. Had it been a group effort?

"Ari - what is it? Tell us!"

Her head was spinning. How had she not realized it sooner? She grew up with her nana and papa, living under their roof practically her entire childhood. She knew them, every detail - didn't she? No, it must be a monumental coincidence. Ricco and Natalia were really her grandparents?

It explained so much about herself, yet left her with so many more questions. Was she even related to them? Or had she been placed with them for safekeeping since they knew her?

If she told them who they were to her, would everything still happen the way it was supposed to? Like how Will had told Aurelia of their relationship's eventuality before it had happened - had it disrupted her future with him and that was why things had ended the way they did?

But keeping a secret like this from one of her best friends - or rather, her grandmother, would be impossible, and could potentially fracture their relationship if she kept it from her.

Everything seemed connected. She had literally unwittingly led them all up to this moment. Was there such a thing as destiny? And how had she even met Natalia or Ricco in the first place? Both occasions had been whilst traveling somewhere new in time - Natalia while escaping from ancient Mexico, one of her very first experiences as she learned how to travel in time. She ran into Natalia in her home in Russia, then accidentally toppled her back in time hundreds of years to France. What had she thought of at the time that caused her to connect with Natalia?

Meeting Ricco had been when she decisively wanted to go to Italy - imagining her own grandfather's stories of it - thinking of what his childhood must have been like. She had unknowingly calibrated herself to literally land in his childhood.

It had all happened so organically, yet almost seemed too flawlessly executed to be possible. But it was real. Unbelievable, mind boggling and spectacular.

"OK, what is going on Ari?"

Aurelia grabbed Natalia to speak privately from Ricco. He wouldn't understand anyway, and perhaps it was better not to tell him.

"What I'm about to tell you is gonna sound insane. You're not going to believe me."

"Of course I will. What is it?"

"I don't think we should tell anyone. Not even Ricco. I don't even know if I should tell you, but now that I know, you're gonna find out - I won't be able to keep it from you."

"OK..."

"You know how we've been looking for my 'friends' here?" Natalia nodded. "They're more than friends. They're my grandfather's family - my family."

"Oh. OK... so? You know I don't mind. You've told me when you're from."

"I know. You're one of the only people that *does* know. But we wouldn't have been able to find them here until today..."

"I don't understand."

"The Tacciones - Ricco, Giovanna, Marco, Teo, Ilaria - they're who we've been looking for. I didn't realize until now, but they *are* my family. You're all my family."

"What? How?" Natalia was taken aback. "Wait, you all? You mean me too?"

Aurelia nodded, looking at her young friend, who she had always looked at as her little sister, trying to imagine her sixty or seventy years in the future - her nana whom she adored so. Still gorgeous, yet aged with deeply engrained smile lines, her hands frail, her hair grey. It made her want to cry knowing that it was her.

"Nat...You're my grandmother."

CHAPTER 51

IN A FROZEN MOMENT

It was better not to tell Ricco or anyone else about who they actually were or their destiny. Reactions would be mixed, and it could be taken as if Aurelia had purposefully orchestrated it all. Plus, as religious as they were, especially Giovanna, they could either take it as a curse or a blessing - sent by an angel or a demon. It was too risky. Natalia was different - she understood things and had a varied viewpoint, her mind open ever since meeting Aurelia when she was six years old - for her, anything was possible, since the impossible had already happened. The thing that Natalia cringed at, was the newly found fact that she would marry young Ricco. Although she liked him, very much so, it felt strange to know that he was the one she was destined to fall in love with.

For now, the three of them, and Lupo, were safe in this frozen moment. Plus, they were unhindered by others around them, and would be able to move about freely in the busy city. Time had been stopped long enough that it wasn't just a momentary blip in the time stream, such as Aurelia's very first experience with time stopping at the castle in Toulouse, France. Or the next time in Spain when Tess had almost gotten trapped there with her - although in that case, Aurelia didn't know how to wake and sustain someone in a frozen moment, and Tess would've died if not for time starting again immediately. Aurelia had prayed with all her might, and somehow tapped into some sort of energy that listened - starting time again for her. The only other experience with time stopping had been her lonely, miserable years alone in Italy - and in that case, Aurelia was certain that time wouldn't have started again if not for her efforts. Time there was somehow fractured, disconnected from reality. But just like her power to travel through time, it was a learning experience to start time again.

Ironically, with time stopped, they had just that, time. So, instead of pushing the issue of getting time to start ticking again, the three of them took their time strategizing what they would do when it did start.

Firstly, they would need a place for everyone to stay for the night, so they decided to explore the streets in search of a hotel or something of the sort nearby. Then after that, they would attempt to find a real estate office, where they could view potential properties for the family to move into. After that, it would be down to the details - what schools the kids would attend, which hobbies or sports they could immerse in, what job Marco would get. Swiping a blank notebook from a nearby convenience store, Aurelia decided to make a list of potentials for her family, everything from what restaurants looked good, to where they could shop, adding in tidbits that she knew they'd like - based on what her grandparents had told her they enjoyed from their teens, like the french fries at Joe's Seafood, and their friend's at Donovan's Pub.

Time was extremely hard to judge in a paused moment, and distracted by the mission at hand, they almost didn't notice how long it actually took. Overall, they spent a few days walking around the city to make the initial list, although with the unique position they were in of not feeling impeded by anything - exhaustion, hunger, not even so much as a mild toothache, the days flew by.

Deciding not to rush attempting to start time again, they took a few days to sightsee - able to go places and see things that no one else could, such as sneaking into the fanciest apartments they could find, doing cartwheels across the stage at Radio City Music Hall, or going into the Central Park Zoo where Natalia and Ricco could pet the alligators, sea lions and other animals, and even Lupo enjoyed himself, sniffing at the plethora of animals around him. Somehow it seemed that living beings only sprung to life when Aurelia touched them, so Natalia and Ricco had an easier experience, not worried about the ramifications of what would happen if they accidentally touched someone. But the wildest thing they did, was testing out Aurelia's favorite part about time being stopped - walking across the ocean to get to the Statue of Liberty.

New York would change considerably over the next few decades, Aurelia remembering what it had been like in the '70s, but for the most part, the feeling around the city was the same. Electric, fluid, vibrant.

Ricco did have his moments of fun, but his soul was heavy from the loss of his sister. They attempted to have a sort of memorial for her in the still church, praying for her soul under the cross, but without his parents, or his uncle the priest to guide them, such as how he would've in Italy, they were shooting blind. They couldn't light a candle or bury her body. Instead, their ceremony was filled with reading their favorite verses from the Bible, singing hymns and telling stories about Daniella.

Each day that passed seemed to help ease Ricco's emotions, slightly, but being OK after such an event was an impossible task. A piece of him would always be broken and carry the pain. The soul was much like a vase - once broken, it would never be the same. Although it could be repaired, it would still be visibly cracked and glued back together, piece by piece.

Aurelia felt the weight of his grief. Daniella dying was her fault. Once again, Aurelia's life being lived had taken someone else's. She should've saved her. She should've saved everyone in town. How many people had died because of her? Five? Ten? Twenty? More? It was impossible to know how many people had been in town, and who. Every time the thought crossed her mind, the panic rushed in, her hands shaking and her speech impeded. Even without thinking about it all, Aurelia didn't want to enjoy anything around her. It seemed like she was just going through the motions, like she wasn't emotionally invested in anything, though everything they did together should've been incredible.

A small part of Aurelia wanted to stay in their paused moment of time, here, nothing bad could happen. She also loved getting to know every bit about who her grandparents were as of today, but it was an inevitably that they would have to get back to the real world, where the water flowed and the snow was cold.

Aurelia needed to learn how to control it. She needed to be able to easily get herself out of this situation again. So after a few weeks of exploring the city, once everyone felt ready with lists in hand of what to do when time started, the trio headed back to the church in Woodside where the family was gathered, mid-snowball fight, so Aurelia could attempt to kickstart time back into motion.

Aurelia stood up, grunting and shaking out her arms in frustration. What had she done before? What was the key? Why wasn't meditating working like last time? Aurelia kicked at the curb as hard as she could, wanting to feel some sort of pain, which would mean she had done it.

"Go again," Ricco called out, his English slowly improving, him and Natalia sitting under the tree outside of St. Sebastian's.

"I CAN'T! IT WON'T WORK!" Aurelia snapped. She had been trying for weeks, to no avail. Time wasn't listening. She couldn't get it to cooperate. A fire seemed to burn in her chest.

"Good. Be angry. *Forse questo aiuterà,*" maybe it would help, Ricco sighed.

Kicking at the curb again, Aurelia shouted, "I am! I am ANGRY! WHY. THE FUCK. ISN'T IT. WORKING - OWWW!"

Pain seared in her foot from kicking the concrete.

Around her, time had skipped forward by barely a few milliseconds. It had almost worked. Natalia and Ricco jumped up, startled by the brief sudden onslaught of sound and minuscule movement of the snowflakes in the air.

"Do that again!" Natalia gasped at the first success.

Aurelia kicked at the concrete again, although she didn't feel any pain, there was hope. She had almost done it. She could get them out.

It took about a week, but finally, as suddenly as it had stopped, time officially started again. The idle sound around them filling their ears loudly and the cold air whipping their skin. Aurelia was exhausted - and somehow even though she knew she herself had done it, she still wasn't sure how. It was like trying to pinpoint the exact thought and feeling you had before smiling. Intangible, yet substantial. Time had jumped forward a few times the past week before she finally got it to stick, each time coming a little closer and the act becoming slightly easier to access.

Now, the snowballs that hung in the air flung forwards towards Ilaria, Marco and Teodoro, one of them hitting Marco, while the other two's trajectory had been changed during the paused moment and plummeted towards their feet.

Shouting in victory from Aurelia's success of starting time again, Natalia and Ricco jumped up and down, running over to hug Aurelia, then Tess, and Ricco's family. Even Lupo seemed ecstatic, barking along with them, his tail wagging as he greeted Giovanna and Marco again.

"*Cosa sta succedendo?*" Giovanna asked Ricco what was going on as he hugged her tightly.

Ricco held his tongue, remembering that Aurelia and Natalia had decided not to share what had happened, "*Niente Mamma! Tutto bene!*" nothing, everything was fine, he lied.

Tess could see through the illusion. Walking straight up to Aurelia, with a crinkled forehead, Tess didn't have to say a word before

Aurelia answered with a nod.

"How long?" Tess asked.

"Only a few weeks, give or take."

"With Ricco?"

"And Nat - and Lupo too."

A slight pang of jealousy hit Tess's stomach, why hadn't she woken her up too?

"Are you OK?"

Aurelia nodded. She was OK. It hadn't been as horrible of an experience, since she had her friends - or more accurately, her family, to share it with. In addition, it gave them time to work out a definitive plan of how the Tacciones would start their new lives in the '50s, as the Quinns. They had scoured the town to make their comprehensive list of every place they deemed important for the family. The next few nights, they would stay at the Plaza Hotel, while they made an offer on one of the many houses for sale that the three of them had toured while stuck in time.

Natalia and Ricco knew the plan and what to do, and Aurelia and Tess would only help them get on their feet for a few days before they would need to leave. Every minute spent with the family in public put them at risk. The last thing Aurelia wanted was to accidentally lead the future back to the family yet again. The consequences could be catastrophic. She had already lost Daniella because of her carelessness, she couldn't lose anyone else.

Although Aurelia felt it wasn't a good idea, Natalia made her promise that she and Tess would visit her at least once a year to check in on them, since the family wouldn't be able to follow the girls wherever they were going. But Aurelia knew that Natalia would be safe, and most importantly, happy, here with the family. In fact, she would get everything she had once dreamed of - an education, her own house, stability. She would find love with Ricco, have a healthy baby boy, and eventually, even a granddaughter.

Saying goodbye was never easy - but knowing that you would see someone again made it tolerable. Aurelia couldn't help but cry as she hugged Natalia once more, after all that they'd been through together, their lives so intertwined. From first meeting Natalia at age six, the entitled royal brat she was initially, to practically raising her for a year in France, and then accidentally stranding her there for years alone. Finally coming back to her just before she would've been married off at only 14 years old, and taking her to the future where she nearly died of the Nantong virus, saving her by bringing her to Eloise for treatment in B-udo, then their time in Italy together, up until this moment here in New York.

Somehow Aurelia knew that their journey wouldn't end here. Besides Natalia raising Aurelia as her granddaughter in the 21st century, she was certain there was more to come between them. But for now, the two would part ways.

Aurelia held Natalia's shoulders as she gave her some advice before she and Tess left, "Listen, you have to be smart. Smarter than everyone here in this time. Don't spend too much of that money - keep it in the bank and don't tell anyone how much you all have. And when you're at the bank, you should put your tiara and all of our Okliots in what they call a 'safety deposit box', so no one steals it - crime is big here - and maybe put my necklace and things in there too, since they're from so many different times.

"Photographs and cameras are your worst enemy, so don't let anyone keep photographs of you-" Aurelia stopped herself, realizing that her grandparents had been repeating her own advice to her. Every time she had posted on social media, they had a conniption. It also explained why there had barely been any photos of themselves, her parents, or her family, besides one or two photo books that her grandmother kept locked in her closet. None of her extended family was even on social media. All along, they had been protecting her and themselves from the future.

"Don't slip by *ever* saying your real name. You're not the Grand Duchess Natalia Petrovna of the House Romanov anymore. You're not Russian - or French - you're American. You're Dottie Smith from Arkansas."

"*D'accord.*"

"No, you can't speak French anymore. You shouldn't speak anything other than English. In fact, you're gonna need to change your accent, fast, Nat. You should also go to that language coach we wrote down for the Tacciones. And remember - whatever you do, don't let on where or when you're from."

"OK."

"It's better to make everyone think you know less than you actually do, so they underestimate you. *You* know who you are. But the less attention you can draw to yourself, the better." Natalia nodded.

"We don't know who, or how many, people could be from the future. Be suspicious of people. Trust no one. If you get too comfortable with someone, you might slip up and say more than you should. Really, you shouldn't drink alcohol, at least not too much, because you need to stay in control and keep your eyes open, always-"

"I know, I know."

"I know you do. You did fine without me for almost seven years - but I would feel remiss if I *didn't* say it. I love you, OK?"

"I love you too, Ari."

"Are you *sure* you want to stay?"

Natalia nodded with a bittersweet smile, looking around at the new three story house the family had purchased only a few days ago, excited for her new life here, yet terribly sad that Aurelia and Tess couldn't stay with them.

"I want this. I'm sure."

"OK... OK. We should go. Tess?" Aurelia wiped the moisture from her eyes as Tess nodded.

Tess held her hand out to Natalia to fist bump her, which Natalia looked at suspiciously.

"It's called a fist bump. You punch it. It'll be a thing soon," Natalia punched at Tess's hand harder than expected, but Tess just laughed. "Maybe you should try boxing here! See ya later, Nat. Be good."

"Bye Tess... bye Ari."

Turning to Giovanna and Marco, and their three kids next to them, Aurelia and Tess said goodbye.

"*Grazie*, Aurelia, Tess," Giovanna said, kissing them on each cheek.

"*Mi dispiace così tanto per tutto quello che è successo,*" Aurelia expressed how sorry she was for everything that had happened. If she could go back and change what happened, she would, "*Se potessi tornare indietro e cambiare tutto, lo farei.*"

Giovanna's voice cracked as she told her she appreciated the sentiment, "*Grazie, lo apprezzo.*"

The girls hugged Teodoro and Ilaria, before Aurelia turned to Ricco, spending a bit longer with him than his siblings, for obvious reasons only known to her and Natalia.

"*Ciao* Ricco."

Aurelia hugged him, knowing full well who he would one day become. Her beloved grandfather. It was funny to think about. How much he would grow, how different he would be. Now, he was a quiet, mild-mannered, introverted kid, but in time he would become an author whose goal in life was to express himself - mainly through his writing and cooking. Although shy upon first impressions, he would turn out to be quite the jokester, intent on making others happy, someone who Aurelia was able to trust explicitly during her childhood. Now that she could see his childhood essence, most of his future personality actually made sense.

When Aurelia was growing up, she was tighter with him than her nana, but as of today, she was closest to Natalia - Aurelia had barely been able to bond with Ricco here. She wondered if Natalia would feel saddened by the fact that the two of them weren't as close when Aurelia was little. So many tiny dynamics were in play, shaping their lives around them.

Their goodbyes said, Aurelia and Tess looked around the unfurnished room at the family and sweet Natalia. Was it right to leave them, Aurelia wondered? Before she could give it too much more thought, Tess hopped onto the stairs next to them, motioning for Aurelia's hand. It was time. They had to go. They had pushed it, staying so many days as it was. But thankfully, no one had recognized them. They had managed to stay under the radar the past week, barely leaving the hotel room, until the family closed the sale on their new house. Luckily, during that time, because they stayed behind as the family had purchased the house and set up other details, Tess hadn't found out about the family's new identities, which saved the awkward lie or explanation from Aurelia.

Staying any longer would be pushing their luck. They had to keep the family safe from further harm.

Fitted in their dresses from the 1800s once again, their personal belongings safely stored with Natalia, they themselves were only stocked up with some waters, sandwiches and some of the family's money from Italy that Ricco had managed to bring, all shoved inside of Tess's bag she'd held onto since Tianjin. Unsure about their decision to split up, Aurelia hesitantly grabbed Tess's open hand and began walking up the stairs. Before the surroundings shifted, Aurelia turned to take one final look back at the family - her family, the Quinns. Waving warmly, the family smiled goodbye. Natalia reached for Ricco's hand, which he took willingly, blushing. It felt like a relief, like a weight had been lifted on Aurelia's shoulders, because in that moment, she knew they would be alright. Aurelia had brought them home.

CHAPTER 52

THE PUB

The stench of sewage and horse manure was overwhelming, flooding their senses. Horse-drawn carriages rumbled along, amidst a steady menagerie of pedestrians that ranged from the poor, beggars, vendors and animal herders, yet also a mix of rich socialites and businessmen. Every square inch of the street seemed to be covered in some sort of filth that clung to the soles of your shoes and was tracked into each building, spreading the smell.

In retrospect, London in the late 1800s hadn't been the greatest choice, but the girls decided to stay for a night or two, so they could get their bearings and decide where they would head next. Living a life on the run wasn't easy, and rarely was it planned.

After a few tries, Tess and Aurelia found lodging which would accept their Italian lira currency that the family had given them, and would accept two young, unmarried women, lying that Tess was Aurelia's lady's maid so they could avoid assumptions. They would have to stay in separate rooms, to help maintain the appearance, but at least they would be close together. With that part of the night worked out, and no other responsibilities, the girls found their way to the nearest pub that would have them. Bribing the bartender to serve them without a male escort, the barkeep finally gave in, and poured them cups of neat whiskeys, per their request. After only two small drinks, the bartender decided the girls had imbibed enough, and their feminine bodies couldn't bear much more, compared to their male customers, so the girls walked to another establishment, then eventually another, where they could continue drinking, convincing and bribing as they went.

Now finally, they had landed in one final pub for "one more drink" before the night was through. Only a handful of customers remained as the night drew on. The alcohol here was especially potent, and it wasn't long until Aurelia and Tess had consumed a bit too much to drink.

"No... no, I'm good..." Aurelia waved her away as Tess handed her another drink that she had somehow ordered, without her noticing.

"You *need* it. We both deserve this," Tess chuckled, tapping her glass to hers and downing it.

"I don't think I've ever even been drunk before," Aurelia laughed, gently taking another sip, secretly hoping to feel what it was like. Tipping Aurelia's cup upwards, Tess made her finish the liquid, motioning to the bartender for another refill.

"Let's change that. Today is a good day to drink," Tess slurred slightly, still only tipsy, yet considerably more affected than Aurelia.

Aurelia didn't realize that the nanobots in her system were working hard with her body to process the alcohol coming in, easing the effects, though not entirely, making her a bit more of a heavyweight than she should've been. As the bartender poured more into their cups, Aurelia's smile fell, the reality sinking in again.

"Tess, I don't think I can do this anymore."

"Drink?"

Aurelia shook her head, no, that wasn't what she was referring to, "Run from my future. Have people we love die because of it."

Aurelia held back tears, the pain of it all weighing her down.

"It's not *your* future. It's *our* future. I told you, I'm with you. Whatever we do, we do together," Tess was foggy from the whiskey, but truthful.

Aurelia managed a small smile, before it faded back into sadness.

"But that's my fault. You shouldn't even be living this life with me. I forced you to choose me over your home-" Tess laughed, unintentionally blatantly loud, the patrons around the girls turning to see what had happened, which caused Tess to laugh more, Aurelia joining in with a chuckle. "Why is that so funny?"

"That was my *choice*, Ari! I don't regret it."

"You don't?"

"No. You need to stop blaming yourself."

"I can't, not when it's my fault."

"What is?"

"Johanna dying. All of the townspeople. Dani."

"That's not your fault!" Bringing her voice to a whisper so no one would hear them, she continued, "You didn't pull the trigger to shoot Johanna, did you?" Aurelia whimpered in response, the vision ringing in her mind. "You didn't start those fires. You didn't lock people inside to die. You're the one that dragged me out and saved my life. You *didn't* kill Dani, they did. Stop blaming yourself. If you want someone to blame, it's the Guardians. They're the ones you should be angry with. They're the evil ones."

"What if they're just reacting to me?"

Tess sighed in exasperation, "Are you kidding me? You? Come on. Think about it. Peaceful leaders don't respond with violence. There's corruption at the top of ZhēnZhū."

"You think the Guardians are just following orders?"

"Of course they are. Who do you think has control of them? The top of the food chain. The Lapites. It's no wonder the heir won't come forward to the public. She's too ashamed of what goes on behind closed doors. She knows that they need to be stopped."

"She? How do you know the heir is a she?"

"Sorry 'PC police', but everyone knows that yellows mainly identify as 'feminine'. I guess it's just an assumption..."

"No, but how do you know what color she chose if she hasn't revealed herself?"

"Uh... the annual briefing? She's always in it, but she keeps her face covered with her second skin suit...? Where have you been the past decade?"

She had been in the 21st century. Tess felt the nagging feeling again that Aurelia was lying, or hiding something from her. Why did she always seem so confused when conversation about ZhēnZhū came up?

"Ari... I need you to be honest with me about something."

"Of course."

"Why don't you speak Mandarin?"

"We're back to that again?" Aurelia laughed, hoping to brush off the subject. "I didn't have the time."

"...Don't you trust me?"

"What? Of course I do, Tess!"

"Then why are you lying?"

A wash of anxiety overcame Aurelia. Tess was too smart. Plus, the addition of alcohol made her brutally honest and straight to the point.

Tess continued, "I need to trust you too, Ari, but I can't, when I know you're keeping things from me. It's too hard."

Should she reveal what she had been keeping from her for so long? What if it fractured the relationship of the only person who chose to stay by her side? Would she lose Tess's friendship?

"I - I'm not... I'm not lying."

"Bullshit!" Tess yelled, the few customers around them turning towards her in response. "Sorry. Sorry, my bad," she apologized in a horribly attempted British accent, before turning back to Aurelia with a whisper. "That's bullshit. You 'didn't have the time' to learn Mandarin? Ari - the primary language download starts when you're three years old. How the hell did you not have the time?"

"I... It's..." Aurelia was out of ammunition. She had entangled herself into a never ending web of lies. Trying to make up false scenarios wasn't doing her any good - it was just perpetuating the inevitable. "I've never used a download."

Tess laughed, before she realized Aurelia wasn't joining her, "Oh, you're serious?"

"Growing up, I learned things one by one, day by day. So, I didn't have the time, or quite frankly, my family didn't have the money, to put me in extra classes, and public school barely even taught me Spanish."

Tess let it sink in.

"School...? How...? Does that mean...?"

Aurelia nodded. There wasn't any point in hiding it from Tess anymore. Not after everything they'd been through together. It had been the nail in the coffin with her relationship with Will, but Tess had seemed more evolved on the subject throughout their discussions, and continued to open up as they befriended more and more permanents. She would either hate Aurelia from this point on, or learn to accept her for who she was.

"Oh my God, I'm so stupid!" Tess ran her fingers through her textured hair. "How did I not realize it sooner?" Aurelia's breath quickened. She shouldn't have told her. She would lose her best friend just like she'd lost Will. "It was *so* obvious - you don't speak Mandarin, you didn't know the history of the *Jīqìrén* Wars, you always stick up for the permanents - because you *are* one."

Aurelia nodded again, her eyes filling with tears. She knew what the outcome would be, why had she pushed Tess away?

"I'm sorry," Aurelia gulped.

"I can't believe you lied to me for so long!"

"I know. I'm so sorry. I just didn't want to lose you."

"Lose me...? Ari, would you stop crying?"

Aurelia sniffled, attempting to blink away the moisture building up, "I'm not crying."

Tess sighed, "Uh huh. Why would you think so little of me that you couldn't tell me?"

"I don't think little of you! But you hate the permanents. I didn't want you to think differently of me. I didn't want you to hate me like Will does."

Tess's eyes darted back and forth, stupefied at the situation, "... Is that what happened between you two? He found out?"

"Yes," Aurelia's voice cracked, holding back crying again. Her insecurities telling her emotions they should stop, she wiped her tears away before they fell. "I understand if you changed your mind and want me to take you back to B-udo. I'm sure that you could explain what happened, and how I fooled you into following me... and then you could go home."

Without a word, Tess wrapped her arms around Aurelia in a hug, "Thank you."

"So, that's a yes...? You want me to take you home?"

"What? No! I can't... I don't want to live there anymore. Not after knowing what they did to Dani and me. I *meant*, thank you for telling me."

"You're not... mad? You don't hate me because of who I am?"

"Who you are? You're still the same Aurelia I know. Aren't you? Sure, I'm mad that you hid it from me - that part sucks - and for the record, I hate that secretive part of your personality - but I don't hate *you*."

Flinging her arms around Tess again, Aurelia sobbed happy tears into her shoulder, "You have no idea how happy I am to hear you say that. I've dreaded this conversation for so long... and especially after how it ended with Will and me. He made it seem like I was some kind of demon out to get him, just because I was a permanent."

"Well that's his loss. Point me in his direction and I'll give him a good smack upside the head to get him to see straight," Tess still didn't know that Aurelia's Will was her cousin. "So, when are you from?"

"I'm fr-"

"No actually wait - let me guess! Obviously not as far as the mid 2100s. You had no idea what was going on there. But I don't think you're from too long before that, not with your way of thinking. Maybe 1900s - max," Tess gasped, a lightbulb going off. "We were trying to find your friends in the 1950s! That's when you're from, isn't it?"

"Well you're close by a few decades... Actually, since we're being honest, there's something else I should tell you about who I am. Something I just found out myself."

"What?"

"The family we were looking for in the '50s... they're *my* family. The Quinns. My grandparents, and their family."

"How did you *just* find that out?"

"No, no. I knew that part. I was expecting we would find them and meet most of them for the first time. What I didn't know is that we wouldn't have been able to find them there, because we already knew them."

"Huh? What do you mean?"

"I thought I knew who my family was, but I was wrong. My grandparents' identities were fake. They're not actually Federico Quinn and Dottie Smith. That's just who they became. Those are merely random aliases that some waitress in a diner chose for them."

"Stoppp..." Tess's bewilderment built up. "So Giovanna and Marco?"

"They're my great-grandparents. My grandparents are Ricco... and Natalia."

"Holy shit! *Natalia?* Does she know who she is? Does Ricco?"

"Nat does. We found out when time was paused. But we decided to keep it from Ricco."

"And how did she react? Was she freaked?"

"Actually, no. She was a little flummoxed by the fact that she would actually marry Ricco - but she was chill - better than I would've reacted if I found out something like that."

"So you're their... granddaughter. Wow. So if we left them in the '50s... when did you grow up? The '90s? 2000s?"

Aurelia confirmed she had hit the jackpot, "I was born in 2000. Presumably. Who knows if that's even the case, now that I know who my family is."

"What about your parents...? Have you already re-met them in the past? Are they from another time too?"

"No. They're actually permanents. I guess...? ...I wonder if they knew about it all. About who I am. About who Nat and Ricco are. I hadn't thought about that."

"You'd think if they did know about it all, that somehow they would've slipped to you. How old did you say you were when you left home? 19 years old? That's a long time to keep something from your daughter."

"No... they died when I was six. I barely knew them. My grandparents raised me - Nat and Ricco, raised me. I barely even remember what my parents looked like. And it was too painful for my grandparents to keep photos laying around of them after their son and daughter-in-law died."

"God, I'm sorry Ari, I had no idea."

"It's OK. It happened a long time ago."

"What *do* you remember about what they looked like?"

Aurelia smiled, taking a moment to try and recall their details, "My dad had short, light brown hair, and my mom had long, black hair with bangs. And she'd wear these little cat eye glasses cause apparently she was blind as a bat. I'm surprised I don't have trouble with *my* eyesight. But her smile. God, her smile still sticks with me."

"How did they die?"

"Car crash."

"And you're sure it wasn't...?"

"The Guardians? No. I don't think so. Apparently at some point in my future, Will and I closed all of the portals during my childhood. Hence, why I grew up unhindered."

"So you know that you'll reconcile with Will then, since he did that with you."

"Ughh... I don't know. I don't understand how it all works. Have I changed our future together? Or was he meant to break my heart, for it all to happen the way it should? He told me in our future we're supposed to get *married*!"

"What? When were you gonna tell me that?"

"I know... it's insane. But honestly, I don't know if I want to forgive him after how he acted about me being a permanent. Plus, I don't think *he'll* forgive me. We have some pretty major, seemingly irreconcilable differences right now with his viewpoints on permanents - he basically thinks I'm a plague on society."

"This is all the Lapite's fault. If they hadn't spread such hate, and prejudice, and misinformation about permanents, you wouldn't be in this situation. Will wouldn't have hurt you like that. None of this would've happened. You and I wouldn't be on the run. Daniella wouldn't be dead!" Tess's voice cracked for the first time at Daniella's name. "Dani wouldn't be dead."

"I know," Aurelia put her hand on her shoulder, hoping to tell her that she wasn't alone in her grief. "The problem is that no one stands up to them and tells them what they're doing is wrong. Even though I don't understand how they would even be able to justify burning villages and *killing* people, it's all just based on this unwarranted hatred that they're spreading."

"You're right... OK, Ari. I'm in," Tess raised her glass to her in a toast, downing a large gulp.

"You're in? What are you talking about?" Aurelia wondered what she had just said to illicit Tess's response.

"No one stands up to them. Not many people even know about what's going on. But we do. We have a responsibility to make change. We can be the leaders that the future needs. No one has the guts to fight them."

"And we do? Tess - are you crazy? Remember, these are the same people that your mom was working with!"

"No, they're the people that brainwashed her into thinking you're a terrorist. That capitalized on time technology and didn't even try to go back and prevent the events that led up to our planet dying and civilization scattering."

"You said it yourself - we can't change what's already happened."

"And who do you think claimed that?" Tess's hands seemed to clamp to themselves, her fingernails digging into her palms. "The Lapites. Aurelia, it's all because of them. They could've used their new knowledge of time travel to save humanity. Instead they started a vacation company and decided that permanents were worthless, belittling their lives to create a feeling of generational entitlement.

"They've taken away our personal freedoms so that everything is monitored, segregated us from the other colonies and even amongst the levels in ZhēnZhū, and now we know for certain that they kill blindly, without remorse. How can we stand by and let it happen, when we're some of the only people in the world that know the truth?" Tess ranted.

"You really think that the past can be changed? The corruption stopped? What about the paradox you said would happen if we knowingly tried to change things?"

"Maybe we can't change the past. But we *can* expose what the Lapites and the Guardians are doing. We have to try. Otherwise what hope is there for the future?"

"Tess, if we do this, we become who they claimed we were. We become renegades. They'll claim that *we're* the evil ones."

"But don't you understand? That's who they *already* think we are. We *are* renegades. Why not accept it already and fight to stop them? We need to stop running. We can't hide from them forever, eventually they'll find us, and do exactly what they've proven to do with our friends - kill us. I don't know about you, but I'd rather die fighting for the future than running from it."

"I don't want to die - period! Tess, I can't be a soldier in this war. The future isn't our fight."

"*Isn't our fight?* They've made it our fight! They're not just in the future, they're everywhere. And I'm not saying we'd be soldiers, Ari. We'd be the leaders."

"What? Me? You, I could see, but me?"

"Ari, you're more of a leader than anyone I know. Plus, with your 'abilities', you're the only one that stands a chance leading us against them. I'm with you."

Aurelia's head was spinning. Fight the future? Fight the Guardians and the Lapites? They could die doing so. They could get even more people killed.

They didn't have an army. They didn't have a plan. They just had a vision for what they thought the world should look like. But who were they to shape peace?

"Tess, if we fail-"

"If we fail - we fail. At least we tried and we'll go down fighting. But if we succeed, we'll have changed the world. We'll have exposed the corruption. Maybe we'll even be able to change the future. Maybe ZhēnZhū never has to be created and no one has to live miserable lives underground. Maybe Earth can prosper."

"But if we change the future like that, wouldn't you cease to exist? Would I?"

"It's a small price to pay for humanity."

Tess was willing to risk it all, even her own life. She had come a long way from the 16-year-old girl Aurelia had met in B-udo. That version of herself wouldn't have dared to say such a thing.

But Aurelia knew she was right. The Lapites had to be stopped. If left to their own devices, who knew what they would do? How many more people would they have the Guardians kill for their own gain?

Right now, they were the only ones willing to do it. But they had to fight. They had to be the leaders of the change.

Aurelia could feel the spark igniting in her body. She couldn't live her life safely as it was, and she couldn't ever be with Will without danger, as much as she despised him at the moment. She couldn't even have friends without worrying that her friendship with them would get them killed. The Lapites had created that misery for her.

She had to fight. *They* had to fight.

Aurelia stood up, raising her cup, which Tess followed, "I'll be your rebel."

"Ok 'rebel'. I'm with you."

"And I'm with you, Tess. Always."

"Always," clanging her glass to hers, the girls toasted.

Around the room, the phrase echoed from the mouths of others.

"Always."

"Always."

"Always."

Chills rushed down the girl's spines.

"Uhhh - Tess... is this your doing?" Aurelia whispered.

"No," Tess looked just as stunned as Aurelia.

The room was unknowingly filled with people that they somehow knew, from their future. Were they here protecting them? Or to show support? To lead them to battle? Whatever it was, it proved that they were on the right path. They were there because they believed in their leadership. To fight the future would be no easy task - but finally, they weren't alone.

The bartender slid them a piece of paper, a silver pocket watch on a long necklace chain, and two bands containing second skin suits, then lifted his drink to them, acknowledging them with a wink.

"Always."

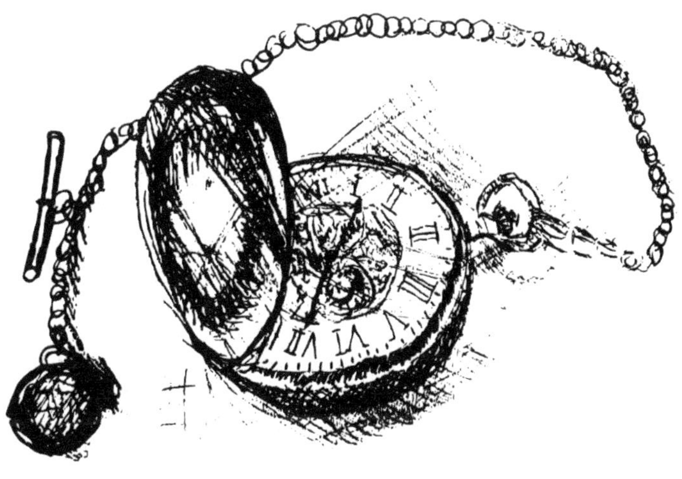

CHAPTER 53

THE FIRST MISSION

"Who the hell are you? Who sent you, huh? What does 'P; HQ T; 43-7-301-18-N/A-N/A' even mean?" Tess screamed at the bartender, the only one left to question, since the other guests had completely dispersed from the pub just seconds after they had ominously all said the same signal word.

But the bartender was silent. His eyes down, wiping the bar of invisible crumbs.

"Tess, stop. He's not gonna tell us. This is meant to be a code for us. I know what it means. It's simple," Aurelia had been staring at it for the past few minutes, but now that she had figured it out, it almost seemed to be *too* obvious.

"You do?"

"'P' - Place. 'HQ' - Headquarters. 'T' - Time. And these numbers - it's like the clocks on the doors of the official company portals - the first two are the year. 43-7. The future. The rest are the date. Day, hour, minute, millisecond."

Behind the counter, the man smiled, affirming it with a single, silent nod before he left the room.

"...And you trust some random guy who just hands you a coded message?"

"'Always'."

"Why?"

"No. Tess. 'Always'. Do *you* even know what that means to me?"

"What? No!"

"It's Will. It has to be. It's our phrase - Tess. 'Always'. We used to say that to each other. And then there's the watch! It's him," Aurelia put the necklace over her head, tucking it into her dress.

"So now you love him again? Now, you're willing to jump blindly for him? Did you forget how you felt *ten* minutes ago? You said you didn't even want to forgive him!"

"And I don't forgive him. Not yet. Tess - I may be mad - no, *furious* - at him... but I still trust him - future him. If he's the one who tried to get me this message, it must be for a reason. Maybe this is how we start fighting back. We didn't have a clue where to start, and now we do. We have a time and place."

"And not an inkling about what we're walking into."

Aurelia and Tess changed up their second skin suits' color palettes for anonymity, Aurelia choosing a shade of green - still unsure what it meant, and Tess from her usual purple to a blue.

They weren't sure how to land in the exact time and date without much to go on, so shooting blindly, Aurelia opened a portal from their hotel in Victorian London and thought about whatever details she could of when they were trying to get to. 43-7. Tess would've only been 13-years-old there. It was the year before the vacation company, Adventures In Time, officially launched, three years before Tess had met Aurelia for the first time, and six years later than the very first time Aurelia had visited the future in 43-1. Trying to use those events as a benchmark, they stepped into the future.

It was strange, but as they walked through time, a new sensation arose. The pocket watch that Aurelia wore around her neck started to whir against her chest. Taking it off and opening it by pressing in the knob, the time on the clock's face had jumped forward by hours. Basic watch technology had never been influenced by the portals before, why was this one? Tess took it to further investigate, but it just seemed like a normal watch, that now clicked along steadily.

"Try going forward in time again..." Tess said, still holding the watch.

Aurelia stepped forward, holding Tess's hand. Sure enough, the watch's hands spun out of control, jumping forward to the time they were in.

"Oh my God! Ari - it's calibrating to when we are!"

The watch was meant to be a guide.

"What? How?"

Aurelia stopped, looking at the watch again, trying to see any defining features on it, but none stuck out. It was an unbranded, silver, vintage pocket watch that only seemed to tell the time, with three hands for hour, minute, and second. But somehow, its technology had been modified for their aid.

"I don't understand. So it knows *when* we are?" exclaimed Aurelia.

"Yes! Look - go forward again," Tess held the watch up for Aurelia to see.

Stepping forward, the watch repeated its motion, winding itself around to the current time. Aurelia stepped backwards, trying to test it further, and the watch spun backwards with them. For the first time, Aurelia had something definitive to help her navigate her ability, although since it only had hours, and not days or years, it would only help them once they were relatively close to their destination.

"Who *was* that guy? What is this?" Aurelia whispered, dumbfounded.

"Who were any of them? Ari - they knew us - or they *will* know our future selves. They had to. This was all planned for us to get to where we're going."

It seemed too good to be true. Finally, after all this time, having to figure things out on their own, they had help from the future?

"Alright. I'm gonna try to get us as close as I can to 43-7. Then we can ask someone or something to see when we are-"

"-Try to think of New Year's Day. Remember I told you about the annual briefing the Lapites do? That's when everyone's out of their homes to watch it - every level is packed with people in the Core. It'll be easy to blend in, and we can pretty easily see the year there."

Now that Aurelia had finally revealed when she was from, she didn't have to worry about seeming like she didn't know what happened in the future.

"OK. New Year's. Let's try."

It took a few tweaks in the new portal to get them to the exact time, but they had managed to get to New Year's Day, after Tess described what the celebration was like each year, giving Aurelia a visual to work with. It only took a peek outside the portal, to see everyone's second skin suits personalized for the event, plastered electronically with the phrase, "Happy New Year 43-8!" written on dozens of people. If the girls weren't on a mission, they would've liked to have stayed to enjoy the event. Towering free food for all to show prosperity, the air sweet like candy, the lights in the Core pink for positivity.

But they had to get where they were going and avoid distractions. Using the portal again, Aurelia went as slowly as she could, backwards in time, as Tess counted out the rotations of the watch. 128 rotations backwards, and the girls stopped at 5:45 p.m., slightly early so that they could figure out why they were sent here. Before entering, they covered their faces with their second skin suits, and Tess tapped her band to Aurelia's, showing her how to link with each other so they could use the suits to hear each other clearly, the future's version of a com system. Ready to go, the girls stepped out into the belly of the beast, Headquarters.

It was already packed to the brim with people, so it was easy to just fall into the crowd and stay unnoticed, especially with their suits covering their faces. Tess held the sides of her wristband, then triple tapped it with two fingers and traced a line on her forearm, the suit morphing from blue to white where she had touched.

"So we can spot each other if we get separated," Tess whispered, motioning for Aurelia to do the same.

The space was decorated to the nines with history themed decor, different centuries and cultures all splattered together in the same room like a Jackson Pollock painting. On one side of the room, freshly painted Ancient Egyptian artifacts were displayed, while just next to them was a medieval throne, and a London phone booth. An incandescent lightbulb pulsed with energy on a wooden stand next to a Hindu shrine of Ganesha, and a Sioux Indian's leather outfit was displayed on a mannequin, complete with an authentic war bonnet headdress filled with feathers for bravery.

The displayed food was just as diverse. Appetizers of traditional Korean dumplings, small bowls of curry and rice, pozole, fried plantains, Kaab el ghazals, and even hot dogs. Malva pudding, steaming hot croissants, custard and baklava were just a few of the treats to grace the dessert table, making their mouths water at the sight.

A glass staircase had been constructed in the middle of the room, that went up and ended abruptly, going nowhere. Above them hung banners greeting the Members, and high-top tables crowded the floor of the main room in Headquarters, each with pamphlets similar to the ones Aurelia and Tess were used to in the welcome packages, however these were electronic, made of a flexible paper-like substance which displayed what the event was about...

The Members' launch of Adventures In Time.

CHAPTER 54

AIT Members' Launch

The girls weren't sure why they were there. Was there something they needed to see about the launch party? Someone they needed to meet?

Aurelia's eyes darted beneath the second skin suit covering her face, trying to examine every bit of the party for a detail that stuck out. Everything around them was kitschy, commercialized, yet fun and interesting.

"There's my Uncle Alex," Tess motioned ahead of them, near the wall, where Aleksander stood watching the event with Eloise, his apprentice.

Aurelia wondered if a young Will was here too. But he would only be 11 in this time - he was probably too young to be allowed in such a prestigious Members only event.

Trying to look for more familiar faces, Aurelia noticed the wall of colorless, silver suits near the back - the Guardians. Panic seemed to rip through her body.

"Tess. This place is crawling with Guardians."

"I know. It's because of the high profile clientele. If I didn't know any better - I'd say ninety percent of the people in this room traveled up from level A."

"Why?"

"Because they can do whatever they want, they own it all. All of the technology. All of ZhēnZhū."

"Are they the Lapites?" Aurelia asked.

"Maybe some, but everyone else probably just works for them. Most Members have been grandfathered into the company, taking over their parent's job when they retired."

"Wait - so you're saying the 'Members', are people that work for the company - for the Lapites?"

Tess chuckled, "In a way, that's who we all work for in ZhēnZhū. Think of the Members as the... upper level management. The influential, invisible hand moving the chess pieces."

"Membership is a title?"

"Well, yes and no. There are two types. There's the 'membership' that Adventures In Time claims you have, which is just a fancy way of delineating your status and letting the guides know which level you live on as you travel in time. And then there are the 'Members'. The ones *actually* in control."

Coming from a slightly raised platform to the left, a booming voice interrupted their conversation, "Hello, and welcome Members!"

The audience clapped at the announcement. No microphone was held, yet her voice was amplified as if it played through a stadium's speakers, just by using the technology in the suits.

"Most of you know me by now, but for those of you who don't, I'm Gira Obicroft, Operations Research Analysis Manager here in B-udo," she paused to let the audience roar again.

This was Gira - Aleksander's boss that Aurelia had heard about. She had a short, stocky body, and long, sleek, black hair tied into a straight low ponytail. She had designed her suit with shades of purple, yellow and pink, indicating that she was romantically fluid, and leaning feminine, her voice was inherently humorous and bouncy, yet her tone sharp and tongue quick, "Through my team's extensive efforts, and our brilliant scientists, we are so pleased to officially present what I know you've all heard the rumors about."

The crowd bubbled with comments.

"Now, now, hold your questions. You don't want to hear about it all from me, trust me. It's almost time for the moment you've all been waiting for, but first, we have a little surprise for you... let me introduce the person that made it all happen. Please, let's all give a warm welcome to our *gorgeous*, incredibly talented and generous CEO; Madame Shǒu Jūn Ai."

The crowd went wild, surprised at the announcement that their CEO would be there. Stepping onstage, a woman wearing a light pink suit that covered her head walked to the center where Gira had stood, double tapping her wrist to reveal her face beneath the suit. For having a Chinese name, she wasn't at all what Aurelia expected. It seemed she was perhaps of partly-Asian decent, after centuries of intermingling with ZhēnZhū's locals that varied widely, mixed with personalized genetic modification. She was perhaps in her late-sixties, but seemed decades younger. Her hair was a natural golden blonde, tied back into a low bun, her eyes a dark grey and somehow almost iridescent like rare black pearls, her figure exceptionally tall and slender. She had small, tight lips that pulled taught as she smiled, and a leader's arrogance about her, despite the daintiness that her light pink suit represented.

"Please, please, that's not necessary," Madame Ai said in a calm, sung tone, her voice slow and sweet, the claps continuing.

Waiting an extra moment to revel in the attention, she raised her hand to the crowd, and like a soothsayer, everyone quieted.

"Thank you. As Gira stated, I know you all have heard the rumors. That we've cracked the code on time travel. You've heard morsels of the stories of our supposed 'test trips', and wondered what nonsense your friends have been told, because it couldn't possibly be true.

"I know most of you think today is some kind of a joke. That we've built a fake amusement park inside B-udo to trick the public into thinking they're traveling in time. We've manufactured lies to keep the peace and bring excitement," Madame Ai paused for a moment, the audience hanging on her every word.

"I hope you understand that I wouldn't be here today if any of that were true. We *have* discovered the secret to time travel."

The crowd exploded, the gasps and comments deafening. Raising her hand again, the crowd stopped, and you could hear a pin drop.

She continued, "I know it's all very exciting," everyone laughed, "but everything will be explained in due time. Today, however, I've decided what better way to introduce our new technology than to show you firsthand?"

Everyone whispered to each other, the feeling palpable. They would get to witness time travel?

Gira walked back onstage at Madame Ai's cue, nodding to her superior with a nervous smile.

"Thank you, Madame Ai. If I may introduce one of our lead scientists, Aleksander Kovachev, who will be demonstrating the technology."

Gira motioned to Aleksander, who stepped towards the glass staircase in the room's center, the crowd stepping back from him to allow him to pass.

"Thank you," Aleksander said, shaking, "and before I begin, I would like to extend my sincere appreciation and support of our incredible CEO, Madame Shǒu Jūn Ai, for joining us today, and for leading us with such grace."

The Members clapped in response, Aleksander smiling with nervous gratitude. Madame Ai nodded at Aleksander, and he continued, "If I could, I would like to request the assistance of a Member to demonstrate our invention."

Amidst the crowd, the second skin suits dinged with volunteers who had tapped the alarm on their bands. Choosing a middle-aged person at random wearing a pure yellow suit, showing that they were gender neutral, they stepped up to Aleksander, where he greeted them with a flurry and asked their name.

"Let's give a warm welcome to Mx. Jeong," the Members cheered for their colleague, who smiled at the attention. "Mx. Jeong, I have a difficult task for you. If you could please help us by walking up the staircase, while holding this."

Aleksander handed them an Okliot, which Mx. Jeong examined for a moment, curious as to what the golden, copper ball was. Surprised at the easy instructions, Mx. Jeong walked up on command, waving happily to their friends below. But by the time they reached the top step, they looked back down at Aleksander, confused. Hadn't they been chosen to travel in time, Mx. Jeong wondered?

"You can come back down, Mx. Jeong," Aleksander stated.

"But, nothing happened...?" they said, walking down, disappointed.

"No. Because it's just a stairwell," the crowd laughed at this, sure that they were being tricked. *This* was what they came all this way to watch? "Mx. Jeong, if you could please stand off to the side for just a moment."

Eloise walked up to Aleksander, holding a large, sealed case that she handed him, before walking back to her spot near the wall of Guardians. Every click of the case was audible as he opened it, the crowd barely breathing in suspense. Inside was a compact fusion reactor housed in a newly built protective shell. It was the very same device he had made years ago, trying his theory to modify it to be used for opening a portal, which he deemed as a failure - that is, until he found it ticking in his desk's drawer three years ago.

Setting it gently on the first step of the glass staircase, he placed two metallic beads on top of metal boxes on the sides of the step, before starting up the portable nuclear fusion reactor, which whirred alive. Inside the small, highly insulated machine, the atoms were heated to over one hundred million kelvin - hotter than the sun's core, stripping away the atom's electrons and turning them into a free flowing plasma. Then, with the beads' extreme magnetic properties, Aleksander activated the metallic beads on either side, creating a harsh magnetic field and triggering the fusion process to begin inside the machine.

Aleksander took out the final piece to the puzzle; a container of nanobots and a tablet to control them, that he opened and allowed into the air, which followed his programmed directives. Then, within mere minutes from the entire process starting, the fusion was complete. Aleksander turned off the magnets and removed the machine from the step, immediately securing it inside his case.

The magnets still in place, he took his own Okliot out, before securing all of his technology in his biometric locked case. When he summoned her, Eloise promptly came to get the case and take it away, back to his lab.

"With our efforts, we've been able to successfully tear an invisible, microscopic hole in space-time, which can be stabilized and widened with our nanotechnology, filling the air with particles that exist in not one - but *two* places in time. Not only can we control when we are going, but where, with a one-time calibration with our nanobots, that make it possible to specify where those particle's two places in time are. As of today, we're only able to use this technology to go *backwards* in time, but rest assured, we're working hard to also get to the future.

"It's with this immense discovery, we've been able to create working space-time portals that are safe, stable, and marketable. All you need to access them is what I like to call, an 'Okliot'," Aleksander picked up one of the golden copper balls. "The 'Okliot' is the most important part of the time travel technology that connects you with the nanobots in the air, reading your DNA and telling the nanobots to send every part of you from one place in time, to the other. Since the nanobots have attached themselves to the particles that exist in two times at once, so do they.

"Don't worry - if you're an Augment, the technology will still work for you. The Okliot will just read your code instead. Plus, we've made sure the nanobots also bring along anything you're touching, so you'll arrive with all of your personal belongings - and most importantly, your clothes. That was something we fixed right away after our first test!" the Members laughed.

"However, I have to stress how crucial it is to never let go of your Okliot while you're in the portal, and that each Okliot can only transport one person at a time. So, Mx. Jeong, now that the portal is ready, would you like to be our first guest to use it?"

Mx. Jeong stood speechless, unsure whether they wanted to be the guinea pig.

"You're scared to try. Not a problem. I was nervous my first time too. I can demonstrate it for you first," Aleksander held his own Okliot up for the crowd to see, and hopped up the stairs.

Everyone's eyes were glued to him, even Gira, Madame Ai, Tess and Aurelia. Had he successfully created a portal using a fusion reactor? The science of it didn't add up entirely. There was something missing - some secret, magic key that connected it all and allowed it to work. Plus, if the Okliots were only used to read your DNA and connect to the nanobots, why had they also worked in Aurelia's unstable portals that weren't opened with technology? There had to be something that Aleksander wasn't explaining.

But sure enough, as Aleksander stepped up the stairs, his body seemed to fade from view, becoming more and more see-through every step he took. He was traveling in time. Not even making it three-quarters of the way, his body had completely vanished.

What ensued was massive. Aurelia and Tess had never seen such hysteria. The Members around them shouted in wonder. Had it been a disappearing magic trick? Where had Aleksander gone? A few of them even ran up the stairs themselves, to attempt it after him, but they weren't holding Okliots, so they just found themselves on a glass stairway that led nowhere. The Guardians were quick to get them down, and after a minute or two passed, and the crowd's questions grew, Aleksander began to re-emerge, stepping down from the middle of the stairwell. Within a few seconds, he was completely back from wherever and whenever he had gone.

The sound of the shouts was thunderous, and even though Aleksander tried to talk again, no one could hear him. Raising her hand to stop them, Madame Ai held the power of silence.

"As you can see, it works," Aleksander smiled.

"WHEN DID YOU GO TO?" someone screamed.

"A *long* time ago, where we've built something special for this momentous event."

"LET US TRY!"

"HOW DO YOU KNOW IT'S NOT DANGEROUS?"

"CAN WE CHANGE THE PAST?"

Questions flooded the room again but Aleksander spoke over them, "Every test we've done has proven that it's not dangerous in any way. And all of you will get a chance to try it, but first, Mx. Jeong?"

Mx. Jeong stepped up next to Aleksander again, with a quick nod of their head. He handed them the Okliot, and once again, Mx. Jeong walked up the stairs, this time much more cautiously, expecting the process to happen. Their body slowly disappeared, as they were transported in time.

"THE STAIRWELL IS MORPHING AROUND ME!" Mx. Jeong shouted down at the crowd, their voice dull and fading.

It wasn't long before they were gone from view, but this time, the crowd was silent, waiting for them to appear again.

It was a solid thirty seconds of silence, which seemed like an hour.

Running back down to announce to their colleagues, Mx. Jeong grinned in excitement, "It works! It's incredible!"

The crowd flung into sound again, shouting over each other.

"I WANT TO TRY!"

"WHAT IS IT LIKE?"

"WHEN WERE YOU?"

Aleksander yelled over them, "Listen, everyone - as I promised, you will all get to use the portal. So calm yourselves, and we'll do this one at a time. In fact, against this wall, we have some party favors for you all to keep. Just scan your band with the Guardians and you can join Mx. Jeong and I at the 'afterparty'."

Holding their Okliots, Aleksander and Mx. Jeong walked back up the stairs into the portal, once again disappearing from view.

People piled on top of each other, clamoring to be one of the first to get their own Okliot party favor, which was housed in a tiny, beautifully designed, black carbon fiber box. Tess and Aurelia were pushed forward in the crowd, leading them towards the Guardians.

"What if our bands aren't authorized for the Okliots?" Aurelia whispered, still connected to Tess via their suit's intercom.

"Then we run like hell. We can't avoid taking them. It'll be much more suspicious!"

So, waiting their turn as the Guardians handed out the Okliots one by one, Aurelia reached the security checkpoint before Tess, which everyone had to clear before they were able to collect their party favors. Copying the people before her, she held out her wrist for one of the Guardians to scan with a clear tablet. Reading her credentials, it beeped, but the man holding the tablet paused, looking at the tablet.

"Can you remove your head covering for me?" the man asked Aurelia.

Her false identity must have been compromised. She had been

found. Stepping back slightly, unsure whether to run like Tess had suggested or stay and fight.

But no one was detaining her. The man barely even looked up at her from his tablet. What if it was just protocol?

Double tapping her band to reveal her face, the man looked at the screen, then to her face, his expression unchanging.

"OK, you're all clear Eriq. You can put your covering on again, if you'd prefer," he had just needed to verify she was who her band said, Eriq?

Double tapping it quickly, and moving along, another Guardian scanned her wrist again, tapping his tablet to the carbon fiber box, which opened on command to reveal the Okliot inside.

"It's biometric?" Aurelia asked.

"The box is," the man said in an obvious tone, handing her the open carbon fiber box.

"Thanks," she smiled, the digitally ingrained face on her suit copying her.

She had gotten it. She had been able to get past the Guardians without issue. Who had created their fake identities, she wondered? Why had they needed to come today? Had it been to see how Aleksander made the portals? Was it to get two Member's Okliots?

Waiting for Tess to clear the checkpoint, she could hear her side of the conversation with the Guardian checking her credentials.

"What? Why? Is there a problem?" Tess asked defensively.

Knowing she would hear her since their suits were still connected, Aurelia whispered to her, "Tess, do what he says, it's just for him to verify you're you."

Hesitating for a moment, Tess unveiled her face, without issue. She stepped up to receive her Okliot, and quickly found her way to Aurelia.

"Thanks," Tess said, sighing from stress.

They had gotten their Okliots. They had remained unnoticed in a room swarming with Guardians. They were doing incredibly well on their first "mission" - in fact, they felt like they were already professionals - that is besides their bodies' reactions; sweating profusely, their hearts palpitating from stress.

Tess briefly released her head covering to pull the pocket watch out that hung around her neck, under her suit, putting the head covering back on immediately. Taking their new, shiny A class Okliots from their fancy case and placing them in Tess's bag for safekeeping, their nerves amped even more.

Now, standing at the bottom of the glass staircase, they wondered what awaited them on the other side.

Where or *when* were they going?

CHAPTER 55

TSUMAMI

Tess marveled as the pocket watch spun backwards in time, vigorously. It almost seemed as if it would break from such exertion. Whenever they were traveling to was a *long*, long time ago.

The glass staircase shifted into white, the room opening around them to reveal what looked like a circular, almost donut shaped building, the entire exterior flooded with light from its paned windows molded with white trim.

The windows stretched from the floor, then curved upwards above their heads, revealing the blue sky. Outside, they were surrounded 360 degrees by an ocean, with dozens of sandbanks stretching out in a row.

The floors and curved interior walls were all painted a flat white, the color mimicking the sea foam forming on the sand outside. They seemed to be on an island somewhere in the middle of nowhere, and the modern building they stood in appeared placed on top.

When were they? As far as she knew, nothing like this could've been built in Aurelia's time, or before, but the pocket watch had made it seem like they went back millennia.

There were already dozens of Members that had beat them to the punch, filling the room with a buzzing happiness. They had traveled in time.

The bits and pieces they overheard of the conversations around them all sounded the same. "How was it possible?", "When were they?', "What would the profits look like if it was able to be sold to the public?", "Could they change events in time?"

Just like at the previous location, there was a bevy of food and drink, with waiters passing out what looked like champagne, but was in fact a much stronger alcohol, that had become popular in the 24th century.

Unsure what to do, Tess and Aurelia walked around the building, trying to attempt to be cognizant of their surroundings like a spy in the CIA would. Peeking in one of the two doors, they watched as the staff used a service entrance's stairwell into the building, appearing from thin air on the steps - obviously traveling in time to get there, perhaps from another portal in B-udo, or somewhere else. The only other door they found was for a restroom. So it seemed there were a total of two entrances. The stairwell portal Aleksander had just opened that they had used, and the staff entrance. Besides that, the circular, donut shaped building was completely uniform as it wrapped around itself.

Aleksander was there, surrounded by a dozen Members who had all turned into adoring fans, and Gira joined him after a while. And yet again, there were Guardians posted every few feet, among them, a familiar face that Aurelia never wanted to see again - the man who killed Johanna. Helios.

It seemed like the company's CEO, Madame Ai, hadn't come to fraternize with the Members, and another face that seemed to be missing was Aleksander's apprentice, Eloise. Aurelia remembered that in Eloise's future with them, she had seen the sun for the first time when they went to Tangier, so perhaps she wasn't allowed or invited because she wasn't a Member.

As they walked around aimlessly, one of the servers came up to them to offer them drinks, with only one glass remaining on his tray, "Priyar?"

Tess shooed him off, "No, no. We're fine."

"You sure?" the man handed her a glass and a napkin.

With a mild annoyance, Tess took it, "Thanks."

"Of course. Always."

Aurelia perked at the phrase as the man walked away, "What did you just say?" but he didn't answer, instead tucking the tray under his arm and heading for the main portal.

"Uhh... Ari?" Tess held up the napkin he had just handed her.

On it was written, what they assumed was, a time, "14:09" - 2:09 p.m. Popping open the pocket watch, the current time read 2:02 p.m.

Whatever they were there for was supposed to happen in seven minutes.

Looking around the building to try and predict their near future, the girls couldn't figure out what the time on the napkin meant. Nothing had changed. Plus, they couldn't understand how the waiter had recognized them, even with their suits covering their faces and heads.

But with only three minutes remaining until 2:09, they stuck together and waited to see what would happen, standing just next to the crowd surrounding Aleksander and Gira. Weaving through the Members, a Guardian approached Aleksander.

"Sir? Sir, we have a problem," the Guardian said a little too loudly.

Shushing him and excusing himself from the conversation with a smile, he stepped off to the side to hear what had happened, Aurelia and Tess getting as close as possible to them without arising suspicion.

"How?" Aleksander asked at full volume.

Little pieces were audible, but for the most part, they couldn't hear what was being said besides, "Can you fix it?", "All of them?" and "Tell Gira".

Something was happening.

Behind them, near the stairwell, a Member tried to leave and go back to B-udo, but was held up by a Guardian.

"Tess, look, they're not letting him leave."

"...I think we need to get out, Ari. We only have about two more minutes before it happens."

"But *what* happens? Aren't we supposed to find out? Isn't that what the message meant?"

"Or it meant 'leave before this time'."

Hearing the ruckus of the Member wanting to leave, another person came over to ask the Guardian what the issue was, then another, until the situation elevated, and finally someone pushed past the Guardian, holding his new Okliot and running down the stairs to use the portal.

But nothing seemed to happen. The portal had stopped working.

Chaos seemed to erupt faster than a lit match in a haystack.

With the realization that the portal had stopped working, panic ensued and spread through the crowd like a virus. First affecting five people, then fifteen, then fifty.

"Tess, follow me."

Grabbing Tess's hand, the girls ran through the crowd to the stairs of the service entrance, where they had witnessed another portal. But it was filled with Guardians and staff, seemingly all trying to use the other exit, with no luck. Someone had closed their way out.

They were all stuck here.

"Ari, thirty seconds!" Tess shouted, unclear what they should do.

Could Aurelia open the portals again? But if she could, she would be compromised and reveal herself to the hundreds of Members and Guardians in the building. Attempting to run down the staff stairwell, Aurelia decided that she had to try something, but Tess grabbed her arm to stop her.

"Are you *crazy*?" Tess hissed. "They'll see you!"

"We have to get out! Something bad is happening, I know it!"

"Ari - if it works, they'll catch you."

"I know. But I'll get you out - and you'll run, OK? Don't let them get you too. Come on," switching Tess's grip to her own, Aurelia grabbed her arm and pushed to get past the guards, the stairwell beginning to morph, slightly.

"Go! Go! Leave!" someone shouted in front of them, stopping them from going further and grabbing Aurelia's shoulder's, holding her in place and attempting to push her back up the stairs.

"LET GO! We have to get out!" Aurelia shouted, pushing him off of her.

He ran past them, and Tess noticed that everyone had reversed their direction and was running up, out of the stairwell. Looking down, Aurelia realized why. There was a bomb about to detonate. Aurelia pushed Tess's arm back, making them backtrack up the stairwell with the crowd. There wasn't enough time to run down the stairs, making a portal to travel in time.

"TESS - RUN!"

In the panic of the moment, and the speed they raced up the stairs, she nearly tripped, but they made it to the top of the landing before the bomb blew, the shock of the force sending their bodies flying into the main room.

The building's exterior glass nearby shattered from the explosion, but quickly resealed itself with nanobots to stop the air from escaping, and allowing toxic gaseous compounds to enter the building from the Earth's budding new atmosphere outside.

Like Aurelia and Tess, a handful of the Guardians and staff had been wearing their suits over their head, which helped to insulate their bodies from the shock. But otherwise, around them, lifeless bodies littered the floor. Someone shook Aurelia to check that she was alive, and she nodded, taking a deep breath that hurt tremendously, as she attempted to stand. She definitely had some broken ribs, and perhaps her leg, if not more. Even though her suit had covered her head, her ears rung so much that she couldn't hear anyone's voices.

Immediately, Aurelia's mind went to Tess. Where was she?

Tess had been in front of her, Aurelia taking the brunt of the explosion between the two of them. Dropping to her knees and looking frantically beneath the rubble, Aurelia found a body, but it wasn't hers. Where was Tess?

Questions shot through her mind - why had they been tricked into coming? Should they not have trusted anyone?

A hand on her shoulder startled Aurelia, and she looked up to see a person with a blue suit above her. Looking at her forearm, the blue had a streak of white. It was Tess. She was alive. Jumping up to hug her, Aurelia still couldn't hear what she was trying to say to her. It seemed like Tess had injured her shoulder - it looked dislocated, and she pushed Aurelia away from the pain. But she was alive.

They were disoriented from the blast. Aurelia tried to motion to Tess to follow her away from the blast site, and she hobbled off, leading the way. Every breath hurt, her broken ribs stabbing her lungs.

A few random Members that were unharmed from the explosion rushed over to check on the survivors, Aurelia shooing them from herself, but Aurelia didn't notice that behind her, Tess accepted their help, and in the chaos of the moment, they were separated.

Almost everyone around her had activated their second skin suit's head coverings, hoping to protect themselves from the debris in the air, and the potential leaks from the windows.

She still couldn't hear, the temporary tinnitus barely dissipating. It was hard to concentrate, and the confusion seemed to be taking hold. But as she walked aimlessly through the crowd, away from the explosion site, a bright light in the distance turned her head to see what had happened, as her suit thankfully shielded her eyes, otherwise she most likely would've been blinded from the harsh light - at least for a few hours or days.

It was a second attack. Another bomb. This time behemoth in size.

A mushroom cloud rose miles away, followed by an initial shockwave that shattered every window and sent every person flying down to the ground. Then finally the sound waves hit, shaking every bone in their bodies, which Aurelia could hear, even though her eardrums still rang from the initial explosion. There had been a nuclear bomb somewhere in the ocean. Crawling onto her knees to look, Aurelia could see that the worst was still on its way.

Not only would there be more shockwaves, but the ocean waters receded around the sandbanks, the ground trembling, the water in the distance swelling towards them. The signs were clear. The nuclear blast had caused a tsunami, and they had no way out.

The people around them screamed bloody murder in panic, jumping on top of each other to try and escape through the broken portal. They were trapped. All of them. There wasn't enough time for Aurelia to even *get* to the only remaining stairwell, let alone save everyone by bringing them with her. Plus, where had Tess gone?

The roaring sound of the ocean coming filled the room, the empty glass panes attempting to repair themselves again, only to be continually shattered by the vibrations.

"TAKE COVER!" someone shouted.

Aurelia loved the ocean. Growing up in California, it was a part of existence for her. She had never been afraid of it, as she was now. But looking out at the monstrous, unstoppable wave that grew by the second, she knew that it would take her life. She knew that it would take all of their lives, washing them away with its force alone enough to kill them.

There had to be a reason Aurelia was chosen to be there. Why would they have used her phrase, "Always", if it wasn't meant for her to trust them? Why would they send her and Tess to die?

Aurelia was powerful. She had surprised herself again and again with her abilities with time; from the portals, to starting time again. Something inside her was connected to a larger force than herself. Maybe she was meant to save everyone. But, weren't the Members the very people that Aurelia and Tess needed to stop? Weren't they evil? If so, were they even worth saving? But then Aurelia thought of Tess. Of Will losing his dad. How many people in the room were fathers, mothers, husbands or wives? Assuming that everyone agreed with the Lapites and the Guardians wasn't right. Maybe they were too scared to stand up to them. Most of the Members had just found out about time travel today. Perhaps they didn't even realize the corruption right under their noses. The Members weren't as integral to the company as Tess had led Aurelia to believe. They were innocent, they had to be.

Revealing her face to see everything more clearly and not be blocked by the second skin suit, Aurelia stood up, despite the force of the shockwave still pushing her back, looking at the impending wave in front of her. Holding out her hand, unsure what it was she was doing, she imagined the fire burning in her chest, pleading with every atom in her body to help her.

Running for cover, Aleksander saw Aurelia standing in the middle of the emptied room, and he tried to grab her to pull her to safety.

"NO, STOP!" she shouted, holding her stance.

She had to try and stop it.

Just realizing who she was, Aleksander stepped back, "IT'S YOU! MIANA."

She couldn't hear his words, but she knew he had recognized her. He called for the Guardians to come assist him, and a group of them ran to his aid.

They grabbed her, but she snapped at them, trying to keep her attention focused, "I CAN STOP IT ALEX. I CAN SAVE US."

Aleksander didn't understand what it was she meant, but anything was worth trying. They would all be dead in less than a minute anyway. He nodded to the Guardians to step back.

Releasing her, Aurelia turned to face the wave, which was now on the sandbanks, standing over one hundred feet and quickly increasing as the water was pushed upwards over the sand. Holding up her hand once more, Aurelia thought about the feeling she had traveling in time. Going backwards to before the wave formed, before the nuclear bomb exploded, before the first bomb exploded in the stairwell. She thought about the space between time, the golden thread connecting the seconds together. About the feeling when time was stopped and she'd managed to jump back seconds in time.

She didn't want to die.

Aleksander ducked to the ground for cover, the tsunami feet away from crashing through the windows, standing above them larger than a skyscraper.

But the wave didn't crash.

Aleksander looked up to see what had happened, but the wave stood still, like a wall of water outside. The Guardians near Aurelia and Aleksander stood up in awe. How had the wave stopped? Looking around the silent room, they realized that everything, and everyone else around them was frozen, just like the wave. Only a handful of them were awake. Their breaths were now challenged, and they quickly became lightheaded from the lack of new oxygen.

Aurelia could feel her nose bleeding, the blood dripping from her face. Somehow, she had stopped time. It was her doing. Never before had she been able to *intentionally* stop time, rather than restarting it.

"How is this possible?" Aleksander was awake.

Looking around, Aurelia realized that everyone standing within a few feet of her was awake. But she hadn't connected them to the energy. They would die soon.

"Was this you?" the obfuscated Aleksander whispered breathlessly.

Aurelia had to stay focused. Her hand still held up as if it were holding the wave, she imagined the seconds rewinding, just as she was able to go back in time in a portal. Stepping forward towards the wave, as if it were an animal she was trying to tame, it listened. The water began to move backwards, reversing its direction and going back into the ocean. She was controlling time.

Within a few seconds, the window panes repaired themselves, the shockwaves going back to the blast site. The mushroom cloud condensed again, swallowing itself into its void. To their left, the bomb in the stairwell reversed, along with all of the people that had flown out of it - although Aurelia no longer saw herself as one of the victims. Aleksander and the Guardians couldn't believe their eyes. They were witnessing time moving backwards.

Aurelia could feel the tax it had on her body. Every second that she reversed felt like sandpaper in her veins. With it, she innately knew that she shouldn't have stopped what was meant to happen. She wasn't sure how she knew, but she wasn't supposed to interfere with time. With herself, Aleksander and the Guardians all broken away from the timeline, she had changed time.

But she had to. She had to save everyone. Collapsing to her knees, she tried to get them back as far as she could, each minute terribly difficult to reverse. It felt wrong. It felt as if she was breaking the gears around her that tried to move in the opposite direction, and she was forcing them backwards. What ramifications would it have?

She managed to get the group of them back at least twenty minutes before the initial blast. Before the portals had closed. They could get out.

"Get everyone to leave," Aurelia croaked to Aleksander, her chest hurting and breath shallow from a punctured lung. "Now. Before it happens again."

The last thing she saw before she passed out from exhaustion, was the calm ocean outside resuming in time. She had done it. She had saved everyone. She had changed time.

CHAPTER 56

All Lies?

An electric burn on her arms startled Aurelia awake. She was surrounded by dozens of people - half of them Guardians all with second skin suits covering their faces, posted against the stone wall. Attempting to get up out of the chair she was in, and run out the currently open, barred cell, she was abruptly stopped by metal cuffs on her arms and legs. Where was she? When was she?

Someone had taken her second skin suit, and she only wore the corset and knee length knickers from the 1800s that she had worn underneath, the cream fabric stained with her blood.

Everything was dark and dimly lit, her breath quick from fear. A single electric lightbulb buzzed above her, dangling out of the dirt packed ceiling by a wire. The room didn't have a single window, just dirt, and stone walls surrounding and suffocating them with claustrophobia. She hated the darkness they were enveloped in.

Once again, Aurelia felt the charge that had awoken her, screaming in excruciating pain that seemed to come from the electrodes she was hooked up to, with wires leading to a machine to her left, where a woman adjusted the voltage.

"Sir. She's awake," a voice from outside the hall said, to someone.

"Keep increasing the voltage until she wants to talk," both voices sounded familiar.

But her thoughts were cut short as another charge ripped through her body. It only lasted a single second, but the electric shock was enough to make her vision dance with white snowflakes, her mouth dry and teeth metallic.

"Why...? What...?"

Her brain was foggy, disoriented from the pain. Her ribs still hurt, healing in the wrong position, their sharp shards still rubbing against her lung.

Without warning, another shock coursed through her, her hands inadvertently grabbing the chair, her muscles spasming, this one lasting a few seconds.

"Stoppp!" Aurelia squeaked, as soon as the charge had ended and she could speak again. "I'll talk! I'll talk. Just stop."

The guard nearest the door motioned to someone outside, and Helios walked in, picking up a wooden chair in the corner and setting it just in front of her. She would never forget his face. The sound of her footsteps running in the rain seemed to flash before her eyes, the image of Johanna fresh, once again.

"Let's start with an easy one," Helios's deep voice resonated in the air, "what is your name?"

He didn't know her name yet. Had they not met before?

She searched her mind for the false identity her band had in B-udo.

"...Eriq."

Helios motioned to the woman controlling the machine, and she shot her with another quick charge, this one not as bad, but still horrible.

"Now the truth."

"...Miana. It's Miana," she lied again.

His eyes attempted to see into hers, but she couldn't look at his face. His striking, yet weathered appearance and dark eyes reminding her of her loss.

"And where are you from, *Miana*?"

"B-udo."

"*When* are you from?"

"The 43's. Same as you."

Helios looked to one of the Guardians in the room, who held a tablet as they spoke.

"Anything?" Helios asked him.

"I have no record of a 'Miana' from B-udo, Sir, besides one scan at Headquarters in 43-1 from a Miana Reynolds. It seems like it was a temporary authorization."

They had record of her time in B-udo with Will and Aleksander.

"That's her, but she's not from the 43's. She's from the past," a voice from outside the room said, stepping into the room.

It was Aleksander.

"Sir, how do you know?" the Guardian asked him.

"Because I was there. I issued the security clearance."

Aleksander was working with them. Aurelia's mouth seemed too dry to speak. Will's dad was helping the Guardians - he was helping

Helios.

"You *know* her?" Helios asked him, his lip twitching beneath his grey stubble beard.

Aleksander nodded. To him, she was his key to everything. She had been to his future and had the knowledge of how to replicate his time technology.

Turning back to Aurelia, Helios continued, "You heard the man. When are you really from, Miana?"

"What does it matter?" she asked, defiantly.

"How did you get to B-udo if you're from the past?"

"I used a 'time machine'," she gasped, sarcastically, acting as if they didn't know time travel existed, laughing through the pain at her own joke.

It wasn't the time to be making jokes, but things felt out of control, and her nervous system resulted to making light of the situation to try and ease her fear.

Helios held his hand up to the woman, with four fingers, who repeated the voltage to him, "Here's four thousand, Sir."

She sent another, larger shock through Aurelia's body, her limbs convulsing and head shaking. It was significantly longer than the previous ones. As it stopped, and her vision slowly cleared, she realized she tasted blood. She had bit the sides of her tongue.

"When are you from?"

"...What?" she gasped, trying to remember what they were talking about. "You're Helios... aren't you...? Where am I?"

Her memory was stunned from the last intense electrocution, but it slowly came back as the shock wore off.

"How do you know my name? Have we met?"

Helios hadn't met her before this. He hadn't killed Johanna yet.

"You killed her."

Helios looked at her, trying to understand what she meant. Who had he killed that she knew?

"Who?"

Aurelia fell silent. She wouldn't give him the satisfaction of her name.

"When are you from, Miana?"

Her memories scattered, she knew she had just been in the 1800s. Was that when she was from?

"1889."

"Where?"

"I don't... I don't remember."

Helios turned to the woman next to them, whispering his instructions, "Less charge next time. It's affecting her memory." The woman nodded. "Who are you working with?"

Aurelia started to remember flashes of what had happened. She was with Tess.

"What? Working with? Working with for what?"

Everything seemed clearer by the second. She wasn't from the 1800s - but her lie had gotten by effortlessly.

"Who got you into Headquarters today?"

"I have no idea."

It was the truth.

"Helios, I need a minute with her," Aleksander said, standing over him. Nodding, Helios stood up. "Alone."

Aleksander. Will's father. Will. His face came into view in Aurelia's mind.

With apprehension, Helios motioned for the Guardians to go outside with him. The woman running the electrocution machine got up, and within a minute, they were alone.

"Alex. You have to help me!" Aurelia whispered to him. "Get me out of here! I haven't done anything wrong."

He nodded to her, "I know you haven't. But I need you to be honest with me."

He was going to help her escape. She was sure of it.

He continued, "What technology did you use to stop that wave?"

"What?"

"...How did you manipulate time?"

"I didn't. I don't use any technology."

Standing up from his chair, slowly, he stepped over to the machine. Aurelia sighed a breath of relief, knowing he would disconnect her and get her out of this horrible place.

Her body shook from the long electric shock he sent, her fingernails digging into the wood of the chair. He had shocked her. Aleksander had shocked her.

"Next time, maybe the truth?"

Her ears seemed to ring, and spots of white floated in her vision.

"I... I told..." speaking was difficult. She knew what she wanted to say, but it wouldn't come out, her voice slurred and tongue numb.

Why was he doing this to her?

"What technology are you using?"

She wasn't using any technology. It was inside of her. Her own body was what was able to stop time.

"I'm not."

"Someone is. Someone reversed time. So who are you working with? What technology are *they* using?"

"Alex. Please. Think of your son. Think of Will. Don't do this to me."

He slammed his hand on the machine's table, angry from her response, "If you don't know, then you're of no use to me. Why don't you think about that next time you answer, huh?"

Increasing the knob on the machine, he blasted her with another electric shock, this one much more intense than any of the previous ones. She couldn't feel any pain during it, her vision completely white and the sound around her not making it to her brain. But after it happened, she knew she couldn't move, the feeling overwhelming like it had been in Tianjin when she was temporarily paralyzed from the car accident. Her head slumped over, her body limp, her nerves in her wrists sizzling from the electrodes where they had burned her skin. Her heart raced in her chest - was she having a heart attack, she wondered?

Assuming she had passed out, Aleksander left the room, stomping down the hallway. Coming back in, Helios scoffed at Aleksander's methods. He wouldn't be able to interrogate her for a while in her current state.

"Get her head secured," he pointed at one of the Guardians, who promptly lifted her head, strapping it into the leather band on the chair.

She couldn't talk. She could barely see. She could hardly remember why she was here. All she knew was that she was trapped.

A few hours passed, and Helios entered the room again, Aurelia's body able to rest from the torture for a short while.

A Guardian sat at the machine, ready to pick up where the woman and Aleksander had left off. Double tapping his band, the second skin suit retracted from his head, revealing his face. Aurelia was seeing things. She had to be. His messy brown hair, his blue eyes.

It was Will.

"Start us at twelve-hundred," Helios instructed Will.

Aurelia couldn't believe it. Will was here to save her.

She tried to make eye contact with him, smiling from the

excitement, but he wouldn't look at her, his eyes focused on the machine.

"What are you doing?" she asked him, wondering what his next move would be to get her free.

"Twelve-hundred, Sir," Will repeated, as he pressed the button on the machine, sending an electric shock through her body.

Her body shook with electricity. What was happening? The shock calming down after the surge, she tried to make sense of why Will was here. Why was he working for Helios?

"Awake now?" Helios chuckled, looking at Aurelia's stunned face. "This doesn't have to be difficult Miana. Who are you working with?"

Will was just pretending. He had to be. But why wouldn't he give her a sign to tell her to trust him - a wink, a look, something?

"Who set those bombs?" Helios rattled on, but she couldn't concentrate on what he was asking her. "Increase to fourteen-hundred."

Will turned the knobs, keeping his eyes on the machine.

"No," Aurelia looked at him, hoping to convince him to stop. "No, no, no - stop! Please!"

The shock pulsed through her limbs again, her teeth chattering. As it stopped, she felt weaker than she did before, the residual effects not entirely subsiding. Why wasn't Will helping her escape?

"Miana," Helios physically turned her head to look at him and not what he assumed was the machine, "I just need you to work with me, so we can get through this faster. The longer you wait, the more pain you'll feel before the end."

"The... end?" Aurelia almost didn't want to know what he meant.

"We can either draw it out, or if you cooperate, give you a quick death. It's your choice."

Helios was going to kill her. It didn't matter what she said.

"Why? Why would you kill me? I haven't done anything," Aurelia pleaded, her eyes darting from Helios to Will.

"Miana - you and whoever you're working for, attempted to assassinate all of the company's Members, and countless Guardians. That's not a crime we take lightly. We're just lucky that Aleksander realized the bombs when he did and got everyone out."

"What?!"

She hadn't planted the bombs - she would never.

She had saved everyone, not Aleksander. That was the inciting incident that caused the Guardians to think of her as a terrorist?

Something she hadn't even done?

"It wasn't me! Helios - it wasn't me! I saved them! You don't understand, you have it all wrong!"

Helios held up two fingers to Will, and he increased the charge to two thousand volts.

"No, no - I'm begging you! It wasn't me! Helios! Please!"

Will sent two thousand volts through her, still less than before, but terribly painful and damaging. Her body couldn't take much more, even with the nanobots in her system, which seemed to be working much slower ever since Aleksander's large shock.

Will was taking orders from Helios. He wasn't there to stop him.

The future Will that Aurelia knew had been kind, gentle - he never would've intentionally hurt her. Was it all an illusion? Had he been working with Helios - with his father - with the Guardians, the whole time?

No. He had loved her. She had loved him. He was hers and she was his, always. Always. Had "Always" been a trick all along? Had she and Tess been manipulated by the phrase to send them to the company's launch in B-udo? She had been so blinded with love that she hadn't seen it.

Things had ended so badly between them last. Had she accidentally changed their future so severely by telling him she was a permanent? Did he really feel nothing between them? Not even a flicker of remorse for her? A pang of guilt?

They were supposed to fall in love. Will told her they would get married. Had that been a deception too? Had future Will fabricated their relationship? If so, why? Was he trying to get close to her just so she would reveal who she was working with?

First Aleksander had betrayed her, now Will. No one even knew she was here, wherever "here" was. No one was coming to save her. She would die at the hands of the people she had trusted. She would die knowing that the man she loved had deceived her. Will had deceived her.

Was everything a lie?

"I think she's gonna be out for a while, Helios. Should we pick it back up tomorrow?" Will said, looking at Aurelia's unconscious body.

Helios nodded in agreement, standing up and stretching out his limbs from sitting so long. They had been at it for hours, without getting much of anything out of the girl. Will disconnected the leads from Aurelia, trying to hide his shaking hands from Helios, so he didn't see his weakness. Under each lead, her skin was charred and melted from the heat of the electricity. He tried not to look at the gruesome burns as he removed the wires.

"No need to do that, kid. Less work for us tomorrow."

"Should we grab a drink before heading back?" Will asked, stepping away from Aurelia.

Helios nodded, "I haven't gotten the chance to say it to you much, but I'm proud of you, Will. I'm happy to have you on the team. You've come a long way from when we first started working together - especially from the young version of you in B-udo now."

Helios referred to the fact that he currently knew two versions of Will - the 25-year-old future version in front of him, that had come back in time to apprentice with Helios, and the 11-year-old kid, currently oblivious at home in 43-7.

"Thank you," Will said.

Helios started to walk out, and Will paused for a moment, his eyes settling on Aurelia's face. She had trusted him. She had believed he would help her. She had begged him to stop.

"Son? You coming?" Helios asked him, standing in the door of the jail cell, about to flip off the light switch inside the cell.

"Yup."

Following him out and closing the cell behind him, Will slipped a metal plate between the door latch and the doorframe without Helios seeing, stopping the door from closing entirely.

Aurelia slipped in and out of consciousness, the room spinning. The permanent nanobots in her body tried to recalibrate from the electric pulses that had reset their directives, again and again - most of them fried, others still, luckily, operable - barely.

Aurelia felt betrayed, her trust in humanity shattered. Will had broken her heart, her spirit, her soul.

She was delirious, but it seemed like the cell door creaked open. Opening her eyes, wondering if she was hallucinating, she watched as a group of figures came inside.

"No more. No more. I don't know anything," Aurelia whimpered, closing her eyes, knowing the pain that was coming again.

Her perception of reality warped, a minute slipped by unnoticed, her mind waking up again.

She could feel someone's hands on her, fiddling at the leads. With her mind grainy and vision spotty, she opened her eyes again, trying to see what was happening in the dark room, the single lightbulb above her turned off. The residual light from the hall seeped in and gave her just enough to see shapes and shadows. There were three figures in the dark room with her - no, four.

"What have they done to you?" a woman asked, her hand stroking her cheek. The shadow of a woman's black hair was discernible amongst the darkness, her voice like a lullaby she had once heard. Her pleasant tone reminded her of Eloise, her soft hands brushing her face intimately like her mother had done once upon a time.

Was she imagining things? Was anyone actually in the room with her? Familiarity creeping up on her, she attempted to study the woman's face, her eyes barely able to hold focus. But, it couldn't be. It wasn't possible. She had died, hadn't she? Was her mind playing tricks on her? Or had they been reunited on the other side? Was this heaven?

"Mom? Are you here?"

"Yes, Lia. Always."

Aurelia's vision darkened again, and the moment around her faded away.

End of book one. To be continued...

See upcoming books/releases in the AIT series and continue the journey into the world of Adventures In Time at;

AdventuresInTimeSeries.com